To Joe,

Hope you
This one too!

CW01020094

HOW THE TIGER FACED HIS CHALLENGE

Sarah Brownlee

ISBN: 978-1518811401

For my father, Paul Brownlee
who taught me to stand and fight

ACKNOWLEDGEMENTS

With special thanks to Carlene Welch, Bianca Marzan and Walton Mendelson for their valued input and assistance.

'They shall not grow old, as we that are left grow old
Age shall not weary them, nor the years condemn
At the going down of the sun and in the morning
We will remember them.

They mingle not with their laughing comrades again
They sit no more at familiar tables of home
They have no lot in our labour of the day-time
They sleep beyond England's foam.'

For the Fallen
Robert Laurence Binyon

PROLOGUE

The night was still. Darkness swallowed the gothic-style mansion that lay at the heart of East London with an ominous terror that was not unfamiliar to many citizens of the city. It was not the darkness itself that posed as the greatest threat; it was the thugs who roamed the streets, searching for victims during their nightly prowls. Stay inside or possibly die. For many, living under siege was better than losing one's life.

Lord Pearson sat in his chambers, the silk-flame lamps flickering bright orange throughout the otherwise dark room. He was waiting for the visitor. The visitor who had sent him such an intriguing message with promises that Lord Pearson—though he would never admit it aloud—could only dare to hope would be fulfilled. And if these promises did not ring true…why, he would simply have the visitor killed and that would be the end of that.

"My Lord, he has arrived."

"Show him in."

The servant gave a low bow and left just as quickly as he had entered. Lord Pearson sat there, waiting, his fingers drumming the table beside him as he sipped on his glass of sherry.

"May I introduce Professor Xelopis Dragoon."

A small, scrawny-looking man draped in a black cloak entered the room. His face was worn and haggard, his nose long and protrusive like the beak of a vulture and his eyes were bloodshot, yet there was a sly, hungry look behind them that Lord Pearson did not fail to notice as the professor advanced towards him, bowing deeply.

"My Lord Pearson," said the man in a silky voice, his head thrown so far forward that the few stray hairs on his almost bald head were practically touching the toes of his boots, "it is a great honour, a truly cherished experience to finally meet you, to find myself in the esteemed House of Pearson and at the feet of a lord as revered as yourself—"

"Rise," said Lord Pearson carelessly. "Your overdose of flattery is not necessary. Tell me of your proposal."

Obediently, the beak-nosed professor lifted his head from the ground and stared squarely into the eyes of the imperious man before him.

"From my message, My Lord, you will have surely gathered that I am aware of your predicament," he said. "Lord Renzo has enlisted help from the Chinese Emperor; you and your men find yourselves in a bit of trouble. Reinforcements have been scattered around the country and it is only a matter of time before they attack. I can only imagine negotiations between Lord Renzo and the Emperor has been going on for years, despite the pact between you. Such a sly, dishonourable act!"

"Get on with it," said Lord Pearson coldly.

"Yes, My Lord. Your men have naturally sought retaliation—

the fire at Notting Hill and the murder of Sir Branswick, one of Lord Renzo's good friends. Such retaliation will not keep the Chinese at bay, nor will it keep you safe in your position. Forgive me, but you need a much wiser strategy. I can provide you with this. I have brought the results of my experiment with me today."

Lord Pearson was a man of impeccable control. In almost every situation he found himself in, he was able to wear a mask of steel to ensure his every emotion was hidden. He could not contain his heart quickening its beat beneath his chest, nor the surge of excitement that shot through him upon hearing these words. But he could hide it.

"Oh yes?" he said coolly. "Perhaps you would care to be a little more explicit with your intentions? Your message hardly conveyed much detail."

"Morphers, My Lord," said the professor. "As I am sure you are aware, Professor Polgas created a formula that could transform a man into his inner beast within seconds. This extraordinary ability has passed down, generation to generation—"

"I did not call you here for a history lesson. I am fully aware of what Morphers are and the gift they possess. What I want to know is what this has to do with you and how you can be of assistance to me."

"Of course, of course. Let me explain. I myself am a professor of able ability. Having followed the works of Professor Polgas for most of my adult life, I embarked upon a mission to devise my own experiment. It is true that Morphers can transform into animals, but what of the DNA that gives them the ability to do so in the first place? It was five years ago when I asked myself this:

would it not be possible to transfer this DNA into the body of another so that they, too, will have the gift of transformation? Perhaps you see where I am going with my story, My Lord?"

"It sounds to me that you are claiming to have discovered a way to change ordinary people into Morphers," said Lord Pearson, unable to keep his heart from quickening beneath his chest again. "But these sound like wild claims to me. History tells us that all the documentation of Professor Polgas' work was destroyed in Firefly House centuries ago. Intrinsic details about Morphers have vanished. You would have had to start from scratch, would you not?"

"Ah—a good professor never reveals the secrets of his success!" said Professor Dragoon, in an attempt to be humorous. Catching sight of Lord Pearson's unimpressed expression and cold eyes, he hastened to explain himself.

"Not all the documentation was destroyed. The professor's assistant kept certain records, copies of which are available to the public in the museum dedicated to him, north of the country. Combined with this knowledge, plus my own skills, I am happy to inform you that I have indeed succeeded in my goal. Not only that, but I have the results here with me today."

With that, Professor Dragoon gestured to the servant who was standing by the door. The servant nodded and scuttled off. The professor turned to Lord Pearson and spoke in that oily voice once more.

"The last few years of my life have been spent in Mongolia. It was there that I chanced upon a young man—a descendant of one of the original Morphers. His spirit animal is the beaver. I was fortunate enough to acquire his DNA. With this DNA, I knew I would be able to inject it into an ordinary human being, which would give them the power to morph. But to confirm this, I needed to conduct a few experiments."

The servant re-entered the chamber just then, but he was not alone. Beside him were three small children. Two of them were horribly disfigured; one sprouted hair from his face and he had two elongated front teeth that ended just below his chin, the whites of his eyes were showing and he was clearly blind. The other child, perhaps a girl but it was difficult to tell, was missing an arm and her lips sagged in an odd manner as though they were made of wax. The third child, a boy, looked completely normal—but terrified. He was sniffling quietly as the professor gripped hold of his arm.

"As you can see, My Lord Pearson," said Professor Dragoon, shunting all three children forward; the blind boy stumbled, his arms scrabbling the air helplessly, "I have had to go through quite a few, um, guinea-pigs in order to achieve results. I hope you do not object to my methods? It is ever so much easier to attain results with children than adults—and I found during the course of my stay that I had very little trouble obtaining these children for the right price."

He was unable to hide a wicked smile. Lord Pearson carelessly flicked his hand to show he was not perturbed. It was all one and the same to him what this shrivelled bootlicker did with his business; his only interest lay in the results.

"So go on. Explain."

"Yes. After extracting DNA from the Beaver Morpher, I then proceeded to inject it into others. It was a long and lengthy process. My first attempts were complete failures, resulting in death or vegetable states. However, through sheer perseverance, I struck gold. This one—" he pointed to the blind boy— "and this one—" he gestured to the girl with the missing arm— "were my last attempts before I met success. I will now show you the full extent of my achievements."

He shoved the normal-looking boy forward; the boy was still crying quietly.

"Come on now," Professor Dragoon told him coaxingly. "Time to transform. Quickly now."

The boy continued to sob, his hands covering his eyes, trembling. Lord Pearson stared down at him, a frown forming on his face. Professor Dragoon looked up at him, smiling nervously, before sweeping towards the boy and leaning over to whisper in his ear.

"Now remember what we discussed," he said, gripping the boy's arm tightly, "you have to do as your told. You know what will happen if you don't do as you're told, don't you?"

The boy began trembling even harder. Professor Dragoon nodded before straightening up and speaking in a louder voice.

"Now let's try again then, shall we? Forgive me, My Lord, this will only take a moment. The boy is nervous, you see. He has never transformed in front of anyone other than myself before. Now, on the count of three. One…two…three!"

The boy shot one petrified look towards the professor, his entire body shaking uncontrollably, and terror consuming him. Then, quite suddenly, he was gone. A heap of tattered clothes fell to the floor. Lord Pearson gripped the edge of his seat.

A split-second later, a small, brown animal emerged from the ragged clothing. A beaver cub. It looked up and sniffed, its body darting this way and that for several seconds. A triumphant expression appeared on Professor Dragoon's face. Lord Pearson continued to look passive, but his pupils were dilating widely as he surveyed the scene before him.

"As you can see," said the professor, swooping down and clutching the beaver in his hands, "my experiment was a success. This boy now has the ability to transform into a beaver at will. My formula, taken from the DNA of the man in Mongolia, gives an ordinary human the power to shape-shift. I have essentially expanded on the genius of Professor Polgas and managed to, shall we say, upgrade his accomplishments."

He looked extremely impressed with himself as though he expected a round of applause to break out at any moment. Lord Pearson did not respond for several minutes. Overwhelming thoughts of endless possibilities, of what he could do with this break-through, of how he could use this to thwart his enemy once and for all...These thoughts swirled round and round in his mind so that he was rendered speechless.

"Tell me," he said eventually, "this DNA...you can take it from any Morpher and inject it into an ordinary person? Or does your formula extend to the DNA of the Beaver Morpher alone?"

"Oh, no, My Lord. I am able to extract the DNA from any Morpher and the result will be the same."

"So if, for example, I was to hand another Morpher over to you—one that could turn into a dog, for instance—you would then extract his DNA, inject it into a normal human, and they would then be able to transform into a dog on command?"

"That is correct."

There was another ringing silence throughout the room. Professor Dragoon, still holding the now motionless beaver cub, eyed Lord Pearson slyly.

"Am I correct in presuming that there is a Morpher you have in mind, My Lord?"

"You shall presume nothing that is currently not your business," said Lord Pearson with a slight bite to his tone. Professor Dragoon bowed low, apologizing. Lord Pearson stared calculatingly at the beaver cub for some time. Then he said,

"Well, Professor Dragoon, you were correct in thinking that the results of your experiment are of interest to me. I am, however, keen to hear the rest of your plan. I assume also that this proposal of yours will come at a price?"

Professor Dragoon hastened to explain that the honour of being able to serve was a reward in itself, but Lord Pearson cut him off swiftly.

"Do not insult my intelligence," he said, his eyebrows furrowing. The professor's eyes widened in horror and he began to babble on about how he would never dream of doing such a thing, but Lord Pearson rose a hand to silence him, before speaking in that cool voice once more.

"It is riches you seek in return for your services. Save your faffing around and get to the point. How much?"

"Well, My Lord, seeing as you mentioned it…"

In a servile manner, Professor Dragoon told the lord in front of him the price of his services. Several servants in the room widened their eyes, shooting their master a quick look to see how he would react. Lord Pearson felt a small smirk hover about his lips.

"If I hadn't already seen the miracle you just performed, I would have your legs ripped from their sockets simply for your sheer audacity," he said in an amused tone. "But I cannot fail to be impressed by what you have to offer. I take it we are on a similar wavelength with regard to what you can do for me? I am interested in discussing this further, but not here."

He clicked his fingers and one of the servants who were standing in the shadows to his left came hurrying over.

"Tell the chef to prepare dinner—we have a special guest dining with us tonight."

The servant bowed and nodded, scuttling off.

Lord Pearson turned back to Professor Dragoon, who was too slow in disguising the glee on his face.

"I assume your boy can turn back into a human?" he said to him.

"Oh yes, My Lord! I will show you now."

He placed the beaver cub down and pulled on its tail. The cub let out a yelp. Moments later, the beaver disappeared and a small, naked boy lay on the floor, shuddering, tears streaming down his face.

Lord Pearson sat back in his seat with a satisfied countenance.

"Good," he said, picking up his sherry from the side table and taking a sip. Then he turned to another couple of servants who were on his right.

"Clothe the boy. Take these children to a room and keep them there until our business is finished."

The servants nodded obediently. One of them stepped forwards and took hold of the blind boy and the girl with one arm, escorting them from the room. The other servant moved towards the small boy who was still lying on the floor before yanking him to his feet. At that moment, the boy's quiet cries turned into loud sobs and he began to scream, flailing his arms in resistance.

"*Ma! Ma!*"

The servant hurriedly began to drag him from the room; Professor Dragoon eyed the boy, a thunderous expression on his haggard features. Lord Pearson, however, continued to watch passively as the children were taken away, the boy's screams echoing loudly throughout the room and down the hall, until the door closed shut and the chamber was silent once more.

Rising from his seat, Lord Pearson approached the professor, who lowered his greasy head.

"We will resume this conversation over dinner. But first, a drink."

He gestured to the butler who was standing by the door. The butler hurried over with a silver tray, several glasses and a bottle of whiskey balancing precariously on it. Two drinks were poured. Lord Pearson took one and placed the other in the hands of Professor Dragoon.

"Here's to new beginnings…and final solutions," said Lord Pearson, raising his glass, that familiar cold smile beneath his beard.

"Indeed, My Lord."

They clinked their glasses, the sound echoing throughout the chamber.

CHAPTER ONE

"Now, the most important thing to remember when dealing with a dissatisfied customer are these four steps: L.L.D.R. When you are here in this office, nothing means more than the L.L.D.R. What is the L.L.D.R, you may ask? It is everything. It is the foundation of excellent customer service, it is the mantra you repeat to yourself every day—believe me when I say it is the path to success. I would not be where I am now if it weren't for these four— *excuse me*, Miss Archer, but would you like to tell me why your focus appears to be on something high above my head and not actually on me? What did I just say about the L.L.D.R?"

The angry, biting voice of her manager came bursting into Skye Archer's thoughts, breaking into the current daydream she had been engaged in for the past fifteen minutes. Shaking her head slightly, she peered into the face of Ned, who was looking seriously annoyed. Her co-workers turned to stare at her.

"Erm…the L.L.F.R…" she began blankly.

"*D*, Skye! Not *F! D!* D, which stands for 'Discuss!' Something you appear incapable of at this moment! Tell me, Skye, how much does this job mean to you? How much drive and passion do you truly have to be the best customer service agent you can be? Because right now, I am not convinced of your commitment!"

Skye swallowed, trying to ignore the many pairs of eyes that were staring at her.

"I'm sorry," she said, clearing her throat, trying to mould her face into an apologetic expression as she looked back at her irate manager.

"I should think so," said Ned with a huff.

Shooting her a filthy look, he resumed his speech about the L.L.D.R (whatever that meant) to the twelve customer service agents sitting at the meeting table. Many were rubbing their eyes, struggling to stay awake; others were staring blankly at the holographic monitor behind Ned's body, trying to make head and tail of what he was saying. Skye felt her nostrils flare.

Typical, she thought as Ned continued to drone on and on about something neither she nor her colleagues understood or, at that time of the morning, cared to understand. *Love the way he chooses me to pick on—at least I'm actually awake!*

She snuck a brief glimpse at her Customer Service Supervisor, Miles, who was snoozing in his seat.

Still, Ned was pretty snappy with her these days and she knew why. Ever since the appearance of Raphael Renzo in her life (just the thought of him created a flutter of butterflies somewhere in the region of her stomach), Skye's enthusiasm for her job had somewhat faltered. Not that it had ever been particularly high; being yelled at and bombarded with a barrage of verbal abuse from angry customers on a daily basis was hardly something that made you want to wake up in the morning. Furthermore, having to pander to her manager's fervent, almost obsessive megalomaniac desire in achieving nationwide status as the 'Best Customer Service Team' of the year was truly nauseating. These were dangerous times in London, but the way Ned behaved, anyone would think he hailed from a completely different planet, let alone city; his existence seemed to be dedicated to driving them round the bend, setting them a target of responding to two hundred complaints a day, forcing them to write up one-thousand word compositions on the importance of good customer service and, worst of all, insisting on three-hour long weekly meetings to discuss ways of improving their department. In other words, he was every customer service agent's nightmare.

But Raphael made it all bearable. He made a lot of things bearable. Skye was barely able to hide a cheesy grin as she sat there, pen in hand, robotically watching Ned talking non-stop in front of the monitor, all the while unable to get Raphael out of her head. The smile was quickly wiped from her face when Ned caught a glimpse of her dreamy expression; he glared at her, pursing his lips so tight that they formed a thin line on his face. Skye coughed, willing herself to focus, but still powerless to stop her thoughts from overriding her.

She still couldn't quite believe everything that had happened over the past few months. She could hardly believe it was only three months ago that she had met Raphael Renzo. She could still vividly recall the day she'd been cornered by a gang of thugs down her local High Street—and a strange man with black hair had stepped in, warning them to back away from her. She never thought that this man would be a Morpher like her. She'd had no idea he was a member of the most affluent and wealthy family in the city, a family that directly opposed the numerous thugs and scoundrels that terrorized ordinary citizens. She certainly never would have thought she would fall completely and utterly in love with him.

But yes, that was exactly what happened and, if this wasn't bewildering enough, it was even more incredible that he felt exactly the same way about her. Raphael was strong, good-hearted, fierce and brave; he was also heart-stopping gorgeous. He, like Skye, was a Morpher, someone with the ability to transform into their spirit animal at will. His spirit animal was the tiger. Despite the fact that Skye had very often considered her morphing ability as a curse because of the social stigma that came attached with it, it was more common for her to thank her lucky stars these days that she was given the ability to morph. Not only had it proven crucial during the times she needed it most, it was also the factor that brought her and Raphael together in the first place.

It hadn't exactly been easy sailing in the beginning. Raphael had expressed an interest in her from the beginning, but Skye had rebuffed his friendly attentions repeatedly, determined not to feel anything for him other than mild affability. Her own insecurities would not allow her to dare entertain the thought that he might have a romantic interest in her. But her efforts were futile—she fell in love. Nor was she the only one. Too shy to tell each other how they felt, Skye and Raphael had kept their feelings for one another secret until that explosive night four weeks ago when they had finally admitted their heart's desires. Skye had struggled with the pain of unrequited love for some time, not realizing that Raphael felt the exact same way as she did. She never thought she'd stand a chance with him; she felt he was completely out of her league in terms of background, appearance and social status—but Raphael hadn't cared about any of that. And that was one of the (many) things she loved about him, his ability to look beyond outer appearances and his appreciation of what was inside. If anything, he had shown her that it didn't matter who you were, where you came from or how you looked—no one was exempt from feelings of insecurity, especially when clueless about how the other person felt. He had opened her eyes in more ways than one; she had learned a thing or two.

What should have been a blissful time between two people who felt themselves struck by Cupid's arrow for the first time was marred, however, by the impending civil war that was slowly, but surely, brewing. It was four weeks ago that Trey Renzo, Raphael's elder brother, had returned to England with news that the Emperor of China was willing to assist the Renzo family and their army of supporters in the inevitable battle that would take place with the thugs. London was in danger. More danger than it had been in for the past twelve years—and that was saying something, considering the turmoil it had been suffering from for a number of decades. Law and order was practically non-existent in the metropolis, but it was about to get a whole lot worse. Things really started to kick off when random explosions up and down the city began several weeks ago, not quite on the horrifying scale that occurred twelve years prior when the thugs and lowlife had organized a disastrous killing spree across the city, but there was widespread panic among the citizens when they realized that history was likely to repeat itself—this time, in all-out war. Grisly murders had increased ten-fold, including the death of Sir Branswick, a close friend of Lord

Renzo. He was found in his home with knife wounds to the chest, charcoal smeared on his face. The thugs had recently taken to rubbing charcoal on the faces of their victims in order to mark their presence; why they used charcoal, no one knew, but it was chilling nonetheless. The death of Sir Branswick, who was a good and kind man, sent sorrow and shivers up the spine of every decent citizen of the city, especially Lord Renzo and his family who had known and fought by his side for many years.

Currently, and ever since Trey had returned a month ago, the city appeared to be under some form of 'terrorist siege'. Random attacks occurred here and there, but war had not been declared officially. Already, a small number of London citizens had evacuated, many fleeing to sunny Spain, which was where the English tended to lodge themselves whenever there was a threat to their livelihood (these evacuees consisted only of the wealthiest families in the city, whose lives had never been directly targeted by the thugs, but who weren't willing to stick around for a full-scale war). Lord Renzo was in constant talks and meetings with the Chinese Generals who had flown in and secretly deployed their men all around the city, discussing strategies on the best way to attack the thugs. What Lord Pearson was doing, Skye had no idea. She didn't want to know. The same sinking feeling and nervousness that had gripped the nation was just as strong inside of her as well. She counted her blessings for the time she had with Raphael, for she knew it would not last. For now, they had to carry on as normal (at least, as normal as was possible under the circumstances), go about their daily lives and try to stay calm. And all the while, tensions were getting higher, crime was increasing and war was coming. But what else was there to do except wait?

Oh, and continue attending Ned's painfully tedious meetings every Monday morning.

"Repeat after me," Ned was saying, clasping his hands together before pointing to the holographic sideshow presentation behind him, which was presently displaying the enormous letters 'L.L.D.R'. Skye shook herself in another valiant attempt to pay attention to what he was saying.

"Listen, Learn, Discuss, Resolve! Ready everyone? Listen, Learn, Discuss, Resolve!"

"Listen, Learn, Discuss, Resolve," chanted the Trixaction Cinemas Customer Service Team; Skye sighed inwardly, sneaking a brief glimpse at the clock. Only another hour and fifteen minutes to go…

"Good, Good! Listen, Learn, Discuss, Resolve! L.L.D.R—the secret to success! Again everybody! Listen, Learn, Discuss, Resolve! Listen, Learn, Discuss, Resolve! One more time everyone!"

The meeting dragged on; the minutes ticked by. Skye occasionally slipped into a daydream about Raphael, remembering how he would be meeting her after work that day. She could barely contain her excitement; and it certainly provided some relief to the monotonous, droning tone of Ned's voice.

Finally, midday hit and the meeting was called to an end. The customer service agents had relieved expressions on their faces, many yawning and stretching; Skye herself snapped out of her latest fantasy, one where she and Raphael were enjoying an enormous raw steak between them, and she hurriedly packed up her notepad, preparing to leave the room.

"Miss Archer, a word if you please!"

Skye groaned silently as she looked up to see Ned, who was staring at her with a deeply disapproving look on his face.

"In my office," he said shortly, snapping his fingers and gesturing for her to follow.

Grumbling to herself, Skye reluctantly followed. No doubt Ned wanted to give her an hour-long lecture to criticize her yet again for her lack of drive and ambition. She stopped briefly in her tracks. Maybe he was even going to fire her? Welcome as this prospect appeared, in the sense that she would no longer have to attend mind-numbing meetings or be yelled at every day, her rational side opposed it with every fibre of her being. Jobs weren't exactly easy to attain these days and Skye knew if she lost this role, she was in trouble. Unable to prevent the worry creeping up on her and now silently rebuking herself for becoming so lax, she entered Ned's office and took a seat opposite him, while he placed himself in his white, swivel chair.

"Now Skye," he began, resting his hands on the desk in front of him and looking at her with a serious, sombre expression, "I think it's about time we have a little chat, just you and me."

Bracing herself, Skye's hands tightened into balls on her lap.

"Mm-hmm?" she said.

Nothing to panic about, she told herself, *you have to have at least three warnings before you're fired and I've only got one. He probably just wants to tell me off about daydreaming again...I really need to quit doing that during meetings!*

"I've been feeling for some time that your performance is not up to scratch," began Ned, looking Skye directly in the eye, "and I'm afraid I have no choice, but to have this talk with you now. Rest assured that it brings me no pleasure to discuss this with you."

Oh my God…he is *going to sack me!*

Skye cleared her throat.

"Oh right?" she said, wildly thinking in her head about how she would have to express feelings of extreme remorse in order to convince Ned to let her stay on.

"Yes. This is not a conversation that I anticipated having with you, but it is clear to me that lately your enthusiasm for this job has been, shall we say, not quite up to par. Therefore, I think it's time we have a chat about…"

Skye's muscles tensed; this was it. She was about to be given the boot.

"… relationships."

Skye blinked.

"Relationships?" she repeated blankly.

"Yes, Skye. Relationships. I am becoming increasingly convinced that the reason for your current rebellious behaviour is due to your relationship with the young man you have recently become involved with. Now don't get me wrong. When I was your age, I had my fair share of girlfriends. I know how easily one can be swept away in the heated passion of love."

He smiled at her indulgently. A myriad of emotions ran through Skye at that moment. Shock was one of them; another was relief; but, most of all, was a cringing embarrassment. Having a discussion about boyfriends with her manager was not something she could have ever foreseen—or wanted. She wondered what was worse, being sacked or engaging in a conversation with Ned about the 'heated passion of love'.

She squirmed in her seat.

"Erm…" she said, unable to think of what to say next.

"It's quite alright, Skye," said Ned with a smile; Skye was greatly perturbed by this new, smiling, understanding Ned and half-wished he would revert back to being the angry one who shouted at her all the time. "I know what you are going through. I truly do. You see, when I was nineteen, the same age as you are now, I had a girlfriend. Her name was Laura, a stunning, breath-taking woman. I may not be the strongest of men, nor even the most handsome, but my wit, my charm, my drive for ambition, all these admirable qualities drew her to me."

"Oh right?" said Skye, wishing she could leave.

"Yes. How many men vied for her attention? But who was it she chose? It was me. Yet it was not in my destiny. You may have been wondering for some time, Skye, why I, a successful businessman, have been single for the last fifteen years of my life?"

Skye, who had never wondered such a thing, felt there was no choice but to nod.

"It is because of my career. My desire to succeed. Laura wanted to tie me down. She wanted me to sacrifice everything for her. She wanted to distract me from my dreams, my desires, and my goals. And do you know what I said to her?"

Skye shook her head.

"I said, 'No, my love. I won't. You must go out into the world to find what you seek, for it is not I. And what I seek is not you.'"

He heaved dramatically.

"You see, Skye? I sacrificed everything for my job. Because I knew I had potential. I knew I could achieve. Now look at me—Manager of Trixactions Customer Services. Head of twelve agents. My sacrifice was not in vain; it was the best decision I ever made in my life. Oh yes, sometimes I think about her. Sometimes I wonder…but no. I made the right choice. It was not meant to be."

He paused for a moment, his gaze taking a far-away look, his hand vaguely stroking his receding ginger hair. Skye could not recall a time she had felt more uncomfortable.

"Er…" she said, while Ned continued to stare at the wall behind her back. "Well, that's really good…"

He snapped out of his reverie and fixed her with a piercing, determined look.

"And why did I tell you my story? Because I know you're a good agent. I know you love your job. I know being a Customer Service Agent brings meaning to your life. Learn from my experience, Skye. Do not allow the whims of teenage lust to distract you from what brings true fulfilment—a career. A career in Customer Services. I once told you that I thought you had Supervisor qualities, but this half-hearted behaviour, zoning out during my meetings, coming in late—these flaws do not make you worthy of a Supervisory position! Tell me, Skye, what are your thoughts? Do you understand how distracting relationships can be? Do you understand the commitment your job demands of you? Tell me, do you *truly* feel you are on the right path?"

The only thing Skye truly felt in that moment was the need to transform, if only to use the power of her wolf legs to sprint from the room and get as far away from her manager as possible, but a sudden, ear-splitting scream from somewhere in the building saved her from answering these highly awkward questions. She wasn't the only one who heard it. Her hearing was a lot more sensitive than that of her colleagues, but even they did not fail to hear the terrified scream that had just resounded throughout the hallway. She could hear the hubbub of frightened voices outside. Ned, too, abruptly snapped his eyes away from Skye and turned towards the door, looking uncharacteristically disturbed.

"What was that?" he said, unable to hide the worry on his face.

His question was answered seconds later. Skye, who was quick on her guard these days, rose from her seat, preparing herself for transformation. She had expected an attack; the thugs knew she was a Morpher and she'd figured it was only a matter of time before they found her at work and tried to kill her for the second time. She still had the scar from when Finn Pearson and his gang had stabbed her in the side a couple of months ago. Due to the adrenaline pumping through her, her brown eyes flashed bright blue; she stepped towards the door, her hand on the doorknob. Ned gulped, pulling on his necktie.

She pulled the door open by a crack, her heart pounding; she could see her colleagues staring towards the open corridor, extremely worried expressions on their faces. Even the holographic customers had momentarily stopped complaining and were gazing in the same direction with great concern.

Moments later, a woman burst into the office. It was the receptionist for Trixaction Cinemas HQ; beads of sweat were dripping down her face, her hands flailing about in sheer terror.

"Help!" she screamed at them. "There's some kind of—

ARRRRGGGGGHHHHH!"

Almost everyone jumped up from their seats, petrified. Skye pulled the door open even wider, Ned cowering behind her, his teeth chattering. Skye's luminous blue eyes scanned the woman, her colleagues and the room, her heart thumping so fiercely she was afraid it would blast right out of her chest. This was it; the thugs were attacking! She was just as terrified as everyone else, but she was a Morpher; and if there was one thing she had learned over the past few months it was that Morphers had a duty and responsibility to protect ordinary people.

Then she saw the reason the woman had screamed. She saw why the receptionist had now flung herself into the office, landing in a heap on the lap of Lucas, one of her colleagues, still screaming shrilly. A small, hairy, brown animal with very large teeth had darted into the office, sniffing the air in panic, its enormous tail shaking very fast.

"HELP!" the woman screamed, grabbing Lucas, almost knocking the wind out of him. "There's an animal! Quick—do something!"

Everyone yelled in fright; some people jumped on their desks in case they thought the creature would run up their legs. Skye's heart almost leapt out of her chest as she tried to make sense of what was going on. There were no thugs. There was something else. She yanked the door open completely and took a step towards the cause of all the commotion. Looking closely at the animal, she could see it was a beaver, a cub by the looks of things. She was stunned. What was a *beaver*, an animal that had been wiped out from the country for over a hundred years, doing in her *office* of all places? Her blue eyes flashing at the creature, she moved even nearer to it. Her wolf senses were picking up on something...this was no ordinary animal...there was something strange about it, and not just the fact it had randomly appeared in the building...

Then it hit her. This was a Morpher.

"Oh my God," she gasped.

And yet, despite her inner assertion that she was right, there was something else that was bothering her. This was a Morpher...and yet it was not. She couldn't explain it. Her human mind could not process the information logically or even make sense of this instinct that was running through her. There was a human inside that beaver's body...but there was something else, too...something that wasn't right...but what?

She knelt down, her body trembling.

"Here," she managed to call out, trying to keep her voice gentle and low. She made some clicking sounds at the beaver, which stared right at her, frozen. "Here...over here...don't be scared..."

"What are you doing?" screamed the receptionist, who was still sprawled on Lucas's lap, holding her skirts high in the air and staring at Skye as though she was insane. "Don't encourage it!"

Skye was unable to prevent the scowl that appeared on her features as her eyes darted to the receptionist.

"It's just a little animal—it's not going to hurt you!" she snapped at her.

However, upon catching sight of Skye's blazing blue eyes and dilated black pupils, the receptionist screamed even harder.

"Oh my God!" she shrieked. "What is wrong with your *face?*"

Everyone else in the office turned to look at Skye's face. Many recoiled when they saw her eyes which had transformed so dramatically. Dread set into her heart as she realized the entire department was now aware of her ability. Skye had never before revealed to her colleagues that she could morph. The only people at work who knew about it were Ned and Lucas. Ned because it was compulsory by law for every Morpher to put it on their job application, and Lucas because of that unforgettable night five weeks ago when Raphael had almost attacked him, having transformed in a fit of rage; Skye had had to morph into her wolf in order to prevent Raphael from causing her colleague any bodily harm. However, neither Ned nor Lucas had told anyone else in the department about her secret; Ned was obliged to keep it confidential due to the *Morphers Rights Act 2121*, and Lucas spent every working day avoiding Skye whenever possible, so his determination to act like she didn't exist also extended to pretending that explosive night had never happened.

She froze momentarily, realizing what she had done in the heat of the moment, knowing that due to the impending war it was practically inevitable that one day everyone around her would know what she was; but she wished it had not happened like this. Keeping her morphing a secret was something she had done ever since she was young, only ever choosing to reveal it to those select few, her nearest and dearest. If everyone at work had to find out about it, she would have rather it happened when she actually had to transform—such as if the thugs had broken into the building and launched an attack. Not like this, with her eyes changing colour because the receptionist had raised hell due to a small beaver running around the building.

Should have controlled yourself better! She told herself furiously.

Calming herself, she felt her eyes switch back to their usual brown. Her colleagues continued staring at her in horror. The receptionist was still yelling her head off. Skye turned back to face the beaver, but it was gone.

Rising from the ground, she was unable to prevent the anger bubbling within her; the receptionist had created all this chaos because of *this?* Because of a tiny animal? Fair enough, it was unusual—downright absurd even—for a beaver to be wandering the halls of Trixaction Cinemas HQ. But Skye had been convinced the thugs were attacking, that the moment had come when she would have to transform at work and fight them off. There was never any absolute guarantee that they would, but she knew the chances were high. She had spent enough sleepless nights lately thinking about the ultimate showdown, when war would officially be declared, when her area of the city would be directly attacked, that at any moment she could lose her life because a gang of thugs might choose to attack the building or set it on fire (even with all the extra security the majority of London businesses had hired lately, the villains still found a way to thwart them). Raphael had been adamant from the start that she should evacuate the city, the country even (in fact, this was the cause of any argument they ever had) but Skye's stubborn nature prevailed and she had put her foot down; she would continue life as normal but, most of all, she would never give the thugs the satisfaction of knowing she had fled because of them.

"When it all kicks off, there's only two people who are leaving this city," she had told him, referring to her mother and best friend,

Daphne, who had so far defied her attempts at evacuating them, but whom she made promise that as soon as war was declared, they would go. "And neither of them is me. I told you, Raphael, I'm staying, and that's that."

Frustrated, but unable to convince her otherwise, Raphael had ordered even more extra security outside her place of work and commanded that the garrison which had defended her home ever since the day she was attacked by Finn Pearson stay put. Skye had not objected; any extra protection for her mother and her colleagues was highly welcome as far as she was concerned.

But back to this fiasco in the office. False alarm. And all it had done was expose her as a Morpher far sooner than she would have liked and created total uproar in the building—all for a small, brown animal that was plainly even more terrified of the humans than they were of it!

"Where is it?" screamed the receptionist. "Where is that disgusting overgrown rat?"

"It's a *beaver*," Skye snarled at her, her anger amplified by the fact that she had a deep love of animals of all kinds; the woman's derogatory, disgusted tone enraged her.

"Who cares what it is!" screeched the receptionist. "It's a nasty vicious animal! How did it get *in?* It's probably got rabies—it could have bitten me! And you! What is up with *you?* Your eyes were blue a second ago—now they're brown! What exactly are you?"

"Wow, are you, like, wearing those super cool colour-changing contact lenses or something?" said Miles the supervisor, gawping at Skye gormlessly.

Everyone stared at Skye, some still with fearful expressions on their faces. Then one of her colleagues, a girl called Aurora, said in a quiet, trembling voice,

"Skye…are you a *Morpher?*"

Skye looked helplessly around at the numerous pairs of eyes that were staring at her. This was the very thing she had tried to avoid for most of her life—but there was no point denying it now. It was going to come out sooner or later.

She nodded. The receptionist gave a small scream.

"I don't believe it! You mean to tell me I've been working in the same building as a *Morpher* all this time? Oh my God! I swear that's not safe? I swear it's against company policy? They're not stable—I've heard about them—"

As the receptionist continued ranting about the dangers of Morphers and her colleagues continued to stare at her in simultaneous awe and fear, Skye felt her cheeks burn and her hands curl into fists. This was why she kept her Morphing ability a secret; because of reactions like *this.* Ordinary people never understood. How many times had she been cast out, judged and segregated for her ability to morph? Gossiped about, whispered about and viewed as though she were some monstrous man-eating machine because she had the power to change into a wolf? It had happened in school, it had happened during her brief stint in college—and now it had happened at work. Since meeting Raphael, she had learned to cherish her gift a lot more than she used to, taking pride in it just the same way he did; she came to recognize how fortunate she was in being able to transform into a powerful beast that was able to protect herself and those around her; she embraced her ability now that she had found someone who was just like her.

She had forgotten the very reason she had been so determined to keep it a secret from society in the first place. Now, amidst the fearful gazes of her colleagues and the shouting woman who was looking at her as though she had some kind of disease, she remembered why she had so closely guarded her ability to morph all those years; horrible memories from her past came flooding back and, to her horror, she felt unwanted tears sting her eyes. Furiously, she fought to keep them in.

Who cares what she thinks? She thought angrily. *She's a stupid woman who caused havoc because of a beaver cub—a Morpher— and now she's scared it away! I'm going to tell this silly cow exactly what I think of her...*

Just as she was about to unleash a back lashing diatribe against the receptionist, who was now ranting about how Morphers were a danger to society and how she would be raising Skye's employment with Head Office, Lucas suddenly stood up; the receptionist, who had still been clutching him in an almost absent-minded manner, promptly slid to the floor.

"Look, shut up, would you?" he said to her. "Skye's not like that, alright? She's not a danger to society or any of that stuff. So just leave it."

The receptionist stared up at him in outrage; Skye gazed at him in shock. *Lucas* of all people—defending her? After what happened a few weeks ago? After Raphael had almost attacked him at her birthday party? After he had spent every moment pretending she didn't exist whenever they were at work together? Skye had tried to apologize to Lucas on several occasions for what happened, but he had brushed her off every time. She was convinced he hated her. So to have him defend her caused her to stare at him, open-mouthed. Lucas shot a brief glimpse at Skye before turning his back on them, swivelling in his chair to face his computer again.

The receptionist, who had recovered herself and was now standing up, opened her mouth to launch a verbal attack on him, when another colleague suddenly shouted out,

"Look! The animal! It's out there!"

Everyone raced to the window where the colleague was pointing in awe at something outside; Skye scanned her eyes around at the pavement. Sure enough, the beaver cub was racing down the road as fast as its little legs would carry it. It bolted behind a row of trees and disappeared. Skye felt her heart sink; she knew it was a Morpher that had caused the disruption in the building and now she would never have the chance to find out more about it. It was not that she had ever been particularly partial to meeting other Morphers, but the circumstances surrounding this one were too unusual for her to dismiss. What was it doing there at her workplace? And why was there something "off" about its scent? She felt oddly drawn to it…but something wasn't right…

"Alright, people!" came the blustering voice of Ned, his small body shakily storming towards them. "Show's over, time to get back to work! And my *dear* ladies and gentlemen," he added in a grovelling voice, bowing in turn to the several shocked holographic customers who had witnessed the entire thing, "may I offer you free cinema tickets in order to apologize for this unseemly incident? I assure you, this is not common of our Customer Services department! We in Customer Services take the words and wishes of our customers *very* seriously and I would hate for you to think that this is an everyday occurrence; you see, the needs of our customers are our topmost priority, this is most out of the ordinary…"

While Ned continued apologizing to the customers, everyone else resumed their seats, muttering quietly to each other, shooting Skye odd, furtive looks every now and then. The receptionist backed away as Skye walked towards her own desk, eyeing her in terror as though she was going to be attacked any second. Skye resisted the temptation to transform and give this woman something to really be scared of; simultaneously she tried to ignore the glances and whispers among her colleagues. She sat down, willing herself to concentrate on her computer screen.

"As I said," began the receptionist in a shrill, ringing voice, once she had safely made her way towards the door, "I will be raising this issue with Head Office! The rest of us who work here can't be expected to feel safe in our positions when someone like *that* is free to roam the building!"

With one last fearful, disgusted look at Skye, she stalked from the office. Skye remained rigid in her seat; her balled fists were clenched so hard her knuckles had gone white. Slowly, the department returned to its usual routine and the whispering and staring subsided. At one point, Ned approached her with a rather stern expression on his face.

"We will have to continue our discussion another time, Skye," he said, "and I don't want you letting this whole business affect you, do you understand? We have a job to do, a department to run, a service to deliver. I don't want you letting what Simone said about you to cause your performance to dwindle even further. Is that clear?"

"Yeah," replied Skye, rather hoarsely.

With a pompous nod, Ned strode back to his office. Skye returned to her screen, wishing she could just forget what the receptionist, Simone, had said about her. Why should she care what she thought? What did the receptionist know about her? Going on as though Skye would hurt anyone just because she was a Morpher—didn't the stupid woman know that she only wanted to protect people, not hurt them?

Yes, she shouldn't care. She really shouldn't. What did one person's ignorance mean to her anyway? But despite telling herself this, she still couldn't stop the flashes in her head of playground bullies years ago and their spiteful jeers; of her friends' parents dragging their children away by the hands when they discovered what she was; of people in college whispering about her, their expressions identical to the last one the receptionist had shot at her, that same fear and loathing…the same flashes that had gone through her mind when her colleagues were staring at her only fifteen minutes ago. She was angry with herself for letting it bother her. There were bigger things to worry about now. What did it matter?

Trying hard not to think about these things, nor about the strange creature that had entered the building or about how Lucas had so unexpectedly come to her defence, Skye pressed 'Accept' on her computer as it rang loudly to let her know there was a customer on the other end of the line.

Don't let anything affect your performance at work, she thought to herself grimly, echoing Ned's words in her head and realizing it was easier said than done.

CHAPTER TWO

At last, it was seven o' clock in the evening, marking the end of the working day. The usual resounding sigh of relief from the department was punctuated with the occasional whispering, which Skye was only too aware of. Hurriedly, before anyone could approach her on the subject of morphing (as she was sure they had been dying to do since the fiasco that morning) she switched off her computer, grabbed her bag and rushed out of the office. She stopped off in the toilets, peeking out at the corridor to keep an eye on who was walking through the halls. There was one person she wanted to talk to before she left, but she wanted to speak with him alone.

Finally, she saw him.

"Lucas—wait!" she called out, banging the toilet door open and racing after him.

He stopped in his tracks, turning to face her reluctantly.

"Skye," he said with a nod, not looking at her. "I'm kind of in a hurry…"

It was the first time he had spoken to her in weeks. Skye carried on in a rush.

"This won't take a minute. Look—it's what you did back there. I wanted to thank you."

"No worries." He turned away and continued walking down the corridor.

"Wait—I just…Look, about what happened at my birthday…" She trotted after him to match his long strides.

"Skye, there's no need to talk about it."

"But there is—I mean, what Raphael did…Lucas, I am truly sorry. We both are. He still hasn't forgiven himself for what he did. He's vowed never to lose control like that ever again. And I should have, you know, not given you the impression we were anything more than…friends. Honestly—I am sorry. And that's why…well, I'm surprised you defended me. I didn't expect that. I thought you hated me—well, maybe you do. But I'm still sorry and I'm grateful for what you did," she finished lamely.

Lucas stopped walking as they reached the doors to the building, finally turning to face her.

"I'm not looking for an apology, Skye. And if you're wondering why I stuck up for you it's because I'm the one who should be grateful to you, not the other way round."

Skye stared at him, confused.

"Grateful to me? But why?"

"Look," Lucas regarded her, his tone extremely uncomfortable, "I acted like a real prat that night. I had too much to drink, I came on too strong—I didn't expect some guy would show up and turn into a tiger. But I saw it in his eyes, Skye. When he transformed—he was going to kill me. And I'd be even more of a prat if I didn't acknowledge that the only reason he didn't kill me is because you stopped him."

Whatever Skye had expected, it was not this. She wasn't entirely sure what to think or say.

"Lucas," she muttered after a moment, "it was my fault it happened. If I hadn't given you the wrong idea…"

"Come on, Skye. I knew you didn't like me like that! You'd been avoiding going for a drink with me for weeks. I'm not stupid; I knew you were trying to make your boyfriend jealous when you started getting chattier with me that night. So I thought I'd take advantage of it. I'm not proud of it. But that wasn't an excuse for me to try and kiss you when you didn't want me to—like I said, I drank too much and I acted like an idiot. I haven't been talking to you because I felt ashamed. Yeah, so…now you know."

Skye shook her head.

"You shouldn't feel grateful to me. I transformed because I had to. There wasn't any choice. Do you see what I mean?"

"It doesn't matter either way. Fact is you did it. So when Simone was talking about you, I wasn't going to just sit there and listen to that crap. By rights, I shouldn't even like Morphers. Trust me, ever since that night I've been telling myself not to. It was a Morpher who tried to attack me…"

His expression hardened.

"But it was also a Morpher who saved my neck. I can't just forget that. I am no fan of your boyfriend. I wouldn't mind seeing him locked up; and I already know the guy's sorry—you know how many times he's approached me to apologize while he's been waiting for you after work? I'm not interested in his apologies or speaking to him. I don't even want to speak to you, Skye. But whatever the circumstances, whatever I feel about it all, I can't just disregard what you did. You transformed to help me out. This is how I feel about it. I don't know if any of this makes sense, but you have your way of looking at things and I have mine."

He stopped talking, running his hand through his hair, a frown on his face. Skye could tell this was something that had been playing on his mind for a long time, that perhaps he had wanted to say it for a while. She didn't know what to say.

"Look," Lucas said, "what's done is done. I've rambled on enough. I don't even know why I told you all that. I'd better get going."

He turned away from her. Skye reached out and took his arm.

"Lucas...thank you. You're right—I still don't really understand. I don't really know what to think. The only thing I know right now is that I'm glad you told me and—and I'd like us to try and be friends. If it's OK with you."

She looked at him nervously. He was silent for a while and then sighed.

"I dunno, Skye, let's just see how things turn out, OK? Anyway, I really have to get going. I'll see you tomorrow..."

He turned away from her and strode quickly towards the exit. Skye lingered on the spot for a while, staring after him. She could not believe that Lucas felt indebted to her in some way. What had been the alternative? Leave Raphael to kill Lucas? Let Lucas die? Allow Raphael to possibly face execution for attacking a non-Morpher, as the law states? As she had told him, there had been no choice and, regardless of Lucas' words, she knew she didn't deserve his gratitude.

Shaking her head, she made her way to the exit doors. Despite the general gloom she had felt throughout the day, that familiar, tingling excitement within her belly began to bubble once more when she realized she would be seeing Raphael very shortly. He would be waiting for her outside, as had been the case for the past several weeks. Due to the city being labelled 'high risk' lately, he had refused to allow her to go home on her own. Her natural independent streak objected fiercely to this, but at the same time she couldn't deny the thrill that shot through her; after all, it meant she would spend more time with him…and that could never be a bad thing.

However, it was not Raphael who was waiting to greet her when she stepped outside into the cool twilight breeze, but the unexpected form of Simone and a couple of other women who were huddled by the exit; Skye recognized them as the other receptionists who worked in the building. Her heart sinking, she swallowed as she tried to walk past them undetected, but Simone caught sight of her at once.

"There she is!" she shrieked.

The other receptionists followed her gaze, their expressions also mingled with fear and terror.

Ignore it, just ignore it, Skye told herself, determinedly not looking at them and walking towards the line of lampposts, which was where she and Raphael had arranged she should wait for him in case he was ever late in picking her up.

"I think it's disgusting how they allow people like that to work with the rest of us," Simone was saying loudly as Skye stalked past, "and I've already spoken to Head Office about it. Seriously, if we haven't got nasty animals wandering into the building then we've got nasty animals actually *working* with us. It's wrong on so many levels. I heard this story a few years ago about a Morpher who transformed and killed loads of people—they're dangerous and uncivilized! They shouldn't even be allowed in the country!"

Skye willed the anger in her temple to disappear as she came to a stop under a lamppost, but if anything it thumped even harder.

"What makes it even worse," Simone's loud voice carried on, practically booming through the air for all and sundry to hear, "is that we normal people aren't even informed about these weirdoes because of the law that was passed; you know, the Act that Old Parliament made when that other Morpher killed himself years ago! So basically, we're being forced to sit in the same building as these unstable animals; God knows what they're capable of—what if it suddenly gets hungry, do you know what I'm saying? I seriously don't think I can work under those conditions."

"Do you think we should be talking like this though?" Skye heard one of the other receptionists whisper fearfully. "I mean, if she hears us she might get mad and kill us?"

"Yeah, Simone, be careful," said the other one, her eyes round with anxiety.

"Thanks girls. But don't worry. Like I said, I've already spoken to Head Office and I know they're going to be doing some serious investigating into the Customer Services department—I mean, her eyes actually switched colour! I saw it! How are we supposed to feel safe at work with that thing running around?"

Skye knew she should have ignored it. She knew Raphael wouldn't be long and she knew that it was stupid to engage in pointless negative fights with people like this. But not for the first time her temper got the better of her. She turned round and faced the women directly, breathing hard.

"I was wondering," she said, forcing her voice to remain as steady as possible, "if any of you have actually met a Morpher before?"

The receptionists, who froze when they realized Skye was addressing them, regarded her in silence for a moment, simultaneously backing away. Simone fixed her with a glare as the other two huddled behind her.

"No," she replied coldly.

"Then how," said Skye, her teeth grit extremely hard, "can you talk about Morphers like that when you've never even met one?"

"I don't need to have met one," hissed Simone, her face turning hostile as her fear became more prevalent. "We all know about Morphers—and what about you? Look how aggressive you are! You're a perfect example of why Morphers shouldn't mix with ordinary people!"

"I'm not aggressive," Skye snarled. "It's just hard not to get annoyed when some idiot is making you out to be some kind of vicious monster. I'm pretty sure I've been working here for the last year and never attacked anyone. But maybe you're too stupid to realize that?"

"Look at how she talks to people," said Simone, her voice shaking with both fear and fury. "She's calling us idiots and stupid. See what I mean about aggressive? Come on; let's get out of here. And don't even *think* about attacking us!" she added, staring Skye squarely in the eye, trembling fiercely as the three of them backed away. "I have my tag device in my hand and I'm calling emergency services right away if you dare to transform!"

"Take a look around you!" Skye said furiously, her fists clenched as she subconsciously started walking towards them; they shrank back in terror. "Do you have any idea what the hell's going on in this city? There are thugs out here who'll slit your throat just for looking at them the wrong way—there are people dying 'cause armies of scum are running around, setting fire to our homes— people are going to die because there's going to be a war! And you're talking as though *I'm* the one you have to worry about? Do you have *any* clue what's going on?"

"Don't come any closer," said Simone, her face white, holding out her tag device threateningly in front of her as though it were a sword. "Take another step and I'm calling emergency services, I swear I will. Everyone knows the thugs respect Morphers, I wouldn't be surprised if you're all in the same league—"

The suggestion that she might be on the same par as the very people who had caused both herself and those she loved such unimaginable pain, whose only goal in life was to maim, murder and destroy, caused Skye to lose her self-control; the words spilled out before she could stop them.

"The thugs murdered my dad!" she bellowed. "They killed my dad! Do you understand that? And you're saying we're in league with them? You ignorant—you foul—you—"

"I said, back off!" said Simone, shaking uncontrollably, for in her rage Skye's eyes had flashed luminous blue and strange tremors were shooting through her body, a sure sign of the beginning stage of transformation. "Back off—come on, let's go!"

The other two receptionists, who looked as though they were

about to faint from terror, nodded and the three of them turned on their heel and fled.

Skye stood there, watching them dash off into the night; her heart pounded as the anger coursed through her. She continued to breathe heavily, at the same time rebuking herself for her outburst. Now it wasn't just the morphing they had cause to gossip about, but details of her private life that she did not want anyone to know about.

"Skye? What's wrong?"

Her heart leapt at the sound of the familiar, husky voice behind her. Despite her rage, she felt something inside her purr softly, the butterflies in her stomach flittering around once more.

She turned round and saw Raphael standing there, a concerned expression on his face.

As usual, whenever she was in the presence of the man she still couldn't believe was hers, Skye had to refrain from melting on the spot (something which she would never have believed of herself prior to meeting him; playing the giddy, love-struck teenager was not really in her nature—but Raphael was the exception that had defied all ration and reason.)

She swallowed and moved towards him.

"Raphael," she said, unable to keep out the warmth in her voice, her heart pounding for a different reason this time.

"Skye, what is it? I pulled up just now and heard you shouting. Are you OK? Is it the thugs? I'm so sorry I'm late—I got held up on the road—a building had caught fire and the whole place was in chaos—what happened?"

"It's fine. I'm fine," Skye replied, shifting uneasily as the recent memory of Simone and the others replayed itself in her mind.

Raphael stepped towards her and gently touched her cheek; she felt her entire body tingle. He tilted her chin upwards with one hand, his penetrating green eyes piercing her own as he pulled her closer with his other arm. She stared up at him; his gaze was intense.

"What is it?" he said firmly.

"It's nothing. Can we go to the car please? It's pretty cold."

She avoided his stare as he took her by the hand and led her to his car. She debated whether or not to tell him about what happened; Raphael had always been very vocal about taking pride in being a Morpher. To him it was unfathomable that anyone would actually view morphing as a bad thing and he had reacted with both shock and disbelief whenever Skye had reiterated the bad experiences she'd had when others found out about her ability. But as she had told him on many occasions, his experiences had been different to hers and, whereas Raphael had been met with respect and reverence, Skye had faced fear and persecution. He had told her repeatedly not to allow it to bother her when people said negative things about her morphing; but she was not quite so thick-skinned and this was something that had not changed, despite his influence.

"You going to tell me what happened?" he said as he switched on the engine after they got into the car. Skye glanced sideways at his beautiful features while he backed into the road; it wasn't long before they were cruising down the streets of London, streets that were currently quiet and extremely empty.

"Don't worry about it, Raphael, it's nothing…"

Raphael sighed.

"Skye, you were shouting in the street. Your eyes were blue

when you turned to look at me and your body was shaking. Tell me."

"It's nothing, honest…just something happened at work today and it set me off, that's all."

"What was it?"

"I…look, something really weird happened at work. I was in a meeting with Ned when suddenly there was all this screaming. At first I thought it was the thugs; that they had broken in—"

Raphael's eyebrows shot up in alarm.

"Impossible! Not with all the extra security we've placed around the building—"

"It's OK," Skye hastened to reassure him. "It wasn't them. It was a beaver."

"A…what?"

"I know. I was shocked too—I've never even seen one in real life before, let alone seeing one in my office. So there was this beaver cub running around. The receptionist—" Skye forced herself to keep the anger out of her voice as she thought of Simone—"started screaming; the whole department panicked."

Raphael shook his head, puzzlement filling his handsome features.

"Something's not right about this. What's an animal like that doing in your building?"

"Raphael, I don't think it was an animal. I think it was a Morpher."

"A *Morpher?*"

"Yes. There was something about its scent that was human. But there was something else…I can't describe it. It's like it was a Morpher, but at the same time it wasn't. Does that make sense?"

"No. I have no idea what you mean. All I know is that it's too much of a coincidence that a Morpher appeared at your work." His expression hardened. "Pearson and his men better not be up to anything funny."

"Pearson? What's he got to do with it?"

"I don't know. I just know the whole thing is bizarre and that it makes no sense; I don't trust anything that doesn't make sense right now. What happened to the animal?"

"It ran away," Skye replied. "It ran out of the building and disappeared."

There was a slight pause.

"I don't like this," Raphael said eventually. "All of it…It's just odd. Another Morpher turning up at the same place where you work? If you see it again, don't go near it."

"But why not?" said Skye, who had already told herself earlier that day that if she saw the Morpher Beaver again, she would try and find out who it was and why it had been there. She had been both intrigued and curious and had fully intended to quell this curiosity if the opportunity should present itself. "It's a Morpher, Raphael. Like us. I don't know what it was doing there either—but it was scared. It wasn't dangerous. It was just a little beaver."

"It doesn't matter. If you see it again, I want you to promise me that you won't go near it."

Skye's eyebrows furrowed as they reached the traffic lights, which were glowing red. Raphael turned to face her, but she avoided his gaze. She couldn't quite explain it, but, aside from her curiosity, there was something that made her feel oddly protective over the beaver cub whenever she thought about it. It was a cub…it must be a very young human. It was frightened; when it had appeared in the office, Skye had not felt remotely threatened. She had wanted to reach out to it. As she thought about this, she resented the way Raphael was telling her to stay away from it. It was a little Morpher…what harm could it possibly cause them?

"It's just a cub," she muttered, looking out the window, trying to ignore Raphael's frowning reflection in the window. "It's not dangerous…"

"Skye, it doesn't matter. Something doesn't feel right. Will you just promise me that if it turns up again, you won't go anywhere near it?"

He took his hand off the wheel and placed it upon her own.

"Promise me, Skye."

She turned to face him.

"Fine," she said reluctantly, meeting his gaze. "I will probably never see it again anyway…but I promise. I just don't know why this bothers you so much."

He gripped her hand tighter; his eyes bore deeply into hers.

"You know what you mean to me," he said, his gaze fierce. "If there's a chance, any chance at all, that this is something… *untoward*, then I don't want you under any risk. It's bad enough that you won't leave the country to go somewhere safe…"

"Don't start that again, Raphael."

"I know. You won't go. But that doesn't mean I'm not going to do everything I can to protect you."

The lights turned amber. Raphael removed his hand slowly and placed it back on the steering wheel.

"So is that why you were shouting when I saw you? Something

to do with that."

"Sort of. My colleagues found out I'm a Morpher. When the receptionist screamed, my eyes changed colour. I thought I was going to have to transform, I thought we were being attacked. The receptionist…well, she doesn't really like Morphers; she was talking about me. She was there outside work while I was waiting for you."

"So you were shouting at her?"

"Yeah…"

"Well, what did she say?"

Skye hesitated.

"Just some stuff," she muttered, "about how we're dangerous and how we shouldn't be allowed to work with normal people. It just…got under my skin, that's all."

"Skye, why do you let what other people say bother you so much? You shouldn't care about what other people think—what do they know?"

"I know," said Skye, her irritation rising; she was not irritated at him, but at herself; telling him what happened meant having to acknowledge how foolish she was to have risen to the bait. "I just couldn't help it. Raphael, how can they talk about me like that when there are thugs running around killing people? Like *I'm* the one they need to be afraid of? I've been there a year—I've never hurt anyone! But she treated me like I was seconds away from attacking her!"

"I know. I know it bugs you when people talk about us like that. But don't let it. People's small minds and harsh words shouldn't mean anything to you; you're better than that. You've got your morphing—and you've got me."

He clutched her hand again and Skye felt the warmth rush through her.

"We're all under pressure," he told her, his voice gentle now. "All of us. Don't lose your cool over people like that. It's not worth it. You can't keep throwing stones at every dog that barks."

"Don't insult dogs please, Raphael."

He grinned.

"Sorry. Listen—are you still OK to come over tomorrow night?"

Skye nodded. She hadn't forgotten. Tomorrow night, the Chinese Emperor himself (who had flown in for a week's visit), plus a number of other special guests, would be visiting the House of Renzo for a formal dinner party to celebrate their alliance. It felt weird for Skye to attend the dinner party at all; she couldn't help feeling she would be out of place in such a grand scenario, plus it felt bizarre to think of such formalities when things were so tense and brutal outside. Still, Daphne, her best friend, would be there and so would her mother, who had been formally invited by Lord Renzo, much to Mrs. Archer's flustered delight.

"Yes of course," she replied as they turned into her road. Six foot soldiers were standing guard outside the premises as usual. "So who exactly is going to be there?"

"The Emperor, as you know…his nephew and niece…my dad and brothers…a couple of lords…your mum and friend…"

"They're very excited to be invited. That was really nice of your dad to invite my mother."

"Yeah, well he figured it was long overdue that they should meet," Raphael smiled, "and what better place to do so than at the dinner? As for your friend, it wouldn't be right if she didn't come, considering how she's in a relationship with Ricardo. It's tradition for our family to request the attendance of our significant others during formal dinner parties."

"So Trey and Joey won't be bringing anyone?"

"Trey doesn't have time for girls. And Joey, er, well, you know what he's like. I don't think there are enough seats at the table for the amount of "girlfriends" he's got. Here, I'll walk you to your door."

He parked up outside her house and stepped out of the car. Skye did the same. As he walked her to the doorstep and Skye could see her mother inside making the usual cup of evening coffee for the guards, Raphael turned to face her and pulled her close to him.

"Tomorrow, after dinner, there's something I want to give you," he said in a low voice.

Skye felt her heart skip a beat as he moved his face closer to hers; she gazed into the beautiful green eyes that were staring back at her, the familiar tingles racing through her.

"Oh right?" she managed to say. "What is it?"

"Not saying," he said, stroking her cheek and giving her a teasing smile. "But I hope you like it."

He cupped her face in both hands.

"I really love you. You know that?" he whispered.

Skye nodded, feeling herself melt into his eyes.

"Me too," she said, clasping her palm over the hand that was holding her cheek.

He leaned in and placed his lips upon hers, kissing her softly, before pressing her against his strong body and kissing her with more ferocity, more hunger. She responded in turn, her wolf senses magnifying, the blood pulsing through her veins; she was excited as she felt him react to her with even more vigour and ardour.

He pulled away, panting very slightly, his hands gripping her waist; his eyes were almost a luminous auburn in the darkness.

"I should go before I let my animalistic passions run away with me," he said, smiling. "I'll see you tomorrow, OK?"

"OK," she murmured.

He pulled her hand to his lips and kissed it before walking away into the night. She watched him as he stepped into his car and drove off, thinking for the thousandth time about how she still couldn't believe he was hers.

She rang the doorbell and her mother answered, a wide beam on her face.

"Skye!"

"Hi, Mum," Skye said, stepping into the house.

"I've just made the coffee for the guards. It really is so nice of your boyfriend allowing them to stay here. Did you have a nice day at work, dear?"

"Yeah, wasn't too bad. So what's for dinner tonight?"

"I got you some lovely Beef Carpaccio—makes a change from the usual steak! I also need you to help me decide what to wear tomorrow; I'm still amazed I was invited! It must be a very formal dinner if the Emperor himself will be there! I can't even remember the last time I wore a dress!"

"Er—well Raphael said we can wear whatever we like, although I guess it is going to be pretty formal...I was just planning on going in my leggings and a top."

"Oh, Skye, no! You can't wear leggings to a dinner at the Renzo mansion! I insist you wear a dress—go on, we can wear matching ones. I'll go to the store tomorrow while you're at work and purchase a couple. I saw a beautiful gown in town today; it was purple with miniature hearts. We could wear that!"

"Mum, I am not wearing a dress," said Skye firmly, thinking that she would rather die than wear a matching dress with her mother, especially one with miniature hearts splattered all over it. "You know how much I hate dresses."

"But dear, I am sure Daphne will be wearing a dress!"

"Yes, but that's *Daphne*. She loves dresses. She looks good in them. I don't."

"But you *do*, my dear. You have a lovely waist—"

"Mum, no. Just no. Absolutely not. I'll wear a long top over leggings, OK? Then it will look like I'm wearing a dress. And I'll wear my wolf boots."

If there was one thing Raphael liked doing ever since they had become a couple, it was buy Skye presents. This was despite her protests, as she was not used to being showered with gifts and, furthermore, these tended to be rather expensive presents that she had no idea what to do with; for example, the state-of-the-art 'Water into Wine' Blender, which he'd presented her with two weeks ago and which did actually turn water into wine due to the fact it came equipped with a kilogram of Vonash, a rare and highly costly mineral that made this otherwise impossible feat a reality. Not being much of a drinker, Skye had given it to her delighted mother who took great joy in showing it off to her friends whenever they came round for their poker night. For Skye, the greatest gift of all was just having Raphael in her life and this was something she told him repeatedly. It didn't make the slightest difference, however, and he continued to surprise her with the odd present here and there; from what he'd said earlier, there was another one coming tomorrow too. She still maintained that her favourite gift from him was the painting of the white wolf he had given to her on her birthday, but without a doubt her second favourite had to be the pair of wolf boots he'd handed to her not long after.

They were beautiful, thigh-high furry boots with a sharp heel and spikes sticking out at the back. Not only wonderful to look at, but extremely handy for kicking into the crotch of any thug who might sneak up behind her and try to attack her. She had nicknamed them 'wolf boots' because their colour matched her own when she was in wolf form. Being quite extravagant-looking, she had not yet worn them out in public. So far, she had only worn them in the presence of Raphael at his home, though admittedly wearing very little else at the time, something which he had no objection to; indeed, he had been quite vocal in expressing his approval…

She flushed with pleasure and, avoiding her mother's questions about what she was blushing about, she hastily changed the subject and instead moved onto the topic of dinner.

They discussed a few more things over dinner an hour later, Skye's mouth full of Beef Carpaccio, walnut bread and homemade creamy mushroom soup. Mrs. Archer was in full flow, talking relentlessly about the dinner tomorrow night and how she was looking forward to meeting the rest of the Renzo Family.

"I take it Raphael's brothers will be there too?"

"Oh yeah," said Skye, thinking of the infamous twins, Joey and

Ricardo Renzo. "I'm pretty sure the twins will be there..."

"One of them has partnered up with Daphne, hasn't he? Quite remarkable, considering word around town seems to be that those two boys aren't the type to settle down! I do hope Daphne isn't setting herself up for heartbreak."

"Yeah, it is kind of weird, but I wouldn't worry too much, Mum," said Skye. She herself couldn't deny she'd had similar concerns when she first found out that one of the most prolific Casanovas in the city was dating her best friend, but, thus far, Ricardo Renzo had proven himself to be a highly attentive and, as far as she knew, faithful boyfriend. At any rate, he seemed to be a lot better than Daphne's ex, Edge, whose possessive, borderline-stalker behaviour had really been to Skye's distaste.

They said goodnight to one another not long afterwards and Skye crawled into bed. She lay awake for some time, thinking over and over about the events of the day and what she wished she had said (or hadn't said) to that Simone. Trying to calm her mind, she tried reading for a while and listening to soothing meditation music, but to no avail. She turned off the lights and, eventually, after much tossing and turning she fell into slumber, her sleep filled with dreams of Raphael, and punctured by nightmares of her city burning in flames to the ground.

CHAPTER THREE

In the year 2118, a man named Sylvester Nuppets changed the fate of many Morphers, both for those who lived in the early 22nd century and those who were not yet born, such as Skye and Raphael. The UK media, which was still in existence during the time, had a field day with the total uproar that exploded throughout the country—and all because of an incident that occurred when Mr Nuppets arrived at his job one day in early springtime, the same job he had been in for ten years.

Sylvester Nuppets worked for a construction site in North London which was dedicated to building homes for refugees that had flocked to the city in 2101, the same year that a terrifying plague, Levola, had rampaged throughout the entire kingdom, killing millions in its wake. For two years straight, the plague swept through the lands, until 2103 when the disease suddenly abated. During this time, over three-quarters of the population died. London was the only city that had been locked under quarantine due to lack of funding and lack of resources, thus leaving the outer skirts completely unprotected. Several million people from surrounding towns and villages had managed to flee to the capital and successfully been approved as having no sign of the disease, but the time came when the city completely shut itself out from the rest of the country. As a result, almost everyone who did not live in London, and who had not managed to flee the island itself, died; a nation that was once famed for its overflowing population now faced a total populace of almost eleven million. A vaccine for the disease was developed in 2105 and every citizen within the country was ordered to take it. Consequently, London remained the only place in the United Kingdom that stayed populated for many years to come; even a century later, the rest of the island was mostly deserted and barren, though many of the evacuees that had fled to the city then sought their fortune overseas. A forty year struggle with economic collapse followed due to the loss of resources throughout the country; but thanks to wily, clever leadership, forged connections with other nations and the invention of highly advanced technology, London stayed on her feet and slowly, but surely, began to rebuild once more.

There were rumours abound during the time that the disease had spread due to a certain ethnic group. However, there was no evidence to support these rumours, which had in fact been fuelled by thugs and racists; they, in typical fashion, sought any excuse to air their prejudice, but the rumours were further played upon by certain newspapers, and this increased suspicion within the city, spreading belief that people of a certain ethnic background were responsible for the devastating plague that had stolen so many lives. As a result, it was not uncommon to hear of racist attacks and, in more extreme cases, murder.

It was this type of attack that Sylvester Nuppets walked in on during that fateful day in Spring. Being a man of peaceful disposition and gentle demeanour, he was horrified to stumble upon the sight of five men brutally kicking one man who was lying on the ground, his face smeared with blood. What made it more horrifying still, as Mr Nuppets stared in shock at the spectacle taking place on his work-scaffold, was that he recognized the men as his colleagues; furthermore, the man on the ground getting his face beaten to a pulp was Paulo, another colleague of his and one he considered a friend. They had shared many coffee breaks together and several discussions on the current climate as well as the low pay that scaffolders were subjected to.

Shy by nature and naturally avoidant of conflict, Sylvester would have preferred to walk away in a situation like this, but the sight of his friend lying half-dead on the ground as these brutes kicked and beat him left no room for doubt. Springing into action, he ran towards the group, yelling at them to stop.

"Hey! Hey stop that, all of you!"

The men turned to glare at him.

"Back off, Nuppets," said one. "This doesn't concern you."

"I said stop," said Sylvester, his voice shaking, but holding his ground. "Stop right now or I will report you."

The men laughed raucously.

"You gonna report us, huh, Nuppets? Good luck with that. This piece of crap here is the whole reason everyone died. Foreign trash. Should never have let trash like him in the country. Now get lost or you're next."

With that, the men continued kicking Paulo; one stomped on his face and there was the sickening, cracking sound of his nose breaking. Sylvester's stomach churned as Paulo managed to raise one lazy, purple eye to look at him, attempting to open his mouth and speak, but it was too full of blood. In that split-second, Sylvester did the only thing he felt he could do and the one thing his instinct was screaming at him. He transformed into his spirit animal.

Like many Morphers, Sylvester tended not to reveal his special ability to others, especially not at work. Nobody, apart from his good friend, Pete, knew he was able to do this. He was not someone who ever sought the spotlight and had fully intended to keep it that way, ever since he discovered at the age of five that he bore the same ability as his grandfather before him. So it was a complete and utter shock to the gang of men when the usually meek and mild-mannered Nuppets was suddenly replaced by the gigantic form of an Irish wolfhound, his builder's outfit bursting to pieces and landing in shreds on the ground.

The Wolfhound bounded towards them, teeth baring, standing protectively over the bloodied and bruised man on the pavement. Simultaneously, the colleagues gasped in horror and ran off without another word. The dog watched them go, his eyes flashing. Then he turned round to look at Paulo; he looked half-dead and was losing blood at an alarming rate. The Irish wolfhound began to bark loudly, that deep, rumbling bark that only a Wolfhound possessed. Moments later, other scaffolders appeared to see what all the noise was about. Their eyes widened in shock when they saw the shape of the enormous dog and the man lying beneath him. They shrank back fearfully, but the dog abruptly stopped barking and began to whine very softly, before licking Paulo's wounds. Then he barked once more and hurdled past the newcomers, who leapt to the side to avoid him. Not long afterwards, they rushed towards the man on the ground and called an ambulance.

News of the incident spread fast among the scaffolders and, soon, it reached the ears of the media. Nuppets suddenly found himself thrown into the very spotlight he had hoped to avoid his whole life. At first, he was the subject of much praise and congratulations from various reporters who took the side of the majority, the ones who were fully against the racism displayed towards men such as Paulo. But it wasn't long before other forms of the media, those that either secretly or openly agreed with the thugs, were writing highly provocative articles, condemning Nuppets for his involvement and subtly inciting further hatred towards the ethnic group. To add fuel to the flames, these same people began an open vendetta against Morphers, digging up stories (whether real or imagined) of the dangers they posed to society, and about how dangerous and unstable they were.

As a result, Nuppets soon found himself the victim of a smear campaign, championed by those racists within the media and various thugs and scoundrels who, even then, were multiplying throughout the city. Going into work became a nightmare with people shunning him or whispering about him; the same thugs who had beaten Paulo to a bloody pulp had been fired, but they often turned up outside the construction site, cracking their knuckles and glaring fiercely at Nuppets. On numerous occasions, Sylvester experienced verbal abuse in the streets; glass bottles and beer cans were thrown at him so often that it became a habit for him to stake out every street he turned into before walking onto it; people screamed at him to get out of town and even sent him death threats; bricks were hauled through his window. In time, even his own company turned against him and he was sacked by his superiors, who cited his presence was 'no longer befitting at this present time.' In short, life became a living hell.

For Sylvester, who was an extremely sensitive and gentle-hearted soul, such life became unbearable. His had been a simple one, going into work six days a week and occasionally spending a quiet Sunday afternoon with a cup of tea, a newspaper and the odd daydream about inviting the lady who worked in the local pharmacy for dinner, something he had always been too shy to do. His Morphing was something he had considered a well-guarded secret up until that fateful day when Paulo was attacked; he very rarely transformed, but, in that moment, he had reacted with pure instinct—never to hurt the men, simply to scare them away, for even in his canine body he could not bring himself to harm another person. Slowly, he felt his life spiral out of control as the harassment and abuse stretched into weeks, months…and it was on one particularly grey evening that Sylvester Nuppets, no longer able to handle the hatred that was coming in at him from all sides, decided to take his own life by wrapping a noose around his neck and hanging himself from his living room ceiling.

News of his death reached the ears of the entire country. The media cooked up a storm; the majority drowned out the minority, citing how disgusting it was that a man—who by all accounts was a hero—should feel driven to suicide due to a few nasty reporters and thuggish bullies. A witch hunt began in order to crack down on those media outlets who had made Nuppets feel so far removed from society; for the first time in history, thugs were driven into hiding for fear of the angry mob that created uproar up and down the country; the mob was made up of equal rights activists and ordinary citizens who were furious that Sylvester Nuppets saw no other way out than to end his life. Campaigns began; 'Justice for Nuppets' slogans were commonplace during the time. Several large companies boycotted the construction site Nuppets had worked for as an act of defiance against his unfair dismissal. Politicians were angrily accosted by activists who demanded that they provide legal rights for Morphers; Paulo, the man Nuppets had saved, spoke out of his distress at the death of his friend and he became the voice for many others who were anguished by such a senseless waste of life. The public increasingly became sympathetic to Morphers. Public mood was hostile and eventually the government had to take action.

So, several years later, a law was passed that all Morphers should have the same rights as 'ordinary people'; that they should not be treated with prejudice in the workplace or elsewhere; that anyone who physically or verbally assaulted a Morpher should face prosecution. This became known as the *Morphers Rights Act 2121,* an Act designed to ensure all Morphers were treated as equals at work, and outside it.

Of course, public mood is constantly changing and the subject of Morphers once again took a dramatic shift seven years later when another shape-shifter, a man called Eric Bolan (who had the ability to transform into a jaguar) killed twelve people over the course of three weeks. He became known as the Shifter Serial Killer and was wholly responsible for the entire country plummeting into fear and panic during the time he was active. When he was caught (during a police operation that saw him eating the remains of a man while in his animal form), word that he was a Morpher was quickly revealed to the public. It was Eric Bolan and his twisted ways that prompted the government to pass yet another law concerning Morphers—that if any Morpher should attack another human being during transformation, they would be sentenced to death. It was during this time that people's tendency to sympathize with Morphers now turned into a deep-rooted fear of the whole lot of them; it highlighted how, once again, the act of one person could have such a profound impact for all.

This way of thinking towards shape-shifters lasted for decades afterwards. Ironically, the very thugs that had persecuted Sylvester Nuppets grew to respect Morphers as time went on. However, like the majority of people, the majority of Morphers were decent human beings and one thing they did not like was to be associated with thugs and scoundrels; it was for this reason that the few shape-shifters who existed in the country kept their morphing a secret—with the exception of those who had the power and status not to fear, or even care, about what the public thought of them. One example was the Renzo family, whose members had always worn their ability with pride.

It was because of the tragic suicide of Nuppets and the *Morphers Rights Act 2121* that, almost a hundred years later, Skye found herself hauled up in front of the C.E.O of Trixaction Cinemas and two Head Office managers, one of whom was a female pursed-lipped one, the other a young blonde man. Beside her, Ned was jittering subtly around from foot to foot, plainly nervous. It was the day after the bizarre incident with the beaver. Ned had spoken to her early that morning and informed her she was required to speak with the highest managers and the owner himself for a disciplinary hearing.

"Now make sure you conduct yourself professionally in front of them," Ned had told her primly. "I'm sure this is all just one big misunderstanding that will be resolved in no time at all."

Even so, they were both shuffling rather worriedly as they entered the Head Office meeting room where the panel was waiting for them.

"Now Miss Archer," began the female Head Office manager; Skye did not fail to notice as soon as she walked in that the female manager was eyeing her with a look of intense dislike, but she told herself she must be imagining it. The woman didn't even know her…

"We received a complaint this morning regarding your behaviour," continued the female manager. "Apparently, yesterday you threatened to transform into a wild beast and attack your fellow colleagues. Is this correct?"

Skye didn't know whether to be shocked or angry—or both—at this fabricated tale. She knew Simone had reported her for being a Morpher, but she hadn't known she'd actually made up a story that Skye had threatened to transform and attack her!

"No, it is not correct," she replied, fighting to keep the infuriation out of her voice.

"Well, it says here that you became rather aggressive during an incident that occurred in the Customer Services department yesterday. It says that several of your colleagues encountered you outside work premises when your shift was over and that you threatened to transform into a…I'm sorry, what animal is it you are able to turn into?"

"A wolf," said Skye, fury now bubbling iside her. She could not believe that Simone had reported such a lie! At what point had she threatened to transform and attack the receptionists?

"Ah yes. Well, as you can imagine, such behaviour is not tolerated or acceptable in this line of work." The Head Office manager peered at her in disapproval. "The company has been gracious enough to employ you, despite being a Morpher, but we certainly do not expect to hear such shocking accusations regarding your behaviour towards normal citizens. We have come to the conclusion that—"

"Wait a moment," interrupted Skye, her anger now directed towards the manager who was sitting there staring at her with such an unfavourable look on her face. "What do you mean, *despite* being a Morpher? When I put in my job application over a year ago, I didn't realize that being a Morpher made me any different to anyone else who wanted to work here! I thought I was being judged on my merit and achievements—not whether I'm able to transform into a wolf! So I'm not sure what you mean by 'despite'?"

"What I meant or did not mean is irrelevant," said the manager coldly. The other manager shifted uneasily, as did Ned. "The point is that this company has allowed you to work with us in the belief that you would act in an appropriate manner—this does not include threatening members of our workforce!"

"I didn't threaten *anyone.* That's a complete and utter lie."

"Three people have said the exact same thing, Miss Archer, that you threatened them yesterday evening after your shifts were over. Why would all three of them say exactly the same thing if it is such a lie?"

"Well, because they don't like Morphers, of course! They were treating me as though I was going to attack them, but I didn't lay a finger on them and I never would in a million years!"

The manager glared at her.

"You need to understand that our priority is to ensure our work environment remains safe and secure for all of our staff," she said. "We cannot have people like yourself threatening the well-being of our workforce."

"I've been here for over a year and I'm pretty sure I've never threatened anyone's well-being!" retorted Skye hotly.

"We have eye-witnesses who say you threatened them. We take such accusations very seriously."

"I really must protest," came Ned's voice; he was sweating profusely as the managers and C.E.O turned to look at him. "I hired Skye because she had an excellent record in her previous customer services role. The fact that she is a Morpher was highly irrelevant— and, in my humble opinion, still is. During the incident with the animal yesterday, Skye did not threaten anybody. I feel the young lady downstairs may have over-reacted somewhat—she was extremely hysterical when she entered our office, you see—"

"You should have informed your superiors that you hired a Morpher," interrupted the purse-lipped manager sternly; Ned gulped. "We were completely unaware of this. In future, you will ensure that all potential employment is cleared with us first."

Skye felt her blood boil. Ned might be pompous and irritating at times, but he had at least made an attempt to defend her. This manager of Head Office seemed determined to tarnish Skye with a brush that she did not feel she deserved; she was adamant that Simone and the others had been telling the truth without even hearing Skye's side of the story. What's more, Skye could now see that her initial suspicion had been correct; the woman did not like her. She immediately suspected it was because she was a Morpher and, judging by the woman's attitude towards her since the start of the meeting and the derogatory tone in which she spoke about Morphers, she was more convinced than ever that this was the reason for the waves of dislike she could feel directed towards her; like the receptionist, it appeared that the Head Office manager did not feel it was correct or natural for Morphers to integrate with the ordinary populace.

Once again, in the face of such prejudice, Skye's temper shot to the surface.

"Isn't it the job of Head Office to double-check records on each employee though?" she questioned innocently, unable to hide the sneer in her voice. "I mean, you clearly have a major issue with hiring people like *me*; I'm surprised you don't diligently search through every single CV to make sure it doesn't happen. Maybe you might want to try doing your job properly in future?"

The female manager stared at her in shock, plainly amazed by her audacity. The other manager's eyebrows shot upwards; the C.E.O stared at Skye rather blankly. Ned was unable to stop himself from smacking his hand to his forehead, before shaking his head in a rather despairing manner. Skye herself was shocked at her own gall and inwardly cursed herself for not holding her tongue, but at the same time she couldn't suppress the satisfied feeling currently racing through her for rendering the Head Office manager speechless—with rage, by the looks of things.

For a moment, silence continued to reign throughout the room. Then, clearing her throat and a small smirk developing on her lips, the female manager turned to her colleague and the C.E.O.

"Your thoughts?" she said, fixing them with an intense look.

The male manager cleared his throat.

"Well, perhaps it would be beneficial to hear Miss Archer's side of the story…" he began, though his voice faltered when the female manager's steely gaze turned into a full-blown glare.

The C.E.O, a large balding man in his late forties, nodded.

"It is hardly fair to take the word of one side without actually hearing what the other side has to say, Regina," he said, looking pointedly at the female manager.

Regina managed a strained smile.

"Of course," she replied.

She raised her eyebrows at Skye.

"*Well* then," she said; it was clearly giving her great difficulty maintaining the politeness in her voice, "why don't you tell us what happened yesterday—according to you?"

"No problem," replied Skye, not looking at her.

With that, she launched into a brief description of what happened, beginning first with the beaver incident ("It is true my eyes switched colour, but to be honest I'd thought we were being attacked by thugs and this is what happens when I prepare myself to be on guard") and ending with the confrontation outside the gates ("I won't deny that the receptionist and her friends were saying some nasty things about me because of my ability to morph and that it made me angry; and yes, my eyes did switch colour again. But I would never have laid a finger on them. There's absolutely no way I would ever hurt an unarmed person while in my animal form. I know the law. And I just wouldn't do it. It's not in my nature.")

The panel sat looking at her in silence once she'd finished. Ned coughed in an exaggerated manner before speaking up.

"I absolutely cannot imagine Skye attacking anybody in that way," he said, trying to sound firm and confident, but still unable to keep his knees from knocking together, "and quite honestly, Simone downstairs was saying some rather horrendous stuff—my entire team heard it. As did some of our customers who were unfortunate enough to witness the incident. I find it very difficult to believe that Skye would ever threaten anyone in the manner she has been accused of. It is true that she can be stubborn…and that there are occasions when she has complete disregard for the rules—and, may I add, she appears to have her head in the clouds half the time, especially in the mornings—"

Great time to get it all off your chest, Ned, Skye thought wryly.

"—But it is preposterous to think that she would ever attack someone or threaten to! And that is why I really must object to these accusations. For all her many flaws, she is still one of my best agents and has contributed more to the department than she has harmed it!"

His voice became stronger at the end, his chest puffing out, peacock-style. Skye felt strangely touched. Ned annoyed her just as much as she annoyed him on a daily basis, but when push came to shove, the Customer Services Manager was ready to defend his employee and she knew it would be incredibly churlish not to feel grateful for that.

Regina the Manager, however, did not look impressed.

"Yes, well, as you are aware this hearing has nothing to do with how good or bad your agent is at her job. It is about a threat she has been accused of making. One we consider such a serious one that we called for disciplinary action almost immediately. Furthermore, such threats are also taken seriously by the authorities, whom we are still deciding whether or not to involve."

Skye's eyes widened in disbelief. A threat made by any Morpher towards an ordinary person was enough to land them a jail sentence—she had never heard of an incident where this particular law was put into effect (there were hardly any prisons in the country, let alone the city) but, nevertheless, if she was arrested then it would cause a good deal of problems for herself and her mother, problems they could do without right now. She felt anger burn inside her once again. There were bigger things to worry about—she didn't want her own flesh and blood dragged into this, certainly not because of some spiteful lie!

"Since when was it acceptable to involve the authorities in something where there's no evidence for it whatsoever?" Skye burst out. Ned shot her a worried glance. "All you've got is the word of some dumb girl who hates me for being a Morpher, some stupid cow who—"

"Skye!" hissed Ned. Regina fixed her with a hard, cold look. The male manager and C.E.O shook their heads.

"You are aware of the *Execution Act 2130*, I trust, Miss Archer?" said Regina, the coldness still prevalent in her eyes.

"I am, thanks. I did study history in school, you know. And I take it you're aware of the *Morphers Rights Act 2121?*"

"Obviously," responded Regina icily.

"Right. Well that Act says that Morphers are to be treated as equals—including at work. And right now, I don't feel like I'm being treated like an equal. For one thing, you're quick to believe the receptionist even though she has no evidence to support her claims and you've totally disregarded my side of things!"

"The *Execution Act* states that any Morpher who attacks an ordinary person in deliberation is to be sentenced to death," said Regina, ignoring Skye's words. "It also states that any Morpher who *threatens* an ordinary person with violence is to be tried and sentenced as is befitting to the crime. Clearly, you have little comprehension of how serious the issue is—"

Skye almost laughed out loud.

"So now it's a crime I've committed? What, for defending myself? Because if my memory serves me right, the only thing I did was defend myself yesterday—*not* attack anyone or make any threats to attack!"

"According to *three* people, you made it very clear that you were about to transform—"

"Yes, three people who have something against Morphers—why? I have no idea, seeing as they made it pretty clear they'd never met any before!"

"I will not tell you again, Miss Archer, the first priority of this company is to ensure the well-being and protection of our staff and, frankly, judging by your attitude I do not find it hard to believe that there is truth to their story—"

"Can we cut the crap? You haven't liked me since the moment I walked in—you make it pretty obvious! And, can I also point out, for someone who's so concerned about the protection of your staff, you've somehow managed to forget that the extra security around the building lately was put in place by Lord Renzo—who happens to be a Morpher himself! Funny how you manage to ignore that fact while you're busy judging me for being different to you!"

"OK, I think it's time we call a halt to this meeting," came the voice of the C.E.O as the furiously frosty Regina stared daggers at the irate, fiery-tempered Skye, and vice versa. "Miss Archer, thank you for coming in to speak with us. You too, Ned. We will review your side of things and come to a conclusion by the end of the day."

This was the sign for Skye and her manager to leave the room. Ned, who was perspiring heavily, managed a weak 'thank you' before the two of them left the room. Skye stared silently at the ground as they walked down the corridor, until Ned was no longer able to restrain himself.

"What in the *world* is wrong with you?" he exploded, dabbing his sweaty forehead with a tissue and glaring at her. "What possessed you to behave like that towards one of the most important managers in the company—and in front of the C.E.O of all people?"

"She's prejudiced against Morphers," Skye growled.

"I don't care what she's prejudiced against! I couldn't care less if she's prejudiced against Morphers, non-Morphers, black people, white people, fat people, skinny people, people with three heads—I absolutely do not care! The point is, she is the manager of H.O— and you have made things a hundred times worse than what they were by failing to control your temper and talking back in that appalling way! What's more, you have managed to put your job on the line—and mine, come to think of it!"

"Simone's whole report was a lie, I was trying to do the right thing by defending myself," began Skye fiercely, but Ned abruptly cut her off.

"This isn't about doing the right thing! This is about doing as you're told—something you clearly have serious issues with! Didn't I *say* beforehand to act professionally? Where, in that head of yours, did you think for one moment that behaving in that dreadful manner would in *any* way help your cause? Don't you *care* about this job, Skye? I seem to find myself asking you that question more and more!"

"Of course I care," muttered Skye sullenly.

"Then I suggest you start acting like it!" snapped Ned. "This whole thing has blown far out of proportion—not to mention, it has taken up valuable time that could otherwise have been spent on more worthwhile things! I planned an entire slideshow this morning, a highly informative three-hour projection series highlighting the pros and cons of verbal holographic ticket machines; but instead of being able to present it to the department, I was stuck in a disciplinary meeting!"

Thinking about how her colleagues were probably cheering and celebrating at managing to evade one of Ned's long, laborious pre-lunch slideshows, Skye was unable to suppress a grin. This did not go down well with her manager.

"It isn't funny!" he said furiously, misjudging the reason for her sudden beaming; the smile immediately vanished from Skye's face. "Don't stand there smirking at me when we have such a serious matter on our hands! I am now going to have to move the slideshow to the beginning of next week, which also means delaying the monthly Customer Service IQ Challenge! Do you have any idea of the disruption you have caused?"

"It's not my fault Simone decided to make up lies about me," flared Skye, her temper swiftly returning.

"But it *is* your fault for not keeping your head screwed on properly during the meeting back there! This will mean more disciplinary meetings, more delays—not to mention *I*, of all people, being criticized by Head Office! *Me!* Regina made herself abundantly clear that I will have to clear all future employment with her—I don't know where that woman gets off telling the Manager of Customer Services what to do, even if she is a manager of H.O…"

His face went extremely red as he puffed up with indignation.

"Nevertheless," he continued huffily, "this one fact cannot be denied. If you had just apologized and told them how much you regretted the incident, they would have dropped the whole thing. Unfortunately, the opposite has happened!"

"Apologized for what though? Like I said, it wasn't true—"

"Once again, you are completely missing the point!"

They arrived outside the Customer Services office.

"Now, Skye, I suggest you get your things and go home."

Skye looked at him, horrified.

"You're not *firing* me, are you?"

"No, I am not," snapped Ned. "However, your emotions are clearly all over the place today and the last thing we need is you creating a scene with one of the customers. If anything like *that* happens you can be sure Head Office will terminate your employment to immediate effect! I suggest you take the day off, clear your head and think about your priorities!"

"Look, there's no need for me to actually miss work—"

"Not another word, Miss Archer! Now collect your things, if you please!"

Still glaring, he opened the door and the two of them walked inside. The other Customer Service agents stared at Skye curiously. She didn't return their gazes.

Making sure her computer was switched off and gathering up her bag, Skye walked back to the door where Ned was still standing, a very stiff expression on his face.

"Look," she muttered, rubbing her neck as he continued to hold the door open, "I also wanted to say thanks, Ned, for defending me back there…"

"I am your manager, Skye, you are a member of my team," responded Ned shortly. "It wouldn't have made sense if I *didn't* inform them of your more redeeming qualities—few as they are. Goodbye and I will see you tomorrow—bright and early!"

With that, he slammed the door in her face.

CHAPTER FOUR

"Skye! Hurry up, the car's outside!"

"I'm coming, Mum!"

Skye ran down the stairs as fast as her wolf boots would allow her, almost tripping on the last step but catching hold of the banister just in time.

"Goodness me!" exclaimed Mrs. Archer as her daughter steadied her balance, looking slightly dishevelled. "Do be careful, Skye! Those boots of yours have got spikes on them—it's almost like an accident waiting to happen! Well," she added, "I must say, you look very nice, dear, but I still think the purple dress would look absolutely lovely on you…"

"Thanks, Mum, but I'm OK with this," said Skye in a rushed way, before her mother could get any ideas about that horrendous purple dress with pink hearts dotted on it; ever since she'd been sent home from work, her mother had eagerly tried coaxing her into wearing it for the Renzo dinner, stating "I've bought it now, you might as well wear it!" but Skye had been firm in her refusal.

They left the house and stepped into the dark, empty streets that were lit with faint firefly lamps. The streets were always empty at this time of the evening; quiet, too, except for screaming that could be heard on regular occasions, a sure sign that the thugs were at work. Of course, there was very little anybody could do, except sit huddled in their homes, thankful they were not the unfortunate souls caught in the crossfire of the villains' evening prowls. Skye instinctively sniffed the air as she always did whenever stepping outside her house at night. The guards still stood vigilantly outside the house and the chauffeur Raphael had sent to pick them up was standing by the car only a mere thirty seconds away—but it would take less than thirty seconds for thugs to spring up and attack them.

She took her mother by the hand and hurriedly pulled her towards the vehicle. The chauffeur bowed and opened the door for them. Mrs Archer looked rather awed as she stepped into the car, noting its splendour with rather flustered intrigue. Skye was somewhat more indifferent as she got in next to her mother; she was used to being chivvied along in Raphael's numerous vehicles (besides which, this one was not as grand as past cars had been; the Renzo family had sold a number of their more prestigious possessions in order to fund the less wealthy citizens of the city who had expressed a desire to evacuate the country, but could not afford to.)

They arrived at Notting Hill Meadows, the place where Raphael lived, within ten minutes. Fire torches were glowing outside the mansion but, like the rest of the city, the streets were deserted. This was a relatively odd and eerie sight in itself as the area surrounding the Renzo territory had always been considered a safe one by the Londoners during nighttime. But now, even here was no longer deemed safe to roam.

The chauffeur escorted them to the door. Mrs. Archer looked extremely excited.

"Do I look OK?" she asked Skye anxiously, patting her dress to smooth it out.

"You look beautiful, Mum," replied Skye with a smile. And it was true; she had not seen her mother look so dressed up, or glowing as much as she was tonight, for a long time. The purple dress with hearts, while it would have looked monstrous on Skye herself, suited her mother very well; like Daphne, dresses were very becoming on her. Ever since Skye's father had been killed by thugs twelve years ago, Mrs. Archer had not bothered herself with making the most of her appearance; so it warmed Skye's heart to see her mother looking so alive and vivacious, something she especially appreciated during these uncertain times.

The chauffeur rang the doorbell and, moments later the butler opened the door.

"Miss Skye and Mrs. Archer have arrived," the chauffeur told the butler.

The butler nodded and bowed slightly to the two ladies.

"This way please, Madams," he said.

They followed the butler down the long, red, velvet carpet hallway. Mrs. Archer mouthed the word "Madams!" to her daughter; Skye grinned back at her. As always whenever she entered the Renzo mansion, Skye noted the numerous paintings and tiger statues in various places down the halls. The spirit animal of Lord Renzo, like his son and also like his great-grandfather, Janus Renzo, the original Morpher, was a tiger and he had a special liking for them.

They walked for a couple minutes more before coming to the dining room door, which was slightly ajar. They could see candlelight flickering and hear soft piano music coming from inside; there were voices talking in low tones. The butler pulled open the door and beckoned them inside.

"Skye!"

As soon as Skye stepped into the room, her best friend, Daphne, came scooting towards her. She looked as pretty as ever in a blue sequined dress and the enormous beam she was wearing on her face.

"Hi, Daph," Skye said with a wide smile as her friend gripped her in a big hug.

"So glad you're here!" Daphne exclaimed, releasing her friend before hugging Skye's mother. "You too, Mrs. Archer! Wow! You both look really lovely—and those boots are amazing!" She lowered her voice. "I'm really glad you arrived, you'll never guess who's here—"

"You made it," came a warm voice next to them.

Skye spun round and saw Raphael standing beside her, a rose in his hand.

"For you, my lady," he said, bowing slightly towards her.

Daphne giggled as Raphael handed his girlfriend the rose, a smile on his lips as he stared into her eyes. Skye felt herself blush as she took it from him.

"Thanks," she told him, pink-cheeked.

"My pleasure," he said, reaching over and kissing her. His eyes roved over her. "You look beautiful."

He turned to Mrs. Archer who was watching the two of them with the widest smile, as she always did whenever they expressed public displays of affection.

"You look lovely too, Mrs. Archer," said Raphael, kissing her hand.

"Oh, flattery will get you everywhere, Raphael!" trilled Skye's mother.

Raphael grinned.

"Come with me, ladies. There are people I want to introduce you to. My father especially, Mrs. Archer, he's very much been looking forward to meeting you."

"I'll see you in a bit, Skye!" said Daphne, waving.

Raphael led them through the splendid dining room that was adorned with red velvet curtains, a long marble table with candelabras on it, and various framed portraits on the walls. Several butlers were standing with trays of *hors d'oeuvres* and glasses of champagne; to the left, a man sat playing soft melodies on a large, ancient grand piano. A few people were standing around in pairs chatting quietly to one another, mere silhouettes among the candlelight.

They came to a long, plush couch at the far end of the room where two people were talking amongst themselves; they looked up when Raphael and the others approached them.

"Dad," said Raphael, addressing a man with greying hair who was holding a silver cane, "Skye and her mother are here."

Lord Renzo rose from his seat, a smile beneath his beard.

"My dear Mrs. Archer," he said in that low, gentle voice of his, taking Mrs. Archer's hand and kissing it. "Our meeting is long overdue. It is a true pleasure to meet you at last. It is quite clear to me now where Skye gets her beauty."

Mrs. Archer flushed a bright, beetroot red, unable to hide her delight at being greeted so courteously by the famed Lord Renzo.

"The pleasure is all mine, I assure you!" she said, rather breathlessly. "And please—call me Lillian!"

"Lillian it is then," smiled Lord Renzo, bowing to her before turning to Skye, stepping forwards and kissing her on both cheeks.

"And it is lovely as always to see you too, my dear. You look as wolf-like as ever; it is most endearing."

His eyes twinkling, he turned towards the man who remained seated on the couch.

"Miss Archer here is also a Morpher," he told him. Skye turned to look at the other person on the couch for the first time and her eyes widened as she realized that the older man in magnificent yellow robes wearing a red and black crown was undoubtedly the Emperor. Seeing him in the flesh was quite overwhelming; there was something inherently regal about him, not just his fine clothing, but also his general demeanour. This was the man who headed the most powerful empire in the world and Skye couldn't help feeling intimidated in his presence.

Frantically trying to decide whether to bow, curtsey or hold her hand out for a handshake (how exactly *did* one greet the Emperor? She'd forgotten to ask Raphael and it wasn't exactly something they taught you about in school), Skye was saved the trouble of speaking as the Emperor rose grandly from the couch.

"It is an honour to meet you," he said to her; he had a strong gravelly, Eastern accent that Skye had never heard before. "In my country, Morphers are held in great admiration."

"Oh, er—we are?" said Skye, feeling tongue-tied and cursing

herself for not knowing what else to say.

The Emperor nodded, a faint smile on his lips.

"Yes. It is almost like a legend, is it not? To transform into the animal of your spirit? We hold such an ability in high esteem. Our ancestors were strongly connected to twelve animals in particular, one for each year—"

"Oh, the Chinese Zodiac!" blurted out Skye enthusiastically. "I love that! I was born in the year of the tiger—Um, I mean," she said, her voice faltering, "sorry to interrupt you—and it is an honour to meet you, too, by the way, I forgot to say it earlier…"

She went pink, highly embarrassed about her bumbling and feeling more out of place than ever; she shot a desperate glance at Raphael, who was chuckling quietly, a fond expression on his face. Skye flushed even more.

The Emperor must think I'm such a…urgh, I don't even know what! She groaned to herself. *Can't even hold a proper conversation!*

The Emperor, however, was all smiles.

"Ah…fierce tiger lady!" he exclaimed. "Such women are feared where I come from for their strength and tenacity."

"Makes perfect sense to me," said Raphael, stepping forward with a grin. "Anyone would think she's the tiger round here; but nope, she's a wolf. Though they're just as, ah, tenacious, to be honest."

"As you may have surmised," said Lord Renzo to Skye and her mother, "this is His Royal Highness, Emperor Jin of China. Emperor Jin will be staying with us for the next few days. We are, of course, deeply honoured by his presence. Emperor Jin, this is Skye Archer, my son's partner, and her most charming mother, Lillian Archer."

Emperor Jin inclined his head towards them; Mrs. Archer curtsied, plainly overwhelmed, while Skye bowed, thinking the whole time about how surreal this all was. As the media had been outlawed many years ago, neither she nor her fellow civilians had ever seen pictures or programmes of the Emperor, nor even the country he hailed from. There were a few history books portraying China, its culture and people, but these had been printed a couple of centuries ago and representative of Ancient China back at the start of the last millennia, not modern-day China as it was now. Ordinary citizens were mostly cut off from the outside world—so to meet Emperor Jin, a ruler so famed and revered, was deeply unnerving. Royalty, or stories of royalty, often struck a chord with Skye. She could recall, many years ago when she was very young, her father telling her stories about her own country's Royal Family; of how, seven hundred years before, a king sat on his throne, a king who had six wives throughout the course of his reign and whose country fought many wars; she could recall tales of a queen who turned her country into a mighty nation, fending off invaders, using the sea as her weapon; she remembered how she would lie excitedly in her bed, waiting for her father to enter the room and tell her more tales; legends that, in these times, had long been forgotten by so many people, like a dusty book placed on a dusty shelf .

Now there was no Royal Family left in the UK. In a surprising move, when law and order began to disintegrate to severe levels, they had evacuated to a place of safety in New Zealand. The United Kingdom remained the United Kingdom, but in name alone. They had not returned since. Skye, in her older years, wondered if they ever would. She thought it unlikely, especially now, on the brink of civil war. But during the times she allowed her mind to wander in this direction, she wished they would someday, if only as a reminder, to show how things had not always been the way they were now, to bring the people a sense of pride, a sense of worth that no one in this day and age could ever recall having. All people knew now was fear. Fear of thugs. Fear of losing their lives to criminals and their vile vices. And, more recently, fear of all-out war. What was there to be proud of now? A broken city, terrorized by hooligans and lowlifes? Pride was alien; fear was a way of life.

"Skye? Are you alright?"

She heard Raphael's voice murmuring in her ear. Blinking, she shook her head slightly and realized she was still in a bowing position, having been lost in thought; the same strange cycle of thought that had taken hold of her more often than usual lately.

"Oh—sorry," she said, looking embarrassed as she straightened up. "I…It is a real honour to meet you, Your Highness."

"As I said, the honour is mine," said the Emperor, inclining his head once more. "I hope to become far better acquainted with you all in the future."

"Skye and Lillian, I do hope you have a pleasant time with us this evening," said Lord Renzo. "There are many more guests that I am sure will be eager to meet you. Lillian, I would be very happy if you would consider being seated next to me at dinner later; I am eager to hear your thoughts on many things, including Morphers, especially as you have managed to raise such a charming one of your own."

"Oh—I would love to!" replied Mrs. Archer, unable to contain the delight on her face.

Lord Renzo nodded pleasantly before turning to his son.

"But where are your manners, Raphael? Mrs. and Miss Archer are without a drink. And might I add," he added, smiling at Skye and her mother, "the *hors d'oeuvres* are really quite delectable. I highly recommend the quail eggs in avocado."

"Oops, sorry!" said Raphael. "Come with me, ladies. Dad, Emperor Jin," he nodded, bowing his head. Skye and Mrs. Archer thanked Lord Renzo and the Emperor before following Raphael across the room again.

"Here you go," said Raphael, leaning towards one of the trays a butler was holding, picking up two glasses of champagne and handing them to Skye and Mrs. Archer. "Hey Tom, you got any more of those quail egg in avocado things?"

Tom, the butler, shook his head solemnly.

"My apologies, but I am afraid we have run out, Master Raphael," he replied.

"Oh right, OK," said Raphael.

He turned to Skye and her mother.

"Not really a big loss," he told them. "To be honest, I thought they were kind of disgusting. So! What do you make of the Emperor?"

Skye and her mother both agreed it was quite an amazing experience. Raphael nodded.

"He'll be staying with us for a few days. There's going to be an official meeting of introduction with a couple of government representatives to discuss strategy, but, of course, that's all for show. Most of them are corrupt and eating out of Pearson's pocket; the rest are eating out of ours, such as the ones we'll be meeting with. That's the dirty world of politics, though. Others have sided with neither ourselves nor Pearson—they're mostly the senior lot. They're still deluded into thinking they have any type of hold over this city, when in reality they're pretty ineffective. Still, they're always looking for opportunities to uphold our joke of a law."

He lowered his voice.

"That's why I had to be so careful a few months ago. If the law brigade, combined with Pearson's allies on the inside, found out that I was transforming and killing thugs in secret, things might have turned out differently. So that's another good reason everything kicked off as soon as it did. Anyway, we just have to hope that our own manpower, plus the Chinese reinforcements, are enough to squash Pearson and his men for good."

Several weeks ago, Chinese reinforcements had been scattered around the city, waiting for the official order to strike. Skye had expected the fighting to commence immediately, but, oddly, this had not been the case. Someone, somewhere was clearly formulating a plan. While she was curious to know what Lord Renzo's course of action would be, she had not yet asked Raphael and he had not brought the subject up. If secrecy was a key essence to victory, then she could understand the silence. A part of her didn't even want to know. It was easier to continue living, pretending everything was normal, at least for now.

Raphael cleared his throat.

"But let's not ruin the evening by discussing politics. Mrs. Archer, did you enjoy meeting my father? I believe he has taken quite a shine to you."

"Oh, well, I can't imagine why!" said Mrs. Archer, all a fluster. "He really is the most remarkable man—all those wonderful things he's done for the city, fighting against those dreadful thugs—and so polite, too—"

"Mum's his number one fan," grinned Skye.

A voice spoke behind them.

"Raphael, there you are. Skye, hello, how have you been?"

They all turned to see Raphael's eldest brother, Trey, standing there with that usual serene expression of his which masked a much more shrewd and vigilant character. Lord Renzo's eldest son, like all the males in the family, possessed the same handsome good looks that the Renzos were known for, but while Raphael was fierce and headstrong and the twins were wild and carefree, Trey was calm and diplomatic, the voice of reason amidst the chaos (as Skye had recently witnessed on several occasions when the twins felt compelled to tease Raphael mercilessly on just about anything; Raphael's hot temper was only soothed by Trey's peaceful, calm intervention). It was these qualities the eldest Renzo brother possessed that had played such an instrumental role in assuring the support of the Emperor. Skye always enjoyed being around Trey who, like his father, had that same quiet confidence and authority that instilled a sense of security in those around them.

He was not alone. Behind him stood two people, both clearly of Chinese descent; one was male and looked as though he might be in his mid-twenties; the other was a girl who looked about Skye's age.

"Trey, hi," said Skye with a smile as Trey kissed her on the cheek. "I'm OK, thanks. You? Oh—this is my mother. Mum, this is Trey, Raphael's brother."

"A pleasure to meet you, Mrs. Archer," said Trey, imitating Lord Renzo and holding Mrs. Archer's hand to his lips, who beamingly told him to call her Lillian. He acknowledged this with a gallant smile before gesturing to the people behind him.

"I would also like to introduce you all to a couple of people who have just arrived. This is Kai, the Emperor's nephew, and Lo Wen, his niece. They will be staying with us for a few days."

The nephew, Kai, stepped forwards, smiling at them and holding out a hand to Raphael.

"I must apologize for our late arrival this evening," he said in that same strong Eastern accent; like the Emperor, his English was excellent. "When we learned our uncle was visiting your country, we had to come along. London is famous for its sight-seeing, is it not?"

"Well, once upon a time, yes," replied Raphael, taking the hand that was held out to him and shaking it in a friendly manner. "Unfortunately, a lot of landmarks were destroyed some years ago. I take it you were out in the city this evening then?"

"Oh yes. We did not see much because our bodyguards permitted us to move very little, but it was still worth visiting places where famous monuments once stood. We even found a teashop during our outing; tea drinking, something our nation and yours have in common. With the exception that we do not take milk in ours." He chuckled.

"To be honest, I don't take milk in mine either," said Raphael.

"As for me, I don't even drink tea so I'm afraid I cannot comment," said Trey, jokingly apologetic.

The three men chortled, as did the Emperor's niece, Lo Wen.

Skye couldn't help noticing that the niece was extremely pretty, dressed in a lavish, sparkling white dress that ended just below her thighs; she also couldn't fail to notice that Lo Wen's eyes had been firmly fixed on Raphael the entire time and had, on more than one occasion, roved around his muscular torso in a not-so-subtle manner. Skye was used to the attention that Raphael received from other women by now, but it still didn't stop her eyes narrowing.

"I'm Raphael, by the way," said Raphael once their chuckles had subsided, "and this is Skye, my girlfriend, and her mother, Lillian."

"I know who you are; your brother has spoken most highly of you," said Kai to Raphael. "And I am charmed to make the acquaintance of you all," he added with a bow in the ladies' direction.

Daphne came over at that moment. She hailed them and the usual introductions commenced.

"Speaking of tea," said Raphael, reaching into his pocket and pulling out a small, plastic bottle with liquid inside it, "that makes me think of bubble tea. Which makes me think of bubbles. I don't suppose you...?"

He held the bottle out to Kai enquiringly. Bubble blowing, the replacement for smoking cigarettes which had been in effect for almost a century now, was a popular habit among many Londoners and it appeared the Chinese also enjoyed the same past-time.

"Indeed I do," was the response. "Shall we step outside?"

"Sounds good to me."

"May I also join you?" said Lo Wen, fixing Raphael with a coy smile and stepping forwards; her English was slightly less pronounced than her cousin's and uncle's, and her voice was soft, an almost musical purr. "I love to blow…and I would especially love to blow yours."

Skye almost choked on the champagne she was in the middle of sipping. Somewhere beside her a snort erupted, but a millisecond later Daphne turned it into a series of coughs. Skye, however, did not find it remotely funny. Under any other circumstances it may have been an innocent enough statement but, coupled with the 'goo-goo eyes' the Emperor's niece was making at Raphael, she could not help the first thought that came into her head after hearing this. She felt her nostrils wildly flare as she tried telling herself to be rational.

Calm down…it's not like she was trying to hint anything. She was talking about bubbles, for Christ's sake! Bubbles! Though it might help if she wasn't looking at him with those blatant seductive eyes!

If anyone else was thinking the same as her, they were hiding it very well—except Daphne; the corners of her mouth were fighting to stay down. Raphael nodded and said it would be a pleasure for her to join them before holding his arm out to Lo Wen; she took it, wearing that same coy smile; Skye felt her inner wolf growling and downed her drink.

"Skye? You coming?"

Raphael was looking at her expectantly. Skye swallowed, immediately moulding her face into a grin, but unfortunately it came out more of a grimace.

"Oh, um, no…I'll wait here for you…"

Raphael hesitated, clearly sensing something was wrong. Skye ordered herself to get a grip.

"Have a nice time!" she said, beaming a little too forcefully at him, Lo Wen and Kai. Kai smiled and thanked her; Lo Wen's gaze flickered over her in a brief, careless way—further feeding Skye's suspicions that the comment had not been entirely innocent—before she turned to Raphael and began engaging him in conversation. The three of them took off towards the patio doors on the other end of the room and Skye turned back to the others, the smile vanishing instantly from her face.

"How are you ladies enjoying yourselves so far?" said Trey, reaching towards the champagne tray, picking two glasses up and holding one of them suggestively towards Skye, who took it with a little too much haste.

"Very much so," replied Mrs. Archer enthusiastically; a solemn-faced butler appeared by their side holding out a tray of sashimi which Skye, momentarily forgetting her disgruntlement, eyed with glee. Raw fish. Nice.

"It's wonderful to be here," continued Mrs. Archer, while her daughter helped herself to almost half the tray of sashimi, wolfing it down; Daphne looked at the remaining slimy fish, her nose wrinkling. "You have a lovely home, Trey; such incredible décor!"

"Ah, it is very kind of you to say so. Though I haven't actually called this my home for quite some time. The last three years of my life were spent in China. I visit whenever I can, though of course my reasons for being there took first priority. Our alliance with the Emperor is a crucial one and may well change the course of our futures."

"Raphael said you were sent there to convince the Emperor to join forces against the thugs," said Skye, her mouth full of raw salmon. "And it looks like you've done an amazing job, Trey—the

Emperor even came over to visit!"

"It is true that we have been very fortunate in forging an alliance with His Highness, but…" began Trey.

He lowered his voice, gathering them closer in confidence.

"Just between us, the real reason the Emperor came wasn't so much to exchange pleasantries; it's because he wants to make sure we're going to win. That's the reason for all this—the dinner, introducing him to officials. The Emperor isn't going to sacrifice his men for a lost cause. That's part of the reason there's been a delay in giving the order to attack; His Highness positioned his troops around the city, but he would not permit the order to attack. Before today, that is. After today, I am quite certain he will."

"But what was the point of positioning the troops a few weeks ago if he wouldn't let them attack?" asked Skye surprised.

"Merely as a sign to confirm our alliance. Also, the Emperor himself is a good man, but his advisors…well, let's just say they want to make it very clear who holds the power. The official council were completely against the alliance in the beginning; it took a long time to win them over, believe me. They were also extremely vocal in their displeasure at the Emperor coming here himself, but Emperor Jin insisted. And, of course, Kai, his Majesty's nephew, has been a big help. During my time making negotiations, he supported me one hundred per cent and played a key part in convincing the Emperor to overrule the council and deploy forces. We owe him a lot."

Trey took a sip of champagne before continuing.

"My father himself is being quite cautious with regard to advancing an attack. It's difficult to commence battle when your opponent is scattered, mingled among civilians without any way to identify them; to attack outright would mean too many civilians getting caught in the crossfire and one thing we don't want is the senseless slaughter of innocents. Now that we have this chance, it is crucial we get it right. There has been some disagreement on how best to proceed, but…Anyway, I hope now you see why it is so important for us to keep up a show of confidence. It is important to show the Emperor and all those who have flown in with him that victory will be ours; keeping up appearances and friendly relations are essential components to our cause."

He smiled around at them, his eyes lingering on Skye for an extra second of two. A brief flash in her head told her that Trey's last comment may have had something to do with her reaction to what Lo Wen had said earlier; Trey was extremely sharp and it wouldn't have surprised her if he had noticed she had been less than happy by the niece's implications, whether innocent or not. Word of Skye's infamous temper had no doubt travelled to his ears, but she didn't want him to think she would ever cause a dent in the relations he had worked hard to build.

"Yeah, that's true," she said, coughing slightly, grabbing more sashimi from the silver tray.

He inclined his head, still smiling and took another sip of champagne. Mrs. Archer suddenly pointed to something behind his head and she spoke in a voice tinged with excitement.

"Oh my goodness—that painting! Is that…?"

"Yes," replied Trey, having turned around to see what had caught her attention. "That's *The Burning Eye* by Robert M. Mansford. His original work, painted at the end of the twenty-first century. My grandfather was a personal friend…the story goes that Mansford had a dream one night that the London Eye was burning in flames; it distressed him so much that he shut himself away and spent an entire week bringing his dream to life in a painting—that painting. Afterwards, he was adamant that the dream was no mere dream…a prophecy, if you will. Naturally, society ridiculed him; back then, they were a lot more sceptical than we are now, hence the twenty-first century most commonly being known as the Age of Scepticism. Anything 'out-of-the-ordinary' was treated with scorn and derision…"

Skye's attention ebbed away as she caught sight of Raphael, Lo Wen and Kai re-entering the room; their chatter and laughter was highly audible. Lo Wen's hand repeatedly touched Raphael's arm as she burst into frequent fits of giggles at his jokes. Skye swiftly turned her head away, clenching her teeth.

"… Of course, it looked like Mansford knew a lot more than the so-called 'leading experts in thought' at the time," Trey was saying, while Mrs. Archer continued to stare at the painting, enraptured. "Twelve years ago when thugs burned the London Eye to the ground, scholars were shocked to discover that eye-witness accounts and photographs reported an almost exact scenario of the painting; men in balaclavas surrounding the Eye, the red sunset and strange half-moon on the right hand side of the sky…and, most chillingly, the small child in the background clutching her teddy-bear. You do get the odd doubter who insists the whole thing must have been concocted in order to coincide with Mansford's painting, but I think that's stretching it a bit. I mean, how can you say the moon was positioned to look that way on the night or that it's a mere coincidence, what with all the other factors involved? Some people will refuse to believe the impossible, even when the impossible is staring them right in the face…"

"Fascinating," said Mrs. Archer, nodding her head in enthusiastic agreement. "I learned about the painting during my schooldays; our teacher thought Robert Mansford crazy, but then, of course, the riots happened. I had no idea he was a personal family friend! May I have a closer look?"

"Certainly," replied Trey, holding out his arm. "Would you like to come with us?" he added, turning inquisitively to Skye and Daphne.

"Oh, I'm OK here, thanks!" said Skye, privately thinking that she wanted to keep an eye on the little group by the patio doors; Lo Wen's wandering hands were showing no signs of relenting their pawing of Raphael's biceps. Daphne, who had spent many hours learning about the London Eye's grisly fate due to being a History student at college, had no desire to relive a lecture during her leisure time and she also politely refused.

Trey and Mrs. Archer walked off towards the large painting on the other side of the room. Skye's eyes flashed towards the tray of sashimi, which she noted with disappointment, was now empty. Daphne helped herself to another glass of champagne.

"It's very exciting all of this, isn't it?" said Daphne, moving closer to her friend and gazing around at the room and various chatting guests, her eyes sparkling. "So many influential people! The Emperor…I can't believe he's actually here!"

"Agreed," replied Skye, though she was only half-listening as her eyes remained locked on the group by the patio; Raphael had leaned over and Lo Wen was whispering something in his ear in a giggly manner.

Catching sight of Skye's stony expression, Daphne's eyes trailed towards where she was looking. She was unable to suppress a grin.

"I wouldn't worry about it, Skye," she told her, and Skye immediately snapped her gaze towards her friend.

"Hmm? Worry? Worry about what?"

"That Lo Wen girl."

"Lo Wen? I'm not worried—why should I be worried?"

"Well, judging by the daggers you're shooting her I get the impression you think she's got a thing for Raphael."

"Of course not," said Skye, ruffled. "She's only just met him, hasn't she? Even if she does come out with some, well, *certain* things that might suggest otherwise…"

Daphne burst out laughing.

"You mean what she said back there? About his, er, bubbles? Get your mind out of the gutter, Skye!"

"Me? What about you, Daphne? I heard you snorting with laughter after she said it. You were thinking the exact same thing that I was, don't pretend you weren't!"

Daphne continued giggling uncontrollably to Skye's half-irritation, half-amusement.

"Well, anyway," Daphne managed to wheeze out while Skye continued looking at her with raised, unimpressed eyebrows, "even if she *did* mean anything by it, it's not like it matters! But I'm sure she didn't mean anything, you know? There's that language barrier thing going on—"

"Her English seems totally fine to me," responded Skye with the faint trace of a snarl as she caught sight of Lo Wen, yet again, stroking Raphael's arm with her delicate fingers; she didn't even bother holding back her suspicions anymore as the words came tumbling out of her mouth.

"I mean, what you say might be more believable if she wasn't constantly looking at him with those bedroom eyes or touching him up every five seconds! But nope, there she goes again! Seriously, could she make it any more obvious?"

"Yes, but the point is, *he's* not responding to it. Raphael's with *you*, Skye, don't forget that. He's with you, not her, and he chose you over all those other bimbo—oh my gosh! I forgot to tell you, I can't believe I forgot—"

"Yes? What is it, Daph?" said Skye, alarmed by her friend's sudden change in tone as Daphne began to babble incoherently, her expression switching from light-hearted to panicky in an instant.

"I wanted to tell you earlier, but then we got interrupted, sorry, I wanted to say but—oh my gosh, you won't believe it, but *she's* here—I should have told you earlier, I wanted to warn you, I'm not sure where she went, but—"

"Daphne, *who* are you talking about?"

"Well, well…hello, *Skye.*"

Skye froze in horror at the sound of the familiar, snide voice from behind her that had spoken her name. Immediately, she knew exactly whom Daphne had been referring to.

I don't believe it, she thought, disbelief surging through her veins. *I don't* believe *it.*

With extreme reluctance, she turned slowly to face the person who had suddenly appeared behind them, simultaneously noting the worried, guilty expression on Daphne's face as she, too, turned around; their sight landed on the stunning blonde who stood before them dressed in a tight, beige dress and four-inch stiletto heels; there was a wide smile (or rather, smirk) on her full red lips and a crafty look in her almond blue eyes.

"Hello, Sasha," said Skye stonily, unable to suppress the instinctive loathing that raced through her as she clapped eyes on her arch-nemesis. She had not come face to face with Sasha for weeks; the last time they had crossed paths was before she and Raphael had admitted their feelings to one another—and Skye had been hoping it would stay that way. What in the world was *she* doing there, at the Renzo dinner party? Surely Raphael had not invited her? He knew how she felt about her; he knew what sly and manipulative deviances lay behind those pouting red lips and fluttering blue eyes.

Could this day get any worse?

"I didn't realize *you'd* be here," Sasha continued in a sweet voice that barely disguised her contempt.

"Likewise," responded Skye, still reeling from this sudden, nasty surprise. She remembered what Raphael had said about members of the Renzo family being required to bring their significant others to dinner parties.

Don't tell me she's dating Joey…or, worse, Trey. No way! Trey wouldn't actually go for her—would he? Didn't Raphael say he had no time for girls? And as for Joey, he's not interested in relationships!

She was saved the trouble of racking her brains, because Sasha then launched into a loud explanation of how her father was Sir Kinswood, a close friend of Lord Renzo, and frequenting formal dinner parties was a weekly occurrence for her—especially, she emphasized, at the Renzo Mansion.

"… So as you can imagine it's very, um, unusual to see you here," Sasha was saying, a faint sneer on her features as she flicked her long silky hair into the nearby butler's face. "I mean, I'd never really had you down as the sort of person who'd be invited to these events—especially not one to celebrate the Emperor's visit. Poor people of society don't really get invited, you know? And your outfit says a lot, too."

She didn't even bother to hide a snigger as she stared pointedly at Skye's boots. Skye felt that familiar anger rush through her. Ever since the unfortunate day she had met Sasha several months back, every encounter with her had been gruelling and unpleasant. Sasha had done everything in her power to ensnare Raphael, including putting Skye down at any given opportunity and kissing him at Jinxes during the West London celebrations six weeks ago. Her attempts, however, had proven to be unsuccessful as Raphael did not reciprocate her interest and was, as he eventually revealed, enamoured towards Skye. There was no doubt that the rejection had been a major blow to Sasha's enormous ego, doubled by the fact that her love interest had bestowed his affections on the 'dirty Morpher dog' she took such pleasure in belittling. Skye did not fail to notice that the venom in Sasha's eyes had increased ten-fold compared to the last time she saw her and she steeled herself.

Skye was not the only one whose expression hardened. Loyal as ever, Daphne stood a little straighter, fixing Sasha with a glare.

"Raphael got Skye those boots," she said. "You know, her boyfriend? That's why she's here—because they happen to be a couple."

Sasha glanced at her witheringly, but there was no mistaking the malevolence behind her pupils.

"Sorry, who are you again? Oh wait—aren't you dating Ricardo?"

"That's right," said Daphne firmly.

Sasha let off a sly chuckle.

"Well, you're just one of many," she said smoothly. "And yes, I do mean at the same time. Seeing as how you don't run in our circles, you obviously have no idea what he gets up to. But I have a few friends who would be happy to tell you just how much, erm, fun he can be. In fact," she added, stepping towards them, an innocent expression on her face, "I could tell you myself. Raphael isn't the only Renzo boy I've had the pleasure of getting to know on a more, ah, *intimate* level."

"Like Ricardo would touch you with a bargepole," snapped Skye, noting how Daphne's entire demeanour had gone ice-cold upon hearing these words.

Sasha practically screeched with laughter.

"Oh *please* let's not go there again, shall we? Look at me. Now look at you two—especially you," she said, throwing Skye that usual contemptuous glance she loved to reserve especially for her. "And," she added, lowering her voice, a sly smile on her lips, "can I just add, I *love* the eagle tattoo right below Ricardo's naval. Bye girls—see you at dinner."

She blew them a kiss, flicked her hair one more time and stalked off, hips swinging.

"Urgh!" exclaimed Skye, the growl rising in her throat as she watched Sasha weave her way through the guests, much pouting and hair flicking as she did so. "Of all the people to turn up here—*Sasha!* You have no idea how much I was restraining myself just then, Daphne…Daphne?"

She turned to look at her friend whose eyes were strangely blank; she was breathing rather fast. Skye thought she knew why.

"What she said about Ricardo—it's all lies," she hastened to reassure her. "She loves pulling that kind of crap; she's been doing it to me from the start. I mean, it feels weird…me being the one telling you not to worry for a change…but seriously, Daph, she gets off on it, don't worry…"

"Ricardo only got that tattoo last week," Daphne whispered.

Skye's eyes widened as the realization of Daphne's implication hit her and her mouth dropped open in an 'O'. Quickly, she tried to mask it.

"It doesn't mean anything," she said hurriedly. "She could have got that information from anyone. And Ricardo and Joey aren't exactly shy with themselves, are they? He could've just stripped off and started showing it off…"

"Yeah." Daphne swallowed, her muscles relaxing slightly. "Yeah…you're right. Ricardo wouldn't do that to me. And—and I can just talk to him about it anyway…Hey look, there he is! Him and Joey went to collect some gift they'd bought for the Emperor…Ricardo!"

She placed her champagne glass on the nearest table and scampered enthusiastically across the room to where the twins had just appeared through the door; they were laughing loudly as usual and voraciously greeting the different guests, most of whom were watching them with amused, slightly wary expressions on their faces. As she watched Ricardo envelope Daphne into a big bear-hug followed by a long, smooching kiss, Skye marvelled at the way her friend was able to brush her suspicions to the side, how she was able to trust so openly and honestly; it was something she, Skye, always had such trouble doing. Despite her earnest efforts to dispel Daphne's fears earlier, she knew that had it been *her* whose boyfriend had recently acquired a tattoo in a somewhat discreet area and the local hussy had been implying she'd had the privilege of being given a private showing, she herself would not have reacted with such passiveness, nor would it have taken mere words to quell her suspicions. Most likely, she would have been boiling under the surface for a lengthy period of time, racing thoughts tormenting her mind. She trusted Raphael…she really did. He was remarkable in the sense that he understood these negative aspects about her and he responded with patience and insight whenever her jealousy reared its ugly head. But still, it didn't stop the thoughts occurring, it didn't stop the suspicions forming and Raphael could not help being so attractive that women naturally flocked to him. In that moment, Skye envied Daphne's carefree and trusting manner, wondering rather dully what it must be like to be free of insecurities and paranoia that were constantly threatening to change you from the docile Jekyll into the monstrous, rampaging Hyde in a heartbeat.

There was a loud announcement from the Head Butler.

"Ladies and gentleman," he said from the middle of the room, ringing an authentic, old-style bell. "Please may I have your attention? Dinner is about to be served. Kindly make your way towards the dining table. Seats are arranged by name so please look for your name-tags which are placed in front of each seat for your convenience."

Everyone in the room proceeded towards the long dining table that was alight with candles. Skye finished off her drink, her eyes immediately flickering towards the trio by the patio, but they were no longer there.

Someone poked her waist from behind. She spun round and saw Raphael smiling at her; she was relieved to note that Lo Wen was no longer hanging off his arm.

"Careful," she told him. "These spiky boots you got me, I've got it in my head to kick people with them if they sneak up on me from behind."

"Hmmm…good point," Raphael told her, clipping her chin playfully.

He took her hand and led her towards the dining room table where the guests were chatting among themselves and finding their seats.

"So," she said in an airy voice as Raphael nodded in greeting towards a couple of new guests who had arrived, "did you have a nice time chatting to the Emperor's nephew and niece?"

"Yeah, they're both nice people. Kai's pretty cool. Lo Wen seems like a great girl, too."

"Oh, does she?" Skye was unable to hide the stony look on her face as she said this and Raphael caught it. A slight smile curved his mouth upwards and he opened it to say something, but he was interrupted by Joey, Ricardo and Daphne who appeared at their side as they arrived at the table.

"Alright, you two?" said Joey, punching Raphael fondly on the arm and flashing a grin at Skye. "How you enjoying the party? Actually, 'party' is stretching it—this is one of the dullest things I've ever attended! Am I the only one who's noticed there's no women here?"

"Er, thanks..." said Skye.

"Half the people in the room are women!" said Raphael, his eyes roving around the nametags that were immaculately placed on the table.

Joey's turquoise eyes rolled upwards.

"I'm talking about *accessible* women," he said, the white flecks on his spiky black hair gleaming in the candlelight. "Not girlfriends—" he pointed to Skye and Daphne—"or women who are about three hundred years old—" he gestured to an elderly woman on the other side of the table who was dressed in flamboyant purple furs, who looked very angry and was busy whacking one of the butlers with her cane for bringing her the wrong drink— "or nieces whose uncles would line me in front of the firing squad for making a move. You should've seen the look Emperor Jin gave me when I said hello to that hottie niece of his! If looks could kill..."

"Wow, you're actually developing morals?" said Raphael, staring at his brother in mock disbelief. "Since when did you care whether a girl was taken or what her family member thought?"

"Since that family member happened to be the Emperor of China, that's when! Even Dad wouldn't be able to get me out of that one. And I'm not about to hit on my own brothers' women, am I? Not that I *haven't* thought about spending some quality time with you two fine ladies, of course..." he added with a purr, a devilish look on his face as he gazed in Skye's and Daphne's directions.

Predictably, Raphael did not react well to this.

"Can you not say things like that about my girlfriend?" he said roughly. "She's standing right here, show some respect—"

"Hey, I'm sorry if I offended you, Skye!" said Joey, throwing up his hands in innocence. "You're not mad about it, are you?"

He winked at her. Raphael's nostrils flared. Ricardo stifled a laugh, as did Daphne. Skye, who was used to the twins' brazenness by now, shook her head, though at the same time she was unable to prevent that familiar excited tingle racing through her; she wasn't the only one who got jealous, and while Raphael's jealousy was nowhere near on the scale as her own, his territorial behaviour over her just made her feel more enamoured towards him—even if she would never admit it.

"It's fine, Joey," she said.

"The Emperor's a smart man," Raphael said aggressively, still aggravated by his brother's comment. "He probably saw right through you. Anyway, you're exaggerating as always—there are other single women here..."

At that moment, Sasha came flouncing towards the other side of the table, conversation in full flow; she was chatting to another, much less attractive girl who was gazing at her in a rather star-struck manner. Typically, all eyes turned towards her; she caught Raphael's eye and winked. He coughed uncomfortably and looked away. Skye noticed this and her expression hardened, at the same time shooting Raphael an accusatory glare; she had refrained from speaking to him just yet about how he hadn't told her Sasha would be there, but it didn't mean she was any less annoyed about it.

"Her, for example," she said bitingly, turning to Joey and gesturing towards Sasha, who was attracting admiring glances from a couple of Chinese Ambassadors as she flicked her hair repeatedly. "I'm pretty sure *she's* single."

Joey gave Sasha an appreciative look before flicking his gaze away carelessly.

"Been there," he yawned, "and not too long ago either. The packaging is nicer than the goods. And the goods have been around a bit."

Simultaneously, Skye and Daphne both shot their boyfriends furtive looks as Joey came out with this rather bawdy statement, but both Raphael and Ricardo gave no sign that either of them had participated in this somewhat lewd version of pass the parcel. Raphael merely shook his head, seemingly disapproving of Joey's vulgar expressions, while Ricardo was busy humming a Christmas tune under his breath for some reason.

"Yowza!" Joey exclaimed, his eyes popping open as he stared at something at the far end of the table. "Speaking of packaging—who is *she?*"

They turned to look at whom he was staring at.

"That's my mother!" said Skye, horrified.

Indeed it was Mrs. Archer that Joey was ogling at; Skye's mother was currently chatting excitedly to Lord Renzo who had pulled a chair out for her; she caught them looking over at her and she beamed, waving.

Joey whistled.

"Mother? No way! You look like sisters—she is definitely not dinosaur material!"

Skye didn't know quite what to say to this, other than that she found Joey Renzo's sudden attraction to her mother both weird and disturbing. Raphael, however, was much more vocal in his objection.

"That's Skye's *mum*," he snarled, yanking Joey by the collar in an attempt to stop him throwing suggestive looks down the other end of the table. "Don't even go there."

"Hey, age ain't nothing but a number, buddy!"

"You really cross the line sometimes, you know that—"

"Ahem, ahem!" The Head Butler came over to them at that moment with his trusty bell; he rang it once and it let off a loud, resounding *ding*. "Please be seated, ladies and gentleman. Dinner is about to be served."

"I'm sitting on the other end, pumpkin," Ricardo said to Daphne, rubbing his nose to hers. "No idea why Joey and I have been placed all the way down the other side of the table. I'd've liked to have chatted to Emperor Jin about a few things!"

"Maybe it's *because* you want to chat to Emperor Jin that Lord Renzo put you as far away from him as possible!" giggled Daphne.

"And what's that supposed to mean?" said Ricardo playfully. "Anyway, I'd better get going, our butler's giving me the evil eye. Come on, Joe, let's go before Raph transforms and rips you to shreds."

"Easy, tiger," grinned Joey, slapping Raphael on the back. "You can't blame me for liking beautiful women, can you?"

Raphael continued to glare at him in a threatening manner; Joey smiled roguishly at Daphne and Skye.

"See you later, girls. And Skye, don't be offended, OK? It's a compliment—there are clearly some lovely ladies in your family!"

With that, he and Ricardo sauntered off, cracking jokes in their loud voices as they walked down the long table, their raucous laughter booming throughout the room.

Raphael turned to Skye, looking both vexed and apologetic.

"Sorry about him—obviously he's just messing around, he wouldn't actually—"

"It's fine," Skye said quickly, not wanting to entertain the highly unpleasant images the whole business brought to mind. "Joey's a wisecracker, I'm getting used to it—should we find our seats and sit down?"

They found them seconds later. Skye was seated in the middle of Raphael and Daphne at the centre of the table, which was currently being weighed down by various bottles of wine and champagne; butlers placed wine glasses in front of each guest. The trio took their seats, as did the sixteen or so other people who were attending the dinner party.

To Skye's absolute dismay, Sasha sat down directly opposite Raphael.

"Raphael!" she hissed, just as one of the butlers was pouring white wine into his glass. "What is *she* doing opposite us?"

"I don't know…" replied Raphael warily, taking a slow sip of his wine with the air of a man who knew he had to tread carefully. "Dad organized the seating arrangements, but I don't think he knows much about Sasha…just that she's Sir Kinswood's daughter…"

Skye fell into a frosty silence, deeply unhappy with the situation but realizing she'd just have to make do with having Sasha in her face throughout the dinner. Trying to ignore the way Sasha smiled invitingly at Raphael while simultaneously shooting her a snooty look, Skye nodded to the butler who held up a bottle of champagne enquiringly. Right from the disastrous disciplinary meeting in the morning until now, resigning herself to Sasha leering at her for the rest of the evening, the day was growing horribly worse. The sooner she got drunk, the better.

*

The evening continued, the guests eagerly anticipating the food. Half a dozen butlers appeared in the room, each of them expertly balancing trays of silver plates and bowls on their palms and forearms. Each guest had a silver tray placed in front of them, which was laden with a starter, main course and dessert. Skye eyed hers, momentarily forgetting her resolution to drink her woes away. Her mouth watered; an enormous rump steak still dripping with blood lay on her largest plate.

"It looks amazing," she told Raphael with a smile.

"I thought you'd like that one," Raphael murmured back, gesturing to the steak.

"My lords, ladies and gentleman," Lord Renzo had stood up with his glass of champagne and was addressing the table; the guests fell silent and turned their attention towards him.

"May I take this opportunity to thank each and every one of you for attending tonight's very special event. I hope you have had a pleasant evening thus far and that it shall prove even more pleasant as the night wears on. I will not be so selfish as to spend a great deal of time speaking and deprive you of the splendid food our chefs have cooked tonight, so I will speak only with necessity as it is required. First and foremost, I must mention the threat that currently hangs over our heads, one that not a single citizen of this city is immune to."

Total silence reigned now; people paused in acts of wine sipping, placing their glasses carefully onto the table. Lord Renzo continued speaking.

"No one in this room is unaware of the dangers we currently face, of the darkness that looms ever nearer. Our enemy gathers in force, day by day; increasingly, they terrorize our city with cowardly acts of arson and murder. A beloved friend and comrade, Sir Branswick, recently fell victim to their vile schemes. I think I can speak for all of us when I say that Sir Jonathan Branswick is a man we will never forget, who will live forever as a shining example to all of us, who defied the scoundrels for decades, who played his part in protecting the innocent. May he rest in a much better world than the one he knew before."

He raised his glass. Everyone else in the room did the same, many murmuring the name of Sir Branswick. Skye, who had never met the man who was one of Lord Renzo's oldest friends, saw the sadness in his face and noted it reflected the eyes of the majority of people in the room, who had also been on close terms with the deceased.

Clearing his throat, Lord Renzo spoke once more.

"I needn't stress to everyone how important it is that we remain vigilant at all times. It is crucial that we do not go anywhere alone, especially places where we may find ourselves as vulnerable targets.

It is essential that we choose our friends wisely; as the old saying goes, careless talk costs lives, and any new friends must be treated with care and caution..."

He threw a pointed look at the twins, whose womanizing antics had been known to spread into the enemy camp before and had, on previous occasions, landed them in more trouble than they had bargained for.

"But speaking of new friends," a wide smile appeared beneath Lord Renzo's greying, golden beard, "such a speech would not be complete without welcoming a truly honoured guest to our establishment this evening. Though he needs no introduction, please raise your glasses to his esteemed Royal Highness, Emperor Jin of China."

The Emperor rose from his seat, bowing graciously as glasses rose in simultaneous unison.

"Thank you," he said in that strong, gravelly voice of his. "I could not have asked for a better welcome from the House of Renzo. I look forward to prolonging such friendship in days to come."

There was a round of applause as Emperor Jin bowed again before taking his seat.

"We are grateful and indebted to you for your support," Lord Renzo addressed him, inclining his head. "And, of course," he added, "we are honoured to be graced with the presence of his Royal Highness' niece and nephew, Kai and Lo Wen Chan."

There was another smattering of applause as everyone at the dinner table turned to look at Kai and Lo Wen, the latter of whom was beaming around, her eyes landing on Raphael, her face smouldering subtly. Skye abruptly stopped clapping and kept her eyes determinedly focussed on Lord Renzo.

"It is our wish that you all have as pleasant a stay as possible with us, despite the morbid circumstances surrounding your visit," continued Lord Renzo with a smile. "And speaking of pleasant, the delectable-looking dishes in front of us look far too good not to be devoured right away; I believe this is my cue to end this dinner speech. Thank you all for listening—and tuck in!"

There was a union of appreciative chuckles and immediately everyone began digging into their food. Skye was so busy wolfing down her steak that she refused to socialize for a good ten minutes or so, but during this time she could not fail to hear the various conversations that were drifting all around her.

"That's right, it was Professor Polgas who created the formula years ago," Raphael was saying to the excitable Chinese Ambassador who was sitting on his other side; the Ambassador was clearly enraptured by the subject of Morphers and was currently bombarding him with an array of questions.

"No one knows much about him, to be honest," continued Raphael to the excited man, whose questions were coming in at a rapid speed as he tried to answer them all at once. "He was murdered, you know, and a lot of his documents were destroyed during the explosion that killed him. There's a museum dedicated to him up north, maybe you might find time to visit it during your stay...And yes, it is true that a Morpher's spirit animal can change—anything can trigger it; age, a sudden event, an unexpected change in circumstances; my great-great grandfather could change into three different spirit animals during his life, actually, they were like templates once he acquired them...Haha, no, we can't actually talk to people while in our animal form, though we can communicate with humans through a set of emotions, imagery or words; there's also this thing called the Survival Pact…"

Skye's attention ebbed away, feeling both amused and sorry for her boyfriend as he continued offering explanations surrounding the myths and legends about Morphers, his enormous rump steak currently untouched.

Meanwhile, the loud voice of Sasha was drowning out almost everybody else's conversation as she twitted non-stop about herself to a couple of enchanted guests. Skye tried very hard to ignore her as she scanned her eyes around, still chewing her steak, her eyes landing on the Emperor, Lord Renzo and her mother. Mrs. Archer was hooting exaggeratedly at something Raphael's father was saying and the Emperor had an amused smile on his face.

Her eyesight flitting elsewhere, her gaze next landed on Trey, Kai and the other Chinese Ambassador who were several seats away from her and seemed to be engaged in a much more serious conversation. Skye could just catch snippets of their conversation:

"… But whether the prince does or does not decide to support his father in this war, one fact cannot be denied," Trey was saying, his voice calm yet firm, "and that is the consequences of delay. I understand the need to protect civilians, but surely a mass evacuation is wiser than prolonging this state of inaction?"

"I must disagree," Kai said, shaking his head. "While under more—shall we say—usual circumstances this method may be beneficial, we must remember we are not fighting an organized force who wave a flag and wear a uniform. The enemy mingles with the populace with no definitive way to identify them - other than by their actions, of which it is difficult to catch them at. Their hold over ordinary civilians is strong; this is something we must not underestimate. How many civilians have been secretly threatened, ordered to stay where they are? The enemy knows the public is his shield—it is an extremely tricky strategy to counter. And, let us not forget, recent reports have concluded that the thugs have changed their appearance, as well as their approach; gangs no longer roam as they used to, despite the increase of attacks. This is to confuse us and throw us off. Lord Pearson knows full well that if we were to launch an outright attack, it would put too many innocent lives at risk—and this is what he uses to his advantage."

"I understand what you are saying, Kai," replied Trey, a slight hint of impatience to his voice, "but I feel the more we delay, the greater the risk becomes; the more time they are given to plot and scheme, the more vulnerable we are. Right now, we are living under siege. There is no use denying it."

"Would you prefer an all-out bloodbath where millions in the city will be killed in the crossfire?"

"Of course not, but—"

"Then we must wait," said Kai simply. "Wait for them to attack. I agree with Lord Renzo on this one—a wrong move may prove fatal."

The Chinese Ambassador nodded in agreement. Trey returned to his food. Skye, who had very little comprehension of any type of war-talk, had understood almost nothing of their conversation and she instead focussed on her next plate, one with a scrumptious variety of chicken wings dipped in garlic, honey and lemon arranged neatly on a bed of lettuce.

It came to her attention several minutes later, amidst the various conversations, tinkling of wine glasses and random booms of laughter from the twins at the end of the table, that Raphael was behaving very oddly as he munched away on his steak. Having eventually managed to satisfy the enthusiastic Ambassador's curiosity, he had swiftly began devouring his dinner; but Skye noticed that, every now and then, he would twitch in his seat, as though he had been given an electric shock. She watched him, puzzled, and when he jumped for the third time she felt compelled to ask him what was wrong.

"Are you alright?" she said, eyeing him with concern.

"Huh?" he replied, seemingly distracted. "Oh yeah, Skye, I'm f—*unf!*—fine!"

There, he did it again. Skye continued to watch him in sheer bemusement; his cheeks went bright red as he delved back into his steak, shovelling the food into his mouth even more quickly than before.

Increasingly becoming suspicious and worried, she suddenly heard a snigger come from across the table.

Her eyes shot towards Sasha who was smiling nastily at her.

Without knowing why, but acting on pure instinct, Skye bent over and stuck her head under the table. What she saw caused fury to race through her before she even had time to think.

Sasha's bare foot was rubbing up on Raphael's leg.

Her head came up so fast she banged it on the table. Her wine glass knocked over and champagne went spilling everywhere. She faced Sasha squarely in the eye, breathing hard, her eyes now a blazing blue.

"Get your foot off him," she snarled at her, anger pumping through her.

Sasha stared at her innocently.

"I have no idea what you're on about," she replied in a sweet voice.

"Skye," began Raphael, who had noticed the exchange; he looked extremely wary.

Skye reacted before she could stop herself.

"I said, GET YOUR DIRTY FEET OFF HIM!" she shouted, banging her fist on the table. The entire table suddenly went quiet and all eyes turned towards her. Many gawped in shock at what they saw, for Skye's eyes were now a brilliant striking blue and a long snout was protruding from her face where her nose should have been…

Horror now mingled with her fury. Realizing what a spectacle she was making of herself, she resisted the urge to transform completely and maul the girl in front of her who— unbelievably—was still looking at her with that same snide expression. As the table continued staring at her in silence, she felt sick as the snout and whiskers continued elongating from her face; she stared blankly at the paintings on the wall, willing herself to calm down, trying to ignore the shocked faces of the guests and the deeply worried look on her mother's face. And next to her mother was the Emperor…what must he think? What had Trey said earlier about controlling herself, about putting up a show of confidence? What would the Emperor think of such volatile behaviour? What would he think of Morphers now, when they lose their tempers so quickly, when they come so close to attacking normal human citizens? Would he withdraw his troops? Would he think that Skye was nothing more than a wild animal, one that could attack and kill a normal person at any moment? Why would he want to ally himself with people like *that?*

As the paranoia continued to surge through her, Skye contemplated for a split-second bolting from the room where no one could see what she was. But then a voice called out:

"And *that*, my friends, is what happens when you see a Morpher in action. A rare, but undeniably fascinating treat!"

It was Raphael who had stood up and said it, a wide beam on his face. Slowly, every guest's amazed expression relaxed into smiles of appreciation; Skye, who had managed to morph her face back to its normal appearance, forced herself to smile as though she had planned it all along. However, the fury still beat within her breast, as did the humiliation. She rose from her seat and said quietly:

"Please excuse me, I must go to the bathroom."

Without another word or glance at anybody, she turned on her heel and hurried as fast as she could out of the dining room. She practically fled down the long corridor, not stopping off in one of the downstairs bathrooms, but instead coming to a halt at the billiards room, which the twins were particularly known for frequenting. She was breathing fast, still trying to squash the rage and humiliation that was fighting to explode within her. This was the cherry on the cake. The disciplinary hearing that morning…having to watch Lo Wen subtly yet shamelessly flirt with Raphael…having to watch Sasha not-so-subtly, but just as shamelessly do the same thing…the general fear and terror that was always jittering inside her, threatening to bubble to the surface…it had all come out in that one moment when she had banged her fist down on the table and semi-transformed. Leaning against one of the snooker tables, she continued breathing heavily, trying to force the images that were plaguing her out of her mind.

"Skye?"

Someone had entered the room.

She really didn't want to talk to him in that moment. She was angry with him. Why hadn't he *stopped* Sasha when she did that? Why had he just sat there doing nothing? Why hadn't he *told* her? Suspicion began to rear its ugly head…perhaps a part of him had wanted it…

"Skye?" Raphael repeated.

She heard him walk towards her; he placed a gentle hand on her shoulder.

She shrugged him off.

"I'm fine," she said shortly without turning round. "I just need a second or two."

But he touched her shoulder again, more firmly this time.

"What happened back there, I'm sorry for it. I should have stopped her. But I didn't want to create a scene…"

The memory of Sasha's sneering face flashed in her mind again.

"It's fine," she snarled.

"The Emperor is watching us all the time, Skye. It's important we command his respect. We can't afford to jeopardize that…"

"Well, I'm sorry I messed up!" Skye spun round, staring right into his face, her eyes blazing. "Clearly I'm not good with this type of stuff—there's too much drama with me, you know! I've had a bad day—watching girls flirt with you in front of my face didn't exactly help. You and Lo Wen, you and Sasha—"

She felt the jealousy storm through her and in that moment she wanted to transform and attack him.

"You looked like you were enjoying it! I heard how Lo Wen couldn't wait to blow your *bubbles*, Raphael—"

"Enjoying it? What the hell is wrong with you? She's the Emperor's niece! I have to be nice—don't you understand that?"

"Oh yeah, nice! I wonder how far you'll go to be *nice!* And what about Sasha, do you have to be nice to her, too? You're nice enough to let her rub her feet on you—you weren't objecting to that, were you? Why the hell did you invite me in the first place, when all you want to do is fool around with other girls? Next time, have the decency to do it *behind* my back, rather than flaunting it in my face! Then again, it wouldn't be as much fun for *Sasha* if I wasn't there to watch, would it?"

She laughed nastily. Raphael lost his temper.

"That's enough!" he said angrily, all patience gone. "Stop it! I hate it when you do this! You get angry and jealous—for no good reason! You accuse me of doing things I don't do! Yes, I should have stopped Sasha, but I didn't want to create a scene at the table— I wasn't sure how to deal with it properly, I didn't want to make you upset! And I *have* to be nice to Lo Wen, Skye—that doesn't mean I'm going to bed her! Why do you do this? You know how important it is that we have the might of the Emperor on our side—why can't you support me and understand, rather than blowing up over stupid things that don't matter?"

"So it doesn't MATTER that another girl was playing footsie

with you under the table?" shouted Skye, her eyes flashing blue. The jealousy was unstoppable; she couldn't control it. Nothing he said mattered; all that mattered right then was that one memory of Raphael and Sasha kissing all those weeks ago, her body pushed up against his, their lips pressed together…

Violent tremors rippled through her; her nostrils flared wildly; she felt her facial features beginning to shift.

"Skye—" he reached out to her, but she rebuked him violently.

"Don't come near me, go back to those stupid tarts—"

But he grabbed hold of her wrists, his eyes inflamed; she reacted with extreme force, snarling wildly.

"I SAID don't come near me!"

"No!" he said furiously. "I'm putting my foot down; this has got to stop! The jealousy, the anger—it's all got to *stop.* Don't you *think* if I wanted another girl, I'd go get one? Doesn't it occur to you that if I wanted to play around, I'd be doing what Joey does and sleeping with a different girl every other night? But I don't and I won't, because it's you I want, just *you!* You're the *only* one I care about, I don't care about other girls, I—*look at me when I'm speaking to you!*"

He dropped her wrist and cupped her face forcefully between his fingers, forcing her to look at him as his eyes burned angrily into her own; but she couldn't see him. Raphael was a blur; all she could see was someone who would betray her…Rage coursed through her bones; she was going to transform, any minute now…

"No," he growled, as though reading her mind. "You're not getting angry. You're not going to shift and we're not going to fight. I'm not letting go until you understand this. I love you. No one else.

Just you. I put up with this crap because I love you. If I didn't, I wouldn't. I don't care how long it takes to make you see it, but I *will* make you see it."

"Get off me, Raphael—get off me, I swear it—"

"No! We're staying put, do you understand that? We're staying put until you calm down and listen to what I'm saying! Come *on*, Skye," he said, his voice dropping to a whisper. "Fight it…you've got to fight it…"

He pressed his forehead to hers; the angry throbbing of her temple beat against his own.

Fight it, he said? Fight what? He meant fight him, surely? That's what her jealousy was roaring at her to do, pounding away at her so that her head hurt, all those girls, much more attractive and charming than she was, girls who were actually in his league, not like her. She wasn't good enough for him…she hated him for it…she hated all those girls who made her feel like she wasn't good enough…but most of all, she hated herself.

*But it's not his fault…*A tiny voice in the back of her head suddenly sprang up. *It's not his fault. He loves you. You love him. This isn't right.*

Yet it could not contend with the roaring, nor with the burning jealous fire that pumped thunderously beneath her chest.

It IS his fault! You saw him…he was flirting with them, openly, right in front of your face!

"I love you, Skye. I really love you. I would never betray you. You have to get control. Don't let it get the better of you."

She stared into his eyes, her lips pulled back in a snarl, white-hot jealousy ravaging through her, the urge to attack him causing her to vibrate with relentless ferocity. But he shook his head, pressing his forehead harder into hers; he spoke again and when he did, his voice was a distant plea:

"Please. Do it for me. Defeat it. Please."

Just then, without knowing how or why, Skye heard exactly what he said; she heard him loud and clear. The softness of his voice drowned out the roaring inside her; the tiny voice inside her head that had battled the roars suddenly exploded with triumph. In a flash, the jealousy and rage disappeared and all she saw were the soft brown eyes of Raphael, looking at her with love and pain, someone who would never hurt her, but who cared about her enough to fight her demons with her. In that moment, all she saw was the reality, not the vicious, destructive fantasies that had streaked through her mind and overpowered her with such overwhelming force. She saw Raphael, with all his love, understanding and kindness.

And she saw how much she was hurting him.

"Oh!" she gasped, leaping back as though she had been electrocuted. She staggered slightly, before burying her face in her hands.

"Raphael...I'm sorry..."

Dismay tore through her. Raphael reached over and pulled her close to him again. She wouldn't look at him and kept her eyes covered, but he stroked her hair and kissed her forehead.

"There," he said soothingly, caressing her, "you're back to yourself now. Well done, Skye—you did it. You beat it. The ugly green-eyed monster is gone."

He pulled her hands away from her eyes and noticed the wet glistening on her eyelashes. Wiping them away, he gently cupped her chin in his hand, smiling at her.

"I'm proud of you," he said. "It normally takes a lot longer than that for you to come out of it—for one thing, we skipped an hour of the cold shoulder this time."

He chuckled. Skye finally looked up at him. She looked into his loving eyes and at his kind smile; she wondered what on earth she had ever done to deserve him.

"Raphael…I'm sorry…I just got so angry. It's not an excuse, but so many bad things have happened today and I just…snapped. I'm sorry for the things I said to you…I know it's not your fault…I shouldn't have let Sasha get to me like that. I shouldn't have reacted the way I did."

"Don't worry about it now. It was just an episode; it happens."

"Thank you…for helping me out of it."

"Hey, I wouldn't be much of a boyfriend if I didn't. That's what I'm here for."

She drooped her head meekly. He clasped her hands in his.

"Dry your eyes, Skye. Are you ready to go back to dinner?"

Dread filled her. The dinner. That would mean seeing the Emperor. What must he think of her?

"I think Emperor Jin is looking forward to seeing you," said Raphael, a twinkle in his eye, guessing the reason for her woebegone face. "After you left, he seemed absolutely amazed—in a good way. He's never seen a Morpher part-transform before and it was extremely entertaining for him. I could hear him telling my father as I left. You have a new fan."

Skye stared at him in disbelief. To hear that she hadn't jeopardized the alliance in any way, shape or form was hard to believe, but relief still swept through her. She still felt horribly embarrassed by the whole thing, and she also didn't want to look at Sasha for fear it would ignite her anger again. She squeezed Raphael's hands tighter with more warmth and gratitude than she could have expressed in words.

"If it's OK, I'm just going to get a bit of fresh air," she said, feeling the cool night air would help clear her head.

"Of course," he said, touching her cheek. "It will be good for you to get outside for a bit. To be honest, I would much prefer if we could both transform and go for a run on the grounds. But duty calls."

He took her hand and led her towards the door. They stepped into the open hallway.

"Don't be too long, OK? And stay on the grounds; don't go wandering off. You can never be too careful."

"Don't be so protective." Skye smiled at him. "I know I'm a bit nuts, but I'm still a wolf. Great senses, remember?"

"I know," Raphael rubbed his nose to hers. "I'll see you shortly then. And then after dinner, there's that thing I want to give you...but I won't spoil the surprise. See you in a bit."

"OK."

He kissed her, his eyes lingering on hers for a few seconds before he turned and made his way back to the dining room. Skye stared after him, watching his strong frame walk down the hall. There was no doubt in her mind that the events of the day had helped contribute to her sudden explosion just now; her weakest attributes, the rage and jealousy, had, no doubt, had a field day with her. Only minutes before, she felt her heart might burst with the fury boiling beneath it, but right then, as she watched him turn the corner until he was out of sight, she felt as though it may burst with love instead. More and more, she was learning that love was not so much about the good times as it was about the bad; that it wasn't about the blissful moments spent together or the parts that gave you butterflies—it was about how willing someone was to weather the storm with you, to stand and fight by your side even when it would so be much easier to walk away. Anger, jealousy, fury, and insecurity…these inner demons were in a league of their own; but so was he. He knew how to fight; he knew how to wield his sword and slice right through the darkness that threatened to destroy her. In essence, he knew what she herself was only just beginning to understand: how to love, deeply and fiercely, despite all obstacles.

Skye made her way towards the patio doors at the end of the hall. She opened them, feeling the cold air immediately blast her face. A couple of guards stood outside the doors. They stared at her as she stepped outside.

"Just getting some fresh air," she told them.

They nodded.

"Please do not stray too far from the house, Miss Archer," said one.

They returned to their rigid postures and Skye stepped into the dark garden, her eyes scanning the vast Renzo grounds. It was so still and quiet, you could hear a pin drop. A walk would do her good. As Skye began pacing down one of the dark paths she had taken so many times with Raphael, the guards slowly moving out of sight, she thought about how she would have to return to the dinner party soon.

Just don't lose it with Sasha, she thought grimly. *Just ignore her…I wonder if pudding's already been served…Oh damn, I didn't finish my wings either…I wonder if the plates have been cleared…*

A sudden noise somewhere near the bushes in front of her made her halt in her tracks.

Her wolf senses magnified; her eyes widened; her ears pricked up. Whatever was in the bushes was not natural to the gardens; she knew, without the shadow of a doubt, that this was some kind of intruder. It was making a strange, slightly squealing noise; something she had never heard before.

Swiftly, she turned on her heel, about to bolt into the mansion. But what happened next caused her to freeze on the spot.

A child's face appeared in her head. A boy. He mimed words that she saw in her mind's eye.

Help me…please, help me…

In that moment, Skye knew what had been making noises in the bushes. It was as though a light-switch flipped on in her head; she did not know how she knew or why she was so certain that she was right; but she knew she could not be wrong.

It was the beaver cub from before. And it was calling to her. It was asking for help.

There was no doubt now that this was a Morpher. Morphers could communicate with other Morphers while in their animal form. The *Survival Pact* meant that a transformed shape-shifter could communicate with another Morpher if they were in danger; they could not speak per se, but they could transfer their thoughts and emotions into the mind of another. This also meant that the Morphers who heard them could communicate telepathically, the difference being that they were able to "speak" with human words and did not have to rely on "picture transferences" to convey themselves. Nobody quite understood this phenomenon among them, but it was an ability that they all possessed.

Skye swallowed hard, turning slowly back to face the bushes.

Who are you? She said in her mind.

Another flash appeared in her head. This time, the boy was crying.

A cold shiver ran through her. Every hair on her body stood on end. The image of the crying boy expanded much more vividly in her mind. Fear shot through her, without knowing why. Right then, her instinct roared at her to run. There was something very dark, very evil, and very twisted at work here …

A second later, she discovered what it was.

Another image popped into her head, but not of the crying boy this time. No, of something much worse. They came, one at a time, a series of pictures that told a story, a story the young boy wanted her to know, but one that caused her to tremble and shake with fear and horror…

A man with a greasy baldhead and hooked nose stood in front of seven children. They were naked; several were crying. They were chained to grey walls. The room was dim; a faint silk-flame lamp flickered in the corner.

The man, who wore a white cloak, moved towards one of the children and pierced him through his head with what looked like an injection. The boy screamed.

The boy kept screaming. Seconds later, the whites of his eyes rolled visibly in their sockets. He struggled against the chains, but to no avail. The man continued to watch him passively. A minute later, the boy stopped struggling. The whites of his eyes remained. He could no longer see. He was blind.

The man pulled another injection from his pocket. He strode towards one of the girls who stood, terrified, shaking her head, crying desperately. The man motioned for her to stay still, but she would not. He slapped her harshly. He stabbed the injection into her chest—the girl began to convulse. Seconds later, she dropped to the floor. She was no longer crying, screaming—or breathing. She was dead.

Skye felt sick.

"No," she whimpered, as the moving images continued flashing into her mind. "No—what is this? What the hell is this?"

But the film kept playing.

The man shook his head. He was annoyed. Disappointed, even. Kicking the girl's lifeless body carelessly out of his way, he moved towards the next child. A second girl. Another injection was pulled out. He rammed it into her arm. She shrieked. Her arms went flailing wildly. She reached out and managed to claw the man in the eye. The man jumped back, swearing angrily. He smacked her across the face. The girl began wailing; all around her, the other children started to cry, their sounds echoing across the dark, grey room...it looked like a cell...The man roared at them to be quiet.

The girl grew fur over her hands. Then...nothing. The man shook his head, his lips pulled back in a snarl. He was angry. Very angry. Still holding his wounded eye where she had attacked him, he stormed towards a wooden door, yanked it open and shouted something.

Three bulky men appeared at the door. The man said something to them. They nodded; a couple smiled. The man pointed towards the girl with fur on her hands. They walked slowly towards her; all the children shrank back in terror. The girl with the fur stared at them as they came towards her, her mouth gaping. She began to shake her head frantically, turning towards the man with the hooked nose, her eyes pleading with him as tears streamed down her face. The man watched her coldly.

The three bulky men unchained the girl. Three pairs of hands grabbed her. She began to scream in wild fashion. The other children whimpered in fear, several squeezing their eyes shut. One of the men clamped a hand over her mouth. They pulled her into the middle of the cell and threw her to the floor...She continued screaming, clawing the ground in a desperate attempt to get away, but the men pinned her down; one clamped his huge hands on her furred wrists. The other two knelt down, their hands beginning to grope her...

What Skye saw next caused her to literally vomit. As the sick, vile images forced themselves into her mind, she staggered to the side before hurling up every bit of food she had eaten in the last hour.

"Stop," she croaked, the strong taste of bile on her tongue as the last of her food came regurgitating through her mouth, landed in a sloppy heap at her feet.

"Stop...please..."

And then they stopped. Just like that. The last thing she saw was the image of the dead girl on the ground and a chained, tanned boy at the end, cowering in the darkness, while the screams of the girl in the middle could be heard echoing throughout the cell amidst the grunts of the men…and then, quite suddenly, it all vanished. Skye was left swaying dizzily in the garden under the clear night sky, the stench of vomit wafting up to her nostrils.

Help me…

It was the boy again, miming in her mind. His tanned face was crumpled in despair, his eyes wet with tears.

Help me…don't let him hurt me again…

Skye knew that the beaver in the bushes was the little boy who was speaking to her right now. And she knew that this little boy had been one of the children in that dark, grey cell…

"Oh God," she whispered.

She struggled to pull herself together. Those children…what had happened to those children? Why had that monstrous man, the one with the hooked nose, done those awful things to them? Who was this little boy, this Morpher?

But right now, the answers to these questions would have to wait. Amidst her horror and nausea, that same protective feeling she had felt earlier in the office when she first clapped eyes on the beaver surged through her. This was what her instinct had been trying to tell her: protect this little boy from harm. She did not know who the perpetrators were, but right then, her priority had to be to help him.

Raphael warned you to stay away if you saw it again, a small voice in her head suddenly warned her. *You promised him.*

Raphael hasn't seen what I just saw, she told herself firmly.

She edged closer to the bushes, breathing heavily.

"Alright," she whispered, her whole body still shaking. "Here we go."

She raised her voice.

"H-hello? Are you there? Come out…I won't hurt you."

There was a shuffling noise inside the bushes. Seconds later, a tiny beaver came crawling towards her, sniffing her feet tentatively. Slowly, she reached down and held her hand out; her trembling fingers caressed the small creature gently on the head.

"Don't worry," she said quietly. "I'm going to help you. That man…what did he do to you?"

The horrifying images of the Memory Transference were still fresh in her mind. Her heart felt heavy, as though it was going to crack in two.

"I'm going to keep you safe now," she continued murmuring, still stroking the beaver as it nuzzled her hand. "He won't harm you again…"

"Miss Archer?"

Skye stood up in a flash and whirled round; the beaver cub fled back into the bush. Someone had crept up behind her. Being so lost in the dreadful memories and her determination to protect the child, her alertness had dropped. Her eyes flashed blue as she turned to face the stranger, ready to transform if necessary.

But it was just one of the guards from the Renzo mansion.

"Oh," said Skye, relief sailing through her.

She quickly turned back again to look down at her feet, but her relief turned to dismay when she realized the beaver had disappeared.

"Miss Archer…is everything alright?"

The guard was staring at her with concern. The silver buttons of his shirt with the Renzo crest imprinted on them glittered under the moonlight. Skye swallowed. She could feel herself getting angry with the guard for interrupting her moment with the beaver, not to mention scaring it off, but she knew it would not look good if she displayed any sense of despair. She had to find the beaver again before it disappeared for good—and possibly returned to the hands of that vile man in the white cloak.

"I—look, I've lost something, I need to find it..." she muttered to the guard, starting to make her way through the bushes.

"What is it, Miss Archer?"

"It doesn't matter—I mean, it does, I just need to find it..."

"It is not safe to go wandering around in the dark. I will accompany you."

"Right," said Skye distractedly, making her way down the dark path beyond the bushes; if she wasn't much mistaken, this path led to the Renzo greenhouse where the family kept a variety of wild herbs. "Yeah, that's fine..."

She turned to look at him briefly as he followed her.

"Thanks...Sorry, I don't know your name?" she said.

"It's Thomas, Miss Archer."

"Right...thanks, Thomas."

She began weaving her way through the bushes and down the narrow path. She sniffed the air, but could pick up no scent of the beaver. Her senses were nowhere near as powerful while she was human; should she transform and see if she could track him? He might be far away by now...She remembered what had happened a couple of months ago, when she had witnessed a teenage boy being beaten to death by a band of thugs; she remembered how she had stepped in to save him, how she had attacked the men in her wolf form; she remembered how she had managed to cry out for help as a wolf and how Raphael had heard her, even though he was so far away. This was the remarkable power of the Survival Pact.

I should transform, she told herself, while Thomas the guard continued shadowing her in the darkness. *The boy might be trying to contact me…if I transform, I might be able to hear him…*

She came to a slow halt and turned around to tell the guard that she needed to transform into her inner beast. He stood there, looking at her inquisitively.

"Thanks for helping me so far, Thomas," she began, "but I no longer need your assist—*umph!*"

Skye went crashing to the ground. Someone had hit her over the head from behind. At the same time, a tranquilizer dart had shot into the back of her arm. As she lay writhing on the cold, muddy path, her eyesight began to blur and a sudden, throbbing pain in her head made her want to scream in agony. A strange, drowsy sensation raced through her body; her heartbeat began to slow; there was a strange ringing in her ears. Her eyes felt heavy and the lids started to droop.

Struggling desperately to keep her eyes open, she witnessed two figures of men standing over her.

"This is her?" came the cold, distant voice of one of them.

"Yes, this is the one." Skye recognized the second voice. It was Thomas.

She had no energy to transform. There was no time to feel fear. There was no time to feel anything. The blurry images of the men reaching towards her were the last thing she saw before she blacked out.

CHAPTER FIVE

House of Renzo, September 26th 2217

It was ten o' clock in the evening. The dinner party had been called to an abrupt end earlier when one of the guards who usually stood outside the mansion burst through the doors, saluted to Lord Renzo and swiftly told him that he needed to speak with him as a matter of urgency.

Silence fell upon the dinner party; everyone knew automatically that some kind of tragedy had befallen. Lord Renzo stood up slowly before excusing himself in a quiet tone. Raphael, abandoning his dessert, followed him.

As Raphael followed his father across the room, his heart began to pound in a fast, furious way; a way that he had come to associate with a certain fear that he had experienced only a few times before. Each time, it had involved Skye. He had not forgotten the day that Pearson and his men had broken into her house and stabbed her; nor had he forgotten that if he had not been passing by to check on her,

139

she may very well have been dead already. It was a memory that often haunted him in his quieter moments, though he never spoke of it. What could have happened was too terrible to contemplate.

And now, as the guard led them down the corridor, Raphael felt that fear once again. Whatever had happened, it involved her. He knew it. He did not know exactly how he knew. But he knew. She had been gone too long…it had been thirty minutes since she had left him in the billiards room, right after that latest explosive episode of hers. Thirty minutes too long. During the entire time that he'd been forced to cater to the zealous whims of the Chinese Ambassador, who had once again cornered him and fired multiple questions at him about Morphing, his mind had been elsewhere. As the minutes ticked slowly by, Raphael's worry increased ten-fold. Skye had said she was going out for a breath of fresh air; she had not said she would be gone for a lengthy amount of time. She liked to go off on her own every now and then (especially after one of her jealous rages; it helped clear her head), but something didn't feel right—and he couldn't explain it. His concern had grown so great that he was only seconds away from telling the Chinese Ambassador that he needed to be excused; but at that moment, the guard had barged through the doors and requested to speak with his father.

As they continued walking down the hallway, a sick feeling twisted inside his stomach. He tried to tell himself he was being paranoid. But his gut told him something else.

"My Lord…in here please."

Another guard stood outside the door where they had just come to a stop. He bowed slightly to Lord Renzo and Raphael, nodding to the other guard that had led them there.

Lord Renzo was still for several seconds before he gently pushed the door open; the guard that had first burst through the doors of the dining room followed him. Raphael steeled himself, his mouth dry, wondering if he would be able to handle whatever he saw inside…

"Please go in, Master Raphael," said the guard outside the infirmary.

Raphael swallowed, his heart accelerating.

"Is it her?" he said suddenly, grasping the guard's shoulder.

Before the man could reply, the sharp voice of Lord Renzo called to him from inside the infirmary.

"Raphael, come here. Now."

Raphael released the guard, his heart filled with dread. He pushed the door open wider and stepped into the room.

It wasn't Skye. But a dead man lay on the hospital bed. Both extreme relief and extreme horror raced through him, rendering him immobile. He recognized the bloodied and bruised man on the bed as one of the guards his father employed. The man's eyes were open, lifeless. His body was stripped down to his underwear. He had been beaten badly; but it was a single shot wound in the chest that revealed the true cause of his death.

"Close the door behind you," Lord Renzo told his son.

Raphael shook himself into action and obeyed.

Lord Renzo turned to the guard that had followed him in.

"Tell me what happened," he said calmly.

"We found him outside, Sir," replied the guard. "By the thorn bushes on the other side of the building."

"How long ago was this?"

"About ten minutes ago, Sir. We brought him in and I came to see you straightaway."

"Did you see anyone else?"

"No, Sir."

Silence reigned for a moment. A second later, the doors swung open again. A short, rotund man in a silvery cloak came whizzing in; he wore a velvet green pointed hat, beige fingerless gloves and a monocle that hung from a chain around his neck—the usual attire for all doctors in the country.

"Doctor Jenson," said Raphael, acknowledging him.

Doctor Jenson was the Renzo family's private doctor; he had been pouring over various alchemies in his chambers, but had rushed to the scene as soon as word reached him that a body had been found on the premises.

"Master Raphael," Doctor Jenson nodded to Lord Renzo's youngest son; his expression was extremely grave as he turned his attention to the grim-faced lord who stood by the body. "My Lord...what has happened here?"

"This man is dead. His body was found on the grounds no less than ten minutes ago. I would like you to determine the cause of death."

Swiftly, Doctor Jenson walked towards the body. He grabbed his monocle and peered closely at the wound. Then he surveyed the rest of the man's body, including the back of his head.

"Hmmm..." he said, his eyes returning to the wound where dried blood covered the entire surrounding area. "The wound is an interesting one...he may have already been killed by the blow to his head, but this wound has several pinch-marks on the outer-skirts of it…Ah! Of course! A Tanzer Gun was used."

"A Tanzer Gun?" said Raphael, baffled. "That's impossible! No one in this country has access to those things anymore."

"That is true, but I am quite certain the pinch-marks are specific to the Tanzer Gun. It would also explain why no one would have heard the gun shot…if indeed that is the case?"

Doctor Jenson raised his eyebrows enquiringly to the guard. The guard nodded his head.

"That's right, Doctor. None of us heard the shot."

"There's only one person rich enough to smuggle a Tanzer Gun into the country aside from us and that's Pearson," said Raphael. "He must be responsible for this. But how did he get into the grounds?"

Lord Renzo didn't reply for several moments. When he did, he looked at the guard who continued to stand there, watching silently. His voice was calm, but there was a steely edge to it that sent chills up Raphael's spine.

"Call an end to the dinner party. Send everyone home. Tell the drivers to take them home personally. Everyone who does not leave must stay inside the building. They must not go outside under any circumstances. But do not incite panic; keep things smooth, keep them calm. Let the Emperor and his family sit in the lounge until I am ready to speak with them."

"Yes, Sir," said the guard, turning on his heel immediately and striding from the room.

"Dad," said Raphael, his stomach lurching in that familiar sick way. "I have to go. I have to find Skye."

"She hasn't yet returned?"

"No. She's been gone too long…I don't have a good feeling about this. The guard being killed…Skye being gone for thirty minutes—I have to go out and find her."

He stared at his father, wordless, but his eyes betraying a fear that he himself was afraid to acknowledge. Lord Renzo nodded.

"Do not go alone. Take the guards with you. Search the grounds. Try not to worry too much, Raphael. Remember, Skye is a Morpher, too…"

But the words did not console him. Skye could transform into a wolf, yes. Yet her ability did not make her invincible. The two of them had learned this the hard way.

Without another word, Raphael swept from the room leaving his father and Doctor Jenson alone with the body. The doctor continued examining the corpse before turning to Lord Renzo, his expression extremely grim.

"What do you think, My Lord?"

Lord Renzo surveyed the body thoroughly before straightening himself, his silver cane firm in his hand.

"I think we must proceed extremely cautiously," he replied. "You are sure this is the work of a Tanzer Gun, Doctor Jenson?"

"Quite positive."

"I see. Then there is no doubt who is behind this. I knew this was no mere brawl between two warring guards; I knew it was our enemy. The circumstances surrounding it worry me greatly."

"But how could they have possibly got in? The guard is meticulous in their duty!"

"I do not think this is a question of how, but a question of why."

"I do not follow, My Lord. The enemy have wanted to invade

for some time. Whatever their reasons, it can only be to do us harm. The problem of security is infinitely more important surely?"

"And yet, apart from the tragic loss of life before us now, no harm has been done to us here," murmured Lord Renzo. "One thing I know for certain. Whoever entered our domain tonight did so with the intention of impersonation. Notice his uniform has been removed. It appears the intruder murdered him before stripping him of his clothes, no doubt to impersonate one of our own. But for what purpose? This is what worries me most. Others would recognize a stranger among them. I must order the grounds to be searched."

"You don't think the intruder may have planted an explosive device?"

Lord Renzo shook his head.

"No. Every acre of our land is fitted underground with an explosive detector that automatically detonates any bomb or device. I believe whoever entered the grounds tonight was looking for something. The question is, what were they looking for? The grounds have to be searched. I highly doubt he or she is still among us, but a check must be taken nonetheless."

Out in the grounds, Raphael was searching for Skye with a band of seven guards. Ten minutes passed; fifteen; twenty. After half an hour and still no sign of her, and despite transforming in order to try and track her, as well as attempt to communicate with her in his animal form, Raphael came to the dreaded conclusion that his worst fear had been realized.

But it was when one of the guards reported signs of a scuffle not too far from the greenhouse that his suspicions were well and truly confirmed. A metal crest that belonged to the official uniform of the guard was found half-hidden in the flowerbeds, while unusual footprints were scattered all over the path leading to the greenhouse. Upon inspection, Raphael realized with a sinking heart that these footprints could only belong to one person, because only one person wore boots shaped like this. Skye's wolf boots were one of a kind and there was no doubt that it was this that had made the marks in the ground. Two other footprints accompanied them, but halfway down the path, Skye's prints disappeared. Another pair of footprints appeared on the scene. What happened after the third pair arrived was anyone's guess, but for Raphael, it only spelled disaster.

As well as this, there was something else lying in one of the footprints; the sight of it turned his blood to ice. A random piece of coal was lodged in one of Skye's prints. Slowly, he picked it up. Coal…the trademark fossil fuel of the thugs, left behind as a silent message to others whenever their victims disappeared or were killed…

It took every bit of self-restraint he had not to haul himself over the gates and run through the entire city, yelling her name. He stormed through the doors of the mansion, his heart pounding uncontrollably. He found his father in Rachelle (the war room where many meetings took place); Lord Renzo was giving orders to several senior guards just as Raphael burst in and interrupted them.

"She's gone," were the first words out of his mouth as he charged forwards.

Lord Renzo and the guards turned to stare at him.

"Did you search the whole grounds?" Lord Renzo questioned his son.

"Yes, I did," replied Raphael, through gritted teeth. "She's gone. She's not here anymore. Whoever killed the guard was looking for her and they took her."

"We cannot be certain of that, Raphael, we must stay calm—"

"Stay calm?" bellowed Raphael. "She's gone, Dad! She's gone—and yes, I can be certain of it! I found her footprints in the mud near the greenhouse! There were two other footprints with hers—and this! Look at this!"

He produced the piece of coal from his pocket and held it up, the rock smudging his palm completely black.

"Coal! Whoever sneaked in tonight took her! Pearson's got her—I'm going to East London—"

"Raphael," said Lord Renzo sharply, while the guards stared at the youngest Renzo, deep worry in their eyes. "You will do no such thing. You must stay here."

"I'm sorry, Dad, but that's one order I can't obey," growled Raphael, already turning on his heel towards the door. "Pearson's got her—she could already be dead—"

The notion of Skye being killed at the hands of Pearson was almost too much for him; he choked on his own words before steeling himself, his hand gripping the doorknob.

"Raphael, you must calm yourself. Use your head—why would Lord Pearson kidnap Skye, only to kill her? If she has been taken, it is much more likely that they want her for a specific reason—or that they know she is the bait to lure you in."

Lord Renzo's words rang out into the silent war room. Raphael swallowed. He knew his father was right; he knew that if Skye had been kidnapped, it was more likely that they would use her for bait, ransom purposes or bargaining methods. This was what his logical side was telling him, the same side that listened attentively whenever his father held meetings in this room, whenever he advised on the best course of action.

But right then, this side of him was overpowered by the idea that the girl he loved was at the mercy of their enemy.

"I can't lose her, Dad," he said quietly, before turning the handle of the door.

Lord Renzo strode towards his son.

"Listen to me," he said in a low voice, his hand gripping the back of Raphael's head, forcing him to meet his eyes. "Listen to me. If they have her, they will *not* harm her. Do you understand? They know full well how much she means to you. If they wanted her dead, they would have killed her on the spot. Wouldn't they? They would have left her body here to gloat. That coal would not be in your hands if she were dead. Do not play into their hands. Should you go charging blindly to the Pearsons, alone and on a head full of anger, they will kill you—they will kill you and this will be their victory. Raphael, heed my words. If they have her, then we will get her back. You must listen to me, my son. We *will* get her back."

They stared at one another for some time, their eyes boring into each other, one pleading, the other defiant. Raphael struggled to speak; both fear and rage raced through his veins.

"If Pearson harms her," he finally said, his voice shaking with loathing, "I will kill him. I will tear his body limb from limb. I won't stop until every last piece of his flesh lies in shreds before me."

"And I will be the one to assist you," said Lord Renzo, a rare display of hardness in his voice that very few had ever witnessed.

He turned to his guards who stood watching, silently.

"Assemble a search party," he commanded. "Leave no stone unturned, both for Miss Archer and for the intruder. Do not report back until every corner of the premises has been searched."

The guards saluted and marched from the room. Raphael continued standing on the spot; his face stony and ashen, trying to tame the inner turmoil and fear that was threatening to overwhelm him. He silently cursed himself. How could he have let this happen? How could he have failed in his vigilance and actually allowed Skye to leave the building on her own for a lengthy period of time? Nowhere was safe. *Nowhere.* Not even his own home. He had been meticulous in protecting her at her house, at her work—picking her up every day, ensuring she was always accompanied—he had insisted, despite her occasional protests. And now…for this to happen…to have her snatched away, right under his nose…His nostrils flared, his eyes flashed orange…if they hurt her…if she came to any harm…

He cracked his knuckles, tremors shooting through him. Lord Renzo placed a hand on his shoulder.

"Come," he said quietly. "We must see to the others. We must not alarm them. We must, above all else, remain calm and in control."

Raphael nodded rigidly, feeling that speech was impossible as he continued to wrestle with the powerful urge to just bolt from the mansion and find Skye.

He followed his father out of Rachelle (named after their ancestor, Rachelle Renzo, a war heroine who played crucial roles during two previous world wars) and together they swept down the corridor. Lord Renzo stopped outside the lounge and told Raphael to wait in the dining room while he spoke with Emperor Jin. Raphael nodded mutely.

He entered the dimly lit dining room where several nervous guests stood, plainly wondering what was going on as they waited to be escorted home. The Emperor, niece and nephew had already been led to the lounge and were no longer present.

Among the confused, troubled dinner party were Daphne, Mrs. Archer, Joey and Ricardo, huddled together on one side of the table, clearly in discussion about what had happened and why the guard had dashed through the doors earlier in such an urgent manner.

"But has anyone seen Skye?" Raphael heard Mrs. Archer ask worriedly as he entered the dining hall. "I haven't seen her for a while, I hope she hasn't decided to go for a run on her own, she was just telling me earlier how much she missed running on the grounds…"

Raphael swallowed. How was he going to tell Mrs. Archer that her daughter was missing? That all the evidence pointed towards her being kidnapped by the very people that wanted them dead?

He strode towards the group, clearing his throat, trying to mould his face into a mask of calm.

"Raph!" exclaimed Joey, looking up as Raphael approached them, his turquoise eyes blazing confusedly. "What's going on? Some guards came in and told us the dinner was over—hadn't even finished dessert! The Emperor was taken away—no one's got a clue what's going on! So, come on, tell us; what's this all about?"

Four pairs of eyes stared at him.

Raphael took a seat next to Ricardo, clearing his throat before staring back at them all.

"There's been a…situation," he began in a low voice, his green eyes penetrating theirs. "I'm afraid one of the guards was found on the grounds tonight. Dead."

The alarm on everyone's face increased ten-fold.

"Dead?" repeated Ricardo, his eyebrows furrowed.

Raphael nodded.

"He was found outside, stripped of his uniform. It appears he was beaten and then shot with a Tanzer gun."

The questions came flying in at once.

"A *Tanzer gun?* Are you *sure?*"

"But—I don't understand—why was he stripped?"

"Who did it?"

"We are still not sure of the exact reasons behind it," replied Raphael. "But…but it looks like someone killed him with the intention of impersonating one of our own."

"But *why?*" asked Joey, baffled.

"I don't know," lied Raphael.

He had to keep it secret. At least, for now, in this room, with too many people listening in. When the other guests had gone he could tell them…Tell them that an intruder had broken in…

And taken Skye…

"Raphael," came Mrs. Archer's timid voice, an underlying fear in it that he did not fail to pick up on.

Reluctantly, Raphael met her eyes. They were wide and scared. She knew. He did not know how she knew, but he was certain she did. She knew Skye was no longer with them.

"Raphael…where is Skye?"

Steadily, Raphael kept his gaze fixed on hers, his heartbeat quickening, unsure how to respond.

Mrs. Archer stood up slowly; his evasive silence confirmed her instincts were correct. The group remained quiet, watching the non-verbal exchange between Skye's mother and boyfriend. Something was wrong…very wrong…

"Where is she, Raphael? Where is my daughter?"

"Mrs. Archer," Raphael began, his throat dry.

Daphne's eyes flitted worriedly from Skye's mother to Raphael. Joey and Ricardo stared silently at their brother. Mrs. Archer began to tremble.

At that moment, Lord Renzo appeared in the doorway. He spotted the group and made his way over to them, accompanied by one of the guards.

"Raphael…Ricardo…Joey," he addressed his sons. "Please go into the lounge. Take Miss Beaufont and Mrs. Archer with you."

"Lord Renzo, please. Tell me where my daughter is…I know that something is wrong!"

Turning to face the frightened, shaking woman before him, Lord Renzo made his way towards her and rested a gentle hand on her arm.

"Please stay calm, Lilian," he told her quietly. "I know this is difficult, but please go with my sons for now. Raphael, take them to the lounge and I will speak with you all there" he added, with a meaningful look at his son. "I will follow you shortly, but I must first speak with the other guests."

Nodding, with the understanding that his father was warning him not to speak of Skye's disappearance while he was gone, Raphael headed them out of the dining room. The remaining guests averted their curious gazes from the group and listened attentively to Lord Renzo, who was now speaking to the room at large.

The small group followed Raphael down the hallway towards the lounge. Mrs. Archer was being comforted by a scared, worried Daphne; the twins took up the rear, muttering to each other. Raphael swung open the doors and they were greeted by the sight of Trey and Kai, who were sitting on one of the leather couches, grave expressions on their faces. The Emperor and Lo Wen were nowhere to be seen; Raphael presumed they had retired to their quarters after Lord Renzo had spoken with them.

"Please sit down," said Trey, standing up and offering the couch to Daphne and Mrs. Archer. Joey and Ricardo opted not to take a seat, but instead made their way to a glass table that had a variety of whiskies and spirits laden on top of it. The twins poured themselves a shot each.

"Anyone fancy a drink?" enquired Ricardo half-heartedly, in an attempt to lighten the extremely tense atmosphere in the room.

Everyone shook their heads. Mrs. Archer appeared not even to have heard him.

"I don't understand," she was whimpering, while Daphne continued to place a consoling arm around her shoulder. "Where is she? Why won't they tell me what is going on?"

"I know, Mrs. Archer, I know," said Daphne, her own eyes betraying deep fear and concern. "But Skye is tough…Whatever's happened, I'm sure she's OK…Lord Renzo will be here in a moment, I'm sure he will tell us what's happened…"

Trey excused himself from Kai and the two women on the couch and walked over to where Raphael was standing rigidly by the door.

"Is it true?" he muttered to his youngest brother, careful to keep his voice low so no one else could hear him. "Dad said someone broke in and killed the guard…and that you found Skye's footprints near the greenhouse…that there were signs of a resistance?"

Raphael nodded wordlessly.

"We can assume she has been taken then…and that this is most definitely the work of Pearson?" Trey continued in that low tone. "Their motive for taking her must be for bargaining—or bait, perhaps, to lure you out into the open…"

The way he was talking, as though Skye was a piece of cheese being dangled in the waters above a hungry fish, caused angry flames to leap inside Raphael once more.

"I don't want to talk about the reasons they took her, Trey," he growled, clenching his fists. "I just can't believe I'm standing here doing nothing while Pearson's got her—we don't even know if she's still—"

He stopped short as he caught Mrs. Archer looking over at him, her face still a mask of distress. The sick feeling swooped inside his stomach. Trey looked over to where the guests were still sitting silently on the couch before turning back to Raphael.

"Forgive me, I did not mean to sound insensitive," he said quietly. "Try not to worry. Stay calm. Skye is much more useful to them alive, Raphael, remember that."

"Yeah, Dad said the same thing," replied Raphael, his jaw clenched.

Trey averted his sympathetic gaze away from his brother as Lord Renzo appeared in the lounge, flanked by two guards.

"Thank you," Lord Renzo told his envoy. "Please leave the room."

The guards bowed and left, shutting the door on their way out.

Five pairs of watchful eyes stared at the aged lord as he walked towards the centre of the room. He cleared his throat before speaking.

"As each person here is aware, a situation arose tonight," he said aloud, looking round at them, from the unblinking Kai to the fretful Mrs. Archer. "One of our guards was found on the grounds, deceased. It soon became apparent to us that an intruder had murdered him before stripping him of his clothes with what appeared to be the incentive to impersonate one of our own. Evidence so far points towards Lord Pearson as the perpetrator."

He stopped speaking and approached Skye's mother, who was gazing at him fearfully.

"My dear Mrs. Archer," said Lord Renzo, lowering his voice and gently placing a hand on hers as he sat down beside her. "It pains me to inform you of this and I ask your forgiveness for keeping you waiting. I must further ask your forgiveness for what has happened here tonight, for it appears our diligence and security has been compromised and, for this, I take full responsibility."

"Yes?" whispered Mrs. Archer, her hand trembling beneath it. Daphne, who sat beside her, waited with baited breath.

"Signs of a struggle next to the greenhouse were reported," Lord Renzo said quietly, "and as the mansion and grounds have been thoroughly checked, we can only assume one conclusion. It appears that Skye has been kidnapped by whoever entered our premises tonight."

Mrs. Archer let out a low gasp and clutched her chest. Daphne's mouth dropped open. The twins, still reeling from the discovery that one of their guards had been murdered, stared gobsmacked at their father. Raphael could not even look in the direction of Skye's mother and kept his eyes fixed on the wall.

"Oh no," Mrs. Archer whimpered.

Tears sprang to her eyes.

"No…this can't be true. Please…how could this happen?"

She stared desperately at Lord Renzo and then to Raphael, the tears coming fast and strong. Raphael was unable to meet her eyes; his expanded with every second that ticked by, his anger at himself boiled to the surface with volcanic propensity.

"Mrs. Archer, please do not despair," said Lord Renzo with as much calming fusion as he could muster. "We have every reason to believe that Skye has not met any fatal mishap. I truly understand the difficulty and grief you are experiencing right now; I cannot even begin to expect your forgiveness for allowing this to happen on my territory; but I want you to know that, wherever your daughter is, we are going to do everything in our power to have her returned to us, safe and well."

His words had little effect on Mrs. Archer, who was now openly sobbing into her hands, a similarly tearful Daphne consoling her as best as she could.

Ricardo came over and placed an arm around Daphne. Joey, his whiskey glass gripped in his fingers, walked hurriedly towards Raphael and Trey, who were still standing by the door.

"Jesus Christ," he muttered. "Kidnapped? I just don't understand it. How in the world did they get *in?*"

"That is still under investigation," said Trey. "But the pressing matter right now is how we are going to get Skye back. We must formulate a plan—at once. A convoy may be the best way forward, if indeed this is a bargaining ploy…Moles have already been dispatched to East London to confirm if she is there, and our spies have been alerted…it may take several hours for affirmation on her whereabouts…"

Raphael was not listening.

"I have to get her back," he said under his breath.

His brothers heard him.

"Raph," began Joey in a wary voice, "stay cool, alright? You heard what Dad said. If the Pearsons have got her, she's likely to be alive. This is probably a plot to get to you—"

"Then that's exactly what they'll have."

"Raphael, you will not help Skye by going after her," said Trey sharply. "It won't accomplish anything. You'll be playing right into their hands. You must stay here. Let the surveillance team do their job—only once her whereabouts have been confirmed can we take decisive action—"

"And if they can't confirm where she is?" Raphael snarled. "Then what? I can't just sit here—I have to do something!"

But what? What could he do? His brother was right. What Trey said, as Lord Renzo had said earlier, was the truth. Charging into Pearson territory would mean certain death; even as a tiger, he had no hope of finding Skye in the stronghold where masses of thugs roamed. He would be instantly killed—and then what good would he be to Skye, to his family, to the citizens?

But he couldn't just sit here, waiting. It was killing him, not

Sarah Brownlee

knowing, not acting…

"I know this is hard for you," said Trey urgently, "but you must stay calm. Right now, our best hope of getting Skye back is to wait for the spies to confirm her whereabouts, and then, prepare a rescue mission—"

RAPHAEL!

He heard her voice, as clear as if she had been standing next to him, yelling in his ear.

"Skye!" he gasped, staggering backwards.

It wasn't his imagination. It wasn't delirium. The last time this had happened was several months ago when Skye had transformed into her inner beast and saved that boy from being beaten to death; the memory often played around in his mind—how he had been in his art room, painting, when her cries for help had appeared in his head, photographic slide-shots popping into his mind one after another as she conveyed to him what had happened and where she was…how he had responded to her to let him know he was coming, how he had thrown his paints to the floor and rushed to get to her.

This was the power of the Survival Pact and once more it was in effect, the telepathic connection between Morphers.

Skye! He shouted back in his mind. *Where are you?*

The pictures came fast. A man in a white suit with a long, hooked nose…a darkened cell…the large sign on the door that read TOW-HAM 61…a small, brown creature with large teeth locked in a cage…a needle…

The pictures disappeared instantly; Skye's voice echoed frantically in his head once again.

Don't come for me! Raphael, don't come—

158

Then she vanished.

"NO!" he roared out loud. "SKYE, WHERE ARE YOU? DAMMIT!"

He cursed blindingly, his fist pounding the door, oblivious to the concerned faces of his brothers who were struggling to get his attention, agitatedly asking him what had happened. Mrs. Archer and Daphne were staring at him in shock; Lord Renzo swept across the room as fast as his cane would allow.

"Raphael," he said, his voice quiet and urgent. "What is it? What did you see?"

Raphael struggled to pull himself together.

"She's alive," he said, fighting to get the words out. "She's in her animal form."

"Where is she?"

"I don't know," was the deeply frustrated reply. "She was only there for a second—she didn't tell me where she was—"

"What has happened?" cried Mrs. Archer, who had leapt from the couch and come running over; Daphne, Ricardo and Kai followed, hot on her heels.

"Mrs. Archer," said Raphael, forcing himself to calm down; for her sake, he had to reassure her that Skye was OK.

"Skye managed to communicate with me through the Survival Pact. It was only for a moment. She is in her wolf form. She is alright, Mrs. Archer…"

How much of the last part was true, Raphael did not know. The panicking circumstances surrounding her conveyance, plus the strange, eerie man in the white coat, were grave causes for concern—but she was alive, and that was what mattered.

"Oh, thank goodness!" cried Mrs. Archer, tears welling up again, this time from relief. "Thank goodness…But—but where is she? Who is she with?"

"I'm afraid our exchange was very brief and she was unable to tell me her location. But please don't worry, Mrs. Archer. Skye is OK and we are going to find her, wherever she is, and bring her home."

"Miss Beaufont," said Lord Renzo briskly, addressing a white-faced Daphne, "why don't you take Mrs. Archer down to the tea room and fix yourselves a cup of tea? My dear Lilian," he said, holding Skye's mother by the arm; Mrs. Archer looked as though she was on the brink of collapse. "Please go with Miss Beaufont. I must ask you to try and calm your mind; try to relax, though I know how difficult this is."

"But Skye—"

"Rest assured that your daughter is safe and that we will do everything in our power to ensure she stays that way. As soon as we have decided upon a course of action, we will alert you. Miss Beaufont, if you please."

Daphne, still extremely pale, nodded and placed an arm around Skye's mother.

"Come with me, Mrs. Archer," she said, her voice shaky. "Let's have some tea. Don't worry. Skye's OK…she's in her wolf form—she can handle anything when she's a wolf, you know that…"

The two of them exited the lounge, Ricardo squeezing his girlfriend's hand as she left.

Those who remained in the room stared at Raphael, who had beads of sweat dripping down his forehead.

"Something's not right," he muttered. "The way she was cut off like that—it doesn't make sense—"

Despite the relief he had felt upon learning she was alive, it was quickly extinguished and replaced by the dread that something drastic may have happened to her in the moment she disappeared.

Lord Renzo spoke quickly.

"I want you to tell me exactly what you saw," he said to his son. "Tell me what you saw and what you heard."

"There was a room—no, a cell. It looked like a prison of some sort. There was a man there…I don't know who he was, didn't recognize him. He wore a white coat; it looked like he was coming towards her. Whoever he was, she didn't like him. There was an animal in a cage, a beaver…"

It dawned on Raphael that the small beaver must have been the same one that had caused such chaos in Skye's office the other day. The same one he had warned her to stay away from. How could it be that they were both now trapped in the same place? That suspicious sensation he had felt the other day amplified inside him once more. This beaver was connected to Skye's kidnapping tonight, but how?

"Go on," Lord Renzo pressed him. "What did you hear?"

Raphael shook his head helplessly.

"She only managed to say a few words. She said, "Don't come for me, Raphael. Don't come." Then she vanished. I—I couldn't communicate with her after that."

There was a brief silence.

"Her priority was to warn you," said Trey, breaking into it. "This almost certainly means she is in the Pearson stronghold. She knows that to enter it means certain death. She must be afraid you would go looking for her."

"Perhaps more than that," added Kai. "As we suspected, this could be verification that their plan is indeed to use her as bait. Raphael, the enemy knows full well that losing you would be a major blow to our cause."

Though he knew that both Trey and Kai were right, it didn't stop the anger rising in him when he heard their words. What in the hell did it matter about the reasoning behind it, or how important he was to their continued survival? Skye was in danger! It was his duty to protect her, something he had promised her when they first met. He had failed in that duty; he had to get her back at all costs.

"This man in the white coat," pondered Lord Renzo thoughtfully, "what did he look like?"

"I only caught a glimpse of him. Long nose…practically bald…"

"What was he doing?"

"Nothing—he was coming towards her; I think Skye was being restrained, I could feel that she wanted to attack him…Wait! He was holding something. Some kind of syringe…"

"A syringe?" said Ricardo, baffled.

Raphael nodded.

"Did she manage to hint anything at all about her location?" continued Lord Renzo. "Anything, Raphael. Did you hear anything? Did you see anything?"

"No," Raphael struggled to remember the other details from the flashes. "No, she didn't communicate her whereabouts. But…"

Then it came back to him. The sign.

"There was a sign! Right above the door—it said 'TOW-HAM 61'."

"Tower Hamlets," said Trey straight away, referring to a borough of East London. "But '61'? Which area is that? I'd better check."

"No need, it's in the southern district of Mile End," said Joey immediately.

"How do you know that?"

"Because 'TOW-HAM 61' is the red light zone of East London," Joey replied, the trace of a grin on his face. "Bit of a risk going there back in the day, but well-worth my time…Anyway," he added hastily, coughing as everyone stared, "'61' is definitely Mile End. And if that's the sign you saw, that must be where Skye's being held."

The thought of Skye imprisoned in one of the seediest areas in London only swelled Raphael's almost uncontrollable itch to transform and bound through the city to find her, thugs be damned.

"We know where she is now," he said out loud, facing the others. "There's no excuse—we have to get her. We don't know what they plan on doing with her—we could be running out of time as we speak!"

"We will assemble a rescue squad," said Lord Renzo.

 He turned to his eldest son.

"Trey, call for the special operations team. Speak to the director of MI24, Charles Barlow; explain the situation to him. A rescue mission should be possible, but a stake-out is required first."

MI24, unlike its predecessors such as MI5 and MI6, was the only remaining functioning department of British Military Intelligence left in the country. It was formed in the middle of the 22nd century and its sole purpose was to control the growing masses of thugs and criminals that were slowly infiltrating the population. But with a sorely weakened government, dissention among the political parties, widespread anarchy and the rise of the infamous Pearson family who found their fortunes amidst the chaos, MI24's attempts at maintaining law and order resulted in failure. The department would have gone defunct, were it not for a handful of agents who kept it alive throughout the years, passing their knowledge and skills of surveillance and concealment onto worthy predecessors, ones who cared about the state of their country and wished to see it restored to a time when prosperity, not decline, ruled. MI24, just like the 'government', was obligated towards only one of two factions who held any power at all in the city: the Renzos. With a desire to finally see the victory that MI24 had been striving towards in the first place, the remaining agents of this special branch were at the beck and call of Lord Renzo; other, more unscrupulous members within this secret service had defected to Lord Pearson, and as a result, even intelligence within the branch could be compromised. No one could be trusted. But Sir Charles Barlow, the director of MI24, was a man Lord Renzo placed a great deal of faith in; he knew that if there was anyone who could get Skye out of one of the most dangerous areas of the city, it was him.

Trey nodded, immediately pulling out his tag device. He was on a call within seconds.

"I should go," volunteered Joey. "I know that place like the back of my hand."

"What if you are recognized?" Kai questioned the twin.

Joey laughed.

"No chance of it. You think I ever actually went there with these good looks on display? It's not just MI24 who're skilled in the art of concealment, buddy. Plus, I made a few contacts back then. I'm pretty sure there are a few ladies of the night who would be happy to stab the Pearsons in the back, given half the chance."

He turned to Ricardo, slapping him on the back.

"Think you'd better sit this one out, Ric. I don't think your girl would be too happy about you revisiting our old hot spots. So," he added, facing his father, "how 'bout it, Dad? You going to let me in on this one? Undercover stuff is one of my specialities, you know that."

It was true. Since the arrival of the Chinese forces, each member of the Renzo family had been playing to his strengths—even the twins had cut down on their lavish lifestyles and devoted more time to prepare for the impending war. Where Trey was skilled in diplomacy and forging negotiations, Joey and Ricardo, with their sharp wits and charming flair, had a natural penchant for sneaking and concealment, which made them perfect for reconnaissance missions (something which both had been eager to take part in; the thrill of going undercover was only surpassed by the thrill of chasing women). Raphael, meanwhile, was seen as the natural successor to Lord Renzo; his bold courage, stout heart and fearlessness in the face of opposition meant that many of their allies and supporters flocked to him and viewed him as a leader, someone to rally around in a crisis. Each of the Renzo brothers had been developing their expertise as of late, whether consciously or subconsciously.

Subsequently, Lord Renzo did not object to his middle son's

request; though he did express his reservations.

"I will let you go on the account that you stay focused on the task at hand," he told him. "Do not be distracted by the local attractions."

Joey pretended to look outraged.

"Jeez, you make it sound like I'm going to one of those old-school fairgrounds! Come on, what do you take me for? There's a time and a place for all that!"

Ricardo grinned. The general light-hearted feel to this exchange between Lord Renzo and his wayward son relaxed the tense atmosphere in the dining hall very briefly. But of course, it did not last as the grim cloud settled above them once more.

"I will assign you to the squad," Lord Renzo agreed. "But within reason; at the first sign of conflict, you flee. Let members of the squad trained in combat deal with it, in the event it should happen."

Joey shrugged.

"Fine by me. I've got no intention of getting killed any time soon, believe me."

Lord Renzo turned to Trey, who had just terminated the call on his tag device.

"Have the moles been alerted to confirm Skye's whereabouts in Mile End?" he asked him.

Trey nodded.

"Yes. I sent them a message as soon as it was identified as the location. I have just spoken to Sir Barlow—he is on his way."

"I should go on ahead and make preparations," said Raphael, already halfway out the door. "I'll meet the agents at the entrance."

"Raphael, no. You cannot go on this mission."

At the sound of his father's words, Raphael stopped in his tracks.

"You can't truly mean to stop me?" he said, slowly facing him. "Dad—I'm the only one who knows what the place looks like—and Joey—"

"Your brother has intricate knowledge of the area. His expertise may be invaluable."

"How will they even begin to start looking for her? I saw where she's being held, I need to be there—"

"You must provide us with a detailed description of the place. The team will then use this knowledge to help track Skye's location."

"I can't just sit here and do nothing while everyone is risking their necks to find her!" Raphael exploded. "Not now that I know where she is; not now that I know she's alive!"

"Raphael, consider the circumstances," said Lord Renzo sharply, while everyone else in the room shifted uncomfortably. "In the split-second that Skye was able to communicate with you, it wasn't to ask for help, it wasn't to tell you where she was being held captive, it wasn't to let you know who her kidnappers were; it was to warn you. Warning you was what she considered to be the most important message to get across—more important than anything else. She would not have done this without very good reason. Has she been told that she is the bait to reel you in? Is she aware that your presence in Mile End would result in your imminent death? Are *you* the true target? If indeed any of these theories ring true, wouldn't it be madness to walk straight into the enemy's lair and hand yourself in on a plate?"

"I could transform," Raphael growled. "You know full well I

could transform and that my strength would be crucial to the team—"

"And have a fully-grown tiger ravaging throughout the town? This would cause disaster on an epic scale and would put both yourself and those who are with you at risk! Think, Raphael—think! Your emotions have clouded your judgement. You are too emotionally invested in this and this is precisely why you must not go. I will not allow it."

"It is my choice to make!"

"Should you choose to defy me then do so at your own peril, for it is I who you must go up against—I will not send my own son to his death."

Both Lord Renzo and Raphael stood before each other, their backs straight, muscles tensed. Raphael's scorching eyes faced the hardened lines on his father's face; both of them looked as though they were on the verge of transformation; hardly anyone in the room moved or even breathed.

Then Raphael's shoulders seemed to sag and the fierce expression left him; he looked lost, defeated.

Lord Renzo walked towards his youngest son and laid a hand on his shoulder. Mental anguish twisted Raphael's features, but no words passed between them.

Another guard burst through the doors.

"My Lord, Sir Charles Barlow has arrived."

Lord Renzo tore his gaze from his son's face.

"Show him in," he said.

Moments later, a tall, robust man with long brown hair, a thick brown moustache and a commanding presence swept through the room.

"My Lord Renzo," he said with a bow.

Lord Renzo greeted him, shaking his hand vigorously.

"Sir Charles—you are most welcome. Thank you for coming with such speed and at this short notice."

He squeezed Raphael's shoulder before gesturing for the head of MI24 to follow him further into the room; the other men in the room welcomed him as he strode past.

For the next forty minutes, the rescue plan was formulated, a team was assembled and potential action was thoroughly dissected. Raphael remained withdrawn, paralysed to act; he provided as much detail as he possibly could with regard to the contents and appearance of the room Skye had been in, and of the sinister-looking man in the white coat. But aside from this there was little more he could do. Continuing to wrestle with his impulse to throw caution to the wind, he kept praying that Skye would telepathically communicate with him again; his heart felt as though it was being pulled in every direction, made far worse by the knowledge that he was powerless to act.

It was almost eleven o' clock at night when the team were ready to set off, half an hour after Skye had managed to communicate with Raphael. The rescue squad comprised of two surveillance agents, three combat agents, two Shrews (the official name for agents who were responsible for snatching whomever they were rescuing from imprisonment) and Joey Renzo. Joey had been ordered to stand outside the town walls unless expressly told otherwise. He was to be given a Stealth Device, similar in size to the Tag Device, but with a completely different purpose. With a Stealth Device, he would, within a certain distance, be able to guide the agents through the city as if he was there himself by transmitting a holograph of himself among their company. But the key feature of this appliance was the holographic ability to physically touch anything made of stone, brick, metal and even human skin. This was an extremely unique and rare utensil, exclusively owned by MI24. Kai had also wanted to take part, but he had been overruled by the others who stated that his presence was needed at the mansion for the sake of the Emperor.

"Nice!" exclaimed Joey, taking hold of the silver, magnetic Stealth Device, which fit easily into the palm of his hand. "Being able to touch something with my holographic hand in one place and touch something else with my normal hand somewhere totally different? Now *that's* what I call useful!"

"Lord Renzo, what if the mission should fail?" questioned Sir Charles Barlow; his team of agents had arrived some half hour beforehand and he had just finished prepping them on their task.

Lord Renzo paused in the act of strapping the device to Joey's hand before raising his eyes to the head of MI24, his gaze heavy.

"Then it may be the catalyst that begins the war," he said. "We will demand that Lord Pearson releases her. If not, we will have no option but to attack the stronghold."

He stared round at them all.

"Be prepared for anything."

Just as he said that, a commotion was suddenly heard outside the room.

Immediately, everyone turned to face the closed door. Seconds later, a guard banged it open, looking panicking and sweaty.

"My Lord," he gasped, "forgive me, but I must inform you—"

"Yes?" said Lord Renzo sharply.

"Forgive me, My Lord, but we found her like this—in the garden—they dropped her, but they were gone before we could fire at them—"

There was an unnatural, tense chill in the room, a sense of foreboding that not one person present could explain. Raphael felt his entire throat go dry. Moments later, the reason for their misgiving was revealed.

Three guards entered the room. They were carrying something between them. A white wolf, limp and seemingly lifeless, her tongue lolling out on the side of her muzzle, her unconscious, flaccid form giving no indication to whether she was alive or dead.

CHAPTER SIX

"I don't think you'll be needing that now, Joe," said Ricardo quietly, gesturing towards the Stealth Device strapped to his brother's hand.

The twins, along with everyone else in the room, had at first been speechless upon catching sight of Skye in her animal form as she was carried by the perspiring guards and laid gently to the floor. But it was a mere split-second before everyone sprang into action.

Raphael broke out of his immobile state first; his heart, which appeared to have frozen in time due to this shocking turn of events, suddenly kick-started into gear again, racing a hundred miles a minute.

Skye was here. She had come back. The wave of shock and relief that had first hit him upon realizing this was immediately shattered by a terror that engulfed his whole being.

She had returned.

But was she alive?

"MOVE!" he roared, breaking through the circle of MI24 agents who were standing around him, their eyes wide with shock as they stared at the motionless white wolf on the ground.

Skye, be alive. Don't be dead. Don't be dead, he chanted desperately in his head.

He dropped to the ground, swiftly followed by his father, Trey, Kai and the twins.

"Stand aside," Lord Renzo ordered the guards who were ogling at the scene; the guards quickly scattered to make way.

Raphael placed a palm on Skye's furry chest and, with his other hand, he held two fingers beneath her snout. Her heart beat very faintly; she was breathing, but only just.

He choked with relief.

"She's alive," he said shakily, tremors shooting through him as he struggled to gain control of the overwhelming emotions that threatened to consume his entire body. "She's alive—but she's weak—"

"Send for Doctor Jenson," commanded Lord Renzo, also kneeling by the wolf's side.

"On it!" said Ricardo, before dashing from the room.

Raphael pressed his face to the wolf's soft, white fur; her eyes remained shut. He, too, closed his eyes and focused on the delicate fur that seeped gently into his cheeks, blocking out everyone and everything in that room, except for her and the miraculous notion that, yes, she was alive, she had returned; how this had come to be, he had no idea; but in that brief moment he didn't think of that; he only knew that he had lost her and she had come back. He wanted to bellow up at the sky and thank the almighty powers that be, but he restrained himself, burying his face in her familiar scent, his fingers brushing her pointy ears.

"You came back," he whispered. "I thought I'd lost you."

Lord Renzo placed a gentle hand on the back of Skye's neck; there were several strange puncture wounds where her cervical spine was and he regarded them, puzzled, running his gnarled palm over them with concern.

"Joey, inform Mrs. Archer," he told the remaining twin who, like the others, continued to stand over Skye, unable to fathom how the Morpher they had planned on rescuing only moments before had somehow turned up half-dead in the lounge. "She needs to know her daughter has returned. But keep her absent for now; we must first tend to Skye."

"Got it."

Following his brother's footsteps, Joey also bolted at top speed from the room. Lord Renzo turned to the guard that had first appeared with the message of Skye's return.

"How did you find her?"

"In the garden, My Lord. One of the men heard a suspicious noise. He went to investigate and that's when he found Miss Archer lying on the grass at the bottom of the wall. He heard footsteps running outside the premises. When he went to check, he saw a couple of men running away. He took shots at them, but missed. It sounded like the men had thrown her over the wall."

"That would account for her unconscious state," said Trey. "It's a long drop down from the wall. But what are those wounds on her neck?"

"I do not know," said Lord Renzo grimly. "But it appears she has been injected in some way."

Raphael was listening to all this. He caressed the top of Skye's head. He looked at the puncture wounds and thought about how she had been tossed over the wall, like a disposable bin bag. Anger flamed inside him; whoever did this to her would pay.

Doctor Jenson's stout frame came breezing through the door, his silvery cloak billowing behind him. The doctor was unique in the sense that he was the only doctor in the land (and there were very few) who had experience in treating both humans and animals, due to the fact that Raphael and his father, both being Morphers, had sustained their own number of injuries throughout the years while in animal form. Doctor Jenson had been with the family for over a decade now and, as he swooped into the room, his keen, medical eye appraised Skye swiftly.

"You say she was thrown over the wall?" he questioned the guard, reaching over and peering at her with his monocle.

"That's right, doctor."

"I see. Indeed, she would have sustained injuries from this. But it looks as though she's taken a beating too."

"A beating?" said Raphael, through clenched teeth.

"Yes." Doctor Jenson ran his hand over Skye's ribcage. "It's possible she may have put up a struggle and been beaten. I notice there are puncture wounds on her neck. We must get her to the infirmary right away."

With an immediacy that suggested there was no time to waste, several guards advanced forwards to lift the wolf. But Raphael held them back.

"I'll carry her," he said. It may have seemed foolish to anyone else and Raphael certainly kept it secret, but he was afraid of anyone but himself holding her; having come so close to losing her, he only knew that he needed to stay in as close a proximity to her as possible.

He lifted the heavy body of the white wolf around his shoulders as though effortlessly and followed Doctor Jenson out of the lounge without a second glance back. Everyone watched him go in silence.

Sir Charles Barlow and his team were observing this extraordinary turn of events quietly, unsure how to proceed. Lord Renzo approached the head of MI24, his hand extended.

"Sir Charles, thank you," he said; Charles Barlow took the hand and shook it. "It appears we won't be needing your services after all; thank you, nonetheless."

"Thanks is not necessary, Lord Renzo," replied the other man. "You know where to find me if you need me again."

"Indeed." Lord Renzo nodded to show his gratitude.

With a bow, Sir Charles gestured towards his agents and the group left the lounge.

One of the guards approached Lord Renzo.

"My Lord," he said quietly, handing him a small, folded piece of paper. "This was attached to Miss Archer when we found her."

Lord Renzo took the note and opened it. A black scribble revealed the following words:

Lord Pearson sends you this gift as a sign of his appreciation for all the wonders that nature has to offer.

Scanning his eyes over the sentence several times, Lord Renzo's body stiffened, his face taut. The guard watched him with concern.

"My Lord?"

Lord Renzo turned to face him, pocketing the note.

"Double the watchmen, security and patrollers tonight. All areas must be monitored at all times. Inform the Head of Security to implement a surveillance system for a two mile radius outside the grounds."

If the guard was at all surprised by these astringent security measures, he did not show it. He saluted, bowing, before turning on his heel; the other guards followed him and they marched from the room.

This left only Kai and Trey alone with Lord Renzo. Trey approached his father.

"What do we do now?" he asked him.

"Kai," said Lord Renzo, turning to face the Emperor's nephew, "might you go and speak with your uncle? Tell him Skye has returned to us; tell him not to worry and that everything is under control."

"Yes, Lord Renzo."

Kai clicked his heels before he, too, swept from the room.

"Trey, close the door."

Obeying his father, Trey shut the door, a wrinkle in his brow.

"What is it?" he asked, his voice strangely loud throughout the now silent room.

Lord Renzo pulled out the note from his pocket and handed it to his eldest son.

Trey took it, his eyes scanning briefly over the paper.

"I don't understand," he said, puzzled. "What does it mean?"

"It means that the winds of change are drawing nearer," said Lord Renzo, taking the note back as Trey held it out to him, "but which direction they are blowing, I can't be certain..."

Trey remained nonplussed at this cryptic response.

"What are you saying? Are you saying it is time to take up

arms?"

Lord Renzo didn't reply; instead he walked towards the window of the lounge and pulled the velvet curtains back; droplets of rain could be seen spattering the glass pane; a rumble of thunder triggered in the distance.

"Dad—is that what you're saying?" repeated Trey with more urgency, walking towards him.

"I am saying to always be on your guard. Trust no one."

His eyes swept across the vast outdoors; outside, the rain now battered fiercely against the window; gale-force winds resounded throughout the night sky; only flashing lightning bolts that illuminated the darkness rivalled the menacing boom of thunder. Lord Renzo's aged reflection appeared in the window as he turned to face his still mystified son.

"The storm is gathering, Trey," he murmured, "and when it comes, we must all be ready."

*

At first, Skye wondered if she was dead. Everything was in black and white, plus there was a strange man with a very round face and monocle covering his left eye peering down at her and examining her long snout. It hardly seemed real.

"There we go," the man said, rubbing some kind of gel above her nostrils. "This should do the trick. Ah—she's awake!"

Skye's natural defensive instincts kicked in; she snarled wildly and aimed a bite at the man's hovering finger, missing it by a fraction.

"Goodness!" exclaimed the man, looking deeply unnerved and holding his hand high above his head for fear of losing half of it. "Stay calm now. Master Raphael, perhaps you should take over? I do not want to sedate her."

"Skye! Thank God!"

Another man appeared by her side. She sniffed his scent and a feeling of absolute tranquility and happiness raced through her, emotions that seemed completely alien and new. She wagged her tail—feebly. It hurt to wag…she was in a lot of pain…

"Ah, she recognizes you," said the first man approvingly, pulling off his white gloves. "Very good, very good. Her senses are alert."

"Skye—it's me, Raphael," said the second man in a gentle tone, stroking her head. "I want you to know you're OK now. You're safe. Doctor Jenson wants to do a few check-ups on you to make sure you get better. Be a good girl. You've been very brave; I'm so proud of you. You're safe now so don't worry."

His soothing words relaxed her a great deal as he continued to stroke the top of her head and gently scratch behind her ears. She whined softly, enjoying the sensation; it helped alleviate the pain. Raphael…of course she knew who he was. He was wonderful and she loved him more than anything. But what did he mean by telling her she was safe now? Had she been in danger? And why did her entire body, top to bottom, feel sore? Why did she ache so much? She was quite certain she was not dead now…Surely death meant an absence of pain, not the amplification of it?

She couldn't remember a single thing that had happened to her recently…why was she lying on this table and where exactly was she anyway? More than this, why was she even in her animal form? She should transform back—but, on the other hand, it would be pretty embarrassing transforming in front of the strange, chubby man with the monocle and there was no way she could ask him to leave while she was a wolf…and it wasn't as though she could actually get up and leave herself, not when agony ripped through her entire body…

She continued to lie there, dazed, enjoying the feeling of Raphael's fingers smoothly stroking her fur…

"Now then," came the voice of the man in the silvery cloak. He was a doctor; isn't that what Raphael had said? "Just a little pinch here, this should ease the wound somewhat…"

He walked towards her, holding something in his hand. It looked like a syringe.

Right in that moment, everything came back to her. Everything. Fear and terror surged through her veins; the syringe seemed to magnify before her very eyes; along with it came the screams of horror and stench of death from past events; violent memories flooded mercilessly through her brain; now she remembered. Now she recalled why she was in so much pain; now she knew exactly what had happened to her…

She snarled at the doctor so suddenly that he dropped the syringe to the floor, leaping backwards. Struggling to pull herself to her paws, she fought to seize control of her mind, where haunting and vicious memories continued whizzing through her brain. It was getting too much, all of it; she continued snarling fiercely, her snarls evolving into angry barks, feeling she had to attack someone, anyone, because only a full-blown attack could distract her from these torturous thoughts…

"Raphael!" gasped the doctor. "She's losing control—I will have to sedate her!"

"No, wait!"

Seconds later, an enormous Bengal Tiger materialized inside the infirmary. Raphael's clothes landed in a shredded heap on the floor and the powerful feline bounded in front of the doctor who, despite having seen the young master in his animal form many times, could not help feeling rather petrified; he realized the tiger was currently protecting him from the wolf who seemed to be losing her mind, judging by the froth and spit that was swiftly forming around her fangs. Doctor Jenson thought quickly, looking around for his sedation syringe; if Raphael could not control Skye, she would have to be tranquilized; otherwise, there was a risk the animals would fight.

Upon catching sight and smell of the powerful tiger in front of her, Skye's pain seemed to vanish entirely as her automatic survival instincts kicked in; for a second, she lost complete control of her human mind and was left alone with her wolf mind: scared, alone, injured—and in the presence of another predator. She had to attack him—and kill him; it was the only way to survive.

She leapt to her feet on the table and growled savagely, the froth bubbling over her entire mouth. She looked like a rabid monster; the tiger roared at her; the hackles on both beasts shot up; Doctor Jenson didn't dare move from behind the tiger's bulky striped body, but his eyes flashed towards his sedation syringe which was lying on the table beside the wolf. He would never be able to reach it.

Then, quite suddenly, the furious, snarling wolf heard the tiger communicating with her.

Skye—stop! Get control of yourself! He conveyed. *Quick, Skye—tell me what happened! Show me what happened!*

The snarls vanished as quickly as they had appeared. The wolf froze, momentarily confused.

Show him what happened?

Please, Skye! Raphael's desperate conveyance was unyielding; the tiger sat on his hind legs, watching her silently, his orange eyes wide and pleading. *Show me where you've been and what happened. Transfer your thoughts to me!*

Her human mind returned to take control; this was Raphael, the man she loved, who she was snarling at; whom she would have attacked only seconds before. He was trying to help her; she struggled to banish the angry wolf inside her and fully absorb his words. She wasn't in the cell anymore—she was with Raphael. She was safe. He wanted her to tell him what happened.

Part of her screamed at herself not to tell him. She wanted to protect him from the horror.

But she knew she must tell him.

Skye had never actually performed a Memory Transference before. It was an ability that all Morphers possessed. The ability to, while in animal form, transfer your own memories into the mind of another Morpher, so they could see and hear every detail as though they were experiencing it themselves. It was similar to what the young beaver Morpher had performed earlier. From what Raphael —and Lord Renzo—had told her about this before, there was no practice necessary—no rules or regulations about how to do it; just the desire to communicate your memory with another.

So that was what Skye decided to do in that moment. She stopped frothing and clamped her jaws shut, her fangs no longer on display. Sitting back on her hind legs, she stared directly at the tiger, her blue eyes boring into his orange ones. She looked up at the ceiling, forcing herself to relive the memories, horrifying though they were, telling herself that Raphael had to know; she howled, her cries echoing throughout the entire room.

Then, both she and Raphael were plunged into the depths of her memory...

She was in a cell. Skye knew it was a cell because she was chained to a wall. What had happened? One moment she had been in the gardens, searching for the beaver cub...the next she had woken up in this dark, silent cell, her legs and arms attached to cold, grey stone.

There was a sniffling cry somewhere to her left. Skye quickly turned her head to the side. She recoiled when she saw a little boy dressed in rags, crouched inside a cage. She squinted her eyes to get a better look at him; he was about ten years old, small, bony and tanned. He looked up at her, still crying quietly. He was vaguely recognizable; Skye had seen him before...but where?

Then it hit her. This was one of the children from the beaver cub's memory. The same sickening memory the beaver child had transferred to her, just before he had run away and she had blacked out. The scared, tanned face of the boy in the cage was the same as the child who had been chained to the wall...it was also the same child who had spoken to her earlier, pleading for her to help him...

It was *the beaver child. The young Morpher who had appeared on the Renzo grounds earlier and shown her those dreadful images.*

Skye cleared her dry throat, somehow finding her voice.

"Hello?" she called out to him quietly, her voice shaking. "Hello? Can you hear me?"

The boy quickly looked away, still sniffling.

"Please," said Skye desperately. "Who are you? What is this place?"

"Ah...awake at last."

It wasn't the boy who responded; a man had entered the cell. Upon catching sight of him, the boy's eyes widened in sheer terror and he threw his face over his hands.

Within seconds, Skye knew exactly why the boy had reacted with such fear and trepidation. She herself was unable to stop the trembling that vibrated through her body when she swivelled her head to see the thin, baldish man in the white coat who came shuffling towards her, a cold smile on his face, a certain type of hunger and madness in his eyes that sent chills down her spine.

It was he, that evil man from the beaver Morpher's memory...the one who had done terrible things to those children...

A fierce urge to cause this man extreme harm and pain overpowered her fear.

"You!" she rasped furiously, clenching her fists that were trapped inside the chains, tremors rippling through her body.

"You recognize me." The man's smile widened. "Well, of course, I supposed you might. The boy had to lure you out one way or another; I suspected it might be through some kind of memory of me..."

He moved closer to the boy in the cage, who whimpered; Skye felt an overwhelming desire to rip the man's throat out.

"You truly fascinate me, you Morphers," the man continued in an almost benign tone, patting the top of the cage. *"Turning into your spirit animal upon command...this whole business about transferring your memories to one another...being able to telepathically communicate...it really is quite remarkable. Professor Polgas certainly hit upon something special when he discovered how to create this wonderful new breed...Morphers."*

He smiled fondly at Skye as though she were a prized jewel. Skye glared hatefully back at him.

"Who are you?" she snarled.

The man tutted.

"It is completely unnecessary for you to know who I am. All that matters is how useful you are for me. And, as it stands, you are incredibly useful. You have no idea of the miracles that will be achieved, thanks to your co-operation. Well...I say co-operation, but, of course, one must always take precautions."

He smirked at the chains clamped around Skye's wrists.

"We had been trying to get to you for some time," he continued. *"But, goodness me, he certainly had you well-protected, didn't he? Very over-protective, that boyfriend of yours, is he not? So we thought we'd use a little bait; try to see if another Morpher could lure you out instead. And who better to do so than my young boy here?"*

He patted the cage again, beaming.

"Planting him in your office was a great start, of course. I figured you would be intrigued by the brat. But there was no way I could have foreseen that your kidnapping would go so marvellously to plan! We knew you would be at the Renzo mansion tonight; we

figured it would be a good idea to infiltrate the grounds with one of our own soldiers, to pose as one of the Renzo guards; time is running out, you see, and it has been important for us to get you as soon as possible. So we told Thomas—you remember him, I presume?—to keep an eye out; we told him to send my boy here to fetch you; young boy was waiting in the bushes, ready to work his magic on you. I knew beforehand that my boy would play upon your sympathies; women, you know, are rather susceptible to feeling that motherly concern for young, abused creatures. It is a mark of my psychological genius to recognize this quality and, thus, use it to my own advantage."

He smiled smugly, clearly relishing in this self-glorification.

"Well, you know the rest. You went hunting for my boy—and now, here you are. The most shocking aspect, however, is that young Mister Renzo left you alone! You see, we never actually thought things would go to plan. We supposed that even if we did catch you by some lucky chance tonight, Mister Renzo would be with you—at which point, we would have had a slight problem. But there you were, completely free for the taking. We had debated whether we should send young boy into the mansion itself to lure you out. But in the end there was no need—you actually appeared on the grounds of your own accord, alone and unguarded! Did I think the plan would actually work? Did I think that you would talk to the boy and receive his memories? That you would walk with our spy, completely unprotected, that you would play right into our hands? No, I had no idea! But thank you...for you have sped up the process quite significantly. A remarkable, highly fortunate turn of events."

Skye struggled to take this information in. The beaver Morpher had been planted there to lure her out? For these villains to kidnap her? And why? What did they want with her?

"You mustn't blame young boy, of course," continued the man, gesturing to the shaking child. "He belongs to me and exists to do my bidding. I have his Ma, also. One foot out of line and it's bye bye, mother!"

He chuckled. Skye's anger swelled.

"I DON'T blame him!" she growled, struggling against the chains. "I blame you—whoever you are! Let him go!"

"Let him go? What a preposterous request! I paid good money for this boy. His existence is meaningless without me. He is the first of my great accomplishments. Let him go?" he scoffed out loud. "Why in the world would I do that, you silly girl? The stupidity of some people really irritates me at times…"

He looked genuinely annoyed as though she had deeply offended him. Skye looked back at him, her hatred increasing. She did not know exactly what type of twisted psychopath she was dealing with, but she knew that this man had to be stopped.

"If you don't let him go, I'll kill you," she told him, breathing fast.

The man observed her, amused.

"How precisely will you do that?" he asked her.

"I'm a Morpher," she snarled.

"Indeed you are. A Morpher who is chained to a wall. And even if you do transform, you will still be locked in chains. Transformation won't break through metal, you know. But do be prepared to break your own legs; the sudden twists and turns that Morphing entails would almost guarantee excruciating pain within

those chains. However, I am not a cruel man. I may even let you go...just as soon as you give me what I want."

He moved closer to her, his face inches from hers, breathing heavily into her face; Skye almost gagged from the rancid stench of his breath.

"It is true that we brought you here for a sole purpose," he said quietly. "But just between you and I, I'm looking for something more. That boyfriend of yours...Oh, what I wouldn't give to have him here right now. I mean, you are fascinating, of course, but a tiger Morpher? Now that would be a true joy to experiment with."

His gaze hardened.

"Unfortunately, my employer has made it very clear that under no circumstances must the tiger Morpher come here. In fact, no one is allowed to know you are here. It's all very hush-hush. But I must have him...and that's why we have to keep this between ourselves, my dear girl. You see, I left a little token for your boyfriend to make him realize this was a Pearson plot...I hear the young man is very heroic. There is no doubt in my mind that he will come to your rescue...and when he does, well..."

His voice drifted off, his mouth breaking into a crooked smile.

"Don't you dare touch Raphael!" Skye said fiercely.

"I shall do exactly as I please and you shall have no say in it. Just think! A tiger and a wolf—the experiments I could conduct! Still, before this pleasant hour arrives, we must first deal with your sole purpose."

"What sole purpose?" she spat.

"The whole reason for your kidnap, of course. Let me show you what I mean. I wanted to do it when you were awake; it's so much

more fun that way."

He reached into his pocket and pulled out a syringe. Skye's eyes widened in horror and, before she could react, the man grabbed hold of her head and pierced the back of her neck with it; the needle dug several inches into her skin; she cried out in pain, resisting the urge to transform, realizing that if she did, the chains would surely crush her bones.

"There we are…hmmm, that's odd."

Releasing his grip on her head, the man stared curiously at the liquid inside the syringe, the blood he had extracted from Skye's neck.

"It shouldn't look like that," he muttered. "It should be…Ah, of course."

He sighed deeply. Skye continued wincing, the back of her neck throbbing painfully.

"So tedious," said the man, shaking his head.

He walked towards the same wooden door that he had first entered by. Opening it, he stepped outside, slamming it shut behind him.

Skye sat on the cold, stone floor. She didn't know what to make of the astonishing revelations this vile man had made to her; she still didn't know why she was here or why she had been injected. She only knew two things: one, that Raphael must not come to find her; and two, she had to find a way out of this place—and take the boy with her.

She looked over at the boy, whose face was still hidden in his hands.

"Hey," she called to him. "Hey…listen to me. Everything's

going to be OK."

The boy didn't remove his hands from his face. Skye observed her surroundings desperately. How would she get out? She was chained to the wall...there were no windows, no doors apart from the wooden one...she couldn't even transform while she was bound like this. She had to find a way out of here.

The wooden door banged open. The man had returned. He was not alone. Four thugs accompanied him. Skye gasped as she recognized one of them, one who had a nasty scar running down his cheek. It was Finn Pearson, Lord Pearson's son.

"I thought you might like to do the honours," said the man in the white coat, turning lazily to Finn. "Considering how you and young Mister Renzo have a history together..."

"Oh yeah," replied Finn, smiling nastily at Skye and cracking his knuckles, "we've got history alright. I've got history with his bitch, too..."

Skye was unable to prevent herself from trembling. She remembered the first time Finn had tried to attack her in the High Street; he had been thwarted by the appearance of Raphael. She recalled how he had broken into her home and stabbed her; the only reason she survived was because Raphael had come to her aid.

But now...now she was alone. Alone and powerless.

"Not enough to kill her please, Master Pearson," said the man in the white coat as the thugs advanced forwards; Skye shrank back, trying unsuccessfully to mask the fear in her eyes. "I only need her roughed up a bit. Just enough so she can't attack, but enough so she can transform. Does that make sense?"

"Perfect sense," leered Finn.

He, along with the three other thugs, approached Skye.

"Don't come near me!" she shouted at them, trying to sound a lot braver than she felt.

"Hard luck, wolfy. You play by our rules now," said Finn.

With that, he reached over and kicked her viciously beneath her chest, his boot connecting with her ribs; Skye felt a sickening crack inside her as she gasped, doubling over, the wind knocked out of her, pain seeping through her body.

One by one, they kicked and punched her brutally; the man in the white coat stood to the side, watching with a passive look on his face; the young boy in the cage sobbed loudly, his cries echoing throughout the cell. Skye felt the blows again and again, merciless, as feet and fists repeatedly battered her face, chest, stomach and thighs; blood poured from her nose as knuckles smashed into her; she couldn't even cry out, it hurt so much; she would surely die here; she knew she was going to die…

There was a sudden, ear-splitting roar inside the infirmary and the Memory Transference vanished. Raphael had broken the connection. The wolf on the table staggered backwards, almost falling off, her claws gripping wood as the horrifying memories disappeared from her mind, leaving her only with the residue of terror that engulfed her. Raphael's roars didn't cease; the tiger's fury at what he had just witnessed was terrible to behold. Doctor Jenson, who had guessed from the beginning that the two Morphers were partaking in a Memory Transference, now realized he was in a grave danger as he stood, trapped between a fully-grown Bengal Tiger who was now filled with rage and a wolf that teetered on the brink of sanity. With two highly volatile, unpredictable predators surrounding him, the doctor did the only thing he could think of in that desperate moment.

"Master Raphael! Miss Archer! Remember who you are! You must keep control of your minds! Do not let your inner beast control you!"

Perhaps Raphael heard him or perhaps he realized somewhere in the depths of his rational, human mind that the only way to truly quell the fury that was rapidly surging through him was to block the sickening images he had just seen; he had to focus on the present. After a furious internal wrestle with himself, he stopped roaring and leapt towards the wolf that stood silently on the table, her claws digging into the wood. He pushed his orange and black face into hers, nuzzling her, fighting to control the anger that pulsated through his every vein, desperate to squash the fierce urge to find Finn Pearson, there and then, and rip his entire body to shreds.

I'm sorry, he conveyed to her, squeezing his eyes shut, licking her face. *I'm sorry. Keep going. I'm sorry.*

I'm sorry, she conveyed back, and Raphael felt his heart would crack as tears fell from her soft blue eyes, landing with a small splash on his nose. He knew she was apologizing because she had wanted to protect him from what he just saw, knowing how much it would hurt him. This only intensified his own self-rage; he had sworn to protect her and he had failed. To witness the full extent of her suffering took every bit of self-control he possessed.

Please. Keep going. I'm ready, he conveyed, still nuzzling her furry white neck.

Skye's glistening eyes looked into his own. She hated that he now knew what had happened; hated what she had just put him through. If she could have spared him it, she would have.

They stared at one another, their gazes intense. The wolf whimpered several times; the tiger caressed her with his head and the silent promise that everything would be OK, promising it to himself just as much as her.

Then, they were plunged into her memory once more.

"That's enough please, Master Pearson," came the drawling voice of the man in the white coat. *"Any more than that and I'm afraid we may have a corpse on our hands."*

"Right," said Finn.

He held his hand up to the thugs. They backed away simultaneously.

Skye lay on the ground, bleeding profusely; excruciating pain tore through her whole body. She could hardly see beyond the thumping bruises that had formed on her eyelids; pain ripped through her like fire; she didn't move. She couldn't. It hardly seemed real. Surely it was not possible to experience pain such as this?

"One more for luck," said Finn.

Skye didn't even react when the boot stomped into her face, breaking her nose with a sickening crunch. In her mind, she screamed in agony; but there was no life in her to cry out loud.

"Thank you, that will do," said the man in the white coat, reaching into his pocket and pulling out another syringe.

"Anything else you need me to do here?" asked Finn, smirking down at Skye's battered frame.

"As a matter of fact, there may be. Can you wait a moment?"

" 'Course."

The man in the white coat walked to the bloodstained area where

Skye lay, panting, red droplets dripping down her cheeks and lips. He peered at her mangled body, a look of distaste on his face.

"I detest violence, you know," he told her. "It's horribly brutal; barbaric, too. We have not advanced as a civilization simply to execute stone-age customs on our fellow man. However, the ends justify the means. Now, Miss Archer, listen to me closely. I am going to release your chains. And you are going to transform into your spirit animal. Is that clear?"

Skye didn't respond. She could barely hear him. There was a deep ringing in her ears; one of the thugs' boots had stamped her left eardrum so violently she wondered if it had permanently damaged her hearing.

"I said," repeated the man, gripping hold of her limp head and forcing her face towards his, his eyebrows furrowing "is that clear?"

Skye managed a nod.

"Good. Now, it has been necessary to weaken you so that you do not attempt to attack or escape while in animal form. However, should you get any funny ideas, the consequences will be dire."

He looked around at the thugs and pointed to the cage with the boy inside.

"Open the cage and hold onto the boy, please," he told them.

"See now," he said, turning back to Skye; out of the corner of her bruised eye, Skye watched as a smiling Finn unlocked the cage and dragged the petrified boy out by his hair. "Should you make any attempt to attack or resist, any at all, young boy over there will have his neck snapped in two. I take no risks when it comes to my life, Miss Archer. Tell me, have I made myself clear?"

Through her blurred vision, Skye saw the boy being flanked by Finn and another thug; the boy was crying again; the thug smacked him around the face and told him to shut up. Skye felt fury mingle with her pain; she wanted to scream at them to leave him alone, then transform and tear the throats out of each and every one of them.

Instead, she nodded weakly.

"Good girl." The man in the coat patted her on the head.

He pulled a key from his pocket with his free hand and unlocked her chains.

"On the count of three, then. One…two…three."

Summoning every bit of strength she had left in her, while painfully aware of the boy's sobs mere metres away, Skye focussed on transformation. She did not know why she was required to transform; she only knew that the lives of herself and the small boy depended on it.

Seconds later, her clothes burst from her body and a white wolf lay on the ground.

Then, immediately, a thought struck her. Could she call out to Raphael as part of the Survival Pact?

In her daze, she knew she must. She had to try. She had to warn him not to come looking for her.

She focussed desperately on him.

"RAPHAEL!" she screamed in her mind.

A split-second later, his voice appeared in her head.

"Skye! Where are you?"

"Don't come for me! Raphael, don't come—"

Raphael disappeared as the man plunged his syringe into

her neck; the sudden jolt of pain broke the connection; the needle caused her to yelp very quietly, but she did not put up a fight; she felt triumphant. Amazed. Triumphant. She had contacted Raphael. It had actually worked. Now he would be safe. This monster wouldn't get his hands on him…

Her body ached; she remained mute and flaccid, staring unblinkingly into nothingness as her blood was extracted and the man pulled the needle out; inside her wolf mind, she felt happy. Even if she should die here, Raphael would be safe.

Delirium set in. Her swollen eyelids fluttered open and closed at irregular intervals; black spots appeared in front of her eyes; her head felt like it was swimming. She was drifting away somewhere…the room was getting blurrier by the second…

"There we go!" exclaimed the man, his voice victorious as he surveyed the syringe. "All done!"

"So what do we do with this kid?" grunted one of the thugs.

"Oh—put him back in his cage."

Plainly disappointed, the thug shoved the boy back into the cage and locked it.

Finn Pearson stepped towards Skye.

"And what about her?" he said.

"The Morpher will remain here until such time is necessary to take action," replied the man, depositing the syringe back into his pocket.

Finn's eyes roved slowly around the body of the immobile white wolf.

"I'd like to give Renzo's bitch something to really remember me by," he murmured. "Tell her to transform."

"Not right now if you don't mind, Master Pearson," said the man, with a bite of impatience. "Perhaps later. Right now, it is essential that I finish my business here—all, of course, for the sake of your father's wishes."

Finn glared at him. Then, snapping his fingers, he ordered his thugs to follow him and stormed from the cell.

Shaking his head as they left and muttering dark things under his breath, the man in the coat kneeled over to get a good look at the wolf.

"Well, you'll live, of course," he told her. "Though I am not sure how long for. Instructions were to kill you after extracting your blood, but if I did that, how on earth would I ever have the opportunity to meet that lover of yours? We just have to wait for him to arrive, that's all...I'm sure he will come after he sees the coal...and it's not as though Lord Pearson will ever know it was me who planted the coal there...but don't you go telling anyone that, my girl, that stays between the two of us."

Skye had no idea what he was on about. As the cell continued to swim before her eyes, she just wanted to sleep forever, to be free of this pain.

There was a knock on the wooden door.

"Enter," called the man.

An extremely beefy thug with spiky purple hair and a chimera tattoo on his face appeared.

"Lord Pearson wants to see you," he said gruffly.

The man in the coat looked perturbed.

"Now? I am busy with the Morpher, I am sure His Lordship understands this..."

"It ain't for you to decide what Lord Pearson do or don't understand," said the thug menacingly. "He's pissed about the coal. Not just pissed. Livid. Renzo knows the Morpher's here. Lord Pearson wants to know how Renzo knows she's here, when he told you to make sure no one finds out."

The blood practically drained from the face of the man in the white coat.

"Th-the coal?" he stuttered. "I—I don't know what you mean…what do you mean?"

"Look, it ain't my job to explain things to ya," said the thug impatiently. "You better come with me right now, that's all I'm sayin'. So come on—move it."

"R-right, yes…"

Skye watched as the man, whose face was now as white as his coat, stood up and followed the thug out of the cell, the door slamming shut behind them. With each moment that passed, she felt herself slipping further and further away. The black spots disappeared and colours flashed before her eyes…she caught sight of the little boy in the cage watching her, his eyes still filled with tears…she tried to smile at him, but her lips wouldn't move. Things were getting darker…darker…darker…

Then it ended. The memory disappeared and the tiger and wolf returned to the brightly lit infirmary.

For a while, the two great predators just stood there, their heads pressed against each other. Both were reeling from the memory, Skye from reliving it, Raphael from watching it. Neither conveyed their thoughts to the other, but both felt the enormity of their ordeal; and despite the horror, confusion and unanswered questions, one thing remained steadfast: their determination to stay on top of it, no matter how hard it tried to crush them.

Doctor Jenson shifted tentatively.

"Is it safe?" he said out loud.

Raphael briefly pulled his tail between his legs. The doctor breathed a sigh of relief. Years ago, when he had first started working with the Renzo family, it was agreed between Lord Renzo, his youngest son and himself (then a newly-qualified doctor) that a certain set of codes should be implemented so that he could have some form of communication with them while they were in their animal form. One of these code signs was the tail between the legs. When uncertain about his position around the animals or if they found themselves in a somewhat dire situation, Doctor Jenson would ask, "Is it safe?" A tail between the legs meant yes; a tail that shot high in the air meant no.

Skye slid down to the table. After the intensity of the memory, her strength had all but left her. Raphael's orange eyes flashed to the doctor. Immediately, Doctor Jenson strode towards them, his hands reaching out to various alchemy bottles, ointments designed to eliminate pain, and creams specific to healing wounds that were cluttered on the medical table. Raphael left the doctor to tend to Skye and he crept silently behind one of the cubicle curtains; seconds later, he had returned to a man once more, wearing a thin white towel that he'd wrapped around his crotch area.

He emerged from behind the curtain, looking gravely serious.

"Are you able to heal her?" he asked the doctor, upon joining him by Skye's side.

He pressed a loving, gentle hand to her furry forehead.

Doctor Jenson nodded.

"Yes. The most serious wounds are the cracked ribs and damage to the ears. But I believe the ointment will prevent and retract any permanent damage." He hesitated. "I take it that you know the cause of her injuries?"

Raphael's expression hardened.

"I do."

At that moment, the door swung open and Lord Renzo, accompanied by Trey, entered the infirmary.

Lord Renzo's eyes scanned the scenario silently, taking in his son who wore only the towel, the wolf who lay stationary on the table and the doctor applying cream to the wolf's chest.

Trey was more vocal.

"What happened here?" he asked blankly, staring at his brother, noting that Raphael had previously undergone transformation. "We heard noises…"

"Skye performed a Memory Transference on me," Raphael told them. "She showed me what had happened to her during her absence."

Both Lord Renzo's and Trey's stares widened substantially.

"There are things we need to talk about," continued Raphael, struggling not to think of Finn Pearson's foot slamming into Skye's face, nor the other horrifying actions he had witnessed. "Important things…Pearson's plotting something, but I don't know what."

"We must call a meeting at once," said Trey. "Raphael, you must tell us everything you saw."

"I'm not leaving her," said Raphael

Lord Renzo moved quietly towards his youngest son.

"Raphael," he said in a low voice. He, too, placed a hand between Skye's ears, gently stroking her. "It will not help her to talk about things here. Let Doctor Jenson do what he must to make her better."

Doctor Jensen, still busy applying ointment to Skye's wounds, nodded.

"It would be best if Skye has no company for now, Master Raphael," he told the stiff-faced man. "She needs rest, just the same as I need concentration. Please forgive my bluntness, but it would be helpful if everyone dispersed." He paused. "I promise I will not allow her to come to anymore harm under my watch."

"Come," said Lord Renzo quietly, taking his son by the arm.

Reluctantly, Raphael turned away. But not before he leaned over the wolf, his lips brushing her ear.

"I'm not far away," he whispered, caressing her head once more.

Skye's eyes remained closed, but she gave a small, soft whine.

"I promise," Raphael murmured, kissing her muzzle.

Trey nodded to Doctor Jenson, thanking him. Then, the three Renzo men turned and walked from the infirmary.

CHAPTER SEVEN

In Stratford, the storm grew fiercer by the minute. Gales ripped mercilessly throughout the city; a tree outside the Pearson mansion was actually uprooted from its dwelling. Several thugs who were loitering beneath it, swigging numerous bottles of whiskey, yelled as the trunk came crashing down, escaping an otherwise grisly fate just in the nick of time. Seconds later, they were involved in a brawling fistfight, roaring wildly at one another as their inebriation kicked in; their general excitement due to the raging storm only added fuel to the flames and, for a while, raucous bellowing and bottle-smashing could be heard all over East London.

From the top window of his gothic mansion, Lord Pearson watched them passively. Normally it was entertaining to watch the brutes clobber one another over the heads, but today he viewed them for mere distraction purposes. He was still trying to quell the anger he had felt earlier due to that snivelling wretch, Professor Dragoon, whose sneaky, treacherous antics had left him seething with rage. He would have killed the bootlicker, but, of course, ration and sense caught hold of him. He needed the professor, after all…

"More sherry, My Lord?"

"Yes."

Hurriedly, his manservant poured him another glass of sherry. Lord Pearson averted his gaze from the thugs for a moment, swirling his drink around. Then he took a sip, his cold grey eyes returning to the band of idiots outside; a couple sprawled ungainly on the ground looked as though they were dead, but it was hard to tell from this distance. He might have to order them to be separated; if they continued killing each other off like this, there wouldn't be enough of them left to carry out his plans.

This caused his thoughts to return to Professor Dragoon. Another flicker of anger sparked inside him; he sipped his sherry again.

The instructions had been simple. Kidnap the wolf Morpher. Do not allow anyone to know who had done it or where she was being held. Extract her DNA. Kill her.

But no. These very simple instructions had not been adhered to. It was a tip-off from a highly reliable source that had alerted Lord Pearson to the fact that his ingenious plan was about to take a disastrous turn for the worst. It appeared that, a mere hour after the girl's kidnap, Lord Renzo had discovered that he, Lord Pearson, was the perpetrator. No doubt those fools in West London would have considered him the prime suspect regardless, but without proof they had nothing.

And yet, as he discovered while reading the informative tag-text that caused his blood to run cold, they *did* have proof. Someone had planted a piece of coal on the very spot where the Morpher had been seized. Coal, of course, was only ever distributed on his orders; a message to his enemies that the Pearson

Empire was on the rise and all those who opposed it would face annihilation.

The fact that someone had planted the coal without his permission was enough to provoke his fury; but that it had been done with specific intent *against* his instructions almost caused him to murder his unfortunate manservant, who happened to be closest to him at the time of this revelation and had borne the brunt of his master's rage.

But, of course, there was only one person to blame. Having released the throat of his manservant, who had been turning purpler by the second, Lord Pearson ordered that Professor Dragoon be brought to him at once.

The professor had arrived in typical snivelling fashion—but there was no denying the hint of worry in his voice or the fleeting look of fear as his eyes darted nervously around the chambers. To Lord Pearson, this was most certainly an admission of guilt.

"My Lord Pearson," said Professor Dragoon in his usual oily tone, though unable to stop himself from swallowing. "May I ask why you have requested my presence? I am currently in the middle of extracting the DNA—"

"Explain to me why a lump of coal was found on the Renzo grounds earlier tonight," said Lord Pearson, his voice deadly quiet.

The professor gulped.

"My Lord," he said, his throat dry, "I don't know what you are referring to—"

"Lie to me again and I will have your head cut off, plan or no plan."

Professor Dragoon began stammering and stuttering

uncontrollably.

"F-forgive me—now that I think about it—oh yes—how foolish of me to forget—there was a piece of coal—ah, yes, now I remember—it was planted there by that boy, Thomas—yes indeed—it seems he could not resist, oh yes, it was Thomas who planted it—"

Lord Pearson stared daggers at the shaking man in front of him. He was not a fool. And if there was one thing he detested above all else, it was someone implying that he was.

"Are you sure about that?" he said, his eyes glittering dangerously.

"Oh yes, My Lord!"

"But why did you not remove it?" Lord Pearson picked up a glass of wine that his manservant was balancing on a tray, his voice layered with cold fury. "My express instructions were that *no one* discovers we were responsible for the girl's kidnap. If indeed *Thomas*—" he sneered as he said the name— "did plant the coal, why did you, *on my orders*, not remove it?"

Professor Dragoon looked thunderstruck.

"My Lord—f-f-f-forgive me! At the time, it did not occur to me—I was so focussed on the Morpher, I didn't think, you see, I have been so concerned with carrying out your wishes, all my attentions are on this, my only priority is to do your bidding—"

There was a shattering, splintering sound of smashed glass. Professor Dragoon threw his hands over his head, trembling, as did the manservant. Lord Pearson, having taken aim in the professor's direction, his wine glass hitting the tapestry on the wall behind instead, rose from his seat, his normally cold grey eyes alight with fire.

"Do not insult me, Dragoon," he said in a low, dangerous whisper. Never had the lord who ruled over East London looked so terrifying.

"Oh, I would never! I would never—"

"Fool!" Lord Pearson thundered. "Do you think I don't know what you have been up to, you pathetic, sniffling excuse of a wretch! Did you think I wouldn't find out if you went sneaking behind my back, going against my wishes? Answer me with the truth or I will have you killed this instant!"

He snapped his fingers and a man who had been standing in the shadows stepped forward. He was holding an axe. Swiftly, the axe was levelled with the professor's neck.

Professor Dragoon actually sank down to his knees, shaking uncontrollably with terror as the blade just about scratched his skin.

"Oh, you must forgive me, My Lord!" he bleated, his nose pressed against the floor, his hands flailing in despair. "I beg your esteemed forgiveness for my wretched self! I did it for you, I did it with the best intentions! If the tiger Morpher discovered the wolf Morpher was here, he would surely come to save her and then his DNA, too, could be extracted—"

"Fool!" Lord Pearson bellowed again. "Renzo will avoid war for as long as he can because of his pathetic concern for innocents, but a declaration of our involvement in the Morpher's kidnap is an invitation for slaughter! What's more, outwardly baiting his son would leave him with no choice—we'd be attacked before we're ready! Believe me, were it not for the fact that your prolonged life is necessary, I would remove your head from your shoulders this very instant!"

"My Lord, please, I beg you, I beg for your forgiveness!" Professor Dragoon practically wept as he continued lying on the floor, spread ungracefully beneath the lord's feet. "I only did what was in the best interest of your cause—"

"You did what was in the best interest of yourself, you snivelling worm! Do you think I do not know your reasons behind this treachery? This is nothing more than your own selfish desire to experiment on the Renzo boy for your own satisfaction! You would see my entire plan come down in flames just to satisfy your own insatiable thirst for scientific experimentation! I should kill you where you kneel, vermin that you are!"

The blade cut very slightly into the professor's neck; a trickle of blood appeared.

"No, My Lord, no!" howled Professor Dragoon, flinching from the cut. "Forgive me, please!"

"The instructions were plain and simple, were they not, Professor? Kidnap the girl, take her blood, and then kill her. Even if we were suspected, their lack of evidence would mean their lack of action. But thanks to your stupid, selfish antics, killing her is no longer an option. Her murder would bring the entire Renzo army onto us with swift retribution—*if* they are not already making their way here now! Because of you I now have to make amendments to my plan. You bumbling buffoon! Tell me, has the DNA been extracted?"

"Y-yes," sniffled Professor Dragoon, still painfully aware of the sharp axe scraping against his neck.

"Good. You will begin work immediately. And you will release the Morpher and have her sent back to West London—*alive.*

Hopefully, her return will stall the event of an attack and appease our enemy until I can implement our next move—*do I make myself clear?*"

"Yes, yes, of course…"

"Now hurry up and move! Time is running out. And let me warn you, Dragoon, cross me again and I will personally remove your testicles and force you to eat them, before separating your head from your worthless body. *Go!*"

"Yes, My Lord!" gasped Professor Dragoon.

He ducked underneath the axe and fled the chambers, cursing to himself as he ran and furiously wondering *how* exactly Lord Pearson had discovered a piece of coal had been left at the scene of the kidnapping.

In his chamber, Lord Pearson closed his eyes and breathed deeply several times. When he opened them again, he had returned to his cold, collected self, his face a mask of calm.

"Clean up the glass," he said carelessly to his manservant, who was still cowering beside him; the manservant scuttled towards the tapestry and, for the next hour, Lord Pearson spent his time sipping sherry and watching his thugs outside bash each other to pieces, while the howling of the wind grew stronger and lightning flashed across the sky.

Now, as he stood gazing out of the window, he surveyed the fallen tree and possibly dead thugs with little interest; the wolf Morpher would surely be back in Renzo territory by now. Hopefully, that would be enough to appease Lord Renzo and that bull-headed son of his. But they were bound to grow suspicious; now that he thought about it, the accompanying note he had ordered to be sent back with the Morpher may have been a mistake. In it, he had wished to illustrate his superiority, to somehow save face, to at least make it look like her return had all been part of his plan and not a blunder by that idiotic professor. At the very least, he'd hoped it would confuse his enemy so that they would be stuck, not knowing which move to take next.

But what if the note somehow provided them with insight into his plans? Writing about the 'wonders that nature has to offer' was a mistake, he could see that now. And how much exactly of her ordeal did the Morpher girl remember? Dragoon had told him she had no idea why her blood was being extracted…but what if his enemy should guess? Dragoon was not to be trusted, this was plain as day; how much did the wolf Morpher *really* know about her reason for being there?

No, he had to act. And fast. He would have to ensure that, no matter what, his plan succeeded. He had to ensure that Renzo did not launch an immediate attack due to tonight's events—and there was only one way to do this…He needed to get a message to someone. Right away.

The chamber doors burst open just as he was dictating the details of his message to his manservant.

"Yes?" he said with a raised eyebrow, interrupting himself as his son, Finn, came storming towards him.

"The Morpher," Finn snarled, coming to an abrupt halt. "She's gone."

"That is correct."

"I wasn't done with her!"

"So?"

"So I had plans for Renzo's girl—and you sent her away!"

Lord Pearson eyed him coldly.

"Yes, I sent her back because, in case it has missed your notice, we have a city to conquer. I am in the middle of something important so go and occupy yourself some other way."

Finn just stood there for a moment, glaring. Then he turned on his heel, striding angrily towards the door, knocking a table over as he did so.

"One more thing, Finnley," Lord Pearson called out. "Tell your friends outside to stop fighting each other. They will have much worthier opponents soon enough."

Finn gave no acknowledgement that he heard him; he wrenched hold of the doorknob violently and left the chambers, slamming the door behind him.

Unaffected by his son's hostility, Lord Pearson turned back to his manservant, collected as ever.

"Now, where was I?" he drawled. "Ah, yes…"

He spent the next ten minutes instructing his manservant in precise detail of the message he wanted delivered. As his manservant nodded, flushed, hurriedly noting everything down, Lord Pearson smiled despite himself. It would all go to plan. It would all work out fine. Victory would be his.

Not long now.

*

"So let me get this straight," said Joey, blowing on a bubble stick and looking around at the sombre faces surrounding him in the lounge, "you're saying that some nut job scientist kidnapped Skye and then planted a piece of coal at the crime scene—against Pearson's wishes?"

"That's right," said Raphael, sinking into a nearby couch.

"That makes no sense," said Joey, shaking his head; beside him, Ricardo looked bemused. "That professor is working for Pearson, isn't he? Why would he do that?"

"From what I heard, he wanted me. He wanted me to come and find Skye."

"Well, why?"

"I don't know the exact reasons. But I gathered he wanted to…experiment on me."

There was an uncomfortable silence. Joey took a swig from the glass of tequila he was holding. Trey stared, unblinking and pensive, at the crackling flames inside the fireplace; Kai's tag device started beeping and he quietly excused himself from the room. Ricardo was snoozing in his seat. Raphael gazed outside the window where the storm had now abated and the night was eerily quiet; still. The group of them had congregated in the lounge once again. It was about 2.30 am now. Earlier, Raphael had reiterated everything he had seen in the memory; he had been careful not to go into detail about the beating Skye had suffered, if only because he himself could not handle the thought of it. Instead he had told them crucial pieces of information and facts that would hopefully help them unravel whatever schemes the Pearson clan had in mind.

Lord Renzo had said very little after listening to his son's recount of Skye's ordeal. He had quietly ordered the butler to bring some food and drink into the lounge before suggesting they all get some rest. He then departed and Ricardo, who had returned from checking on his girlfriend and Skye's mother (who had been given their own personal bedroom chambers and spent the last hour fretting about Skye and demanding to see her), said he saw his father making his way to the army barrack headquarters next door. This had caused a wave of raised eyebrows among the group who wondered what this could mean; were they finally ready to launch an attack?

"That's what he was doing to Skye though, wasn't it?" said Joey, swigging the last of his tequila and reaching for a bunch of grapes lying on the table. "Experimenting on her. You said she was being injected?"

"Yeah."

"And they were after her—specifically her," Joey continued. "It's because she's a Morpher. Has to be. She wasn't bait, after all. Pearson didn't want Raph rescuing her—and that's what I don't get. Why did they want Skye? Why was this madman injecting her? What exactly is Pearson up to?"

That was, of course, the question on everyone's mind.

"It's the note that worries me," murmured Trey, his hazel eyes still focussed on the flames. "Pearson's note…he said he sent Skye back as a gift. I couldn't make head or tail of it. Dad was being really evasive afterwards. I couldn't tell what was on his mind; a part of me felt like he was ready to attack."

"Lord Renzo may not have a choice," said Kai, who had re-entered the room and overheard Trey's words. "We now know for certain that Lord Pearson is plotting something—whatever sneaky, underhand business he has in mind, Lord Renzo can no longer afford to wait for the right moment to instigate war. By doing so, he runs the risk of defeat even before it has begun. We now, all of us, tread in extremely dangerous waters…Miss Archer's kidnapping…this professor who experimented on her…something is about to explode and none of us know what it is. Rather than be taken by surprise, we may have to attack as a form of defence."

"And of the innocents?" said Trey, raising his eyes to the Emperor's nephew. "You recall our conversation earlier at the dinner table, Kai. Millions may be caught in the crossfire. As you said, how can we attack our enemy when we cannot see them?"

"And that is the most fatal of consequences. Either launch an attack on the enemy and sacrifice countless innocents or wait here, like sitting ducks, and risk total annihilation."

"Doesn't sound like much of a choice," said Joey uneasily.

Trey shook his head.

"I have always felt a plan of attack was the best way forward. Waiting for the right moment or the ideal gateway surely only increases the danger of losing altogether…this seems apparent in light of recent events. We cannot take Skye's kidnap or Pearson's mysterious plans lightly."

"I'd like to know how that Thomas or whatever his name is managed to get into the grounds in the first place," said Joey grimly.

"The beaver kid," said Raphael from the couch. "Doctor Jenson deduced it earlier. The beaver got in through an underground rabbit hole. He was carrying some tiny phial and slipped it into the guard's water bottle when he wasn't looking. It was some kind of sleeping brew. Knocked the guard out cold. That's when they threw Thomas—their spy—over the wall; Doctor Jenson suspects he was wearing Fingle Pads, which is why he didn't suffer any injuries when he landed."

The others looked stunned at this news. Similar to Tanzer Guns, Fingle Pads were another extremely rare, costly commodity, which was not available in their country, incredibly difficult to find in the international trade market. Only the richest and most influential could possibly hope to get their hands on one. Raphael himself had a pair, one of his most prized possessions, a gift from his father on his fifteenth birthday. They were soles that one placed at the bottom of their shoes and made of a special type of foam that had only been discovered at the beginning of the 22nd century. This foam meant that, no matter what height you dropped from, as long as you landed on your feet you would be completely unharmed. The Fingle Pads also had miniature spikes at the bottom in order to balance the wearer and ensure a secure landing, rather than toppling all over the place.

"So that's when he killed the drugged guard and took his clothes," continued Raphael. "It would have happened in the space of two minutes; the area itself is pretty remote, no one ever goes there. The other guards hadn't a clue. All the spy had to do then was keep an eye out for Skye…When he found her, he let a second person in through a gate near the greenhouse. It's old and rusty, hidden almost, can only be opened from the inside…that's how they carried her out."

He felt that familiar blazing anger again. What he wouldn't give to rip into the throat of every thug, lowlife and scumbag under the Pearson regime…

"How in the world did Doctor Jenson discover that?" asked

Joey, wide-eyed.

Raphael swallowed, quickly burying his dark thoughts.

"Another guard found the empty phial earlier; Doctor Jenson ran some tests and realized it was a sleeping drug. He said it would be best to search the grounds for any small openings after I'd mentioned I saw the beaver kid in the cage during the memory…Some of the guards found this rabbit hole. Wide enough for a beaver cub to get through. He put two and two together."

The others, still amazed by this news, were speechless for a moment.

"Who exactly is this beaver cub?" asked Trey. "He's another Morpher, isn't he?"

Raphael nodded.

"Yes. But I don't know who he is or where he came from. He turned up at Skye's office the other day; then he got into the grounds; and then, when Skye transported me into her memory, he was there again—but as a boy this time. He was locked in a cage."

"Sounds like he's a prisoner of this psycho in the white coat," said Joey.

"I think so, too. In the memory, the scientist said something about how he had 'paid' for the boy…and that they had captured his mother. First time Skye mentioned him I got a bad feeling…warned her to stay away if she saw him again. There's something…*unnatural* about the Morpher boy, but I can't put my finger on what it is. But I think Skye's very drawn to him—she wants to protect him, this much is obvious. And I understand why she feels that way." Raphael's expression hardened. "After seeing him in the cage and the way that bastard Finn treated him…Well, trust me, it's not the kind of thing anyone, let alone a kid, should ever go through."

The butler came in with a large tray laden with biscuits, a variety of cheeses and celery sticks. A pot of tea was settled down, along with several teacups. The Renzo brothers, with the exception of Joey and Ricardo (who had just woken up and taken the tequila his twin brother offered to him), and Kai helped themselves. For a while, nothing but the munching sound of celery sticks and sugar stirring could be heard within the lounge.

"How is the Emperor?" asked Trey, turning to Kai as he added a slice of brie to his cracker. "Is he unnerved by tonight's events?"

"Do not worry about my uncle," replied Kai in a reassuring voice. "I explained the situation to him. He feels we took the right action; but he also understands that war could commence any moment from now."

"What do we do in the meantime?" asked Joey, pouring himself another shot. "Just sit around and wait?"

"Dad's not going to wait much longer, I can tell you that much," said Raphael, declining a plate of crackers the butler held out to him. "It's not a question of when anymore, but how. We have to kill the scumbags, but at the same time make sure the innocents are protected as much as possible."

There was a sudden, explosive bang outside which caused everyone to jump.

"What was that?" said Ricardo, alarmed.

Another ear-splitting boom blasted off in the distance, far more deafening than a clap of thunder and much more sinister. Every man in the room leapt to his feet. Seconds later, several more bangs followed. Raphael dashed to the window, his eyes darting frantically around outside to see if he could get a clue of what had made the noises.

"What the hell's going on?" he exclaimed.

And then they heard it. The horn.

It was an ancient variation of a bugle horn that had been in the Renzo family for generations, dating all the way back to the 1600's during the time of the English Civil War when Oliver Cromwell and his Roundheads had fought King Charles I and his Cavaliers. Raphael's oldest of ancestors had been a general in the Cavalier Army; it was said that he had died in battle having leapt in front of the king himself, taking a bullet to the chest. The general had been honoured by the king with a memorial plaque (which was later desecrated and demolished by the Roundheads after the execution of the king) and this bugle horn, which was formally presented to the general's family. For centuries, it remained the most precious of family heirlooms and, in recent times, Lord Renzo had announced that when the time came for arms to be taken against the Pearsons, or when the enemy launched their attack, the horn would be blown, amplified by modern-day technological equipment so the blasts would echo across the entire city.

Now, this same horn resounded throughout the City of London. It penetrated the eardrum of every man, woman and child; and for those within the Renzo stronghold, there was only one possible conclusion they could come to.

"This means..." said Raphael, his voice trailing off.

"Yes," said Trey, sounding gritty and determined.

They stared round at one another, realization sinking in.

The war had begun.

CHAPTER EIGHT

"Sirs—Master Kai!"

A guard had burst into the lounge, panting and sweating heavily.

"Lord Renzo requests your immediate presence in the war room!"

He needn't have bothered alerting them; all five of them were practically already out the door; leftover biscuits and cheese lay scattered on the floor as a reminder of the sudden turn of events that had shocked them all and caused them to hurtle from the room, one after another.

As they ran down the corridor, they were not the only ones the bugle horn had such a dramatic impact on. Maids scuttled like frightened rabbits along the hallway, arm in arm, wild-eyed and panicky; the butlers muttered precariously to one another, wondering which way to turn; the chefs were the loudest of all, having evacuated the kitchens and yelling orders and nonsensical instructions to their fellow cooks, though they didn't pay the slightest bit of attention to each other. One of the chefs, Antonio, who sported an enormous, lopsided white cooking hat and an extremely bushy black moustache, came flying into the corridor, brandishing a large frying pan above his head as though he expected the entire Pearson army to come charging at him down the hall.

"Mister Renzos!" he yelled, as he spotted the running men, waving his pan furiously about like a caveman with a club. "Where those Pearson bastards?! I kill them! I kill them!"

"Good man, Antonio," Raphael hollered back to him. "Stay calm, alright? Tell everyone in the building to keep calm, got it?"

"I got it, Mister Raphael, I got it! I kill those Pearson scum if they come here, I kill them!"

Raphael and the others continued speeding down the corridor; they came to a halt outside the door of Rachelle. Raphael yanked it open.

Lord Renzo stood in the middle of the war room; to his left were Emperor Jin and the two Chinese Ambassadors. To his right, the Head of his army, General Jackson. A proportion of the General's personal unit stood to attention behind their commander, waiting for their orders.

"What's the situation?" said Trey striding forwards, swiftly followed by the others.

"There was an official attack ten minutes ago," said Lord Renzo, wasting no time in explaining. "Three Tic-Tac Flamethrowers simultaneously exploded—one in South London, one in North and one in West. Our units up and down the city were immediately called to action; Ice Walls have been erected to minimize the risk of further Flamethrower attacks, each located within a five mile radius of each other."

"Lucky," said General Jackson in his gruff voice; he was a tall burly man who never smiled and who, in previous decades, had killed more thugs than his entire army put together. "Reports of Flamethrower usage have been unreliable, shaky at best. It's been difficult to gather information regarding the enemy's weaponry; almost impossible to foresee their method of attack. Ice Walls were a stroke of genius."

Trey nodded.

"That would account for the explosive noises," he said. "You are right, General Jackson—Ice Walls were a very good move."

Ice Walls were the only form of defence against the formidable Tic-Tac Flamethrowers. As the name suggested, these particular Flamethrowers were very small, the same shape and size of a Tic-Tac sweet. But there was nothing remotely sweet about this highly advanced piece of weaponry, which, with one squeeze between finger and thumb, had the power to blast an entire row of houses to pieces with great flames of fire. For the past few years, both the Pearsons and the Renzos had been stocking up on various defence and attack equipment to prepare for the impending war. The trouble with this was that neither side knew for certain what the other possessed in their weapons vault. International black trade markets, eager to take advantage of the civil unrest within the city, had presented a variety of weaponry and defence to both clans; official governments within other nations, bar China, refused to get involved. Hence, an unusual assortment of weapons were purchased by both sides; many of these were—luckily—not fatal in the sense of liquidizing the entire island in one go, such as nuclear powers or lethal gases; instead they consisted of traditional military usage: bows and arrows, swords, daggers, revolvers. But these traditional weapons themselves had special implementations due to technology's advancement through the years. The arrow that came with the bow was laced with a temporary paralysis that rendered the victim unable to move for thirty minutes; daggers that, with the push of a miniature button on the handle, could transform into staffs; for defence, there were shields that came with protective shades. The shields would vibrate when someone was sneaking up from behind, able to sense the creeping/running sensation towards the bearer and any weapon that may be swinging towards them; the protective shades gave the wearer four-dimensional ability—able to see the enemy from left, right, front and behind.

Both clans often rejected the more deadly apparatus as the black market trade was dodgy and some of their bigger 'advanced' weaponry was faulty. Even Lord Pearson was not willing to sacrifice his entire army, land, and possibly himself, just to win—because what was the use of winning when there was nothing to rule over?

However, both sides had managed to get their hands on a select few weapons of warfare that *were* considered much more dangerous and out of the norm. Lord Renzo's spies had cited there was a fifty-fifty chance that Lord Pearson had purchased a boxful of highly costly Tic-Tac Flamethrowers; as a method of precaution, Lord Renzo had then purchased a large number of Ice Walls and ordered them to be placed in various hidden points throughout the city, ready for usage if necessary. This was after much debate with his advisors, some of whom strongly opposed spending so much money on something there was no guarantee they would ever use (especially when it raised their ever-increasing debt to the Chinese Empire to astronomical amounts), but Lord Renzo had been firm in his decision. The Ice Wall, an ingenious invention by a Dutch scientist at the turn of the century, was a type of liquid spray that could absorb fire in its particles in the space of half a millisecond. One spray of it covered a radius of 8.4 kilometres and lasted in the air for a maximum of eight hours. At the sound of the first explosion that night, Lord Renzo's men had sprayed Ice Walls all over the city; only two more Tic-Tac Flamethrowers succeeded in exploding before the entire air was spritzed, thus eliminating further threat of fire attacks and saving countless lives in the process.

"The enemy continues to march forwards, but Emperor Jin's forces currently block their route as far as Central London," said Lord Renzo. "Warfare rages in Picadilly Circus. Meanwhile, reports show that more are working in smaller groups and attacking civilians in their homes. Most Londoners have been alerted through the bugle horn and know to stay indoors or evacuate to a Silver Shelter, but with separate bands of thugs hunting them in their homes, the innocents are in serious danger. Reports of these attacks have already been cited in various areas of West London, North London and several in South. Raphael—I want you to take your Bengal Unit and focus on these perpetrators. Use whatever means necessary to stop them. While transformed, you will be able to locate their whereabouts through your senses…and, of course, the screams."

"Yes," said Raphael immediately.

"How many thugs currently march through Central?" asked Trey.

"Numbers estimate at ninety thousand," replied General Jackson.

Everyone who had just entered the room looked shocked.

"*Ninety thousand?*" repeated Trey, stunned.

"There has to be some kind of mistake," said Raphael in bewilderment. "Reports a few weeks ago suggested sixty thousand at the most—and that's counting the thugs who are attacking civilians in their homes!"

"Yeah, well, the reports got it wrong—or Pearson swelled his ranks in the last few weeks," said the General. "There's at least ninety thousand of them fighting Emperor Jin's forces in Piccadilly and we've got a strong tip-off that thousands more are on the move. The attack began swiftly and without warning; we deployed our units as quickly as possible, but much damage has already been done. Their target is this stronghold. It looks like Pearson sent out his entire army tonight."

Ninety thousand. They could hardly believe it. Where had the extra numbers come from?

"What weaponry do they have?"

"Mostly hand-to-hand combat weapons," replied one of the Chinese Ambassadors by Emperor Jin's side. "Daggers, swords, staffs…some have bow and arrows, rifles, pistols…"

General Jackson scoffed loudly.

"Brutes with stones, toddlers with sticks!" he said in a loud, contemptuous voice. "Those thugs have no idea how to fight. We're evenly matched in numbers, it seems, but not everyone has skill with a blade!"

"Do not underestimate the enemy," said Lord Renzo seriously. "If we have been training our forces all this time, you can be sure Lord Pearson has, too—thugs though they be. Now come—not a moment to lose. Change into your armour and get ready to deploy.

Raphael, begin in Brentfordshire—be careful, reports show that thirty homes have been attacked already. Trey, command the archer unit on the border of Central. General Jackson will lead his infantry to Central and join Emperor Jin's forces. Kai, please go with General Jackson."

"And how about us?" said Ricardo, gesturing to himself and his twin brother.

"You are both to stay here."

The twins looked outraged.

"Why do we have to stay behind?" said Joey, fuming.

Lord Renzo regarded them sternly.

"Because I want you here to defend your home. Neither of you command units—there is little sense in sending you both to the front line when your combat skills are not up to scratch. I did tell you months ago—years even—that your time spent partying would be better served in combat training, but you chose not to listen. And there is no need for your espionage abilities at present. No, both of you remain here and hold the forte."

Grumbling mutinously, Joey and Ricardo continued looking stony-faced. Raphael pulled them to one side.

"Keep an eye on Skye," he said in a low voice. "I checked on her an hour ago and she's doing much better—Doctor Jenson's practically managed to restore her to full health—don't let her out of your sight. She'll probably want to join the battle. Promise me you'll keep her safe."

The twins exchanged glances. Then they nodded.

"Let's move out," said General Jackson, turning to his officers. "Down with the Pearson scum!"

His officers, consisting of the most highly trained, seasoned warriors in all of London, nodded and marched from the room to assemble their unit. General Jackson bowed to Lord Renzo and Emperor Jin before he, too, departed.

Trey and Kai also prepared to leave; the twins and Raphael clapped their brother on the shoulder, telling him to take care.

"Trey, remember," said Lord Renzo, placing a firm hand on his eldest son's arm, "the enemy are strong in number, but there is no reason that your skills should not surpass theirs. Logically, victory should be yours; remember, circle them; repel any charges. Be careful of Emperor Jin's and General Jackson's forces; try and lure the enemy into groups before aiming. And one more thing…"

He lowered his voice, his beard almost scratching his son's ear.

"Do not aim to kill. Aim to wound or demand surrender."

Trey looked at him, surprised.

"But why?"

Lord Renzo shook his head.

"I have a strange feeling about this battle. All is not as it seems. Heed my words, Trey—kill only if necessary. Is that understood?"

"Yes, Father."

Lord Renzo embraced him briefly.

"Good luck, my son—take the greatest care."

Trey nodded; then he and Kai both swept from the room.

Raphael was next.

"Good luck out there, Raph," said Ricardo, sounding uncharacteristically anxious.

"Yeah," nodded Joey fervently, "watch your back. We'll see you shortly."

Raphael clapped them both on the shoulders.

"Don't worry about me," he told them. "I'll be back in no time—right after I've killed those thugs. Look after Skye."

Lord Renzo walked towards Raphael and placed a hand on the back of his youngest son's neck, pressing his head to his.

"Stay transformed at all times," he told him quietly. "Your senses are sharper, your reactions quicker. Keep your mind clear always. Do whatever necessary to protect the civilians. Should you require assistance or should anything untoward happen, communicate with me via the Survival Pact. Have your unit stake out each area in case of an ambush. Can you do this?"

"You know I can," replied Raphael.

Lord Renzo nodded, pulling his head back and staring into Raphael's resolute green eyes.

"I have every faith in you. Now go—and God speed."

Pressing his father's hand to his forehead and with a fierce air of determination, Raphael strode from the war room.

Tension was high in the corridors as he sprinted as fast as he could to his Bengal Unit outside, a force of five hundred men and women who had been assigned to him. The Bengal Unit (named so in reference to Raphael's spirit animal) had proven their stealth and combat skills on numerous occasions during training, and also their loyalty (such as the multiple times over the last year when Raphael had been secretly killing thugs in his animal form; a number of his unit were aware of his actions, but none said a word. Their respect and admiration for the youngest Renzo was paramount and, of all the units, it was hard-pressed to find one so attached to their commander as they).

"Oh, Master Raphael!" cried one of the maids as Raphael dashed past, reaching out for his arm and clutching it, stopping him in his tracks. "What shall we do? Has the war really begun? What if the Pearsons should come here?"

"They won't, Eliza," said Raphael, injecting as much calm into his voice as possible while his own heart beat furiously; he patted the woman's trembling hand. "We're going to destroy them. All of them. You'll see. And then we'll finally have a city that's safe to live in. Stay here. It'll all be over soon."

The maid kissed his hand, her eyes glistening with tears.

"Do be careful, Master Raphael. Please stay safe—we will all pray for your safety!"

Raphael touched her cheek briefly and smiled. Then he continued his sprint down the hallway.

He came to a halt outside the infirmary. Swiftly, he opened the door. Doctor Jenson was there; Skye was there, too, still in her wolf form. She had been sleeping for several hours now. Thanks to a combination of Doctor Jenson's talents and his range of superior medical remedies, Skye's wounds had all but healed; even her ribs, which had taken such a beating. After working on her for over an hour, Doctor Jenson had earlier told an increasingly worried Raphael that he no longer had cause to worry. Skye might need a while to rest, but she would be back to full health in no time.

Now, as she lay sleeping, his beautiful white wolf with such a peaceful, content expression on her face, pain stabbed at Raphael's heart. Confident as he was, war meant uncertainty. Nothing was guaranteed. Always expect the unexpected. He had to get out there and destroy those thugs. For his family, for the people…for her.

"Master Raphael!" exclaimed Doctor Jensen, hastily placing the phial he was holding on the table. "The horn! Is it war?"

"Yes. It has begun," said Raphael, striding towards Skye.

He laid a gentle palm on her soft, white coat.

"How is she?"

"Very well," said Doctor Jenson, walking over to stand beside him. "The remedies have had a tremendous effect; after she has rested, I have no doubt that she will be back to full strength."

Raphael turned to face him, his expression pained.

"Doctor Jenson…I must lead my unit against the thugs. I need you to promise me that you will keep her safe. I have asked my brothers to keep an eye on her, but I'd like your assistance, too. For the past few weeks now, Skye has talked about joining the battle when war begins…I can't let it happen. I know it may be selfish of me…I know that Skye is strong and that as a Morpher her assets may be valuable…but I can't lose her, Doctor Jenson. Not now that I know what it's like. I can't do that. Please, promise me you'll keep her safe."

Doctor Jenson nodded, his round face sombre.

"I do not know what strength I have to contain a wolf as fierce as Miss. Archer," he said, "but I will do as you ask, Master Raphael."

Raphael clasped the doctor on the shoulder gratefully.

"Thank you, Doctor Jenson."

He turned back to the sleeping wolf and stroked her head.

"I'll be back soon, alright?" he whispered, leaning over. "Be a good girl. I won't be long, I promise."

He kissed her several times, once on the forehead, another on her muzzle. She stirred softly. He smiled, the look in his eyes tender.

Then he turned away, the familiar pounding resuming beneath his chest.

"Master Raphael—wait!"

"Yes, Doctor?"

"Wait—take this."

Doctor Jenson hurried towards a chest of marble drawers in the corner of the infirmary. He pulled open the top drawer, reached inside and pulled out a tiny package.

"What is this?" asked Raphael as the doctor handed the package to him.

"A Bestia Exalter sweet. As a Morpher it will enhance your senses, amplify your attack power and strengthen your coat. Take it just before you transform. It will last for three hours after consumption and should aid you greatly in battle."

Raphael opened the package and took out the sweet. It was green and square with a fiery orange patch in the middle.

"Doctor Jenson—thank you," said Raphael, pocketing it.

"God speed, Young Master!"

Raphael clasped him once more in farewell. He turned one more time to look at Skye, vowing that when he returned to her, it would be in victory. Then, trying to lift the heaviness of his heart, he departed swiftly from the room.

*

When Skye woke up, it was to see the black and white rotund frame of Doctor Jenson peering down at her, examining her fangs with a magnifying glass.

"Teeth all in order," he muttered to himself. "Molars look a bit jagged, though…"

He caught sight of Skye's bright blue eyes blinking up at him.

"Ah, awake!" he exclaimed, hovering the magnifying glass above her face so that her blue eyeball expanded considerably. "And much sooner than I expected. I trust you are feeling much better?"

In her animal form she could not, of course, talk back. Instead, she wagged her tail, which, she noted, no longer hurt.

"Good, good. Many people have been concerned for you and will be delighted to hear that you have recovered. Your mother and Miss Beaufont in particular have been deeply stressed—I have had to ask them to leave on no less than six occasions; but it's understandable, of course, perfectly understandable…I must say, the Bone Spritz concoction worked better than I had ever guessed—perfect realignment of the ribcage—ingenious! Doctor Parfoot of the Central Americas must be very proud indeed…But dear me, listen to me, rabbiting on like this! You must want to transform, yes?"

Skye's tail wagged again, her ears pricking up.

"Indeed, indeed…Well, I will give you a few moments. A pile of clothes is over there for you on the chair. We are in short supply of ladies clothes, unfortunately, but Master Raphael has provided you with a pair of jogging bottoms and a jumper which he hopes does suffice?"

It certainly did suffice. Her eyes darting to where the neatly folded clothes were resting on the chair, Skye's tail wagged harder. She loved wearing Raphael's clothes…it meant his musky scent stayed with her wherever she went…

"Well, I'll be back shortly then, Miss Archer," said Doctor

Jenson, before exiting the infirmary.

Skye continued to lie sprawled on the patient's table for a few moments without moving; too many thoughts were whizzing around her mind. As soon as the doctor left, the terrible ordeal she had been through returned with unwelcome haste and swiftly threatened to consume her; it took every bit of willpower she had to push the previous events from her head. Instead of allowing the terrifying image of Finn Pearson's boot slamming towards her face, she focussed on how the earlier, agonizing pain was no longer present; her ribs didn't feel like they were on fire anymore. She thought about her mother, Daphne, Raphael…she couldn't wait to see them. She wondered if Raphael had told Lord Renzo about what that man in the white coat had said…she wondered if he had told them about the beaver cub…

The memory of the professor in the white coat caused her to shudder; the image of the small Morpher boy and his flowing tears made her heart hurt. She couldn't think of them right now. Later. Now, she had to focus on transforming.

Closing her eyes, she concentrated on her human self. Seconds later, Skye returned to her bare, physically weaker human body. She immediately began shivering, noting how cold it was in the room without her wolf coat to keep her warm. Hurriedly, she pitter-pattered across the floor and threw the jumper and jogging bottoms on (there was also a pair of boxers and a vest which were far too big, but would have to do).

She heard sudden voices from outside the door. She crept forwards to hear what they were saying.

"…and, of course, that is all well and good," said one voice, which she was pretty sure belonged to Doctor Jenson. "Miss Archer is indeed awake and her injuries almost fully healed."

"Ah, she's awake? Excellent!" said a second voice. "Raphael's told us to keep an eye on her, so we'd better go in."

"Not just yet, Master Joey, please. Miss Archer is changing."

"Have you told her about what's happened?" came another, low voice that Skye had to strain to hear.

"No. Not yet."

Puzzled, Skye stepped into a pair of plimsolls that were lying underneath the chair and which she presumed were for her. She vaguely realized in the back of her head that her wolf boots were gone forever…the monster in the white coat surely had them…

It occurred to her at that moment that there were strange noises coming from outside, somewhere far in the distance. An unusual rumbling noise that sounded like a mixture of shouts and screams. She hurried to the window to try and catch a glimpse of where the odd sounds were coming from, but she could see nothing, except the trees and high wall that barricaded the Renzo mansion from the outside world.

There was a knock on the door.

"Miss Archer, are you dressed?"

"Yes," Skye called back croakily. Her voice always had a slightly papery rasp to it whenever she had been in her wolf form for a long time.

The door swung open and Doctor Jenson, Joey and Ricardo walked in.

"Hey, mini-Raph!" Joey strolled towards her, grinning, and enveloping her in a hug. "Good to see you awake and alive! And you're wearing the pair of plimsolls that I used to wear when I was twelve—suits you!"

"They suit her better than you, Joe," said Ricardo, also grinning and hugging her. "Good to see you awake, Skye."

She smiled at them, but an uneasy feeling was creeping through her. It was natural for the twins to be jovial most of the time, but she couldn't help feeling there was something forced about their grins, something slightly stiff in the way they embraced her; she caught Doctor Jenson out of the corner of her eye, but he refused to look at her and instead busied himself with a stack of papers on his desk. Something came back to her just then, something one of the twins had said outside the door: *"Raphael's told us to keep an eye on her…"*

"It's great to see you both, too," she told them. "Erm, so where is Raph—?"

"Your mum and Daphne are going to be thrilled to see you awake," said Ricardo, throwing an arm round her shoulder. "Oops—is that alright? Sorry, your shoulder isn't in pain or anything, is it?"

Skye shook her head.

"OK, great," said Joey, casually striding to Skye's other side and holding his arm out to her. "Listen, shall we make our way to the lounge? Daphne and your mum are both there, they're dying to see you."

Skye felt afraid, but she couldn't explain why.

"Joey, Ricardo," she said, looking at both the twins and swallowing. "Where's Raphael?"

There was an uncomfortable silence in the room. Doctor Jenson coughed and stopped shuffling his papers.

Joey's turquoise eyes stared into hers; he looked resigned and wary at the same time. Over Skye's shoulder, Ricardo nodded to him.

"Skye," he said slowly, "half an hour ago, the bugle horn was blown."

"The bugle horn…?"

"Yes…thousands of thugs marched from East London through to Central. There was a lot of…a lot of trouble along the way; at first, we thought it was just bands of them kicking up riots again. But there's too many of them…Skye, the war has started. Raphael has taken his unit and gone to fight them."

Skye's blood ran cold.

"Raphael's gone to fight?" she repeated, because she could think of nothing else to say.

"Yes."

Joey and Ricardo shot worried glances at each other. Doctor Jenson cleared his throat and approached them.

"Miss Archer," he said gently, "it is very important that you rest. The remedies have done wonders in healing you, but rest is still crucial at this stage. My advice is to please go with Masters Joey and Ricardo, they can take you to the lounge and also provide you with a meal and tea, which will be very good for building your strength…"

Skye didn't actually hear the rest of what he said. The news was slowly sinking in. The war had begun. The same war that had brewed threateningly beneath the surface had now exploded. Raphael was out there, fighting the thugs. She cast her mind back to the many conversations they'd had; about what they would both do when war hit; about Raphael's Bengal Unit, which he had been training with for a long time. Skye had discovered many things after they became a couple and it had astounded her just how wide and vast the Renzo military preparations were. She remembered their many arguments: how Raphael had been so determined she should leave; how she had fiercely defied him and insisted she used whatever strength she had to fight by his side.

Now Raphael was out there in the midst of battle

And she was here, safe in the mansion.

"I have to help him," she muttered, oblivious to Doctor Jenson's current rhetoric about the benefits of herbal tea.

"Skye, no," said Joey immediately. "Doctor Jenson's right—you have to stay here and rest."

"Raphael's out there—I have to go to him—"

"Miss Archer, it will not help Master Raphael if you choose to take part in the battle," said Doctor Jenson firmly. "The extent of your injuries earlier was critical; you're lucky to still be alive. The remedies have healed you, but your current state is still delicate. Not just physically, but mentally, also. You have been through a terrible ordeal; engaging in conflict so soon afterwards may cause irreversible damage that you yourself would have no control over. You *must* rest."

It was only due to the acknowledgement that the doctor had saved her life that caused Skye to bite on her lip, refraining from fiercely rebuking his words and insisting that she was fine; that she could fight. Instead, she forced herself to breathe calmly, looking squarely into the eyes of the concerned faces around her.

"Doctor Jenson, I'm a Morpher. You know that in my animal

form I can fight; I can evade attack, my defences are stronger—"

"Yes, Miss Archer, I do know this. I also know that, as I have told young Master Raphael on countless occasions, being a Morpher does not automatically make one invincible. Especially one who has recently been through a highly traumatic event."

"Don't worry about Raphael," said Ricardo. "He's a big boy; he can take care of himself. Worry about those thugs."

"He'll come back, Skye," added Joey, holding his arm out to her once again, "and what's more, he made us swear that we'd look after you while he's gone. So come on, then. How about we go to the lounge and see your mum and Daphne? They're waiting for you, you know."

For a second she remained still, thinking briefly about how bizarre it was that the twins, of all people, should be chaperoning her and acting as bodyguards. The urge to transform and join Raphael wrestled with her logic; after all, if she hadn't been so stupid to go wandering off on her own in the first place, she wouldn't be in this position. And what if Doctor Jenson was right…? The horrors from earlier flashed at random intervals in her mind. She couldn't afford to lose concentration if she were out there, fighting the thugs…

Resignedly, she took Joey's arm and looked up at him.

"You sure he'll be alright?" she asked him quietly.

Joey flashed a toothy smile at her.

"'Course he will! He's Raphael, isn't he? The hero of the family, ya-di-ya and all that jazz. He'll be back just as soon as he's done with Pearson—and he'll be thrilled to see you up and about. So—to the lounge then?"

"And if it makes you feel any better, you aren't the only one who's been ordered to stay behind," chimed in Ricardo. "Me and Joe haven't exactly been high in demand. No idea why—we can fight just as good as anyone else!"

"Too much socializing, Master Ricardo," said Doctor Jenson sternly. "Far too much. Your father warned you on numerous occasions, I believe, that sacrificing training for enjoyment purposes would do nobody any favours. Furthermore, landing yourselves in the infirmary on a weekly basis due to being inebriated is terrible for your health—"

"Yeah, yeah," interrupted Ricardo, carelessly waving away the doctor's criticisms. "Already had the lecture from Dad. We get it. No more drinking. No more outings. No more girls—not for me, anyway. I've got myself a great girl—she's all I need."

His eyes melted into a soppy, slavish gaze. Joey mimed puking.

"Spare me the cheese," he said with a grimace. "Skye, let's get to the lounge before Ricardo starts stinking the place out with his cheddar. Thanks, Doc. We'll take things from here."

He nodded to Doctor Jenson, who sighed and turned away, muttering to himself. The three of them departed from the room, but Skye swerved her head to take one last look at the doctor, murmuring, "Thank you." Doctor Jenson merely inclined his head, his expression concerned, before turning away and resuming his business with the stack of papers.

The corridor was still in disarray. Skye, whose senses were always amplified right after being in her wolf body, felt a powerful, emotional wave of panic and fear hit her as soon as she stepped outside the infirmary. The wide-eyed, panicking maids who stood frantically by the kitchen, the butlers who nodded to them as they went past, looking unusually vague; the cooks who were yelling at each other, armed with pots and pans; the guards who were hollering above the rest trying to maintain order. The reality of what was happening hit her more strongly than ever and she swallowed hard as they continued hurrying down the hallway and towards the lounge.

Ricardo opened the door of the lounge. Skye had barely taken a couple of steps forward before the screaming and stampeding ensued.

"SKYE!" was the simultaneous shriek, and then, arms flying around her, faces burying themselves in her shoulders.

"Oh, my dear daughter!" cried Mrs. Archer, tears falling down her cheeks, cupping Skye's face in both hands. "I thought I'd lost you! I thought I'd lost you!"

"It's OK, Mum, I'm here," Skye whispered, unable to prevent the strong wave of emotion that swelled inside her as she hugged her mother and wiped the tears from her eyes. She felt a huge lump come to her throat; it had been close. It really had. She still didn't know why they hadn't killed her. But it was true; the loss had almost become a reality. Skye pulled her mother tight; only now did she realize the full extent of her kidnap and the impact it had on those dearest to her. Blocking the fear of what would have happened to them if she hadn't come back, she continued squeezing her mother, not wanting to let go.

"We've been so worried about you, Skye," said an equally tearful Daphne, who was also hugging her. "We didn't know, you see...you came back and you were all...injured. The doctor wouldn't let us see you…"

"It's OK, Daph," said Skye, releasing one arm that was wrapped around her inconsolable mother and throwing it around her best friend, whose eyes were wet and shiny. "I'm alright now. I'm really sorry you had to worry like this…"

The three continued embracing each other amongst much sobbing, mostly on the part of Mrs. Archer. As Skye stood there holding her mother and best friend in her arms, she realized in that moment that this was where she was supposed to be. Where she had to be. Not out there in the heat of battle away from the two people who, aside from Raphael, she loved more than anyone in the world. But here in this lounge where, in the event that something should go terribly wrong and if the mansion was invaded, she would be right by her mother's and Daphne's side, ready to defend them to the death and fight for them in a way that no one else could. The desire to join Raphael and battle alongside him continued to rage through her; but they needed her more and she had to keep them safe if the situation called for it. Right then, she was glad that her defiance towards Doctor Jenson had gone no further than a rebellious pout; this was her place, there was no doubt about it.

"Ladies, shall we sit down?" said Joey, gesturing charmingly towards the couches.

Skye, Daphne and Mrs. Archer, amidst many sniffles, nodded and broke apart, making their way towards the velvet seats. It was then that Skye noticed they were not the only people occupying the lounge. A few guests who had been part of the dinner earlier were also there, muttering anxiously to one another with the pale, wide-eyed looks of people who'd had too much caffeine; Lo Wen was there, too, sitting next to one of her uncle's Chinese Ambassadors; and who else should be sprawled on the couch, but Sasha. Skye noticed this with surprise, followed by a grimace.

Wonder what she's still doing here, she thought to herself.

She had figured Sasha (who looked very haughty as Skye and the others took a seat on the other side of the room) would have been among those who had left the mansion earlier before the war began.

Sasha rolled her eyes at her before carelessly flicking her gaze towards the magazine she was currently holding. Skye wondered if Sasha knew about the kidnapping earlier; if so, she was probably annoyed to learn she was safe and sound.

Skye was surprised to find herself shaking her head and silently rebuking herself, but the doubt came, nonetheless…surely even Sasha was not as callous as that? Not now that she knew what true callousness was; true callousness was the sort of evil she had been in the cell with only hours before…

The flashes returned. Skye buried her head in her hands.

"Skye?" Daphne said, sounding concerned, reaching out and placing a hand on her friend's arm.

Struggling to pull herself together and ban the images from her mind, Skye took a deep breath and lifted her head.

"It's fine…I'm fine, Daphne," she said, brushing away the beads of sweat that had developed on her forehead. "Listen," she added, lowering her voice, "what exactly is the situation out there? Joey and Ricardo haven't told me much…"

Daphne leaned in closer.

"I heard that about a hundred thousand thugs appeared in Central London, armed with weapons" she said quietly. "Lord

Renzo sent his army out to meet them. They've been fighting for about an hour now. A lot of buildings have been set on fire…"

"Like the riots twelve years ago?"

"Worse. Look out the window."

Skye turned to where Daphne was pointing. The lounge, unlike the infirmary, was facing the east—sure enough, there was a fiery red glow in the sky, marking the horrors that were currently thriving in the city.

"Lord Renzo sprayed Ice Walls all over London when Lord Pearson began his Flamethrower attacks," Daphne continued, her gaze fearful as she, too, surveyed the blazing glow in the distance, which contrasted ominously against the black night sky, "but these were mostly located outside civilian homes and on residential streets. The rest of the city…"

Her voice trailed off. Skye swallowed hard. Raphael was out there, among those burning flames…

Mrs. Archer, who was sitting on Skye's other side, took her daughter's hand and squeezed it tight.

"He's very strong, my dear," she murmured, stroking her hair with her fingertips.

Skye nodded, trying to hide how afraid she really felt.

"I know," she said. "I know."

"Skye, you hungry?"

Ricardo plonked himself down next to Daphne, throwing an arm around his girlfriend's shoulders, his eyes widening inquisitively.

Skye shook her head.

"No thanks, I—"

"Sorry, sweetie, but doctor's orders," said Joey, also appearing and carrying what appeared to be a plate laden with meat, cheese and bread. "Doctor Jenson said you need to build your strength up—and that includes eating. Sorry, I know you like your meat all bloody and stuff, but best we could do right now, I'm afraid."

He handed the plate to her. Skye eyed it nauseously. She didn't see how she could possibly eat a thing. But it was true; she had to rebuild her strength. She was no good to anyone as a sickly patient, delicate and fragile, being tended to by Joey and Ricardo (which, in itself, felt odd and unnatural; the twins weren't exactly the mother-hen type).

"Thanks, Joey," she said, picking up a fork and reaching for the large lump of pork that was sitting next to the loaf of bread. She took a bite, swallowed and immediately felt like she would hurl it up again. Joey beamed at her approvingly. Skye smiled painfully back at him.

The room was mostly silent for a while. Everyone tried not to focus on the flaming red sky outside, or the wild shouts and screams in the distance; the gunshots and clanging sounds, which represented hundreds of blades in action. They tried not to think about what would happen if Lord Renzo and his army lost the battle; tried not to think about the terrible consequences that friends and loved ones, caught in the midst of the killing and fighting, may suffer; tried not to think about what would happen if Lord Pearson's thugs attempted to invade the Renzo grounds.

Tension in the lounge was paramount. People sipped on coffee, munched on snacks, engaged in attempted light-hearted whispers of conversations—but the icy, frigid atmosphere was felt by every single person present, just as the fiery flames of war touched each and every human being who was smack-bang in the danger zone outside.

Mrs. Archer rose from her seat and made her way to the coffee table. Joey got up to join her and Skye watched as the two started chatting, with Joey pointing to various bowls on the table which were filled with different types of tea and coffee beans, and Mrs. Archer nodding her agreement. Skye's mother returned moments later with a steaming cup of tea and handed it to her daughter.

"Here you are, Skye," she said, sitting down again. "White tea—your favourite. There are so many teas there that I didn't know which was which. Joey Renzo explained it all though; he's incredibly helpful, isn't he?"

"Yes," replied Skye wryly; she doubted that Joey's interest in her mother extended purely to helping her choose a cup of tea and she promptly shuddered at the thought. This made her think of Raphael's reaction earlier at the dinner party…Raphael. He was out there. How could she even try not to think of him or think of something else? Her heart began to ache again.

Please be safe, she thought despairingly, looking down into the steamy, silvery liquid in her mug. *Please be OK…*

"As an all-powerful Morpher, wouldn't it make more sense if you were out there fighting, too? Raphael's gone so why haven't you?"

The words cut through the air like a knife. For Skye, it was a double-edged blade, one that sliced deep. Everyone fell silent, turning to look at Sasha who still lounging on the couch, eyeing Skye with a cool, unimpressed expression, her eyebrows raised in mock curiosity which gave the impression that she had enjoyed the effect her words had on the room at large.

Daphne was the first to react.

"Are you stupid?" she said angrily. "What makes you think Skye would go out there and fight? We're lucky to have her back with us!"

Sasha rolled her eyes to the ceiling; everyone watched with bated breath.

"Yes, we all heard about the kidnapping," she said, sounding supremely unconcerned. "But she's not exactly lying paralyzed in the hospital bed, is she? She looks totally fine to me. So what's the big deal? I thought the Morphers were meant to fight—you know, because they *can?* Thought you and Raphael were a team," she added, turning back to Skye with a slight sneer on her lips, "but you let him fight out there on his own. And yet you go on like you're this big bad wolf who's scared of nobody."

"Don't you speak to my daughter like that," said Mrs. Archer who was shaking with quiet fury.

"It's OK, Mum," said Skye in a low voice.

She looked at Sasha, her expression hard. What could she say? That she was safely here with all of them because she was not mentally fit to join the battle? Because she was still delicate? Because, even though she had the ability to shape shift into a wild wolf and take out ten thugs on her own, she had to stay here and rest? She didn't want to say that. It made her feel weak and, above all, it played upon the fear and guilt she felt already.

"You don't have to defend yourself to her, Skye!" Daphne said fiercely as though reading her mind.

Skye placed a hand on her friend's arm. Then she fixed Sasha with a piercing look.

"I'm here because…because, yeah, stuff happened to me earlier and it messed me up…"

She hated admitting it. Sasha narrowed her eyes condescendingly.

"Lord Renzo even *said* that we should be careful where we go, and that included the gardens," she said in a loud voice, "but you decided to go walking off on your own! Seriously? You almost got people killed! I mean, do the same rules not apply to Morphers or something? Or is it just you, *Skye?*"

Daphne and Mrs. Archer had identical expressions of outrage on their faces. The twins looked on, speechless, unsure whether to intervene or not. Everyone else continued staring, their eyes darting between Skye and Sasha at regular intervals.

Skye swallowed. At any other time, the notion of having to defend herself against Sasha in this way would have been laughable to her. But she couldn't deny what had unfolded that night. She *had* wandered off on her own…she *had* put people in danger…she *had* caused people she loved pain and stress from worrying about her…she couldn't deny this.

"It was stupid of me to wander off like that," she said, painfully aware of all the eyes that were watching her. "But I did it because…" She paused; she couldn't talk about the beaver child right now. Couldn't think of him, the young boy who was undoubtedly still locked in the cage…

The needle flashed before her again; a thug's fist came swinging towards her face; the young boy screamed as the other thug slapped him round the face.

She trembled, her eyes watering and switching to blue as she fought to push the images from her mind again. Daphne observed this sudden reaction in her friend, before rounding on Sasha.

"Why don't you just get out?" she snapped. "Seriously, don't you have anything better to do? Like get your precious beauty sleep?"

Sasha seemed thoroughly unperturbed. She opened her mouth to speak again, but Skye spoke first.

"And I'm here," she said, her voice stronger now, having vanquished the memories, "because there are people I care about in this room. And I want to be here in case Pearson comes."

"Oh, please!" Sasha scoffed, flicking her hair. "The thugs aren't coming *here*. Everyone knows we're going to win."

"You seem sure about that," came Lo Wen's voice from the other side of the room. "How do you know?"

Sasha tutted irritably.

"Because in case you haven't noticed, *we* happen to be the one with the trained soldiers. We've got all the weapons, we've got the money—this whole thug thing is a bit of a joke, to be honest. It was only a matter of time before we got rid of them."

"The other side have got all those things, too," said Ricardo with a frown.

Sasha gave a tinkling laugh before standing up, stretching, and sweeping one hand through her long, golden hair.

"So? Everyone knows that my father and Lord Renzo have the best of the best. I've lived here my whole life and never even had any problems with thugs. Trust me, after tonight, that'll be the end of them."

"Maybe you've never had any problems with them because you've never been in a position where you *had* to," said Daphne coldly. "We're not all as privileged as you."

Sasha yawned.

"Yeah…anyway, you're right, I should get my beauty sleep. Not that I need it. Want to join me, Ricardo?"

She turned to the twin, who looked deeply uncomfortable. Both Skye and Daphne stared at Sasha in amazement and anger. Sasha shrugged and glided towards the door.

"Wake me up when it's all over then. Night, night."

With that, she left the lounge. Daphne's nostrils were flaring.

"One of these days," she said in a low, growling voice. "One of these days, I swear…"

"I agree," said Skye grimly. Sasha may not be evil in the same sense as the white-coat…but she was still a first-class bitch.

"What a horrible girl!" exclaimed Mrs. Archer fiercely, clutching Skye's hand in a protective manner. "Saying such nasty things! As if my daughter ought to be out there fighting those hooligans! Lord Renzo has thousands of trained people at his command. How dare she say such things? And after everything you've been through!"

"Don't worry, Mum," said Skye, patting her angry mother on the shoulder. "She and I have never exactly been the best of friends."

"Good! I certainly wouldn't want my daughter befriending someone like *that!*"

"You didn't really listen to her though, did you?" Daphne whispered, her eyes wide and frightened as Mrs. Archer turned away, still muttering furiously to herself about Sasha. "About going to fight because you're a Morpher? You wouldn't, would you?"

Skye hesitated. She had not told Daphne what she intended to do when it came to a final showdown with the thugs. Raphael was the only one she ever discussed it with. She couldn't bring herself to tell her best friend and her mother that she had fully intended to fight when the time came; that that there was a deep-rooted, burning desire inside her to avenge the death of someone she had loved so deeply, but who was stolen from her many years ago. That chances were, if she hadn't been injured earlier, she would have had far more difficulty choosing whether to stay or fight than she did now.

"I'm here, Daphne," she told her. "That's what matters right now. And what about you?" she added, lowering her voice and swiftly changing the subject. "Hope you didn't let what she said get to you, about Ricardo."

Daphne harrumphed.

"No way," she said, turning to look at her boyfriend, whose hand was locked in hers, and who was currently engaged in conversation with his twin brother. "He wouldn't...and besides, there are bigger things going on right now. Bigger things to get upset about."

They fell silent. Their gazes drifted in simultaneous reluctance towards the window again where the blazing red sky flickered above them like a wave of molten lava. The distant yells and shouts continued erupting throughout the city. Inside the lounge, amidst the would-be casual conversations and coffee sipping, the heartbeat of every person present thundered uncontrollably beneath their chest, the panic and tension in the room growing with sickening surety. In the corner, a large grandfather clock tolled its bell four times. 4 am.

One hour since the battle had begun.

I'm here, right here, I'm waiting for you, Skye thought desperately, closing her eyes and seeing his handsome face in her mind, his bright green eyes which crinkled at the sides when he smiled. *Please be safe. I love you so much. And I'll be right here for when you return.*

CHAPTER NINE

Outside, the battle continued to rage. The men and women who had taken up arms only an hour previously were now very different to who they were before they went into the battle zone. Many had never seen war before; most had never been involved in any type of conflict; even the legions of thugs, who had made it their mission to terrorize people for decades, were not used to the enormity and blood-thirst of this particular clash. For those who had trained with the Renzo army, it was the platform necessary to summon all their strength and courage against the enemy, while for Pearson's thugs it brought out the epitome of their brutal, sadistic natures. With the exception of the Emperor's forces, neither side had engaged in a conflict quite like this one before. It was the chance for both to experience something that had previously only existed in their minds—and, like most imagined things that were brought into reality, it was not what any had expected.

War…was there any glory to be had in war? Afterwards, yes. When the names of heroes were toasted; when the fallen were honoured; when their sacrifices were remembered, hailed as the ultimate pinnacle of humanity; to give your life for the protection of others, for freedom, for all that was good in the world. There was nothing nobler than this.

But in the heat of battle, there was only suffering. Suffering, blood and gore. To look upon the face of someone you had just killed, acknowledging that it was either slay or be slain; to watch friends and comrades be blasted to pieces or bayoneted in front of your eyes; to suffer the never-ending flashes and nightmares, always to relive the scenes of horror. To be trapped by your own memories, sometimes poisoned by your own mind. To acknowledge and accept that to defeat a greater evil meant to go through all manners of evil yourself. For the noble, honourable individual who sacrificed mind, body and soul for the greater good, there was no way out; and for the villain who thrived on misery and prolonging suffering as long as possible, they, too, were trapped, albeit in a different sort of cage.

Flames whipped with ruthless ferocity all around. A ring of fire surrounded the two armies. Thugs, quickly realizing they were unable to burn down civilian homes due to Lord Renzo's Ice Walls, turned their attentions instead to shops, stores, monuments and market stalls—those that had not been destroyed by the riots twelve years ago. Central London was a mass of fire and smoke; and right at the heart, Trey and his archers stood scattered in various positions around General Jackson's and Emperor Jin's forces.

He had not been prepared for the sight that met his eyes when he took his force of six hundred trained archers to the scene of the battle via the London Underground Sewers. (The LUS was a failed experiment in the late twenty-first century concocted by politicians who, in an attempt to decrease pollution, decided on an innovative scheme—boats that ran through the sewers, an alternative to trains, buses and cars, where passengers could board and drop off at various Sewage Stops throughout the city. Unfortunately, due to poor sanitation implementation, around fifty people died and the system was shut down. These days, it was used primarily by Lord Renzo whose copper speedboats meant hundreds of people could be transported through the sewers in a very short amount of time.)

The scene that greeted Trey shortly after 3 am was one of shock and horror. Thousands upon thousands of thugs had marched into Picadilly Circus; they carried weapons and were identifiable only by the fact that Emperor Jin's and General Jackson's forces wore uniforms. They had quickly set fire to every building and stall that was not being protected by an Ice Wall, before charging forwards, waving axes, daggers and spears wildly in front of them. The thugs were vicious fighters; their preferred method of fighting was to bite into the neck of their enemy or beat them to death. Lord Renzo's and Emperor Jin's forces were outnumbered, it was true; the sheer mass of thugs was overwhelming. But General Jackson had been right; the thugs were not trained warriors. They relied instead on instinctive brutality and this placed Lord Renzo's soldiers at a distinct advantage. The other blessing was the absence of civilians; due to the time of attack, most civilians were likely in their homes, having been fast asleep when the battle commenced. This meant they did not get caught in the crossfire; but they could not stay inside forever, nor would the Ice Walls hold for long. Unless the battle ended swiftly with a Renzo victory, countless innocent lives would be lost before the day was over.

This was what Trey deduced after scanning his eyes quickly

over the battleground. Seconds later, he and his archers were ambushed by about five hundred thugs carrying machetes who charged towards them, yelling raucously, intent on butchering them to pieces. Swiftly, Trey assembled his archery into three rows, ordering the back row to stand, the middle row to crouch and the first row to kneel.

"Bring them down!" he roared; the archery pulled back their strings as the thugs rampaged towards them. "But do not shoot to kill! Fire!"

A sea of arrows spurted through the air. Thug after thug fell to the ground, writhing in agony as the arrows struck them, the special arrowhead rendering them paralyzed. Trey watched them fall, a great frown on his face. He still did not understand his father's orders to shoot but not kill. How else were they to eliminate their enemy once and for all?

However, this was not the time to question the command. He had his orders and he wasted no time in making some himself. He instructed his archers to divide into groups and locate themselves within various points around the battleground. A few of his more lithe archers climbed the oak trees within the vicinity, able to get a full perspective of the fighting from up above. The tree bowmen were able to take aim at bands of wild thugs, many of whom posed the greatest threat when maneuvering in large groups and targeting individual soldiers; this caused a succession of arrows to rain down on the thugs, and they did this effectively until bullets came flying at them from the ground. Trey watched as three of his archers fell to the concrete; he ordered his remaining bowmen to aim for the gun-wielding thugs. A hailstorm of bullets and arrows commenced. One of the bullets just scraped off Trey's cheekbone and left him with a nasty, bloody graze.

"Take aim!" he bellowed as another mob of thugs started shooting at them.

There were so many of them. But they were unskilled, undisciplined. Bodies lay all around, many having been slain by Emperor Jin's forces. If they could hold out in numbers, this would surely be a Renzo victory…

But Trey started to notice something strange. Amidst the swarms of fighting men and women, amid the clashes of blades and stream of arrows and bullets, some of the thugs were cowering and shaking, their weapons hanging limply by their sides, great expressions of fear on their faces. It was not uncommon for someone to lose his or her nerve in the heat of battle, but for the typical thug who was known for being savage and remorseless, it was unexpected to say the least. Looking closely, Trey saw there was not just fear on the faces of these thugs, but a wide-eyed sort of innocence, too. He watched as one thug, crying and backing away, threw down his weapon and turned to run, pulling what looked like a tag device from his pocket as he did so. He was swiftly halted by another thug who bared his teeth at him, waving his dagger threateningly; the first thug tried to run past him, but the second pulled his arm back and stabbed him. Trey's eyes furrowed as he watched the first thug sink to the ground, blood spurting from his chest. There was a crooked grin on the second thug's face who swiftly snatched the tag device from the dying thug's hand; then he began to drag him away from the battle.

What Trey had just seen—aside from the brutal nature of the

killing—disturbed him greatly. Nevertheless, he dismissed it as fear-paralysis and returned his attention back to the masses upon masses of brutes that were slaughtering and maneuvering towards him. He did not have time right now to fathom dissension among the enemy ranks. A battle had to be won.

He raised his arm.

"Aim!" he bellowed.

The arrows soared through the air, reaching their targets.

*

Before Raphael and his Bengal Unit reached Brentfordshire (Skye's hometown) several things commenced. One was his instruction to his team who were ready and armed, waiting for him to give them the go-ahead to deploy.

"Groups of thugs are breaking into civilian homes," he announced to them as they stood among the dark grounds outside the House of Renzo. He wore only his underwear in order to make transformation easier. His team watched him silently; they could hear the distant yells coming from Central London, just as they were unable to avoid the orange swirl in the night sky, a telltale sign of the fire, which raged throughout the city.

"Our first target is Brentfordshire," he continued, "and from there you must follow my lead. I will be in animal form and unable to communicate verbally. Verbal communication will be done through Paddy; he is my second-in-command during this battle."

Paddy, one of Raphael's oldest and closest friends, stepped

forward. He was usually a jovial, cheeky sort of chap, but there was no smile on his face now. Paddy had known Raphael for the past seventeen years and had sometimes accompanied him during his transformation into a tiger; therefore, he had learned over the course of almost two decades the different actions and signs to watch out for when Raphael wanted to convey something to him. The friends had decided to implement this knowledge into their military training and both agreed it would be extremely useful on the battleground.

"An estimated thirty attacks have already been carried out," Raphael told his unit. Raphael's battalion was made up mostly of swordsmen and women who were also highly skilled in martial arts and, as a result, the Bengal Unit was known as one of the most diverse of the lot, combining classic ninja techniques with the proficiency of medieval knights.

"Homes under attack may be identified by screams, shouts, bodies discarded on the grounds—and, of course, by the presence of thug groups. Lord Renzo has ordered to show mercy where possible and to kill only if necessary."

There was a rather blank stare from members of the Bengal Unit, several muttering confusedly. Showing mercy to the thugs had not been part of the plan, not for the last several months while they had been training. Each had harboured the impression that the thugs were to be eliminated, with the House of Pearson being the ultimate target. None were under any illusions. If the thugs were not killed, they would only return. The fanatical extremism of Lord Pearson's brutes left no room for compromise and it was for this reason that the Bengal Unit found this command to be highly disconcerting.

Raphael knew what they were thinking and he secretly agreed

with them. He, too, did not understand the reason behind this particular instruction. But outwardly he said:

"In my experience, and I am sure in many of yours, I've learned that it is not in the nature of the common thug to show mercy to his victims. However, it would be a disservice to everything we stand for if we stooped to their level. For this reason, I trust that each and every one of you will show compassion where it is necessary."

There were more murmurings. No one had forgotten Raphael's ventures only several months ago when he had transformed in secret and individually targetted Pearson's thugs. This sudden turnaround baffled them. Raphael continued speaking.

"Having said that, your own lives must come first. If you have no other option then you must defend yourselves, whatever the cost. Our ultimate goal is to protect civilians. Let's move out."

His battalion saluted. Raphael nodded to them, patting Paddy on the back. With that, he and his unit made their way to the secret Sewage Stop that was based in the Renzo grounds. It took ten minutes for them to reach Brentfordshire.

The town, in striking contrast to Central London, was eerie and quiet. The streets were deserted; no lights burned in any of the houses. The hairs on Raphael's neck stood up; he thanked his lucky stars that Skye and her mother were safe at his home and not here in this town, a ghost town by the looks of things.

But where were they? Where were the thugs that had broken into peoples' homes? Where were the civilians? Why was everything so quiet…?

They came to a halt at the very edge of Brentfordshire where rows of houses dwelled in the still of the night; several fireflies whizzed around the nearest lamppost; their glow was the only sign of life among the darkness.

Raphael turned to Paddy.

"I'm going to transform," he told him in a low voice. "Something's not right here. Cover me."

Paddy nodded.

"I've got your back," he said, making a waving hand gesture to the troops to let them know Raphael was about to morph.

Raphael removed the tiny sweet that Doctor Jenson had given him. He looked at it briefly before unwrapping it and popping it in his mouth, swallowing it down. Seconds later, he transformed. As he shed his clothes, as the town and Paddy's watchful face descended into night-vision, he quickly tamed the immediate aggression he felt whenever he morphed, quelling the automatic bloodlust that raced through his veins within the first few seconds of transformation.

That was when he heard it. The faint sound of sobbing coming from the end of the street, the same street that Skye's house lay on.

He swished his tail to the left, a clear sign for Paddy (who was standing directly behind him) to follow him and split the unit. In turn, Paddy gestured to four captains of the Bengal Unit.

"Stake out the town," he told them. "If you come across any trouble, alert us right away."

"Yes, Sir."

Without haste, the captains took their individual companies and the unit split up, staking out different areas of the silent Brentfordshire. The remaining force of one hundred soldiers crept behind Paddy, who followed the tiger in front. Raphael stalked through the night, led by the sobbing noises. His company was poised and tense, unnerved by the silence. Whatever they had expected, it was not this.

The crying sounds led Raphael to a small-detached house, three doors down from Skye's. The front door was wide open, but no lights were on. The cries were coming from inside. His heartbeat quickened beneath his furry chest.

His paws padded noiselessly as he slinked through the door, twisting his large, lithe body into the hallway. Paddy motioned a handful of the company forward, those that were particularly apt in stealth, before he, too, followed Raphael into the house. The majority of soldiers stood outside the door, the sobs now audible to them; they braced themselves, keeping a sharp eye on their surroundings, weapons at the ready.

"Check upstairs," Paddy whispered to several of the group that had followed them in. Nodding, they made their way deftly up the stairs.

The cries grew louder; Raphael's ears pricked up, his hackles standing on end. The sobs were coming from inside one of the rooms on the ground floor—the dining room perhaps? Whichever room it was, there was a flashing blue light coming from inside it, the beams bouncing off the walls and out into the hallway. Every fibre of his being was on edge, ready for action. Slowly, with Paddy on his heels, he turned sideways and entered the room.

It was a dining room, to be sure. Four chairs surrounded a round table, the silhouette of a large bowl of fruit in its centre; and crouched on the floor by the legs of one of the chairs was a little girl, probably no more than nine years old, her face buried in her hands, the cries audible through her palms. Next to her feet was a tag device; bright blue light flashed from it, forming a large, holographic circle in the air. Inside the flashing circle was the face of a teenage boy; his eyes were open, unblinking, his mouth formed into a shocked 'O'; a trickle of blood dripped from his mouth. It was clear that he was dead.

"What the hell is this?" whispered Paddy, disturbed, as Raphael stopped in the doorway.

The girl looked up and saw them, her tear-stained face twisting into an expression of terror as she caught sight of the huge tiger. She began to scream.

Paddy rushed forwards.

"It's OK," he said quickly, kneeling by the screaming child; she backed away from him, her eyes still fixated on the tiger, her terrified shrieks shattering throughout the entire house. From behind Raphael, half of his company appeared, their eyes widening when they caught sight of the girl and holograph in the air.

"It's OK," Paddy repeated soothingly, holding his hands up in front of the girl to show her he meant no harm. "Don't be scared, OK? He's a Morpher. Do you know what a Morpher is?"

The girl, almost choking on her simultaneous sobs and screams, managed a petrified nod, her wide blue eyes popping alarmingly. Paddy reached out a hand to comfort her.

"He's not going to hurt you. He's a good tiger. He wants to help you. We all want to help you. But you have to calm down, OK?"

Raphael debated with himself whether he should transform there and then in order to help put the girl at ease. But her screams subsided as Paddy continued talking to her in that soothing tone, her whole body trembling with fright, her face crumpling as tears continued to slide down her cheeks.

"That's better, that's better," said Paddy. He looked at Raphael who now sat on his hind legs, staring at them with his blazing orange eyes. Paddy turned back to the shaking girl, careful to keep his voice gentle and calm.

"Can you tell us what happened to you?"

The girl's teeth chattered uncontrollably.

"B-b-bad people," she sobbed. "B-bad people came."

"To your house?"

She nodded.

"What did they do?"

The girl shook her head, her cries amplifying.

"Please," said Paddy quietly, gently squeezing the girl's shoulder and looking at her with pleading eyes. "You must tell us what happened. We can only help you if you tell us. What did the bad people do?"

"Th-they took Mummy, Daddy and George. George!"

She pointed to the blinking holograph of the dead teenager, weeping uncontrollably.

Paddy swallowed hard.

"That's George? George is your...brother?"

"Yes. They took him...and Mummy and Daddy. George is...he's dead, isn't he? They killed him!"

Raphael watched this from the doorway, his stomach lurching as the little girl burst into a fresh wave of sobs. Paddy tried to console her.

"What is your name?" he asked the girl.

"M-Martha."

"OK, Martha. Where did they take your family? Can you tell us that?"

There was a sudden commotion from outside; a yell in the distance; the sound of smashing glass; the holograph of the dead boy abruptly disappeared. The platoon that had accompanied them into the house wheeled round, before rushing outside. Moments later, one of Raphael's captains burst through the hallway.

"Sir!" he gasped, addressing the tiger, while Paddy stood protectively in front of the crying child. "Captain Elmsvine has reported several almost empty homes with the exception of one family member in each house, usually a child. Captain Flare reported the same during her investigations. She has also informed us that several hundred thugs have appeared at the town's borders to the west and are about to attack!"

Raphael bared his teeth. This was the formal order to counter-attack. The captain saluted before sprinting from the house. The little girl's wails had abruptly ceased; now she appeared to be frozen with terror.

Seconds later, there was the sound of more glass smashing. Then, footsteps thudding throughout the house—but they were not the footsteps of Renzo soldiers.

"Where's that little brat, then?" came the loud, harsh voice of a man from somewhere in the hallway.

"Please," came a woman's crying voice, also from the hallway. "Please, please don't hurt my children!"

"Shut up," rasped another woman, followed by the sound of

someone being slapped. The cries were replaced by a yell of pain.

The man who had spoken first hooted with laughter.

"She finks we're actually gonna spare her brat!" he snorted. "One of 'em's already dead, ya silly cow! He was caught tryna run away! That's why we're 'ere—we told ya what would 'appen if any of ya tried any funny business!"

At this, the cries of the first woman transformed into ear-splitting screams of anguish.

"My son! My son!"

"I said, shut it! Or I'll kill ya where ya stand! Now—where is that brat?"

Raphael bounded silently behind the table, crouching low, his fiery eyes fixated on the empty, dark doorway, claws at the ready. The little girl, whose mouth had dropped open in shock, her eyes glistening with tears, gasped.

"Mummy!" she cried, leaping to her feet, preparing to run towards the voices.

Paddy quickly grabbed her arm and held her back.

"No, Martha!" he whispered urgently. "You have to stay here. The bad people have come back. If you want to help your mummy, you have to stay here and be very quiet, OK?"

Shaking uncontrollably, Martha nodded. Paddy pulled her into a crouching position by a large glass cabinet before he, too, kneeled down behind it, his hand clutching the rifle in his belt.

"Oi, we ain't gonna be able to clear out the town!" came a new, gruff voice from the hall. "Renzo's troops have shown up!"

"Renzo's blimmin' troops?" came the first man's voice, aghast. "What the 'ell are they doin' 'ere? The battle's over in Central, for

Chrissake! Awright, quick—find the brat 'n get outta 'ere! An' don't just stand there gawping, you twat, go tell the uvvers that the Renzos 'ave arrived!"

"No, please, please! I beg you, leave my daughter alone!"

"I said, SHUT IT!"

Moments later, the silhouettes of five grown men and two women, including one who was crying and wailing uncontrollably, appeared in the doorway of the dining room. A light switch flickered on. The first thing the thugs saw was Martha crouching by a glass cabinet, crying into her hands.

"Martha!" screamed the wailing woman as she caught sight of her daughter.

"There she is!" said one of the thugs triumphantly, the one who was in charge of the others; he was short and bald, his grey teeth full on display as he grinned widely upon seeing the little girl. "Now we just gotta do our fing 'n be on our way."

He pulled a knife from his pocket and turned towards the screaming mother who was being restrained by the other thugs.

"Ready to watch your uvver kid die?" he said to her, stepping further into the room.

"Not today, scum," said Paddy, materializing from behind the cabinet and shielding the girl, his rifle clutched in his fist. A split-second later, the enormous Bengal Tiger leaped out from behind the table, roaring thunderously.

The thugs yelled and scattered. The short, bald one dropped his knife to the floor in terror as the tiger hurdled towards him, fangs flashing.

"What the f—ARRRRGHHH!" he bellowed in agony as the

beast's jaws sank deep into his leg.

He dropped to the floor as Raphael released him, still screaming shrilly, blood appearing through his trousers.

"YOOOOWWWWW!" he screeched; the tiger turned on the others, blood staining his sharp teeth.

"It's that Morpher! KILL IT!" screamed the wounded thug.

The female thug, who had bright red hair and a massive snarl on her face, managed to whip out a pistol from her pocket. Paddy, still shielding the girl, watched in horror as she aimed it at the tiger that was about to pounce again.

"Raphael, LOOK OUT!" Paddy shouted, turning his rifle on the female thug and pulling the trigger.

Two bullets shot through the air simultaneously. One hit the red-haired thug right in the back; she dropped like a stone to the floor. The other bullet fired directly towards Raphael's orange and black chest—miraculously, it ricocheted right off him and instead smashed into the glass cabinet; antiques fell out, crashing to the ground. Paddy threw his body over the girl, who was screaming with terror; his mouth dropped open when he saw Raphael was unharmed. Doctor Jenson's Bestia Exalter was phenomenal; it had completely repelled the bullet.

But the tiger did not stop to fathom the gunshot that may have otherwise killed him. The remaining thugs who were still yelling deafeningly were scrabbling over one another to escape the room. They made no more attempts to try and attack Raphael.

Amidst one final roar, the gang of thugs fled, abandoning their bleeding leader. The chaos in the room disappeared abruptly as it had appeared. Raphael continued pacing up and down as adrenaline rushed through him, snarling wildly; Paddy pulled himself off the crying Martha; the thug with the bleeding leg was trying in vain to reach the door; his attempts were futile and he continued to just lie there, moaning and groaning. The red-haired thug lay silently on the ground in a pool of blood; she was dead.

The girl's mother, who had thrown herself to the floor during the brief skirmish, raised her head, momentarily speechless and trembling violently. When she saw her daughter, she began screaming again.

"MARTHA!"

"MUMMY!"

Running towards each other, the woman threw her arms around the little girl and the two started sobbing uncontrollably. Outside, yells and shouts could be heard. It sounded like the Bengal Unit was fighting the thugs that had appeared at the border.

"Madam," said Paddy, acting fast and walking towards the pair, stepping over the bald thug who was swearing blindly. "My name is Paddy and I am a member of Lord Renzo's army. This is our captain, Raphael—"

He pointed towards the tiger that was still pacing up and down angrily. The woman eyed the feline, terrified, pulling her daughter closer.

"He is Lord Renzo's son," Paddy continued. "He is a Morpher and we're here to help you."

The woman's expression relaxed somewhat, despite her shaking.

"Oi, I'm flippin' bleedin' to death over 'ere!" shouted the thug, holding onto his leg in agony.

"Madam, we need you to tell us what happened here tonight," said Paddy, ignoring the thug; Raphael stopped pacing and came to a standstill, his orange eyes fixed on the mother.

"They came while we were sleeping," the mother whispered, stroking her daughter's hair. "A group of them…they took my husband and son away…they said if we didn't come, they would kill our children."

"Don't you say anuvver word, you old cow!" spat the bald thug.

Paddy rounded on him.

"Shut up," he snapped, while Raphael growled warningly at the thug "or else I swear I'll pop a bullet in your other leg. Please go on, Madam," he said, turning back to the terrified woman.

The woman shakily complied.

"They forced me, my husband and son out of the house. Then they separated us. Groups of them were doing the same thing to our neighbours. I was taken to a building on the other side of town. I—I was put in a room with other people, but I couldn't see anything, it was too dark…"

"Where did they take your husband and son?"

"They didn't tell me. My—my son…"

The woman's face became overwrought with fear.

"He said my son was dead!" she burst out, her eyes welling up with tears. "Please—tell me it's not true!"

Both Raphael and Paddy remembered the lifeless face of the boy in the holograph; a sinking feeling consumed them. The little girl tugged on her mother's coat.

"Mummy," she whispered, her tears flowing steadily. "I saw him, Mummy. He's dead. George is dead."

The mother gripped her chest, unable to breathe.

"No," she moaned. "No…Oh, my George…"

Paddy bowed his head. Raphael diverted his eyes, struggling to suppress the killer instincts that were surging through him; the overwhelming itch to rip the throat out of that thug on the ground, of every thug out there, to punish them for what they had done, for separating a mother from her son…it was almost too powerful to contain…

As the mother's heart-wrenching wails and weeping resounded throughout the night, a soldier of the Bengal Unit appeared in the doorway.

"Sir," he said, addressing Raphael, unable to contain the surprise in his eyes as he surveyed the crying woman and child, the bleeding, scowling thug on the ground and the dead redhead. "We've succeeded in running the thugs out of town—most of them fled when they saw us. Captain Flare also reported a warehouse on the north side of Brentfordshire that was filled with people—OAP's mostly. They seem to be in bad shape, Sir. What shall we do now?"

In response, Raphael bounded forwards; the soldier jumped to the side as the tiger leapt out of the dining room and disappeared. Moments later, Raphael returned in his human form, a blue shawl he had found hanging from the banister wrapped round his groin.

He immediately approached the crying mother and her daughter.

"Madam…" he said softly, laying a gentle hand on her shaking shoulder.

"My son…my son…"

Raphael turned to the soldier in the doorway, who was still

plainly wondering what on earth had happened.

"I want a squad to take this lady and her daughter back to our home," he ordered. "Make sure they are safe and fed. Give them a place to sleep. Madam, I'm sorry," he turned back to the sobbing woman, who seemed oblivious to him. "I have to ask you both to leave for a while. It isn't safe for you here."

"George…oh, George…"

Raphael knelt down, his green eyes finding the watery pupils of the little girl. He brushed a tender hand against her wet cheek, wiping her tears.

"You've been very brave," he told her quietly. "Can you be braver for just a little longer? My soldiers are going to take you and your mother to my house—it's a very safe place and you'll be OK there. No more bad people. Can you do that? Can you go with them?"

Sniffling and staring at him with her wide eyes, Martha nodded.

Raphael gave her a small smile.

"Good girl."

He turned back to the soldier.

"Assemble the squad. Then report back to me immediately."

The soldier saluted and rushed off.

Paddy hurried towards Raphael, an expression of grave concern on his face.

"Raphael, something's not right," he said in a low voice. "Why did the thugs round up civilians and take them away? And why did they run away just now without putting up a fight? This makes no sense."

"I know," Raphael muttered back. "I know, it makes no—"

And then, a thought occurred to him, one that was so horrifying that he could hardly bear to acknowledge it.

Ninety thousand thugs had marched into Central London, his father had said. At least thirty thousand more than what they had expected.

Where had the extra numbers come from?

"Oh my God," he whispered, praying beyond all hope that he was wrong.

Paddy eyed him quizzically; the soldier returned at that moment with a squad of eight Bengal Unit soldiers. Raphael motioned for them to escort Martha and her mother away; the mother had taken hold of a picture frame that been sitting on the mantelpiece, one with a smiling, blonde-haired boy waving his hands high in the photo. She clutched it to her chest, her sobs reverberating throughout the house. The squad gently urged her and her daughter out of the room.

Only the soldier who had been ordered to report back to him stayed behind. Raphael watched them go unblinkingly, his entire body stiff. When they were out of sight and the mother's wails became a mere echo in the distance, he turned to face the bleeding thug on the ground. A look of murder appeared in his eyes, a look that also masked the fear that was swiftly expanding inside him.

He descended upon the writhing thug and grabbed him by the scruff of his collar.

"Start talking," he snarled.

"'Bout what?" scowled the thug, his hands drenched in his own blood. "If you're gonna kill me then whatchoo waitin' for? You've already dun my leg in, you prick!"

"I'm not going to kill you, filth," Raphael breathed

threateningly, teeth baring. "Not yet, anyway. Not until you tell me what I need to know."

"I ain't tellin' ya nuffin, pretty boy, more than me 'ead's worth—"

With that, Raphael slammed his hand down onto the open wound where his fangs had left their mark. The thug howled in agony.

"What was that?" hissed Raphael.

"Awright, awright! What the 'ell you wanna know?"

"I want to know why you were rounding up civilians. I want to know why you and your lowlifes threw people into the warehouse."

"Yeah, well, that ain't info I can give ya, we was ordered not to—"

The hand smashed down once again.

"YOWWWWW! Awright, ya son of a bitch, awright! We was told to get people from their 'ouses 'n stick 'em in Lord Pearson's army! We 'adta give 'em weapons 'n make it look like they was fightin' wiv us! 'E told us to put anyone who couldn't fight in the ware'ouse and to leave one kid behind—'coz if any of 'em tried to escape, we 'adta kill their kid!"

Raphael had frozen, his worst fears confirmed. Paddy came up behind him.

"Raphael," he said, his face ashen, "what does this mean?"

Raphael didn't respond. Instead, he leaned in closer to the thug, their noses almost touching.

"You forced civilians to join your campaign," he whispered, his face trembling. "You made them pretend they were fighting for your side. How many of them did you force into battle?"

"I dunno, maybe 'undreds? Fousands? I dun' bloomin' know, we was just told snatch people all over London 'n make 'em join in!"

"Why? Why did Pearson order you to do that?"

"I dun' bloody know, do I? We was just told to do it, innit!"

Raphael spun round and snatched Paddy's rifle from his hands. The next second, the butt of the gun was pressing right between the thug's eyes.

"Tell me why," he said evenly, "or I'll blast your brains out."

Beads of sweat developed on the thug's forehead.

"I toldja," he said in a panic, "I dunno! We weren't told why, we was just told to do it, it ain't like I was gonna ask!"

"You've got three seconds," breathed Raphael, his finger on the trigger. "One…two…"

"I swear, I dunno!" shouted the thug, perspiring heavily. "I dunno, for Chrissake, I dunno! You gonna shoot me for sumfin' I dun' even know 'bout, ya Morphin' bastard!"

Raphael was silent, his tantalizing green eyes burning into the thug's sweaty face. Then he pulled the rifle away and punched him hard in the jaw.

A tooth cracked; the thug went sliding to the floor, knocked out. Raphael stood up, breathing heavily.

"You'll live because I don't want the woman whose son you murdered having to deal with your corpse in her house," he said in a quiet voice to the unconscious man.

"Raph," said Paddy urgently, as Raphael handed the rifle back to its owner, "if what he said is true then some of those people fighting for Pearson out there are innocents…they're probably being killed by our forces as we speak!"

"We've been fooled," Raphael muttered. "Every one of us. That's why they suddenly expanded in number. They hadn't recruited more thugs at all…they forced civilians to jump into the fight and pretend they were thugs themselves!"

All of a sudden, nothing made sense. What was the purpose of it? Purely to make the Renzos feel bad afterwards when they realized they were killing innocents as well as thugs? This wouldn't help Pearson win the war. His army would still lose, especially if it was filled with civilians. It was an illogical, incomprehensible move.

How many of Pearson's army were actually civilians? How many were being killed in the fray? Trey and the others would only see people armed with weapons; with only the fiery flames to light their way, how would they distinguish the thugs from innocents, when even under normal circumstances it was near impossible to tell the difference between the two?

Another thought occurred to Raphael. His father's order: attack, but don't kill. A strange order, one that had made no sense when it was given…

Had Lord Renzo suspected something was amiss? Is that why he told them to spare life where possible? His father's compassion stretched far and wide, but it was laughable to think he would spare the thugs at the expense of sacrificing his own soldiers and innocents in the city. Raphael now saw what he had not seen before—that for his father to issue this command, there had to be very good reason for it.

If Lord Pearson's aim was not to win this battle, then what was it? If his goal was to send his thugs, plus civilians, into war, knowing full well there was no way he could win, then what was the driving force behind his actions?

The churning cogs in his brain began to work furiously.

"They told the civilians they would murder their children if they didn't obey," he muttered, more to himself than Paddy. "That's why Captain Flare reported lone children in the affected homes, they were to be killed if their families tried to escape the fighting...like Martha. People they thought were too fragile or too old to fight...the mothers and OAPs...were bundled into the warehouse...This must have happened in towns and districts all over the city...The thugs who appeared west of the border just now...They hadn't come to fight...They'd come to steal more citizens...That's why they fled when they saw us..."

Raphael knew there was no more time to think about this. He had to act quickly.

He turned to the soldier who was still standing in the doorway, watching in bemusement.

"Tell Captain Flare and her company to ensure the safety of those who were trapped in the warehouse," he told him. "Meanwhile, Captain Elmsvine is to protect the children left in the houses. Tell both of them to them to gather as much information as possible about the thugs' earlier antics. I want the Bengal Unit to surround the town and form a garrison. Make sure no one else tries to enter Brentfordshire. Also, send a squad to clean up the mess in this room—and keep an eye on that scum when he wakes up."

"Yes, Sir."

The soldier saluted and dashed from the house.

"What do we do now?" asked Paddy, stashing his rifle in his

side-holder.

Raphael surveyed the thugs on the ground, one dead, and the other unconscious.

"Now," he replied grimly, "I'm going to Central. There's no time to lose. Paddy, stay here—you're in charge."

"Wait, Raphael, let me come with you—"

"No, you're needed here. And I'll be faster on my own. Have you got my spare armour?"

"Yes, it's with Captain Panopio."

"Good. I'll take it with me. Look after everyone, I'll send word as soon as I reach General Jackson. Have your tag device at the ready."

Paddy nodded, unable to hide the concern in his eyes.

"Be careful, Raph."

"You, too."

With one last nod to his friend, Raphael sprinted from the room, tearing through the corridor and landing outside beneath the burning night skies.

CHAPTER TEN

The bodies mounted; the death toll continued to rise. Despite Lord Renzo's instructions not to kill, this was not adhered to by everybody. While he had the power to command everyone in his own army, he had no say over the Chinese forces—and Emperor Jin had made it very clear to his soldiers that the thugs must be eliminated. Emperor Jin's army fought with a blood lust matched only by the brutes they sought to vanquish. Many of the Emperor's warriors—like Lord Renzo's—wore steel armour; but they had not counted on the sheer savagery of the thugs whose bloodthirsty natures drove them towards committing some very brutal and violent attacks on the Emperor's forces, attacks that not even an armour made of steel could deter.

Thug after thug fell down; Emperor Jin's soldiers fell; General Jackson's fighters fell.

And so did the innocents caught in the crossfire, their presence unknown to all, except those who had put them there.

But this ignorance was not to last. General Jackson and Kai, who were currently engaging in battle on the west side of Picadilly Circus while the Emperor's forces were fighting in the east, were doing their best to contain the overwhelming legions of thugs that seemed to be multiplying by the second.

"We'd do better if we could kill the brutes!" roared General Jackson as his troops, who were outnumbered, repelled the thugs repeatedly with their vast array of weapons, sometimes knocking them out, other times slicing off an arm or hand, but avoiding instant death where possible. The thugs were no match against the General's forces when it came to hand-to-hand combat; it was the sheer volume of them that posed as the greatest threat.

"Lord Renzo has ordered we do not aim to kill!" Kai shouted back, as his own regiment shot countless arrows towards a thousand thugs who were charging towards them. "We must obey him, General!"

This was not to the General's liking. Not to his liking at all. He had already lost almost an entire battalion due to one maniacal thug who threw a bomb their way. The shields that belonged to his forces also had an in-built Exploder Detector (something that could sense the presence of a bomb from fifty feet away and cause the shield to flash blue to warn its bearer) but his battalion was caught in a crush of around a thousand thugs and they were unable to escape the blast. General Jackson could only watch helplessly as his regiment was blasted to bits. A fury streaked through him, one that made him want to personally murder every damned thug in the vicinity. But he was too great and disciplined a general to lose his composure and was instead left firing orders, wondering ever the more bemusedly why Lord Renzo had issued this absurd command.

The reason was revealed to him at about five o'clock in the morning, two hours after the battle began. The thugs were still going strong, coming at them like a colony of determined hornets, refusing to relinquish. General Jackson himself had just disposed of several; though he and his forces were doing their best to spare life, in battle this was an inevitable impossibility. For the first time in his long military career, General Jackson experienced an unknown phenomena. Which direction could the battle possibly go in if they were ordered to spare thugs' lives, while the thugs' only mission was to destroy each and every one of them?

It was the sudden, unexpected appearance of Lord Renzo's youngest son, Raphael, which caused the General to momentarily come to a standstill. Even in the dark and by the light of the flames, Raphael was recognizable from a mile away. He wore steel armour and was making his way towards the battleground, a long staff swinging in his hands.

Cutting his way through the crowds of thugs with ease (his sword-fighting skills were second to none) the General hurried out to meet him. Raphael came to a halt outside a burning flower shop.

"General Jackson!"

The General's hawkish, glaring eyes observed the youngest Renzo.

"Raphael, what are you doing here? Your father gave orders for you to stay in the suburbs!"

"General, believe me, I wouldn't have come unless I had to. I tried contacting you by tag device, but there was no reply—"

"No reply? Of course there was no reply! We're up to our neck in brutes, man!"

"It's the battle, General—it has to stop!"

"Stop? You came here all this way just to tell me that? What do you think we're trying to do? They've already taken out a battalion of mine—it would be a lot easier if we could just kill the blighters—"

"No, it has to stop because some of those thugs you're fighting are actually civilians in disguise! Pearson forced them to pretend they were part of his army!"

Raphael's urgent words hit General Jackson like a ton of bricks.

"Civilians?" he repeated blankly.

"Yes! Something has to be done—we don't know how many people out there are actually innocents!!"

For a brief moment, General Jackson didn't move or say anything, which was in stark contrast to the furious battling and fiery flames all around. Then he sprang into action.

"Dammit!" he roared.

"General Jackson, what has happened?"

It was Kai. He looked sweaty and was panting heavily; a deep graze ran down his face where a dagger had slashed him.

"Innocents!" thundered the General. "Those bastards have forced innocents into their ranks!"

Kai's eyes widened and for a moment he was stunned into silence.

"How do you know this?"

Raphael turned to face the Emperor's nephew.

"We cornered a gang of thugs in Brentfordshire. They told us they'd threatened civilians and ordered them to join Pearson's army."

"How many did they threaten?"

"He couldn't tell me. But we must do something—now!"

Seven thugs charged at them just then. General Jackson,

Raphael and Kai immediately prepared for the fight; Raphael swung round with all the agility of his tiger spirit and avoided the dagger that came flying at him; he whipped his staff high above the thug and smacked it round his head, the thug dropping wordlessly to the ground. General Jackson knocked a rifle out of another thug's hand with his sword, piercing him through the shoulder. Kai swiftly dodged two other thugs who held machetes; he aimed a series of kicks and punches at them; seconds later, both were sprawled on the concrete.

The others were swiftly dealt with. Kai turned back to Raphael, breathing heavily.

"Is Lord Renzo aware of this?" he asked him.

Raphael nodded.

"I was able to contact him just after I left Brentfordshire, but I ran into a gang of thugs and was forced to cut the call short and transform. I lost my tag device during the fight and there was no time to search for it, but I communicated with him via the Survival Pact and told him I was on my way to see you."

Kai was silent for a moment. Then he said:

"I must warn Trey. I will be back shortly."

With that, he darted back into the midst of battle.

Raphael turned to General Jackson whose taut face looked like waxwork among the light of the blazing fire.

"General, we must contact my father again and—"

As he said this, a loud buzzing noise emitted from the General's pocket.

General Jackson delved his hand into the pocket and pulled out his tag device. There were eight missed calls displaying on the screen. Lord Renzo's name flashed before their eyes.

The General pulled Raphael behind the burning flower shop and immediately pressed the 'Accept' button.

"Sir!" he bellowed as Lord Renzo's face appeared in holographic form; the expression on Raphael's father's face was unreadable, but there was a fiery look in his eyes that reflected the bursting flames all around.

"Pearson swelled his ranks with civilians!" General Jackson continued shouting. "Only God knows how many of them were forced into battle!"

Lord Renzo's sharp blue-green eyes darted between the General and Raphael.

"General Jackson, order all your forces to retreat," he said, his voice calm yet firm. "Tell Trey and Kai to withdraw. I have informed Emperor Jin of the situation and we have sent word to his army instructing them to do the same. Raphael, I am glad to see you are safe. Go with General Jackson."

"Lord Renzo, we should issue an announcement over the reverberator to let the thugs know we are aware of their actions!" said General Jackson immediately. "That would expose the scum for what they've done and then the innocents will know we're onto them!"

But Lord Renzo shook his head.

"No. It is too risky. If Pearson discovers we are aware of his plans, it may prompt him into ordering a mass slaughter of civilians. Withdraw your forces and return to Notting Hill."

"But they will only follow us, Sir!" objected General Jackson frustratedly.

"Those are my orders, General. I trust you to do as I command."

With no other choice but to obey, the embittered General nodded his compliance and thrust the tag device into Raphael's hand; then he pulled a silver horn from his side and charged back towards his corps.

He blew the horn three times; the sound echoed across the sky, drowning out the yelling and clashing.

"RETREAT!" bellowed General Jackson, his leathery face glowing amongst the flames. "RETREAT! BACK TO THE STRONGHOLD! ALL RENZO FORCES—RETREAT!"

"Dad," Raphael said, panicking, turning back to his father's holographic face as their soldiers, after a split-second of confusion at this command, turned to flee. "What are we going to do? Even if the battle continues in Notting Hill, there's no way we can tell the difference between the thugs and civilians! People up and down the city are trapped in warehouses—Pearson can order their murders any time he chooses!"

"Raphael, we must not tell anyone that Lord Pearson has sent innocents into battle," said Lord Renzo, his voice urgent. "Those few of us who know must keep it quiet."

"But why?"

"Lord Pearson has laid this trap for us for a reason—whether it was purely for his own enjoyment or for something more, I do not yet know. But, as I told General Jackson, if he discovers we are aware of his plans, he may order the deaths of the hidden civilians. We need time to find them, and the space to look for them—bringing the battle closer to Notting Hill gives us freedom to search the rest of the city undetected. Rescuing the imprisoned civilians and children left behind will hopefully grant those caught in the battle the chance to escape, for there will no longer be the threat of losing loved ones. Then, once at Notting Hill, we can encircle Pearson's thugs and demand they let the innocents go. We can grant the civilians safe passage out of the battle by assuring them of our support and letting them know their loved ones are safe."

"A lot of things could go wrong…" replied Raphael, a horrible feeling settling through him after he listened to his father's plan, unable to stop himself thinking of all the disastrous things that could go awry.

"It is the best chance we have, Raphael. We must try."

Raphael swallowed.

"You're right," he said. "You're right. OK. How shall I—?"

Just then, something happened to turn the tide of the entire battle. Something no one had foreseen.

At first, it sounded like thunder rumbling in the distance. Raphael's first thought was that the storm had returned. But it soon became apparent that the rumbling sounds were actually the beat of drums. Banging, vibrating thumps that echoed across the city as though a hundred drums were playing in unison. The noise was deafening and grew louder with each passing moment.

"What is that?" shouting Raphael, his eyes scanning beyond the battleground.

Lord Renzo's forces momentarily stopped fleeing; Lord Pearson's thugs froze in the act of pursuing them, their heads swivelling simultaneously to the east.

"It is the Pearson signal," murmured Lord Renzo, his holographic brow furrowing. "The signal to retreat."

Raphael could not hear him amidst the ear-piercing drumbeats, but it didn't matter. Seconds later, he witnessed legions of thugs do a complete U-turn and bolt across Picadilly, back towards Stratford, East London, like a herd of wildebeest pursued by lions.

"MOVE IT!" one thug could be heard yelling above the stampede. "RUN, YOU CLOWNS! BACK TO STRATTY!"

What the hell is going on? Raphael thought, mystified, as thug after thug charged past.

Why were they retreating?

Elsewhere, a roaring cheer erupted. It was Emperor Jin's forces who, still blindingly unaware of the masses of innocents caught in the skirmish, were waving their weapons around in victory as they witnessed the enemy fleeing.

Amidst the chaos, Raphael noticed that some of the thugs were not running to the East; they were scattering in all directions, some to the North, some to the West, some to the South. Others flung themselves behind trees or close to ditches. A third, maybe more, of the entire thug army were running in haphazard directions. Raphael was convinced beyond the shadow of a doubt that these were the civilians who had been forced into battle.

"They're running away!" came the distinctive bellow of General Jackson who came charging towards them, bashing his way through the escaping thugs. "I've ordered the troops to stand guard. Why did the bastards run? And where are the civilians?"

"Raphael," came the sharp voice of his father as the drums continued to bang, "return to Brentfordshire and round up your unit. I want you to scope the surrounding towns. Should you find any similar situations to what you found in Brentfordshire, release any innocents who are trapped and escort them back to their homes. General Jackson, the civilians caught in battle have fled; it is likely they are scattered all over the city. Find them. I will send word to Trey and Kai to assist Raphael by scoping other districts. Emperor Jin's forces must return to the stronghold and stay on guard. Is this clear?"

General Jackson rushed off immediately to inform his regiments. Raphael nodded silently, still unable to comprehend what had just happened.

"Return home as soon as you are finished, my son," said Lord Renzo quietly. "Take the greatest care."

His holographic face disappeared. Raphael was left standing behind the burning flower shop, squeezing General Jackson's tag device in his palm. Piccadilly Circus was suddenly a lot emptier than it had been moments before, except for the bodies that lay dispersed on the ground, thugs, soldiers and civilians alike…almost all of Lord Pearson's army and the civilians who survived had disappeared. Further away, the Emperor's forces continued cheering; Lord Renzo's army stood silently in the distance as the distinguishable figure of General Jackson could be seen giving them orders. All around the heart of the city, flames and smoke continued to dominate. Seeing this for what it was, Raphael felt sick; devastation gripped him. There was so much death, blood and fire. Blood had spilled that should never have been there in the first place…and why?

Why had Pearson forced innocents into battle?

Why had he wasted his own thugs and ammunition on a battle

he could have never won?

Why had he ordered their retreat just as it seemed an unexpected victory was his?

Why? Why? Why?

He had expected it to be straightforward. He had felt confident that the combined forces of their own army and the Emperor's would get rid of Pearson's thugs, once and for all.

But it had been anything but straightforward…and now they were thrown into total confusion and disarray.

"Raphael!"

It was Trey. Behind him was Kai. They were sprinting towards him. Raphael noted the nasty scar on his brother's face, and his left hand was a bloodied, mangled mess.

"Are you alright?" asked Trey, as he came to a standstill. "I heard about what happened in Brentfordshire…Civilians, Raphael. Civilians."

He coughed as the smoke continued wafting around them.

"I couldn't believe it when I heard…Of course, we haven't told the troops. It would be terrible for morale if they found out—and the more people who know, the more dangerous it is for the civilians who were captured by thugs. I'm sure Dad's already told you, but if Pearson's holding innocents such as the ones you found in the warehouse hostage, he might order their execution at any time if he finds out we know what he did."

"Yes, that crossed my mind," nodded Raphael.

"Killing innocents…there were things I saw during the battle, things that didn't seem right. But I never would have guessed…"

A fraught look crossed Trey's face.

"Thank God that Dad ordered us to spare life where possible. He must have suspected something. Otherwise…"

He shook his head. Kai nodded, frowning hard.

"Who else knows, Raphael?" asked the Emperor's nephew.

"My unit—they were there when we found out what happened. General Jackson, of course…I'm not sure who else. Is the Emperor aware?"

"Dad would have told him, but I don't think his troops know," said Trey. "General Jackson won't yet tell his soldiers the innocents were forced into battle; he will just tell them they need to find civilians scattered all over the city. We need to keep this information under wraps for as long as we can. Only once we've searched the city and freed the innocents can we reveal what happened."

They stared round at one another; the prospect of telling their soldiers, who had risked their lives to defend civilians, that they had in fact been tricked into fighting the very people they had sworn to protect was not a welcome one.

"Why did the thugs retreat?" questioned Raphael quietly.

"Your guess is as good as mine," replied Trey. "It doesn't make sense—not when they saw we were fleeing ourselves. But we can't waste any more time deducing their actions. Raphael, our combined units should be able to cover the districts in London—if we work quickly, we should be able to stake out the city within the next couple of hours and help the towns and villages that were targetted."

Raphael nodded.

"I understand. I'll return to Brentfordshire."

Removing his steel armour, Raphael's transformation into a tiger was instant. Seconds later, the leftover panic and morbidity that remained in the vicinity hit his hypersensitive senses and he struggled briefly to control his animal mind.

"I'll take care of this," said the now black and white frame of Trey, reaching towards the armour. "Be careful, Raphael."

"Send word once you reach Brentfordshire," said Kai.

Raphael shot them one last look, his eyes fleetingly scanning the burning scenery behind them. Then he bounded away, his sharp hearing just catching the mournful wails of someone on the battlefield who had just discovered the fallen body of their friend.

*

The pounding drums in the distance woke Skye from sleep.

Across the lounge, candle flames flickered gently. Her body was curled on the couch, her head resting on her mother's shoulder. Mrs. Archer was sleeping in a seated position, a pillow propped up behind her neck. On the other end of the couch, Daphne and Ricardo had fallen asleep in each other's arms. Joey was nowhere to be seen. Two other sleeping guests occupied the sofa on the opposite side of the room.

How long had she been asleep? She could not even remember dozing off. She and her mother had been talking about the nightmarish situation they were currently in…

She swallowed; her heart felt like it had dropped to the bottom of her stomach.

The battle. Raphael.

She stood up, careful not to wake her mother. The curtains were drawn, but the blazing glow in the sky was still distinguishable through the silken fabric. What time was it? And that strange, pounding noise from outside…it chilled her with a portentous dread, which she could not understand. She had to find out what was happening.

Silently, she crept across the lounge and towards the door. Opening it, she was greeted with the illuminated corridor; as opposed to earlier, the hallway was now empty and quiet.

Tip-toeing her way down the corridor, the hairs on her neck rising instinctively due to the eerie silence, she turned the corner in the direction of the war room. Skye had never actually been inside Rachelle before, but she knew it was the place that Raphael, Lord Renzo and the others congregated when they needed to discuss war matters.

Would anyone be there? There was only one way to find out.

She came to a stop outside Rachelle, knocking three times.

"Come in," called a voice.

It was Lord Renzo who had answered. Skye slowly opened the door and took in her surroundings. She noted the round table in the centre where meetings were undoubtedly held. The room flickered with white silk-flame lamps, casting an ethereal, almost heavenly glow around the place. Paintings adorned the walls; the statue of a fierce-looking woman stood proudly in the corner. Two guards, which Skye at first mistook for statues themselves, stood erect by the doors; they didn't even react when she entered the room.

And Lord Renzo himself stood next to a small rectangle desk; white sheets of papers were spread across the top, and a strange-looking orb which glowed a faint purple colour resided in the middle.

He looked up when he saw her.

"Skye," he said cordially, his face looking rather worn beneath the white flickering.

"Lord Renzo," she croaked back.

She coughed several times; her throat was extremely dry.

"Sorry," she rasped.

Lord Renzo gestured to a chair by the desk.

"Please, take a seat. Can I get you a glass of water?"

"No...thank you, I'm fine."

"You are feeling better now?" he asked her as she sat down.

"Y-yes, thanks...Lord Renzo, I'm sorry for earlier, for going off on my own..."

Lord Renzo shook his head and placed a gentle hand on her shoulder.

"Do not be sorry. Your safety is all that matters."

Skye watched him as he returned to the front of his desk, observing the purple orb closely. The question was burning inside her.

"Lord Renzo—the battle," she blurted out. "What's happening? Where is Raphael?"

"The battle is over. Lord Pearson's army fled back to the east. Raphael and the others are currently administering the safety of civilians throughout the city."

"You mean...we won?" Skye stared at him in awe, unable to prevent the joyous bubble that began swelling inside her.

But it quickly deflated when she saw the look on Lord Renzo's face.

"I'm afraid," he said heavily, turning to face her, "that it is far more complex than that."

His words sent chills up her spine. What exactly had happened? Now that she thought about it…if they had won, where were the returning victors? Where were the cheers? Where was the good news that should have woken everyone in the Renzo household so they might celebrate the victory in unison?

There was none of that. There was only a noiseless mansion and a leader whose disquieted silence was the only betrayal of the unknown forces at work.

"Lord Renzo," Skye said tentatively, "what do you mean?"

"Tonight, Lord Pearson sent out almost ninety thousand thugs to wage war against us. But not all of them belonged to him. Half of those people he sent into battle were, in fact, civilians."

Skye stared at him in shock.

"What?" she whispered.

Her mind was reeling. She couldn't understand it. Civilians?

"How? I don't understand…"

"A few hours before the battle, Lord Pearson sent groups of thugs into various districts in the city. There, they threatened every able-bodied adult and teenager, forcing them to participate. They left one family member—usually a child—behind, with the threat that if they refused to take part in the battle or were caught trying to run away, those left behind would be killed. Other members of the families, mostly mothers and OAPs, were thrown into abandoned buildings to add greater weight to this threat. As a result, thousands of innocent people were forced to arm themselves with weapons and march into Central London…many of them marching to their deaths."

His eyes gleamed orange beneath the light of the lamps, his aged body stiff amidst the white flickering. Skye couldn't speak. The impact of this revelation had rendered her speechless.

"I had my suspicions," Lord Renzo continued quietly, peering once again into the purple orb. "Had Lord Pearson truly increased his numbers through successful recruitment? Through aspiring thugs? Or was there something more sinister at work? There was no way I could be certain…and when the enemy rides out to meet you with such swift haste, there is little that can be done but to accept the challenge."

He picked up a glass of water that was lying on the desk and took a sip. It was then that Skye noticed just how old Lord Renzo really looked. Old and weary.

"I ordered our forces to spare life where possible…yes, no doubt at detriment to themselves. How much of my instruction was adhered to, I do not know. As for the Chinese forces, they are not under my command. I hadn't the power, nor time, to debate the issue on something that was based purely on suspicion. Emperor Jin ordered the slaughter of those marching from the east—no mercy, no exceptions."

Silence reigned briefly. Skye felt sick. All those people. Ordinary people. People she saw on the bus every day, those she went to work with, kids she'd been at college with…How many of them had been forced out of their homes in the middle of the night? How many had lost their lives in the bloodshed?

"When Raphael confirmed it to me, I ordered our armies to retreat. We expected the battle to resume here at the stronghold; it would have given us time to free the imprisoned civilians. But then something happened…the thugs retreated."

Skye was confused. What exactly did that mean?

"I don't understand…"

"Lord Pearson had no reason to retreat. We were fleeing. These were untrained thugs fighting trained militia; why wouldn't they take advantage of our temporary surrender? Logically, his army would have shown their exuberance at our defeat or pursued us. Wasn't it victory the Pearsons were after? Well, they did follow us—briefly. But moments after we called for retreat, Lord Pearson did, too. The sound of drums is hard to miss."

Outside, the faint banging of drums was still audible in the distance. So that was what the noises were…

"So you and I are in the same boat, Skye," continued Lord Renzo in that quiet voice. "For I, too, don't understand. I cannot understand why, aside from Lord Pearson's personal sadism, civilians were forced into the fight. I cannot understand why the drums rolled only moments after I ordered the withdrawal. Nor do I understand the reasons for your kidnap and sudden return, which I feel has played a crucial role in the unfolding of tonight's events. I cannot understand these things and it worries me greatly, for time is running out."

Skye didn't know what to say. To see Lord Renzo, who was always so calm and confident, in such uncertainty was almost frightening.

"Come here for a moment, Skye," said Lord Renzo, gesturing towards her as he continued to hover over the purple orb.

Skye obeyed and walked over to him.

"You see this?" he said, tapping the orb softly. "With this

device, I am able to track every member of my army throughout the city; indeed, the whole of the country. The tiny black dots represent our soldiers, including the Emperor's forces."

Skye looked closely. The entire orb was covered in dots that were either one of three colours: black, white and orange. The black ones were mostly clumped in bunches, but scattered in various places around the orb.

"What about the others?"

"The white ones are everyone else. Thugs and civilians alike. There is no way to tell the difference between the two."

Skye watched the black and white dots moving in unison throughout the orb. On the right-hand side were a large number of white dots, no black ones at all; Skye suspected this area represented East London, the Pearson stronghold. On the left were large groups of black dots and also a great deal of scattered, singular white ones. They hopped around at frequent intervals.

The orange ones were fewer, but there were a number of them lumped together in the middle; they were not moving at all.

"What about the orange dots?"

Lord Renzo raised his head.

"They are the dead. I have been using this orb for many years. It is how we managed to find those who fell victim to Lord Pearson's thugs. It was how we managed to send their bodies back to their loved ones. A small gesture in the grand scheme of things—but I'm afraid justice abandoned this city many years ago."

For the first time since Skye had known him, Lord Renzo displayed a strong sense of despair, a melancholy that Skye's powerful wolf senses absorbed considerably. He buried his head in his hands and for a moment the room was quiet. Skye watched him, wanting to say something to comfort him, to let him know that she and everyone else were aware of everything he had done to thwart Lord Pearson's attempts to control the city; she wanted to tell him of their gratitude for the strength and courage he injected into them when they struggled to see beyond the darkness. But she didn't say anything, not knowing how to comfort a man such as Lord Renzo.

Moments later, he removed his hands from his head and turned to her, a faint smile beneath his beard.

"Ah, Skye. Do not let the unhappy musings of an old man trouble you. Where justice once existed, it can yet return. We all have our moments. But I do believe, as I always have done, that in the end good will triumph. It sounds very cliché, doesn't it? And yet I know in my heart for this to be true."

Skye nodded and for a while there was only the ethereal flickering of white light and Lord Renzo occasionally tapping the orb.

"What will happen now?" she asked him finally. "Raphael…"

"Do not worry about Raphael. He is currently investigating towns and villages to ensure the safety of civilians. He, Trey and the others should be back soon. You see these white dots, not moving and strangely clumped together in various parts of the globe? I believe these are the trapped civilians; we are able to transmit this information to Raphael, making it easier for him to find them. General Jackson's troops are searching for those innocents who were forced into the fray. The Emperor's forces will be here any moment. They have been ordered to defend the stronghold in case Lord Pearson launches another attack. But it is unlikely. His thugs, like our troops, will be tired. There will be much to discuss when the others return."

Skye stared at one of the white silk-flame lamps, watching its paper ripple gently through the air. Thank God Raphael was safe.

"Lord Renzo," she began hesitantly.

She didn't want to raise the subject. The memory, fresh as it was, still haunted her and the thought of it made her blood run cold. But she knew it had to be discussed.

"The man in the white coat…the one in the cell." She swallowed. "Raphael told you about him? About what I…showed him in the Memory Transference?"

"Yes, Skye. He told me in very intricate detail what happened to you during your kidnap."

"What did he want with me?" Skye's voice lowered to a whisper.

Lord Renzo paused before making his way over to her.

"I do not know," he said. "I only have my suspicions. The one thing I am certain of is that he wanted you because of your Morphing ability. But I am sure that you, too, are aware of this. I have a strong hunch also that your kidnap tonight ultimately led to the battle that was fought in Picadilly…No, Skye, do not look that way. War was inevitable. It was a question of when, not if."

Skye nodded, though still unable to prevent the guilt and shame that showed clearly on her face.

There was a knock on the door.

"Enter," Lord Renzo called.

A guard strode into the room.

"My Lord, a general of Emperor Jin's army wishes to speak

with you. He is outside."

Lord Renzo nodded.

"Skye, may you excuse me for a moment? I will return shortly."

Picking his walking stick from the corner he followed the guard and walked outside, closing the door behind him.

Skye sat silently on her own for several minutes, absorbing everything Raphael's father had told her in the last half-hour. There was a dangerous air about the whole thing, one that made her feel like each and every one of them was walking on a tightrope—and yet, it was as though they balanced the tightrope in the darkness, unable to even see their destination, which made the danger ever the more potent. So many missing pieces of the puzzle, so much confusion. So many lives at stake, so many people under threat. What would be the outcome? Who could say?

As Skye continued watching the rippling white paper-waves that emanated such a beautiful glow, she thought of Raphael. Of her mother. Of Daphne. Of everyone else she loved and cared about. She thought about how, in that moment, she wished she could just bundle them all together and take them to a land far, far away from here, a place such as this room with its tranquil serenity and radiant lights. Away from danger, away from darkness, away from the risk of losing them—she wished she could keep them safe forever in her own personal heaven where nothing bad ever happened and they could be free to live, love and be at peace.

The statue in the corner of the room caught her eye and she went to take a closer look.

Rachelle Renzo, War Heroine, Services: 1916-1918; 1940-1945. CBE, OBE & Recipient of the Victoria Cross, read the plaque at the foot of the statue.

Skye was not entirely sure what the awards stood for (she would have to ask Daphne about it sometime) but as she looked up at the proud, beautiful bronze face of Raphael's ancestor who had lived three hundred years ago, she wondered about the remarkable deeds this woman must have committed, so much that there was a statue built in her honour and a war room named after her. She knew that the dates represented two major world wars from the past. Skye found herself thinking more and more lately about those who had fought and sometimes died for this country, those who had striven through blood and tears to defend everyone they loved and their homeland. A strange wave of misery rolled through her.

So was this what they died for? A broken society and a nation that had spent the last two centuries forgetting their sacrifice? Skye had never learned about it in school. She wondered why this was. And now, war had hit their already ruined city. Why had their ancestors tried to bury this country's history, so much that the perils of war had almost become a myth? Had they really become so lax during peacetime that they thought war could never again touch them with the same poisonous, deadly fingers which only two hundred years later, had wrapped its grip around the throats of their descendants?

So many millions who died. So many millions who chose to forget.

Skye shook her head, angry with herself, knowing that she was one of the latter; she had never been taught and, therefore, never really cared. But she did now. Now that the horrors of war had touched her.

With one last look at Rachelle's proud, strong face, she turned away and her eye caught sight of a large painting hanging by Lord Renzo's desk. Something about the painting ignited her curiosity and, moments later, as she trudged over to it, she discovered why. It was a painting of a young man, probably in his early thirties. But not just any young man. Her mouth dropped open. She recognized him—and she wondered why a portrait of him was hanging in the war room of the Renzo mansion.

The door creaked open and Lord Renzo re-entered.

"Ah," he said quietly as he approached her, following her gaze. "You know who he is, don't you?"

Skye nodded. She had seen pictures of him before, though not quite so large and grand as this one. He had been younger in the photos she had seen, but it was undoubtedly him. His spiky black hair and sharp features that gave him the look of a Native American rather than his Filipino heritage triggered clear memories in Skye's mind; of a time several months ago when she and her mother had been cleaning out their attic and stumbled across a series of photographs, hidden away in a dusty chest.

"He's my relative," Skye murmured, staring into the face of her ancestor whose distinguishable cool, relaxed expression stared back at her. "The brother of my great-great grandmother...He's my great-great uncle. Why is there a portrait of him in this room?"

A smile appeared beneath Lord Renzo's beard.

"Because he was the first Morpher who dedicated his life to vanquishing the thugs of this city," he replied, his eyes scanning the portrait of the confident-looking man. "It was two centuries ago, during the time that Professor Polgas created his fateful formula, that thugs started to multiply. Those in charge at the time were responsible. Like a parent who refuses to implement boundaries or instill morals in their child, or who allows their child to run all over them without fear of repercussion when they do something wrong, this country exploded with swarms of hooligans, plunderers and terrorisers. Too much freedom given to those who didn't know how to wield it, resulted in imprisonment for those who did; and over the years, it grew progressively worse. The plague that hit in the last century wiped out a great deal of people, but the mind-set remained—culminating in what you see before you today. Your great-great uncle, Ash Fernwright, took it upon himself to use his newfound ability to challenge the very first thugs that were slowly breeding in number. Sadly, he paid the ultimate price for it. But many years later, his heroics were discovered and he has long been revered within these walls as an inspiration to many Morphers and ordinary people, a beacon of courage and strength in the face of adversity."

"Wow," murmured Skye. "I didn't know this…"

"When Raphael told me your ancestor was the first wolf Morpher, Blaise Fernwright, I knew, of course, that her brother, Ash, was also a relation of yours. Both of them had a strong sense of justice and a desire to protect the innocent—their blood runs through your veins, Skye. You must always take comfort from that. The two of them have a small gallery dedicated to them in the Polgas Museum north of here, as does my great-grandfather, Janus Renzo. I am surprised Raphael has not yet taken you to visit. Perhaps when this war is over, and providing it is still standing, you would like to have a look."

He smiled at her again, leaving her to her thoughts as he resumed his position by his desk. Her eyes lingered for several more moments on the face of her great-great uncle. She felt ashamed with herself that she had never bothered to delve into her own history—that she hadn't known the extent of her ancestry. She had not even known that they were part of the museum dedicated to Professor Polgas in the north. Curiosity had extended purely to wondering what her ancestors had been through, before brushing these thoughts away and getting on with daily life. Now, she wished she had taken the time to dig deeper; she vowed that, as soon as the opportunity presented itself (and hoping it did) she would do exactly that.

A feeling of pride swelled through her as she took her seat by the desk again, a welcome emotion amidst the horrors of the day. It was the same pride she felt whenever she thought about her father. Courage and strength in the face of adversity…this was the message of her ancestors. Now, more than ever, she needed this; and by summoning it successfully, she was in good company, judging by those who came before her.

CHAPTER ELEVEN

Three hours later, at approximately eight o' clock in the morning, the war room inside the Renzo household was full to the brim.

The majority of those present were, of course, exhausted. Most had not slept for over twenty-four hours; what's more, several of those hours had been spent fighting. The wounded had been taken to the infirmary and were in the capable hands of Doctor Jenson, while others had been transported to the only hospital in West London, half a mile from Notting Hill. Emergency Switches (buttons located around the city which could summon an ambulance through transportation within seconds) were put to good use, even though a number of them had been vandalized throughout the years by thugs. Meanwhile, the dead bodies were still being identified and taken away; the fallen had not yet been counted, but it would not be long before their numbers were revealed.

Lord Renzo sat at the head of the round table. Butlers bustled around, providing water for everyone. Raphael sat to the left of his father and Trey to the right. Emperor Jin, Kai and General Jackson also sat around the table. Standing were some of the Emperor's generals and a number of Lord Renzo's senior officers, those who had come away from the battle unscathed. Behind Raphael stood Paddy and two of his other captains. There was a great deal of talking inside the chamber; in the corner, a tearful soldier was being consoled by his friend; on the other side of the room, tiredness had kicked in and tempers consequently flared. A heated argument had taken place between one of Trey's archers and one of Emperor Jin's lieutenants. Weapons were actually exhibited, until an angry general from the Emperor's forces intervened and pulled them apart.

"Please everyone, let us settle down," came Lord Renzo's voice above the hubbub. "We do not want to spend too long here. Many of you are tired and it is essential that you rest. There are things that must be discussed, therefore I would appreciate the undivided attention from every person in this room."

Everyone turned to look at him and the room grew gradually quiet.

"Raphael, please start us off," said Lord Renzo, turning to his youngest son. "What happened after Lord Pearson's thugs retreated?"

Raphael stood up.

"We scanned as many towns and villages as we could," he began, staring around at the numerous pairs of eyes that were watching him. "We received the information you transmitted to us about where civilians may have been held; as it turns out, the information was correct on nearly all accounts. We released them, of course, and they all told us the same thing: that thugs had come for them in the night and forced them into abandoned buildings, while other members of their families were ordered to join in the fight. A child was usually left behind in the house. They were all told that if they spoke of it to anyone, they would be killed instantly."

"It was a good thing Raphael heard the child crying," Paddy remarked, "otherwise we may never have known."

"What child is this?" asked Emperor Jin.

"Her name is Martha, Your Highness," Raphael told him. "I heard her crying in a nearby town—we were just in time, it seems. Had we been any later, Pearson's thugs would have killed her. Her brother was caught trying to escape the battle and they killed him for it. They were on their way to murder her also, but my unit got there first. Martha and her mother are currently residing here with us—their only remaining living family member is the father, one of the civilians who scattered after the battle."

He turned to General Jackson, a heavy look entering his handsome features. The room was briefly silent.

"As of yet, it is impossible for us to know how many civilians survived and how many did not," said General Jackson gruffly. "We spent several hours rounding them up; they numbered in their thousands. It is likely the dead amount to just as many."

There was another, deeply uncomfortable silence.

"Are our troops aware of the circumstances surrounding the battle?" questioned Lord Renzo quietly.

General Jackson nodded.

"They have been informed," he replied woodenly.

"As have our forces," said one of the Emperor's generals.

"And ours."

"Mine also."

"Ours too."

Raphael nodded once, his eyes focussing on the white marble floor. No one said a word. It was doubtless that the same thought ran through their minds. Every soldier, archer and warrior in the allied forces now knew that they had been fighting—sometimes killing—innocent people. This was not just terrible for morale; it was a personal grievance for the many noble warriors who had pledged to protect the innocents. For the complete opposite to occur meant devastation on a phenomenal scale.

"We could never have kept it a secret from them," said Lord Renzo in a clear voice, "and it would have been a disservice for us to do so. Our forces fought valiantly; the devious cruelty of this calamity is the fault of our enemy, no one else."

"We are fortunate Lord Renzo gave the order not to kill where possible," said General Jackson, in stark contrast to his earlier objections.

There was an almost accusatory tone to his voice and many in the room caught it. This was no doubt directed towards the Emperor's forces who had not heeded Lord Renzo's warning and, under the command of the Emperor, had slaughtered as many of the enemy as possible, thug or not.

The Chinese Ambassadors, both of who sat on either side of Emperor Jin, notably stiffened. The atmosphere in the room was suddenly tense.

"In war, one cannot take chances or afford any situation that increases the enemy's chance of victory," one of the Ambassadors said icily. "Our warriors have been sacrificed so that you and your kin may have liberation. A most generous and benevolent gesture from our empire, wouldn't you say, General? The fact that your civilians were caught in the battle is not, I am sorry to say, our concern; our only concern is victory. Unfortunately, innocent life is always at risk under such circumstances."

"Indeed," replied General Jackson, through grit teeth, "except when it doesn't have to be, of course."

"Lord Renzo, your vigilance undoubtedly saved many, many lives," said Kai, quickly jumping in as the Ambassador and the General continued glaring at one another, "and our deepest sympathies go out to your people. It is deeply tragic that when war hits, we must act as we see fit in order to emerge as victors."

The Chinese Ambassador opened his mouth to speak once again, but the Emperor himself silenced him.

"Lord Renzo, it is with sincere regret that I did not heed your warning," said Emperor Jin in his deep, grave voice, lowering the hand he had risen to silence his Ambassador. "As my nephew said, we must do as we see fit to win this war. I did not feel at the time that altering my army's stance on the basis of a hunch could result in any positive outcome. This does not, however, lessen the tragedy of your loss and my heartfelt condolences go out to your people."

The Ambassador, plainly outraged that the Emperor should feel compelled to apologize in any way, took a deep breath in yet another attempt to speak. But Lord Renzo inclined his head towards the Emperor and said:

"Emperor Jin, your condolences are most appreciated. There is no need to apologize for doing what you felt was right; it is both the virtue and vice of us all, no less applicable to your majesty."

There was quiet again in the room and the tension relaxed, with

Sarah Brownlee

the exception of the Ambassadors who looked distinctly ruffled.

"The way I see it, we have two pressing questions," said Trey, accepting a glass of water that one of the butlers held out to him. "Lord Pearson did not begin this battle with the intent to win, this much is clear. So, what is the true reason behind his attack? And secondly, where do we go from here?"

He placed the glass on the table.

"Ninety thousand thugs fought in Picadilly this morning," he continued. "It is estimated that almost half of those were actually civilians. Which means that roughly forty thousand actual thugs were fighting. Which then demands the question—what happened to the remaining twenty thousand? We estimated weeks ago that Pearson had sixty thousand at his command. Where were the others?"

"But this is mostly speculative," objected General Jackson. "Sixty thousand estimated, yes. But there is equal chance it could be more—or less. We cannot know for sure. Furthermore, these reports were submitted several weeks ago. Pearson could indeed have swelled his ranks—or dropped to the exact amount that fought in the battle earlier. Which means his entire force was out there fighting tonight."

"But why would Lord Pearson have sent his entire force out in a battle he could have never won?" argued Trey. "His thugs could never be victorious against our trained forces. We were tricked, it is true. Our only disadvantage was the sheer *number* of the enemy— many of which turned out to be innocents. But why did Pearson do this? What was his purpose? What, purely to anger us by mingling civilians with his forces? This wouldn't help him win the battle! In fact, victory over this entire war would certainly be ours if this was the case. This is how I see it, General. Either Lord Pearson knew he could never win against our own armies and he wished to go out with a 'bang'—by having us murder our own people—or, and this is what I believe most likely, he has a plan in mind and needed to distract us. And what better way to distract your enemy than by instigating a phony battle?"

There was a brief silence.

"What do you mean, Trey?" asked Emperor Jin, while the Chinese Ambassadors sat either side of him, frowning at Lord Renzo's eldest son.

"I mean that the enemy is clever," replied Trey, "and, logically, none of this makes sense. Lord Pearson would not begin a war unless he felt sure he was going to win. I believe he is plotting something, something completely unknown to us. He initiated the battle, not because he thought he could use brute force to beat us, but because he has something up his sleeve and he needed time to implement it."

His words stunned the majority of people in the room.

"So you're saying the battle was no more than a cover for Lord Pearson's true plans?" said General Jackson slowly.

"Logically speaking, yes. Pearson has invested too much into this city to simply throw it all away on the basis of a seemingly random battle that would see us grieving, yet victorious. There is more to this, I am certain of it. I cannot be the only one who thinks this."

He looked around at the generals, soldiers and leaders.

"There is also the matter of how disciplined the thugs have become," he said. "It has not escaped our notice. In the space of a few hours, Pearson's brutes were able to successfully round up civilians, imprisoning some and forcing the rest into battle. During the retreat, their behaviour was strangely well organized. This is not the behaviour we would expect of what are essentially gangs of hooligans, who have displayed nothing more than violent thuggery and random rioting in the past. These are the actions of men and women who have been trained, who have undergone drills in these certain areas. It would have taken a very skilled military general or elite force to discipline these thugs. Does this not strike anyone else as strange?"

"Where would he have found these resources?" asked Raphael slowly. "There's no one in his camp anywhere near on the same level as General Jackson or Emperor Jin's—"

He cut himself off abruptly, his piercing green eyes widening as he looked at his brother.

"Could Pearson have an ally that we know nothing about?" he said, with a suddenness that perturbed everyone in the room. "We have ours. What's to say he doesn't have his?"

The suggestion that a foreign force was secretly working with Lord Pearson caused a great deal of muttering among the listeners.

"But surely our spies would have reported such a thing?" said General Jackson in a disbelieving tone.

Lord Renzo shook his head, his forehead creased.

"We cannot know every movement the enemy makes," he said, glancing around at them all. "What Raphael says is a possibility, no doubt…and certainly a worrying one."

One of the Chinese Ambassadors scoffed.

"And what foreign nation would dare go up against our

empire?" he said contemptuously.

"One that works in the shadows and has no intention of revealing themselves," said Trey. "If indeed this suspicion has any truth, they will not risk the wrath of the empire by coming out in the open."

"But if there really is a fourth party involved in this, where are their soldiers?" argued General Jackson. "Where's the manpower?"

"Perhaps there is none," replied Trey. "For one thing, deploying soldiers from a foreign nation would most definitely expose them. Secondly, their involvement may just be to assist behind the screens—such as training thugs how to retreat in orderly fashion or, at the very least, passing this information onto Lord Pearson so that he may implement it."

"I don't buy it," said General Jackson, shaking his head.

"We cannot rule out the possibility. The events of tonight are too strange to rule out anything. There is also the subject of Skye's kidnap yesterday evening—this man in the white coat, the child Morpher, the reasons for her kidnap which are still unknown to us…None of it adds up—and yet war began only hours after she was delivered back to us. It is linked, all of it, and yet some of those crucial links are missing. We must find out, no matter the cost."

His concern mirrored that of everyone in the room.

"We ought to attack right away," said Raphael immediately, standing up. "If Trey is right, if he really *does* have secret allies we know nothing about, then we can't just sit here while he carries out his plans, whatever they are. We must attack!"

"Raphael, troops on both sides are tired," said Kai. "We would do better to rest our soldiers and—"

"And if Trey's right?" flared Raphael, turning to face the mild-mannered man on the other side of the table. "We're sitting ducks! It's like we're just waiting for Pearson to hit us with whatever twisted schemes he has in mind!"

Kai lowered his head. Everyone in the room watched silently. Then the Emperor's nephew spoke again:

"Raphael…even if Lord Pearson has something in mind, he cannot execute anything with such a tired force. Nor can we retaliate when our troops are also tired. I am in full agreement now that we must attack the stronghold—like you said, if Trey is right then we cannot just sit here and do nothing. But it would be foolish to attack now. Lord Renzo, Uncle—may I make a suggestion?"

He turned to both Emperor Jin and Lord Renzo. Emperor Jin nodded his head.

"I would like to organize an elite company to infiltrate Lord Pearson's stronghold and discover exactly what he is up to," he told them. "I have a squadron that have undertaken many such missions; they are extremely skilled and experienced in operations such as this. I can have them ready within the hour."

Emperor Jin and Lord Renzo simultaneously nodded their agreement.

"Furthermore," continued Kai, staring around at everyone else, "none of us harbour any illusions about how crucial it is that our troops rest so they are ready for our next course of action. Might I propose we hold a banquet this evening, both to celebrate our victory in this battle and to honour the dead?"

"Victory?" repeated General Jackson incredulously. "This was hardly our victory, Commander Kai! Thousands dead, soldiers and civilians alike. Tricked by our enemy—and we retreated first, not the other way round! What exactly is there to celebrate about this complete disaster of a battle?"

"Forgive me, General, if I came across as crude or insensitive," said Kai with a bow towards the rather hot-cheeked General, "but I do believe that a victory banquet is essential for a number of reasons. The first, of course, is to honour the fallen. Like yourself, I have fought in many battles…as you can imagine, having an empire means engaging often in war…Rebellion sprouting up everywhere. After each battle, it is customary to hold a banquet, regardless of whether we experience victory or defeat. Honouring the dead is essential, both for the fallen and for the living. Secondly, it is important to keep up the morale and mood of our forces. The knowledge that we have been mistakenly fighting civilians has undoubtedly come as a blow. We must keep their spirits up. Sufficient rest and a banquet will lend valuable assistance to this."

There was a murmur of assent throughout the room. The ruffled General Jackson merely jerked his head.

"And then, when the banquet is over, we must attack Pearson's stronghold," said Raphael firmly.

Kai nodded.

"What do you say, Lord Renzo? Uncle?"

Lord Renzo exchanged a glance with Emperor Jin.

"Yes to both requests," replied Emperor Jin slowly, while Lord Renzo nodded and turned to one of the butlers.

"Prepare for a banquet this evening," he told him.

The butler nodded and left the room.

"The Emperor will be leaving later tonight, of course," said one of the Chinese Ambassadors. "It was never the plan for Emperor Jin to be present during the time of battle. Your Majesty," he added, turning firmly to his ruler, "I trust you have no objections to your departure tonight? Your position is now compromised and we cannot risk placing you in danger. Kai and ourselves will take command of the forces in your absence."

"He's right, Uncle," said Kai, also turning to the Emperor. "The circumstances have changed. Don't worry, we will win this. I will make preparations for my men to escort you back later this evening. Is that permissive?"

It was agreed that the Emperor would leave the country later that day and return to China, along with Kai's cousin, Lo Wen. After fifteen more minutes of discussion, there was unanimous agreement that a 'victory banquet' would take place later in the evening and that Kai would arrange a team of spies to infiltrate Stratford, in order to try and discover the full extent of Lord Pearson's unknown plans.

"In the meantime, everyone get some rest," said Lord Renzo to the room at large. "I will be sending teams of guards to patrol the city and check on civilians. Hopefully, many of those who scattered will be reunited with their families by now. Get some sleep. It is likely we will need all our strength later on tonight."

"What do you think?" muttered Raphael to Trey, as one by one they marched from the room. "Is Pearson likely to attack us later today? What if Kai's spy team discover nothing about what he's planning to do?"

Trey shook his head.

"We have no way of knowing what Pearson's next actions will be. We only know that we have to be entirely on our guard—and we must pray that Kai's team manages to extract information for us."

"Whatever happens, we need to attack the stronghold tonight as soon as the troops are able," said Raphael fiercely. "I don't like this—we're too vulnerable. The longer we wait, the more at risk we are of falling victim to a surprise attack. We don't know what the bastard plans on doing."

"You're right, we have no other option now. But at any rate, Pearson cannot launch an attack with his weakened thugs, same as we cannot defend ourselves with our own wounded and tired forces. We need time—time and rest. You must rest yourself, Raphael."

Raphael nodded.

"I'm going to see Skye," he said.

Trey patted his youngest brother on the shoulder and the two parted ways down the corridor.

Raphael knew that Skye was currently resting in his bedroom. Upon his return, his father had told him that she was almost fully healed now and that she had turned up in the war room looking rather disoriented and had fallen asleep there. Lord Renzo had instructed his men to carry her to Raphael's quarters so she could sleep peacefully there.

He hurried down the hallway and towards the stairs that would lead him to his room, though it took him a while to reach them due to being excitably accosted by various maids, butlers, chefs and guards who were eager to hear details about the battle.

"Mister Renzo is alive, thank goodness, thank goodness!" shouted the ecstatic cook, Antonio, throwing his frying pan to the floor and grabbing hold of Raphael, enveloping him in a big bear hug. Loads more followed and quickly surrounded them.

"Master Raphael—is it true we won the battle?"

"I heard that innocent civilians were forced to fight for Pearson—please, surely this can't be true!"

"I knew it, I knew it! I knew we'd send those scum thugs packing!"

"I'm very worried about my sister and her family, Master Raphael, terribly worried. I've tried calling her tag device, but there is no reply. I'm so scared she and her family may have been caught in the battle!"

"Young Master, if there is anything I can get you, please say the word. Shall I bring some food and drink to your chambers?"

"No. Thank you, but there is no need," said Raphael desperately, freeing himself from Antonio's tight grip. "Everyone— thank you. There's been losses on both sides, but we are convinced Pearson won't attack us again today as he does not have the resources to launch an assault. To those of you who asked if civilians were caught in the battle…Yes, I am truly sorry to say that this is true and it breaks my heart to tell you this. But please rest assured we are doing everything we can to keep the situation under control and ensure Pearson is defeated once and for all."

There was an outbreak of frantic murmuring as the faces in front of him paled and various pairs of eyes regarded him with panic.

"More details will be given to everyone at the banquet tonight," he continued, as one of the maids held her hand out to him, tears in her eyes. He took it and squeezed it.

"It is hard right now, for all of us. But it is important we rest and are ready for the next course of action, whenever and whatever that may be. Please, do try to contact any loved ones you are concerned about; but understand, loss extends far and wide…I know how difficult this is and believe me when I say that your loss is mine…"

He hung his head, that icy stabbing pain piercing him, the same one that had plagued him ever since he had discovered the full consequences of the enemy's manipulation.

"Let Mister Raphael rest, you all!" shouted Antonio, picking up his frying pan and waving it around threateningly. "He need sleep! He want to see wolf woman! Go, move, move!"

He shooed everyone away with the pan and the crowd dispersed, their distressed voices echoing through the hall. Raphael watched them go, his face pained and weary. Then he turned on his heel and flew up the stairs, two steps at a time.

He opened the door quietly. Faint sunlight streamed in through the curtains. Then he saw her. Curled up on his bed, her face buried in the pillow, mouth slightly open, a little sliver of drool sliding down her mouth; the latter was something he was always teasing her about and he would laugh whenever she reacted with extreme embarrassment. He smiled, noting how good it felt for the corners of his mouth to turn upwards, and silently crept forwards, removing his boots as quietly as possible so as not to wake her.

But Skye's wolf senses were just as strong while she was asleep as they were when awake.

"Raphael?" she whispered, her brown eyes blinking up at him.

She looked frightened, almost as if she couldn't believe it was really him. In response, he sat on the bed next to her and tenderly caressed her black hair.

"Hi," he said softly, smiling down at her.

She continued to stare at him for a few more seconds, blinking. Then, quite suddenly, she leapt from the bed and threw her arms around him, squeezing him hard and kissing him full on his lips. He gripped her just as tightly in his strong arms, returning her kiss with an ardent passion that was only rivalled by her own, hungrily devouring the softness of her mouth, his hands clutching her waist as he pushed her backwards into the bed; her fingers clenched his hair, her tongue swirling round his, the two of them lost in the moment as they desperately consumed one another.

"I've been so scared," she whispered in his ear when they finally wrenched themselves apart.

"I know," he murmured back, stroking her cheek.

They stared at each other for a long time, their hands intertwining, and his green eyes boring into her brown ones. There was so much to discuss; so much to remember; so much of the horror and confusion to dissect.

"Do you want to talk about it?" she asked him quietly.

He shook his head.

"I want to lie here. With you. For now."

He pulled his arms away, stood up and removed his clothes. She reached out to him and guided his strong, muscular body towards hers. As she cuddled up to his firm, toned torso beneath the covers, his lips found hers once more. No words passed between them for a long time as they continued relishing in the pleasure of each other's company; no terror or devastation plagued them as they explored one another as they had done so many times before. Love was the only dominant force in that magical moment, so powerful that it stopped Time and ordained that war, blood and destruction be nothing more than a forgotten nightmare.

This was how it remained, brief in reality yet infinite in memory, until the two fell asleep in each other's arms.

*

It was around midday that Skye was woken from a dreamless sleep by her tag device, which was beeping noisily on the bedside table. Blearily, she scrabbled her hand around to find it, pressed the 'answer' button and was greeted by the sight of a hysterical Ned who told her not to bother coming into work the next day—or ever again—because Trixaction Cinemas HQ had burned to the ground.

"Along with six months' worth of slideshows and presentations!" he screeched, his holographic face almost demented in its grief.

Skye hurriedly nodded and offered her condolences, quickly hanging up as he was about to launch into a furious, feverish rant. His holographic face disappeared instantly. Skye shot a worried eye towards Raphael who she hoped would have slept through that. Her hopes were dashed though, for Raphael was wide awake, blinking up at the ceiling.

"Sorry," she said to him quickly. Raphael had only been asleep for three hours, if that. "Go back to sleep."

"No, it's OK," he replied, turning to face her, his handsome face peering into her own. "So…looks like you're out of a job."

"Looks like it. The whole disciplinary meeting was a waste of time, at any rate."

"Well, I always felt you were wasted in that place, you know."

He grinned at her. She smiled back.

"Poor guy," Raphael shook his head. "He really ought to get out of this city; less civilians, the better."

"Maybe he will. But I wouldn't be surprised if Ned started single-handedly trying to rebuild the HQ himself; life isn't worth much without three-hour slideshows every Friday!"

Raphael chuckled.

"Yeah…well, hopefully we'll turn this city into how it's supposed to be and then your manager can get you back to those meetings."

"Not so sure about that, Raphael, I think I could probably get used to life without them."

They rubbed noses and snuggled each other; she kissed him all over his face as he stroked the curve of her spine.

"How have you been since the infirmary?" Raphael asked her quietly.

She pressed his hand to her lips and kissed it.

"OK," she muttered back. "I get flashes every now and then. But I've been OK. Your brothers took good care of me."

"Good."

"I went to see Daphne and my mother. Then I went to the war room and found your dad. He told me everything that had happened…"

There was a pause.

"What was it like?" she asked him finally. "The fighting …going out there and meeting them like that. I heard about—about the civilians…"

She regarded him tentatively. She knew how deeply it must

have affected him. The news was shocking and horrifying for them all; but for Raphael, who considered the protection of innocents as a number one priority, she knew how deep the wound must have struck.

"There was nothing we could have done," Raphael murmured, his face taut. "We were outnumbered by what we thought was an army of thugs. Turns out almost half of them were people who'd been forced out of their homes. Hard to see, hard to know who your enemy is in the dark…Pearson always used it to his advantage; he used civilians as a shield…because that's what he's good at…"

His knuckles cracked. Skye wrapped her fingers around his.

"Before the battle, my dad gave the order not to kill when possible. If he hadn't…"

"How did he know?" asked Skye, as Raphael's voice trailed off.

"I don't know. A hunch maybe? He said afterwards that he felt something wasn't right. Still, it wasn't enough to convince the Emperor and his troops. The Chinese forces didn't hold back."

Skye had not been outside the mansion since the battle, of course. But she could have only imagined what it must have been like. She knew the wounded were being treated, she knew the dead were still being carried away…She squeezed Raphael's hand harder.

"Where do we go from here?" she questioned.

"Trey has his own theories about Pearson's reason for attacking this morning," Raphael replied. "He's convinced the battle was nothing more than a ploy—a distraction. That Pearson never had any intention of winning—he just needed time."

"Time for what?" asked Skye, confused.

"We don't know. This is just Trey's theory. But when I think about it more, it makes sense. Pearson couldn't have beaten us with an army of thugs and civilians. So why else would he have attacked us? Just for fun? No. Pearson commands mindless brutes, but it doesn't mean he's one himself."

"Then what is it that Pearson has in mind?" said Skye, her heart quickening for reasons she couldn't understand. "Why would he go to such lengths? Sacrificing his thugs, sacrificing the people—for what?"

"That's what we're trying to find out. Kai is organizing a team to stake out East London and see if they can find out the reasons behind Pearson's actions. Also, Trey suspects a foreign ally might be working for Pearson on the sly."

"A foreign ally?" repeated Skye, her eyebrows shooting upwards.

Raphael nodded.

"But this is all speculation. We don't know for sure. We just have to pray we find out what's going on—and fast. I don't like sitting here doing nothing when Pearson's up to something."

His eyes caught hers and he pressed his forehead gently to her own.

"In the meantime, our troops have to get some rest. All of us need to be prepared for what's to come."

"But what is that?"

"It could be anything. All we can do is prepare for the unexpected. There's going to be a banquet this evening to honour the dead...and raise morale. The troops know innocents were caught in the crossfire...the one thing we'd all hoped to avoid."

Skye's heart sank. She thought about Raphael and Lord

Renzo; about how hard they had worked to keep civilians out of danger. But the enemy's trick had rendered their efforts futile.

"By the end of this evening, we're hoping Kai's team will have some information for us," Raphael continued, "but even if they don't, I'm quite certain we will launch an attack on the Pearson stronghold—and it could be as soon as tonight. We can't afford to wait around any longer. We don't know what other tricks Pearson has up his sleeve—doing nothing at this point would be the worst thing to do."

The quickening of Skye's heartbeat continued to increase. To know that the fighting could start again later that day; that Raphael would be out there battling the Pearsons and their minions, placing his neck on the line once more…she hated it. All of it. The war, the bloodshed, the risk of losing him and everyone she cared about…she hated it all. And now, to discover that the enemy had something in mind, something alien to them, left them in a more vulnerable position than they could have anticipated.

"My mother and Daphne," she said, swallowing hard. "They have to leave. They have to get out. Tonight."

Raphael nodded.

"We'll take them to safety. The Emperor is leaving too. We can arrange something for them as well. But they might not leave without you, Skye."

"No. They promised me they would go when the fighting started."

There was a brief silence. Then, in a reluctant yet firm tone, Raphael said:

"You know how I feel about this. If you would—"

"No." She cut him off sharply before he could go any further. "We're not going through this again, Raphael. I'm staying."

"I almost lost you earlier," retaliated Raphael, his temper swiftly flaring. "Do you know what that was like? You were kidnapped—I thought I'd never see you again!"

"And you could have been killed in the battle this morning! You're asking me if I know what it's like? I know *exactly* what it's like! You were out there fighting—you could have died. I didn't know if you'd come back! The whole time I was sitting here, wondering if you'd make it out alive, wondering if I'd see you again…Yeah, I know exactly what it's like, Raphael! And I'm not going through that again—once Daphne and my mum are gone, I'm going into battle with you."

"No," he growled.

"Yes!" she snapped. "I'm fully healed now—Doctor Jenson did an amazing job on me. You can't stop me. You understand? I'd rather go out there and die with you than be tucked up safely in a corner somewhere alone!"

Neither spoke for a moment as frostiness filled the air. Then Raphael cupped her face gently and turned it towards his own.

"I don't want to argue with you," he said quietly. "I'm afraid, Skye. That's all. I'm scared of what could happen. I'm scared of losing you."

"So am I," she said to him, her expression pained. "But please…don't tell me to go anymore. I won't do it. I'm not leaving you."

He stared at her mutely before burying his face in her hair. Her defiance, while serving as an expression of love, only escalated his fears. As for her fears of losing him, they were only quelled by her fierce determination to stick with him, no matter the cost.

"There's also the matter of what happened to you," Raphael murmured in her ear. "Your kidnap. I know you may not be ready to talk about it…"

"No, it's fine."

"OK. We still don't know why you were taken or what Pearson's exact plans for you were. We only know that he wanted you for your Morphing ability. Skye…have you got any idea at all what exactly it was they wanted with you?"

Skye thought back to her time in the cell. She shuddered involuntarily. But no…her guess was as good as his. He saw the memory just as it had happened.

"He just kept going on and on about how he was fascinated with Morphers. Kept talking about how they'd been planning on kidnapping me for a long time. Told me I was going to help him somehow. But he'd betrayed Lord Pearson, too. Lord Pearson didn't want you to find me. But I don't know…I don't know what it was he wanted with me."

Raphael shook his head.

"We'll find out soon enough. In the meantime, we have to go along with the plan. And, Skye, if you see the Beaver Morpher again…"

"I know. I promised you I wouldn't go near him—and I'm sorry I broke my promise, Raphael, I truly am. But the things I saw…He showed me images, memories of what that professor had done to him. Him and the other children. I couldn't just walk away…"

"It's OK, Skye, I understand. I saw it, too. Some of it."

"I have to get him out, Raphael. I can't just leave him to the professor. That man is evil."

Raphael's face hardened.

"Trust me. That twisted psycho is right at the top of my list for whom I plan on sinking my teeth into, along with the Pearsons. But we need to be patient, Skye, alright? Who is this Beaver Morpher and where did he come from? There's something not right about his morphing ability, couldn't you sense it?"

She nodded.

"You're right. Something about him doesn't add up. I felt it the very first time I saw him. And his abilities…there were things he could do that we can't. But we have to get him away from that professor. They locked him in a cage…"

She didn't finish her sentence. She knew that Raphael was aware of the atrocities. Some of them, at least. And she herself only knew what the boy had shown her, which was surely only a fraction of what the callous professor had put him through.

"We'll get him out," he told her reassuringly, as she rested her head on his shoulder. "We'll find a way, Skye."

They continued to lie there for a while. Skye breathed in his scent, wondering when they might have the chance to lie together like this again, if ever.

"Do you want to get some more sleep?" she asked him softly.

He shook his head.

"I'm fine, don't worry."

"What exactly is going to happen at this banquet tonight?"

"Mostly it will be our soldiers and archers; anyone who is well-enough to attend. We'll honour the dead and toast the fallen. It's

important we keep morale up, especially if we attack again tonight. There'll be food…drink. I know it may sound a little extravagant so soon after the battle, but I think Kai's right. We must keep everyone's spirits strong."

He sat up suddenly, rising from the bed.

"There's something I have to give you—I might not get the chance again."

He made his way towards a chest of drawers in the room, opened the top one and pulled out a tiny package.

"I know you're probably sick of the gifts," he said quietly, handing it to her, "but this was what I wanted to give you."

She held it in her hands for a second, before unwrapping it.

It was a tiny white wolf, carved out of marble, hand-made, and attached to a silver chain. Raphael's talent as a painter was phenomenal; but she had never known him to carve something before. It was beautiful.

"Thank you," she whispered. "It must have taken you a long time."

He gently took the pendant from her and slipped it round her neck.

"There," he smiled. "Now everyone can see how beautiful your spirit animal is."

She smiled back, looking slightly abashed.

"I never have anything to give you…" she said, shaking her head.

He kissed her.

"Having you here is all I want," he told her. "I'm going to take a shower. Skye, get some more sleep."

"No, I'll get ready too. I want to check in on my mum and Daphne."

"OK then, I won't be long. We'll go together. Then we should grab some lunch—I don't know about you, but I'm starving."

"Steak?" She smiled at him.

"Raw." He grinned.

About twenty minutes later, the two emerged from Raphael's bedroom and were making their way towards the lounge. Atmosphere in the halls was mixed. They came across a group of extremely sombre guards who were talking mournfully about the loss of civilians in the battle; closer to the kitchen area, several domestic staff seemed positively—if not forcefully—upbeat, convinced the Pearsons' tyrannical reign was about to come to a close and that the Renzos would emerge victorious. Everywhere in the mansion was tense, however, and the Morphers had to inhale deeply as the waves of tension hit them like a ton of bricks; it was a sure sign that not one person remained in the dark about the uncertainty that faced them all.

"Skye! Raphael!"

They heard someone calling their names from behind them as they crossed the hallway to reach the lounge. Turning, they saw Daphne and Ricardo hurrying towards them.

"We knew you were resting and didn't want to disturb you," said Ricardo, clasping his brother by the shoulder and embracing him; Raphael had not seen either of the twins since his return. "It's good to have you back."

"Good to see you too, Ric. Where's Joey?"

"Well, last I saw he was keeping Skye's mum company," said

Ricardo in an innocent sort of way; Skye's eyes widened and Daphne jabbed him in the ribs.

"But I heard he's having lunch in the dining hall—alone," continued the twin, unable to suppress a grin. "We were on our way to see him, actually."

"Skye, your mum is still sleeping," said Daphne, turning to her friend. "Shall I go and wake her?"

"No, let her sleep," said Skye quickly. It occurred to her that it wouldn't be long before she would have to tell both her mother and Daphne about their evacuation later today, something she knew they would both undoubtedly resist. In that instant, it hit her. She might not see them again for a long time. She might never see them again at all…

"Let's go eat," said Skye, linking her arm with her friend's.

"OK!" beamed Daphne.

They walked down the hall together towards the dining room, the two Renzo brothers following them and talking quietly between themselves. Daphne began to launch into an excitable, low chatter about a scarf that Ricardo had apparently knitted for her himself and presented to her earlier that morning.

Amidst her rather vague bemusement that Ricardo Renzo had a penchant for knitting in his spare time, Skye nodded and smiled at the appropriate intervals as her friend continued talking enthusiastically down the corridor; all the while, a voice lingered in the back of her head, one full of fire and determination.

I'm not letting anything happen to you, the voice said to her chatty best friend and her sleeping mother. *Even if you hate me for it, even if you refuse to go, I'm getting you out of here. I'm not losing anyone else I love to those stinking thugs. I swear it.*

CHAPTER TWELVE

The banquet began at around six o'clock in the evening, just as the first signs of dusk were settling in. The largest dining hall in the Renzo mansion, which had not been used for almost five years, was quickly decorated by the staff with wreaths of poppies strung along the walls. A long table laden with meat, pie, vegetables, fish and rice stood to the left, while on the right an equally lengthy table was heaving underneath an array of drinks. Zen music played softly in the background.

The hall filled up quietly, but swiftly. Unscathed soldiers in uniform, who were strong enough to attend the banquet unlike their more exhausted comrades, stood around in groups, talking to one another. A set of archers approached the drinks table. A few of the Chinese forces had attended also, but most of them remained in the barracks next door to the mansion on Kai's orders; the Emperor's nephew had explained to his troops that there was a strong possibility they would attack Pearson's stronghold that very night and he wanted them on a call-to-action basis. Some of the guests who had attended the dinner party were also present.

"Everyone alright?" said Raphael, approaching a table at the back where Skye, Joey, Daphne, Ricardo, Trey and Paddy were currently seated.

Joey and Paddy greeted him cheerfully enough, both with drinks in their hands. Trey nodded to his brother. Skye, however, barely looked up from the plate of meatballs that was in front of her.

"How are you?" Raphael said to her quietly, kissing her forehead. "Stupid question, I know…"

Skye shrugged her shoulders, trying to control the sick feeling in her stomach that was threatening to manifest itself in physical form. The plate of meatballs remained untouched. She had been dreading the banquet for her own reasons as she had not worked up the personal courage to do what she knew must inevitably be done.

"So who fancies some wine?" said Joey, looking around at his companions with a grin. "Trey decided to bring me a glass of apple juice—not entirely sure what he was thinking, he probably got knocked on the head one too many times during the battle!"

"There's no alcohol tonight, Joey," said Trey, shaking his head. "The troops might be fighting again later. Turning up drunk would be a fine way to lose."

Joey's jaw dropped.

"*No* alcohol?" he repeated, horrified. "So what about those of us who aren't allowed to go out and fight? Dad's got me and Ric under lock and key—I've asked him plenty of times to let us go, he's still not listening!"

"Not a major surprise," muttered Trey. "You and Ricardo are better off here, Joey."

"Jeez, you sound like Dad!"

"Well, Dad gets it right most of the time, you know," chimed in

Raphael, unable to suppress a grin.

Joey rolled his eyes.

"Yeah, yeah. Just you wait. The time will come when me and Ric will be needed for our services. Isn't that right?"

He turned to his twin brother who was busy chomping on a large chicken leg. Ricardo nodded, his mouth full. Daphne shivered against him nervously.

"I just want this to be over," she said, against the background of Zen music. "The fighting, the thugs. I hate all of it. I just want it to end."

"Don't worry," said Paddy, who was shovelling oxtail soup into his mouth.

He swallowed his food down.

"It's tragic what happened today…but we're going to beat them. We lost only a few forces ourselves, while Pearson lost many more. There's no way he can launch another attack on us like that."

"Hell, yes," added Joey, smiling, before sighing deeply and taking a large swig of apple juice. "They'll be defeated, alright. Then we can get back to normal—a different girl every night, a new face to wake up to every morning; no more having to be careful what women we meet in case they slip something in our drinks—right, Ric?"

"Yeah," agreed Ricardo enthusiastically, before catching sight of Daphne's displeased expression. His voice faltered.

"I—I mean—back to normal so we can hang out properly again, not for the women obviously!"

Daphne continued to look on, stony-faced. Joey roared with laughter.

"Are you whipped or are you whipped! Don't worry, sweet-cheeks, he's been a good boy since he's been with you. Don't know how he does it!"

He slapped Ricardo on the back and shot Daphne a wink.

"Yeah, well, you wouldn't," said Raphael, shaking his head while Ricardo started spluttering, having almost choked on his chicken leg as his twin pulled his hand away.

"Too right I wouldn't!" grinned Joey. "Give me about ten more years to settle down—you know, providing we survive this war and everything—and then I *might* consider it!"

"I'm just going to get some tea," said Skye vaguely; she had not been paying attention to the conversation. "Do you want anything?"

"I'm OK for now, thanks," replied Raphael, rubbing her arm. "You want me to come with you?"

He eyed her meaningfully, but she shook her head. Daphne also caught the look on Skye's face; she momentarily stopped glaring and stared at her with concern.

"Skye, is everything alright?" she asked her in a low voice. "You've been really quiet all evening. You're not getting…you know…flashes about yesterday, are you?"

"No, no," said Skye quickly, unable to look her friend in the face. "Anyway…I'll be back in a second…"

She stood up and walked towards the drinks table. She should have done this earlier. She should have resolved to do it the very moment she had them both together in the same room.

But after lunch, Skye's mother had also appeared at the dining table and both Daphne and Mrs. Archer sat either side of her, chattering light-heartedly between themselves, plainly relieved that they were all together again, safe and sound. Skye's courage had failed her; she was unable to tell them that they had to leave that very night.

It wasn't just her courage, though. She didn't want to say goodbye.

"...Yeah, it was messed up. Some of them just dropped their weapons, you know? Just dropped them and ran..."

"I came face to face with this kid, he only looked about sixteen. Just stood there, staring at me with his mouth wide open. Big, beefy sort of kid holding a machete. You know what I did? Just turned away from him. Lord Renzo said not to kill...but even so, I couldn't bring myself to attack him. Saw it in his eyes, there and then—he didn't belong there."

"But we never would have guessed they were civilians..."

Skye was unable to stop herself from listening into the conversation between three soldiers who stood by the drinks table. They were talking about the battle; she listened closely as she poured herself some tea.

"My wife called me today," one of them continued, "said she saw them taking away the bodies. Not as many of our own...mostly civilians...and Pearson's scum..."

"They tried to attack the hospital, I heard."

"They did?"

"Yeah. Shortly after the battle—bunch of thugs tried to storm the place and kill off some of the wounded. We chased them off, though."

"Damn. Bastards. I'll be glad when this is over. They've had it coming for years. This is our chance to turn this city around. I just want to get to the point where I don't need to worry about my daughter leaving the house anymore. I can't wait for that day, believe me."

"Same here. We'll get 'em, Barry, don't you worry. We've got the best lord in the whole country on our side."

"That's the spirit, Tom."

The men shuffled off further down the table. Skye raised her head, watching them go. Then she slowly made her way back to the others.

"I've always wondered," Ricardo was saying, as she took her seat next to Raphael, "how did this all happen, anyway? How'd thugs manage to take over like this? When we took a trip to the Central Americas some years ago, I watched this television show—"

"You've seen TV?" interjected Daphne excitedly.

"That's right, doll," replied Ricardo, throwing an arm around her. "When this is all over, I'll take you to see some for yourself—though, to be honest, I can't really see what all the fuss is about. Anyway, what was I saying? Oh, yeah—so I watched this programme, which showed London as it was centuries ago. Nothing like now! I mean…we had a *queen* for one thing!"

"We still do have a queen," said Raphael. "Or king, rather. They live on the other side of the world."

"Yeah, so, here's the thing—we have a king! So why do we live in such a rubbish tip?"

"It's all thanks to the 'London Blunder', isn't it?" said Paddy, who was on his second helping of oxtail soup.

"The what?"

"Ricardo, haven't you ever picked up a history book in your

life?" asked Trey incredulously.

"Nah. School was never really my thing."

"Well, after the plague hit, the whole country was in trouble," said Daphne, and everyone turned to look at her. "Loads of people died and there was only a few million left. The authorities at the time did a good job of building the city up again, though—they made some great alliances with other nations, such as the Chinese Empire, and managed to keep things moving; taxes went up by fifty per cent, but a few years later someone discovered valuable resources in the north of the island and prosperity grew, because the country could trade once again; people still avoided living outside the city, though, as there was a widespread fear that the plague still lingered in certain areas…"

Joey let out a loud yawn. Ricardo elbowed him in the stomach.

"Go on, sweetie," he told his girlfriend. "My girl's an educated genius," he added, turning to his twin reproachfully, "let her finish!"

Daphne flushed.

"Well, I wouldn't go that far," she said, looking embarrassed. Subtle grins lit up around the table.

"Anyway, even though the city managed to stay on its feet, crime was on the rise. There was this Prime Minister called Octan Freemason who ordered this thing called the Criminal Rehabilitation Programme—it was based on the works of John Mumplane, a psychiatrist who lived a couple of hundred years ago. He wrote the book: *'Evil: Pity, not Punish. Integrate, not Segregate.'*

"Never heard of it," said Joey.

"You wouldn't see any copies of that book lying around now," said Paddy, shaking his head. "Most historians consider it the catalyst that single-handedly wrecked the entire city."

Trey nodded.

"That's right," he said. "Things just went downhill from there…Prisons up and down the city were shut down. Criminals were encouraged to mingle freely with the populace; the police were no longer allowed to make arrests, but instead ordered to treat all bad behaviour with sympathy and compassion; problem is, when you do this for people who treat you the exact opposite, you place yourself in an extremely vulnerable position. On absolutely no accounts were they allowed to use force to stop criminal activity. Books and pamphlets were distributed to the more seedy characters of society; they were required to attend workshops, which would hopefully 'bring them to the light' and squash the dark side out of them. This was all part of the scheme—repercussions for bad behaviour was thrown out the window and anyone who tried to enforce any was immediately ostracized by the authorities and society."

"That's crazy," said Ricardo.

Trey shrugged.

"That was the mind-set back then. Future generations will always view the actions of their ancestors as crazy. To the people of the past, it was normal—but that's because they lacked the foresight to see the consequences. Anyway, what followed was inevitable. Criminal activity exploded throughout the city—thugs multiplied by the thousands. Without fear of rebuke, there was nothing to stop them. It is the ultimate penalty that comes with tolerating the intolerant. The scheme worked on the odd few, of course; but for the majority it was the open doorway to indulge in the very worst of their nature. These thugs weren't interested in tea and sympathy; they were interested in power—and Octan Freemason handed it to them on a plate. So, there you have it. The London Blunder. Old Parliament placed the rights of the criminal above the rights of the innocent and the result is what you see before you today."

"It didn't help that Lord Pearson and his clan found their fortunes around this time," said Raphael, shaking his head. "The government was weak, but they still had to abide by their own laws; that's why our very small police force didn't take action during the riots twelve years ago; what's more, some of the police were as corrupted as the thugs themselves! The nations that helped us out of poverty after the plague were angry that so much money had been spent on this failed programme—they turned their backs—"

"With the exception of the Chinese Empire," said Trey, "but even that came with a price. They demanded that all media outlets be banned, for example."

The others turned to look at him in surprise.

"I thought the media was banned because the government just didn't want TV and all that to exist here anymore!" exclaimed Paddy.

"That was the reason given at the time. But the banning of the media was due to Chinese rule."

"Well, why would they do that?"

Trey shrugged.

"There wasn't much else to enforce upon the island, I suppose. It was already broken and corrupt, thanks to the rehabilitation scheme. It was a stamp of power, that's all. But the Chinese agreed many years ago not to conquer the island and make it a part of their

Empire—this was due to respect for the British Monarchy and the fact that, even till now, much of the Commonwealth stills exists. Our island was pretty much destroyed, but its history still commanded a degree of respect throughout the world. Luckily for us, too. We might be struggling with a broken nation, but at least we can still call it our own."

He shook his head, his face thoughtful.

"I suppose it is kind of crazy when you think about it," he murmured. "Not for over a thousand years was this island invaded. Napoleon couldn't take it...the Armada couldn't take it...Hitler couldn't take it. All those foes that failed to invade...and in the end we were destroyed within our own borders by the very people who were meant to protect us."

"Yep," said Paddy, finishing off the last of his soup. "Now all we've got are some shoddy politicians who are paralyzed to act and civil war on our hands. Wouldn't wanna be anywhere else right now!"

"All this talk of history and politics has given me a headache," said Joey, standing up, stretching. "Ric, wanna help me smuggle in some wine?"

"Yep!" Ricardo jumped from his seat, planting a kiss on Daphne's cheek.

"Thanks for the info, sugarplum," he said to her. "Beauty *and* brains—that's what I like in a woman!"

"Yeah, she's got brains enough for both of you!" smirked Joey.

"Good luck smuggling in alcohol with Dad on the watch," Raphael told the twins.

"Hey, we can smuggle anything! It's one of our many talents, you know."

With identical, mischievous grins, the twins left the table.

Raphael leaned in towards Skye.

"Have you spoken to them yet?" he asked her quietly.

She shook her head, that familiar sick feeling swooping through her solar plexus.

"Skye, there you are!"

They looked up to see Mrs. Archer hurrying towards them.

"You won't believe it, but I only just woke up!" Skye's mother exclaimed as she approached the table; Raphael stood up to offer her his seat. Mrs. Archer thanked him and sat down.

"I've been sleeping for absolutely ages! You should have woken me!"

"No, Mum, you needed to rest," said Skye, trying to make herself sound normal.

This was it. She had to tell them. Both of them.

"Mum," she said suddenly, as the others chatted quietly among themselves. "There's something I have to tell you and Daphne—"

"Attention please! Lord Renzo wishes to speak!"

Skye's voice was drowned out by the Head Butler who was speaking into a megaphone and waving his free hand to gain the attention of everyone present.

The chatter inside the hall slowly died down; the music in the background abruptly stopped playing. Each head turned towards Lord Renzo who was standing alone in the centre.

"Everyone," said Lord Renzo, his pupils scanning the many faces that watched him; he looked tired. Heavy bags bulged beneath his eyes. "If I could just have a moment of your time. I want to thank you for attending this gathering, soldiers, warriors and staff alike. We are brought together for a common purpose—to honour those who could not be here tonight. Some lie in our hospitals, injured; others will not stand with us again for they have fallen into a place that we, the living, have no access to."

There was total silence throughout the hall; somewhere to the left of Skye's table, a sob escaped someone's lips.

"Most, if not all, in this hall know of the tragedy that took place during the battle this morning; how our enemy forced civilians into battle and fooled us into thinking they were fighting for Lord Pearson. We could not have foreseen such a devious, abhorrent act. I want to make it very clear to each and every person standing here now that you fought with valiance and honour; I implore you not to allow the devastation that has hit us to command your senses; I beseech you to remain confident in the knowledge that what happened this morning was the fault of nobody here. Each of you, in the line of duty, has lost friends, comrades, loved ones…and in order for us to bring such destruction to an end, we must remain strong, united in our determination to thwart our enemy, once and for all. I have every faith in you…and I pray that you, too, shall continue to hold the same faith in me."

There was a murmur of assent throughout the room. Lord Renzo's last sentiment was non-negotiable; they would trust in him till the very end.

"So, let us take this opportunity to remember. Remember all those who lost their lives today, so that our tomorrow may be brighter one. Those who fought and fell in the quest for freedom from oppression and tyranny, which our enemy has demanded we succumb to over so many years. Let's remember our unfortunate citizens, whose only crime was to be in the wrong place at the wrong time, to be used at the mercy of our enemy."

He paused briefly. Silent anger filled the air. Lord Renzo cleared his throat.

"But let us not allow the sacrifice, both of our warriors and our people, to be in vain. Our mission has always been to strive for freedom and justice, to bring light to our darkened city. Let us continue towards our goal with strength in our hearts and faith in our cause."

Then, one of Lord Renzo's generals stepped forward, holding the very same bugle horn that had been passed down by the Renzos' ancestors. No longer amplified, but in its purest form, he raised it to his lips and began to play the melancholic, yet beautiful tune of *'The Last Post'*, the traditional tribute song for those who had fallen. Many people in the room lowered their heads; some were unable to stop the tears from flowing as they remembered friends they would never see again and loved ones who were cruelly taken from them.

And, slowly, the grief, sadness and anger shifted into something else. A look of determination entered the gaze of everyone present; they would beat their enemy, even if they were to die in the attempt. They would not allow the deaths of those recently passed to have been in vain.

The final note from *'The Last Post'* was played. Lord Renzo nodded to the general; the general inclined his head, clutching the bugle horn by his side.

"Thank you," said Lord Renzo in his quiet voice.

He turned to face the silent audience once again.

"Despite the tragedy that has befallen, we must take comfort in our own strength and perseverance. We may attack the enemy as soon as tonight. Emperor Jin is now on his way back to China, but the Chinese forces currently stand guard around our stronghold. Please be prepared. Until then, please feast as much as you can—and I thank you once again for your continued loyalty and dedication."

He took a small bow and gestured towards one of the staff; seconds later, Zen music filled the room once more, waterfall sounds emitting soothingly from the melodic notes.

"Lord Renzo certainly has a way with words," said Mrs. Archer, wiping a tear from her eye as chatter in the room slowly began to resume. "I can still hardly believe what happened this morning…Skye, dear, what was it you were going to say?"

"Oh—I…"

Skye couldn't help it. Her voice got stuck in her throat again.

"Yes, dear?" said her mother, looking at her with concern.

"I…It's just…"

"Trey, I must speak with you."

Thwarted for a second time, Skye looked up to see who had suddenly appeared at their table, sweating profusely, his skin rather pale as he addressed the eldest Renzo brother.

"Kai!" exclaimed Trey, rising quickly from his seat as the Emperor's nephew stood in front of them. "You're back!"

Everyone turned to stare. Kai had been absent for the past several hours, along with his surveillance team, in their bid to discover Lord Pearson's next plan of action.

Kai ignored everyone, except Trey.

"I must speak with you," he said to him again, his face a mask of urgency.

Quickly, the Emperor's nephew pulled Trey to the side. Everyone at the table watched with identical worried expressions; Raphael had risen from his seat.

There was a brief discussion between the two. Then, moments later, they both swept from the room.

Those who were left at the table continued to stare after them; nobody spoke and for a moment all that could be heard was the quiet chatter in the hall and the sound of cutlery as people dug into their food. Paddy, who was on his third bowl of oxtail soup, paused midway before gulping it down, wiping his sleeve on his mouth and breaking the silence.

"What was all that about?" he said, mystified.

Nobody replied. Raphael had an enormous frown on his face.

Then his tag device beeped.

Whipping it from his pocket (it had been retrieved earlier that afternoon by a soldier who had stumbled upon it near the battleground), it was clear he had received a tag-text. He scanned his tag device quickly as he read the message.

"Kai's surveillance team was a success," he said out loud, his green eyes lighting up, excited triumph swiftly filling his features. "I can't believe it! They found the—"

His tag device beeped again and he opened up the latest message, cutting himself off mid-way.

The triumphant expression froze on his face; the blood drained from his features. An unexplainable eerie feeling shot through Skye as she watched him. Everyone on the table frowned confusedly at

Raphael's sudden shift in manner and the cryptic tag-texts he had received.

For several moments, Raphael remained frozen in his position, not moving or blinking.

"Raphael?" said Skye tentatively.

Then, without a word, the youngest Renzo turned his back on them and bolted to where Lord Renzo was sitting, talking to one of his generals. Skye leaped worriedly from her seat as the others began muttering amongst themselves; she hurried after him, weaving through the crowds of people.

"...and then I was sent this," Raphael was saying, once Skye reached the table where Lord Renzo and the general were sitting.

Lord Renzo took the tag device that his youngest son was holding out to him. He, too, became strangely immobile upon reading it, his face paling very slightly.

"Raphael, what's going on?" whispered Skye, tugging on her boyfriend's sleeve.

Raphael didn't reply; instead, without looking at her, he took her hand and squeezed it.

"What shall we do?" he asked his father.

"Find me Captain Burgloss," replied Lord Renzo quietly. "Quickly."

Raphael nodded, released Skye's hand and disappeared into the crowds of people.

Skye turned to face Lord Renzo, a look of bewilderment on her face.

"Lord Renzo, what's happening?" she asked him. "Kai came back and Trey disappeared with him—did Raphael tell you?"

"Yes. Raphael told me. Skye, please go back to your table and stay with the others."

"But Raphael—"

"Please, Miss Archer. Do as I ask."

There was finality in his voice; what's more, there was something else there, too, something she hadn't heard before.

She realized it was fear.

She didn't question or protest further, but slowly turned away, not understanding what had happened in the last five minutes, her heart racing uncontrollably as the strangest sense of foreboding filled her entire body.

Raphael came charging back through the crowd, a stern-faced captain in tow.

"Raphael," she said shakily, briefly halting him. "What's going on? Your dad said—"

"Skye, go back to the table and wait for me to join you."

"But I don't understand—" she began frustratedly, pulling on his sleeve again.

"It's a trap," hissed Raphael. "It's a goddamn trap. Go back to the table. Stay there until I return. Keep the others there and don't let anyone else leave the hall."

Without a second glance back, he hurried past her, the captain swiftly treading his heels. Skye stared after him, her heart hammering even faster beneath her chest. A trap? What did that mean? What was a trap?

With no other choice but to return to the table, Skye slowly made her way back to her mother and Daphne, her heart continuing to pound uncontrollably.

*

A full moon had appeared in the sky. It was unusual in colour that evening; bright yellow surrounded by a slight orange glow. Usually, a small white moon graced London's skies; or nothing at all. Cloudy nights often blocked the translucent lighting.

The uncommon sight above was of little interest to Trey. There was only one thing that currently held his undivided attention: what Kai had told him, with such urgency, earlier that evening in the banquet hall.

"We've found the professor!" had been Kai's words, as Trey was pulled to the side by his friend's dishevelled, flustered frame. "The man who kidnapped Skye! Currently unguarded, currently alone, in a small store in Central London. We must capture him— now. My team have him under watch, but it will require force to seize him. You asked me to tell you right away when we made any discoveries—well, this is it, Trey. This is it!"

"Brilliant," Trey had muttered approvingly. "I'll send for my unit—"

"No time. I have a platoon that currently reside only a mile from the professor's whereabouts. They can assist us in kidnapping him. We must go."

With a simultaneous nod, Trey and Kai had vanished from the banquet. They hurried outside to the Renzo grounds, nodding to the numerous guards patrolling the place, some of who held plastic cups in their hands and were, therefore, not excluded from honouring the dead.

A car was waiting for them; Kai's personal valet was behind the wheel and one of his captains was sitting in the backseat. The two men bundled themselves beside the captain, Trey first and Kai following swiftly behind.

"Quick," Kai told his driver. "To the professor."

Now, after driving for almost ten minutes, Trey's sharp mind began working furiously. He had already alerted his brother, Raphael, about the unexpected turn of events.

Sorry to leave so suddenly, he had written to him through his tag device, moments after getting inside the car. *Kai's spy team a success. Professor found. Tell Dad.*

Trey had not known beforehand what Kai could find out during his team's reconnaissance mission; truthfully, he had been doubtful there would be any success at all. Sneaking into the Pearson stronghold undetected was difficult in itself, but to get close enough to make any type of discovery in the space of a few hours was, in Trey's opinion, wishful thinking. Throughout the banquet, he had firmly believed that they would be assembling their forces that same night in order to attack Pearson in his own territory; this, and this alone, had pre-occupied him the entire evening.

So to receive this sudden news from his ally was both shocking and welcome. With Pearson's mysterious professor in their clutches, many secrets would be unravelled and, with them, the key essence to victory. Excitement swelled in Trey's veins.

"Once we have the professor, we can extract information from him regarding Skye's kidnap," he began muttering to himself. "We can ask him about the reasons they took her and what Pearson has in mind. I wonder if he might be able to tell us why civilians were pulled into the ranks—and what Pearson's overall scheme is."

The car swerved sharply to the left, causing the three-backseat passengers to crush against one another.

"Perhaps he may even have information about Pearson's possible foreign ally," continued Trey, undeterred as he almost rammed into the captain on his left. "This professor must surely have knowledge on all aspects of the enemy's plan. What do you think, Kai?"

Kai had been very quiet ever since they started their journey to reach the professor. Rotating his head away from the window to face Trey, he stared at him.

"It's entirely possible," he replied.

Trey nodded.

"Yes—and I am extremely curious to learn how your team found him. I honestly wasn't expecting it, Kai. Do you think—?"

It was then, in that very moment, that Trey realized something wasn't right. Perhaps it was the odd, creeping chill that unexpectedly trickled down his spine despite the warmth of the car; a 'hunch' that he, though not a Morpher, possessed as an ability, just like his father did. Perhaps it was the strange look that had come into Kai's face, one his keen eyes did not fail to miss and one he had not seen before. Perhaps it was the fact that it suddenly came to his attention that they were no longer taking the route to Central London, but were instead driving towards South London, hence the sudden, sharp left-swerve.

Whatever it was, it caused the hairs on the back of Trey's neck to stand on end and sent an uncomfortable, prickling feeling running through his entire body.

"We seem to have taken a wrong turn," he said, keeping his

voice calm.

There was no reply. The driver kept his foot on the pedal.

"Kai," said Trey, more firmly. "This is the route to South London. We have to turn back."

There was a loud clicking sound in his left ear.

A pistol being cocked.

"No, Trey," said Kai, his face blank as he turned to stare at the man next to him. "We are not turning back."

Trey didn't move; he couldn't, even if he tried.

Kai looked beyond the motionless, pale face mere inches from his own and spoke calmly to the captain who currently held the gun to Trey's head.

"Keep the Tanzer ray close to him," he told him. "We don't want him getting any ideas."

He reached over and pulled Trey's tag device from his pocket. Trey, momentarily paralysed mentally, physically and emotionally, unable to comprehend what was happening, was only too aware of the cold butt of the gun pressing against his skin.

He swallowed, his throat extremely dry, slow realization beginning to burn through his mind as the wretched horror of the situation sank in.

This can't be, he thought, the blood drained from his face, *it can't be...*

"Kai," he finally said, finding his voice. "I don't understand. What does this mean?"

"You'll find out soon enough," was the response.

The car continued driving silently down the winding road. It was as though nothing had happened; the valet kept his eyes on the road, his dispassionate expression the same as it ever was. Kai stared silently out the window; Trey stared straight ahead; only the sensation of the cold metal pressing against his skin served as a reminder that this was happening, that it was real...

That something, somehow, had gone terribly wrong.

"We're being followed, Commander," said the valet, his eyes peering into the rear-view mirror.

"Lose them," said Kai calmly.

Sure enough, there was a car tailing them. Kai's valet coughed slightly before suddenly slamming his foot down on the pedal and swerving violently to the right. Everyone in the backseat smashed into one another; the gun was yanked away briefly from Trey's head; Trey, no longer in shock but fully understanding the mortal danger he was in, took advantage of that split-second of frenzy; he threw his fist back and aimed a punch in the captain's face. Blood spurted from the captain's nose and the Tanzer Gun in his hand fell to the floor. Trey scrabbled to reach it, cursing himself for not arming himself before he left the banquet, but immediately an elbow wrapped itself around his neck, gripping him in a tight headlock; he gasped for breath.

"I said, no tricks," said Kai coldly, his grasp almost suffocating the wheezing man beside him.

He turned to the captain whose nose was still bleeding heavily.

"Pick it up!" he snapped at him.

The captain, practically blinded by the blood streaming from his nose, hurried to find the gun, retrieving it moments later.

Trey was turning blue.

"Kai!" he managed to gasp.

The arm released itself; the butt of the gun pressed once more against his skin.

"Don't think about pulling anymore stunts like that," Kai said to him, his gaze malevolent as he looked at Trey, who was now inhaling great gulps of air. "Otherwise, he'll blow your brains out. Did we lose them?" he added, turning to the valet.

"Yes, Commander."

"Good. Carry on to the desired destination. We don't want to keep our dear friend here in the dark any longer."

They carried on driving down the long, dark road. Charred remains from buildings that thugs had burnt to ashes were scattered all over. Silence reigned in the car, but the beat of Trey's heart thumped deafeningly in his ears. Kai...he could hardly comprehend it. It had barely sunk in. The man he thought was both his friend and comrade was neither of these things. There was no captured professor. There had been no raid. He did not know where he was going or the true purpose of this journey. He only knew that he had to find a way to warn his father—and that many lives now rested on the events that were about to unfold.

And the Emperor? What of him? Was he part of this? Or was Kai working alone?

The car came to an abrupt halt.

"Here we are," said Kai, a smile on his face. With the hard cold metal still shoved against his head, Trey stared at him. He didn't recognize him.

"Bring him out," Kai ordered the captain, opening his door and stepping outside.

Nodding, the captain roughly seized Trey by the collar and

practically dragged him from the car. For a second, Trey contemplated whether to attack him, but the gun was still held too close to his head. He complied without struggle.

They were in a forest area; sick-looking trees were all around them. Shards of glass and litter lay scattered over the muddy ground. Only the light of the yellow moon brightened this eerie wood. Trey did not recognize the place, but there was an aura of despair and scent of death about it that told him this forest had seen much devastation.

Kai clicked his fingers and made his way to the boot of the car. The captain kicked Trey forwards and ordered him to follow.

"Come, my dear Trey," said Kai, beckoning him as he came to a stop at the car boot. "There is something I wish you to see."

Trey was shoved forward by the captain. Kai opened the boot of the car.

"Look," said Kai, the faint trace of a smirk on his face. "Tell me what you see."

Reluctantly, Trey leaned over to look inside the boot.

There was a dead man inside. But not just any man.

It was Emperor Jin.

"No!" he gasped.

The Emperor had been stabbed several times; this much was clear. His usually sleek velvet robes were spattered with dried blood; his lifeless eyes were wide open, as was his mouth. His head flopped sickeningly to one side, the sign of a broken neck.

Trey turned his head away, squeezing his eyes shut, horror and shock pulsating his every vein.

"No," he whispered, the sight of the dead Emperor imprinted in his mind. "No…this cannot be. Why? Kai? *Why?*"

"Well, it's very simple why," Kai shrugged. Trey opened his eyes, meeting the nonchalant gaze of the man beside him. He could not believe the callousness with which Kai spoke, he could not believe the cruelty in the face of the man he had worked with, fought with and trusted all these years; he could not believe that the Emperor lay, dead, in the boot of the very car they had been driving. He could only stand there in silence, his mouth agog, his face suffused with disbelief as he stared at the stranger who stood next to him, who peered coolly at the corpse of his uncle.

Kai slammed the boot shut and faced Trey, his brown eyes glittering under the moonlight.

"Why am I doing this? Well, so many reasons, though I am not sure I can be bothered to go into all of them," he continued, speaking in that indifferent tone. "My Empire is too soft, I fear. Look…little islands such as this one exist and people can live as they wish. Granted, this country of yours is hardly a place where one would actually *want* to live, but the fact that they have this freedom at all really raises my hackles. My uncle and his predecessors have imposed no laws, no requirement that you and your kind bow to the Empire, despite the fact that it was the Empire that saved the UK's neck all those years ago after that dreadful disease! No, no. It's time for change."

Trey regarded him, speechless, the Tanzer Gun still pressed against his forehead. He barely felt its pressure now; the words he was now hearing rendered him stunned. After a brief moment of silence whereby Kai seemed to be lost in rather tranquil thought, Trey summoned his voice.

"The Emperor…" he said, his voice barely a whisper.

Kai snapped out of his daze. His face hardened.

"Ah yes," he said coolly, "my uncle. He had to go, of course. He would have had me killed, had he known of my plans. And, also, I never quite forgave my uncle for what he did to my father…"

"I don't understand…"

"A bit of family history, sure to bore you. My father fell in love with a commoner, my mother. They had a child outside marriage— me. My uncle forbade them to marry. As law decrees, a member of the royal household may not marry a commoner. As a result, my mother was forced into marriage with a man who was not particularly nice…he enjoyed kicking her around and one day he went a bit too far. They told me the bruises were so bad that when they found her body, she looked like a multi-coloured corpse…

"When my father, who had fled the royal court when I was born and taken me with him, heard the news, he abandoned me on the doorstep of the palace and threw himself over a cliff. My uncle took me in. Maybe he felt bad about what he did. Or maybe he just didn't want the scandal to damage his reputation. Either way, I was forced to live with the man who had effectively murdered both my parents. And now the perfect opportunity has arisen for me to administer justice on him…Oh, and gain control of this lovely little island."

Trey could not believe his ears. How he could have been hoodwinked this whole time by the one person outside his family that he'd trusted with his life…who, on countless occasions, had proven himself a steadfast ally and loyal comrade…who, time and again, he had shared his concerns, his strategies and his plans. It cut through him like a knife, not only the sickening sense of betrayal, but the danger, the catastrophic danger that his city now lay at the mercy of.

"It's like—what's that wonderful British expression?—killing two birds with one stone. Isn't it?" Kai continued. "I get to kill the Emperor and win the war, all with one shot. You see, Trey, you weren't wrong. I will not lie, I have always been a great admirer of your intelligence. Lord Pearson does indeed have a foreign ally— me. When you arrived at the palace three years ago to submit your request that the Empire aid you in this war, I saw the perfect opportunity to gain control of your island. I saw, also, the chance to take the throne for myself. My men back home are already in the process of disposing of the Emperor's one and only son, my cousin. This leaves only myself to take the crown. From the day you arrived, I worked hard to convince my uncle to assist you. I worked hard to gain your trust. I then allied myself with your enemy, offering my aid, assuring him that when the time came, the Chinese forces would switch sides. In return, he will give me control over your people— and rule this city in my absence. It was the perfect plan—conquering this island with hardly any loss to my own troops. Your city, your country…It *will* become part of my Empire, Trey. Make no mistake about that."

He was mad. Mad, twisted, but, above all, Trey now knew that Kai was the biggest threat to their survival. Now it was not so much about winning the war as it was about escaping the tyranny of this madman. If the Chinese forces switched sides, the Renzo Army would be in a dire situation. He had to warn his father—but how? How could he, when he was out here in this deserted forest, in the presence of a tyrant worse than Lord Pearson himself, the butt of a

Tanzer Gun pressed firmly against his head?

"As I said, Trey, I am a huge admirer of your intelligence—your other theory was also correct, you see. Everyone has been utterly clueless about the reasons why Lord Pearson instigated the battle this morning. They were baffled by his strange movements, by his odd use of civilians, by his reasoning behind what was essentially a pointless move. But you, my friend, got it right. It was a distraction—all of it. Lord Pearson needed time to implement his grand plans and what better way to do it than by instigating a phony battle? Those thugs he sent into battle were certainly expendable, as were the civilians…That was rather a nice touch, wasn't it? Make it look like his army was bigger than it was by forcing ordinary people to fight. At the same time, you wasted valuable resources and warriors' lives on what was essentially a false battle! A stroke of genius, if I do say so myself!"

He beamed, plainly pleased with himself.

"It was our last resort, you see. That professor should never have baited your brother to go and rescue the girl; because of his stupidity, you may have attacked the Pearson stronghold that very night! And *then* what would have become of our plans? No, no. We couldn't have you ruining everything, not when we had come so far—not when I myself had been the puppeteer training those useless thugs how to fight, how to do drills…yet another thing you picked up on. So we decided to put Operation Luna into effect."

"Operation Luna…?"

"Indeed. The last resort. Training those thugs for months on end how to successfully kidnap ordinary citizens and force them into battle in case the situation ever called for it was certainly very straining on my generals. I had secretly deployed them to Lord Pearson last year; though, of course, we couldn't run the risk of the thugs opening their big mouths and blurting out that the Chinese Empire had sent them allies; my generals were disguised as thugs themselves! But it was a success in the end, was it not? All of it a very great success indeed, so that the ultimate plan can run its course."

"And what exactly is this ultimate plan?" said Trey hoarsely.

Kai regarded him almost pityingly.

"That, I'm afraid, is not something you need to know."

There was the sudden sound of a car engine revving somewhere close to them. In a split-second, Kai snatched the Tanzer Gun from his captain, pointing it squarely at Trey's face.

"Investigate," he ordered the captain.

The captain nodded, disappearing into the darkness.

"It appears we may have company," said Kai coldly, his eyes fixed on Trey. "It doesn't surprise me. There are traitors everywhere, you know. But it is irrelevant; they cannot save you now."

There was the sound of gunshots. Minutes later, the captain returned, panting.

"It's Renzo's soldiers," he said breathlessly, another rifle swinging from his hand. "I killed one and shot another; there's a full vehicle of them. They'll be here soon."

"No matter," said Kai, calm as ever. "We'll just have to cut this short. They're too late anyway. The plan is already underway; the guards outside the Renzo mansion will already be suffering the poison we slipped in their drinks earlier. The sun is about to set on the Renzo empire. I confess, Trey, I had grown somewhat fond of you. It is a pity, it really is."

"Kai," said Trey, beads of sweat on his forehead, his throat dry, desperation in his voice now. "Think about what you are doing. You have nothing to gain—nothing from us, nothing from this country—"

"Don't be silly, Trey. I have plenty to gain. Plenty. I have very grand plans for the inhabitants of this island."

A dreamy, faraway look came into his eyes.

"Oh yes…I want the UK. Why not? It once ruled a good chunk of the world and had an empire that could rival my own. Isn't it a nice notch on my belt? Look at it now…ruined, spoiled…pathetic, frankly. Your leaders over the past two centuries didn't care about you. Why should I? And you have a king—well, so what? If your Royal Family cared, they would have never abandoned you. They would stand and fight with you—isn't that what your old kings and queens did? Stand and fight with their people? But now they're gone. It's quite humorous actually. Did you know—and you must forgive me, but I have always been keen on your island's history— the main reason your ancient monarchs voluntarily chose not to use their power and agreed to let Old Parliament rule the country was to stop civil wars from happening in England? But now, look; your parliament is weak and you have civil war…yet where is your king to protect his people?"

He shook his head and sighed.

"Waste, such waste. Most of your historic monuments are destroyed; your island is a wasteland; your politicians were cowards who left you to fall. So what's the point of conquering it? Oh, just for the name. Rule Britannia, Britannia rule the waves, Britons now exist to be my slaves. And you, my dear Trey…you will be the first to feel what life is like under my reign."

There was nothing else for it. Trey lunged forwards in one last desperate attempt to grab the throat of the man before him; at the same time, the popping sound of the Tanzer Gun clicked; and it was the sight of Kai's smiling face that served as the last thing the eldest of Lord Renzo's sons ever saw again.

*

At the Renzo mansion, the banquet was called to a halt due to two shocking incidents that were brought to the attention of all those present.

The first was the appearance of Captain Burgloss who Lord Renzo had sent for earlier when Raphael had shown him the worrying tag-text he had received. The captain had burst through the doors only a mere half-hour after he had left, his shoulder bleeding from a gunshot wound; what's more, tears were falling from the burly captain's eyes. The music came to an abrupt end; everyone turned to stare, momentarily frozen.

"Lord Renzo," he gasped, his face pale, dropping to his knees

Lord Renzo and Raphael were first by his side. A circle quickly formed around him. Skye stared at the wounded man along with everyone else in the hall, their faces horrified.

"Captain Burgloss!" exclaimed Raphael. "He needs a doctor—quick, let's get him to the infirmary—"

But the captain shook his head, anguish twisting his features.

"Forgive me, Lord Renzo. There was nothing I could do…"

"What happened, Captain Burgloss?" said Lord Renzo in a quiet voice.

"Please forgive me," wept the captain. "I followed them, just as you asked me to. But we were too late. It's Trey, my lord. He is dead. He was killed by Commander Kai."

His words rang out in the silent hall, words that pierced the heart of every person present, faces aghast, but none more so than Lord Renzo, who could only stand there, white-faced, upon hearing the news that his eldest son was dead.

"Trey…dead?" Raphael managed to say, looking strangely gaunt.

He turned to face his father, who continued to stare at the captain, unmoving.

"Kai has betrayed us," said General Jackson, his face puce, his hands pummelled into fists. "That bastard!"

"Where is he now, Captain Burgloss?" asked Raphael, finding his voice.

"His captain killed one of my men before shooting me. I ran back to my squad to get help…but by the time I returned, Kai and his men had gone. He has been working for Lord Pearson. Only Trey was left…My Lord, I am sorry. So, so sorry."

He began weeping once again, guilt tearing through him.

Lord Renzo moved forward; he placed a hand on the shoulder of the sobbing captain. Then he turned to look at the hundreds of pairs of eyes that were staring at him, shock and horror showing plainly in their distressed faces; several of Trey's archers stood at the back, openly crying.

Though ashen-faced, Lord Renzo managed to speak calmly.

"We must assemble our forces," he told them at large. "We must launch a defence barrier around our stronghold—"

But, just then, there was a deafening crashing noise outside the hall. Seconds later, a man staggered inside, a smashed, empty glass in his hand. It was one of the Renzo guards who normally stood protecting the mansion.

He collapsed to the floor.

"Poison!" he gasped.

There was nothing anyone could do. He shuddered several times, foam frothing at the mouth; everyone watched helplessly as he gave one final gasp and died before their very eyes. Several maids screamed, covering their faces with their hands.

"What the hell is the meaning of this?" whispered Raphael, as several soldiers rushed towards the dead guard and a few more ran out the doors to discover the cause of this sudden blow.

Before anyone could fathom what had just happened, another guard flew into the hall; it was the guard who stood in the watchtower and surveyed the land, keeping an eye out for enemy attacks or otherwise.

He made a beeline for Lord Renzo.

"My Lord—we are surrounded! The Chinese forces are attacking us from the back of the mansion!"

There was a frightened, panicking murmur from the domestic staff in the room; the soldiers present stood to attention, wide-eyed, ready to accept command. Skye stood rigidly behind Raphael, fear pulsating through her veins.

"General Jackson, order all units to defend us from south of the house," said Lord Renzo, immediately turning to the General. "We must defeat the Chinese forces before Lord Pearson's thugs attack us from the front—"

"My Lord, we are being attacked from the front as well!"

"So Pearson's scum have already arrived!" thundered General Jackson. "We'll have to divide into two, kill off the thugs to the north—"

"General, no!" exclaimed the watch-guard, his entire forehead perspiring heavily. "The ones attacking us at the front…they are not thugs!"

"Then who are they?" demanded General Jackson.

The watch-guard took a deep breath, before turning to face Lord Renzo.

"My Lord…they are *wolves.*"

CHAPTER THIRTEEN

There was a stunned silence all around.

"Wolves?" repeated General Jackson blankly.

The watch-guard nodded frantically.

"Yes—thousands of them—and more approaching from the borders of Notting Hill!"

"I don't understand," said Raphael. "Wolves? What—?"

"Lord Renzo, Master Raphael, General—please, we have no time to talk! We must launch an immediate counter-attack. I have alerted our soldiers and archers in the barracks. But with the Chinese forces switching sides, plus these creatures attacking us from the front—not to mention our wounded who lie in the hospitals—I fear we are greatly outnumbered!"

The frightened murmuring in the hall increased. Panic swiftly filled the air.

"How many are estimated to be attacking us from the front and back?" Lord Renzo asked the watch-guard.

"Some twenty thousand Chinese forces *at least* are currently storming the mansion," replied the watch-guard. "As for the wolves, there are too many to count; they are jumping the wall—they will be on us at any moment!"

"My Lord! Our guards surrounding the mansion are dead—they have been poisoned, every one of them! Animals are trying to get inside! We are unprotected!"

It was one of the guards that had ran from the room earlier who had just appeared with this news, having investigated the troubles outside. At the same moment, Joey and Ricardo Renzo came bursting into the hall, panting and sweating heavily. Ricardo had a smashed wine bottle swinging from his hand, while an enormous, painful-looking gash on Joey's right arm dripped with blood.

"Jesus Christ!" Joey yelled, running towards them, droplets of blood scattering behind him, Ricardo hot on his heels. "Close the doors! Close the damn windows! There are hundreds of massive dogs out there—they look like Skye when she's transformed, but way uglier! We were out near the wine cellar and one of them just attacked me—"

"I killed it with this," said Ricardo, waving his smashed wine bottle around fervently. "At least, I think I killed it, I mean, it dropped to the ground—"

"Not just that, but we saw Kai!" exclaimed Joey, his eyes darting wildly around. "He was on his own, just walking all cool and stuff among these animals! We called out to him—but he pulled out a gun and aimed a shot at us! Then he shouted, 'Kill them! They killed the Emperor!' We only just managed to throw ourselves inside before all these animals lunged for us. What the hell is up with that?"

"Killed the Emperor?" exclaimed General Jackson, eyes

popping. "Then Emperor Jin! He must be…"

"Dead," finished Lord Renzo.

"So that was Kai's plan all along," said Raphael, a snarl marring his features. "He was planning on betraying us all this time—he joined forces with Pearson, killed the Emperor…" His expression distorted, heavy anguish and sorrow replacing his rage. "He killed Trey…"

Joey and Ricardo froze.

"What?" they both whispered.

"Trey…dead?" said Ricardo in a numb tone. "Dad?"

He turned to his father, looking almost helpless. Daphne moved towards her boyfriend and embraced him.

"We must hurry, Lord Renzo," muttered General Jackson, his usually red face stark-white. "Forgive me—but they are coming!"

Lord Renzo's eyes left his twin sons who, for once, were speechless and immobile.

"Our only option is defence," said Lord Renzo. He raised his voice, speaking to the hall at large; the soldiers and warriors stood to attention.

"The archers must attack the wolves from the top balcony. All other forces must defend invasion from the Chinese. Everyone else must be evacuated via the Silver Tunnel."

"And what of Pearson's damned thugs when they arrive?" said General Jackson, who was already arranging units to fend off the Chinese forces. "Who'll fight them?"

"Nobody," came Skye's quiet voice. "The thugs *are* the wolves."

Only Raphael heard her. He spun round.

"What did you say?" he said, stunned.

She had suspected it ever since they heard wolves were attacking them. It was at that moment, when the watch-guard had blurted out this startling revelation, that everything seemed to piece together in her mind. She remembered the professor, extracting her blood…she recalled how he had talked about a secret plan that Pearson had…she remembered the young beaver Morpher, whose morphing ability had seemed so unnatural…she recalled the memories he had shown her where children were being injected…no, not just injected; experimented on. She thought about how strange it was that only a percentage of thugs had taken part in the battle, with civilians to swell the numbers…she thought about all these things and realization hit her with a sickening thud.

"The thugs," she said, her face deathly pale. "The ones who didn't fight during the battle. They were being injected with my blood, Raphael. That professor was turning them into wolves…an army of Morphers!"

Raphael could only stare at her.

"My God," he whispered.

If estimates were correct, there were at least forty thousand thugs who had fought during the battle; and if the others had been injected, that meant some thirty thousand savage, bloodthirsty wolves were running rampant outside.

So that was the reason behind the battle. It was the distraction. Pearson had needed enough time to inject the rest of his thugs so they may attack the Renzo stronghold, not as men, but as wolves. Strong, powerful, their senses drastically increased, one wolf could take down ten men—and with the sheer barbaric nature the thugs possessed, the murderous intent of their enemy had increased ten-fold. Now Raphael and Skye both knew. They knew why the professor had found her so valuable. They, more than anyone else, understood just how dangerous a city filled with murderous wolves was.

They had to act. Raphael, in the absence of Trey, was now in charge of commanding the archers that would attack the wolves from the front.

"Dad," Raphael hurried over to Lord Renzo, his face ashen. "The wolves outside—they're thugs! Pearson's professor injected them with Skye's DNA. He's turned them into Morphers!"

Lord Renzo stared at his son.

"So that was his plan," he said quietly.

"What shall we do?" came Mrs. Archer's scared voice.

She, along with Daphne and some of the staff members who were huddled together, stood petrified in the hall while crowds of soldiers and archers moved out. Skye spun round to face her, pain showing clearly in her eyes.

"Mum, you have to go," she said swiftly, striding towards her.

General Jackson, who was busy arranging the soldiers in the room and speaking a hundred miles a minute into his tag device to one of the captains in the barracks so they might deploy the troops who were fit enough to fight, scooted towards Lord Renzo.

"The stronghold is lost," he told him, his voice low. "There's no point in denying it. Our only hope of attacking Pearson tonight was through the element of surprise. With the Chinese forces and those beasts combined, we're finished. The most we can hope for now is to get everyone else out safely. We must give them time to evacuate—we cannot allow the enemy to invade the mansion and slaughter everyone in sight!"

Lord Renzo gathered together everyone who was not part of his armed forces. He turned to Ricardo, who stood, pale-faced, clutched by a frightened Daphne, and Joey who stood by his twin's side.

"Ricardo, lead them to the Silver Tunnel entrance. Take some of the men with you for protection. Hurry—the Tunnel will take you outside the city. Seal it. From there you know where to go. We will join you afterwards."

Ricardo nodded, swallowing hard. The Silver Tunnel had been implemented by Lord Renzo many years ago in the event that an emergency evacuation needed to take place. The Tunnel began in the basement of the Renzo household, ran underground and ended outside of London, into the deserted wastelands of the rest of the country. In the event of a successful invasion by any foe or enemy, Lord Renzo had instructed that all evacuees must be taken out of the city and hidden in the forests in the central and northern parts of the country. Ricardo and Joey had both travelled this Tunnel many times during their more wild escapades, but never before had it been used for its original purpose.

"And me?" Joey asked his father.

"Your assistance would be greater if you helped your brother command the archer unit…now that Trey is no longer with us," Lord Renzo told him. "But if you must go with Ricardo, then do so. What do you choose?"

Joey stared at his father.

"I'll stay," he replied, looking uncharacteristically blank.

He turned to Ricardo.

"Don't even think about getting yourself killed, alright?" he told him, smacking him on the back. "I'll see you on the other side— of the country, that is! We're not bound for Hell just yet!"

"Be careful, Ricardo," said Raphael, clasping his brother by the arm. "Look after them. You know the Tunnel better than anyone."

Ricardo nodded, his face sweating. He embraced his father before turning to his twin. It was the first time the two of them were to be separated.

"Joe," he began anxiously. "I—"

"Oi, no soppy goodbyes!" said Joey, playfully punching him. "Get the hell out of here already!"

Ricardo gulped, strangely mute. He hesitated briefly, before turning away and rounding up the evacuees, who continued to stand like a herd of frightened sheep in the hall, trembling and crying amongst themselves.

"Mum—Daphne—go!" Skye said, whirling on her mother and friend.

"Yes, Skye, let's hurry!" said Mrs. Archer, clutching tight hold of her daughter's hand.

"No, Mum—I'm not going with you."

They stared at her.

"What?" said Daphne, plainly confused. "Skye, what do you mean? Of course you're coming!"

"I can't," said Skye, fighting to hold back tears, unable to look them in the eye. "Don't you understand? We're outnumbered! The Chinese forces have switched sides—there are wolves outside, ready to kill us all! I have to stay. I can't let them get you, you understand that? We need to hold them off—"

"Skye, no!" gasped her mother in horror. "No—you cannot do this! I will not allow you—as your mother, I forbid it!"

"I'm sorry," said Skye, crying now, the tears falling swiftly. "But I'm staying. You have to go with Ricardo—"

"No! Skye, no!"

"I can't let you die here, Mum! Not like Dad. Please understand. Please—just go!"

She wrenched herself from her mother's grasp. Mrs. Archer continued to stare at her in shock, her lips trembling, while Daphne now sobbed openly.

"Ricardo, look after them! Promise you will!" Skye turned away, blocking her ears to her mother's pleas and to Daphne's cries.

"Raphael! Please—do not let her stay!" cried Mrs. Archer, as Ricardo and the other soldiers began escorting them away.

Raphael could only watch helplessly. Skye turned to face her mother and friend one last time.

"I love you," she whispered, her eyes blinded by her tears as the blurry view of her mother struggling frantically against the soldier, screaming her name, and Daphne weeping, staring back at her, shaking her head in disbelief, caused her to want to pull her heart from its socket and rip it out, if only to end this terrible pain that scraped the very essence of her soul; the image of them being pulled from the hall, pleading to her and crying, would be one she knew would haunt her forever. "I really, really love you. I'm sorry."

"I will look after her, Mrs. Archer," Raphael said as Skye's mother reached out to him, begging him to keep her safe, beseeching him to make her see reason. He grasped Mrs. Archer's hand and kissed it, as though to seal his vow. "I will not let her come to any harm. I promise."

Skye's mother and Daphne were led from the hall, their cries still audible even from the hallway. Ricardo, chalk-faced, took one last look at his brothers and father before he, too, left. Skye turned her head away; she couldn't bear it.

"Skye," Raphael pulled her by the waist, his voice hushed. "I don't want you to do this. You know my feelings on the matter—"

"I must protect them," she gulped, almost choking on her sobs. "I must. You know I must. I have the right to!"

He wrapped his arms around her, tremors shooting through his body as his inner beast showed its face, resigned to the one thing he had prayed would not happen.

"I know," he said, pressing his lips firmly to her head as the agony continued seeping through her. "You stay with me, Skye. You stay by my side. Don't you dare leave me."

She nodded, still taking great gulps, sweeping her hands across her tear-stained face.

"Ricardo will keep them safe," he told her. "Once they are in the Tunnel, there is no way anyone can follow them. Ricardo will seal it as soon as the last person walks through."

They stared at one another, realizing exactly what this meant. They could die here. Both of them.

"I wish you would have gone with them, Skye," he whispered.

She shook her head, her wet hands clasped around his bronze cheeks.

"I have to stay with you," she whispered back, her eyes shining. "For you. For them."

"Raphael!"

It was General Jackson who barked his name.

"The archers must shoot from the top level—the wolves are breaking in! You must counter-attack—now!"

The General turned to face the soldiers standing behind him.

"Follow me!" he bellowed. "Take no prisoners!"

With that, General Jackson charged from the hall, his units following swiftly behind, to face the Chinese forces that were on their doorstep. Lord Renzo, flanked by three soldiers and Joey, stood before Skye and Raphael.

"Raphael, hurry," he told his son. "Hundreds more wolves have appeared and our defences can only hold for so long. Bring down as many as you can. Joey, go with him. Skye, you can transform?"

For a moment, Skye was confused as to why Lord Renzo was asking her that. She was a Morpher. Of course she could transform. Then, in a flash, she understood the reason for his question. The last time Skye had experienced some kind of trauma (though, looking back now, on a much smaller, and even insignificant, scale) she'd had trouble with transformation, which had almost resulted in her own death. Lord Renzo must have been worried that the experiences she had gone through while locked in the cell may have triggered that same glitch inside her once again, the one that rendered her immobile to switch into the physical entity of her inner wolf.

But it had been different last time. Last time, she had felt hopeless. Despairing.

This time, she felt compelled to act. Driven to fight. Above all, determined to protect the people she loved.

She nodded to him.

"Then it is best you transform right away," Lord Renzo told her. "As a wolf, you are stronger and much less vulnerable."

Raphael and Skye turned to face one another.

"Whatever happens," he told her fiercely, pulling her close, "I love you. I love you and nothing, not this war, not even death, will ever change that."

She stared back into his glowing green eyes, determined to hold back the tears that were threatening to consume her again.

"I love you, too," she said.

They kissed—brief, passionate, a sign of their union and of their love; the small glimmer of light among the thunderous storm that tore violently around them.

"Let's go," he said, as they broke apart. "Remember, Skye. Stay with me."

She nodded. The hall was almost empty now; the shouts and snarls could be heard clearly from outside as the enemy tried to break through the Renzo forces and into the mansion.

Only Raphael, Skye, the archer unit which stood silently waiting for Raphael's orders, Joey, Lord Renzo, and his personal guard remained.

"Take the greatest care," Lord Renzo told them. "I must go to General Jackson. We have to give the evacuees time to escape—but at the first opportunity you must run. Do not stay to fight a losing battle."

"Be careful, Dad," Raphael told his father, their gazes holding each other.

He clasped him briefly.

"Look after each other," Lord Renzo said, his blue-green eyes also piercing through Skye.

The three Morphers stared around at one another, their ferocity and determination plain to see, whether subtle or prominent. Lord Renzo then turned to Joey, embraced him and warned him to be careful; Joey nodded wordlessly. Then, Skye's entire body trembled violently; her clothes burst into the air and a split-second later, a white wolf stood in her place. At the same time, two of the soldiers flew into the hall, one with Raphael's armour, and the other with Joey's, which was hurriedly secured. Raphael, with Skye running beside him and Joey trailing rapidly after, dashed from the hall, the archer unit following with swift heed behind them.

*

In the space of twenty-four hours, the City of London had gone from being a divided city as contradictorily erratic, yet stable, as it had been over the past twelve years, to a Metropolis lit with flames and drenched in blood, where it seemed Lord Pearson was to emerge as the ultimate victor. Kai's betrayal, the loss of civilians, Trey's death...Not one person inside the Renzo stronghold, or indeed their many supporters throughout the city, could have fathomed or predicted such catastrophic consequences. And now, with London teetering on the edge of total destruction, with every villain and cad already celebrating their impending victory, hope and faith for the losing side seemed to have all but vanquished.

At the front of the mansion, General Jackson and his units fought valiantly, fending off invasion with all the strength and might they could muster. But they were outnumbered—the Chinese forces had seen almost no losses during the battle earlier that morning, whereas the Renzo Army had suffered far more, primarily due to the order to attack, but not kill. Placing themselves at risk to save civilians caught in the battle (though they had unwittingly done so) was a sacrifice that now showed its detriment in full entirety; for every Renzo fighter there were at least five Chinese soldiers. Moreover, these were not undisciplined, barbaric thugs, but skilled, organized warriors who had seen numerous battles and won most of them. As such, General Jackson was under no illusions. He knew there was no chance of winning; the most he could do was buy time for the evacuees. How much time, though, was something he could not be sure of. He was joined shortly by Lord Renzo, who brought with him hundreds of fighters from the barracks, but it was still not enough. Meanwhile, up and down the city, terrified civilians were being rounded up by packs of enormous, vicious wolves on the orders of Lord Pearson, before being marched into East London and thrown into specially designed warehouses meant for intensely sinister purposes.

On the top balcony, Raphael's archer unit were raining arrows upon the hundreds and hundreds of wolves that had leaped and bounded their way over the wall. The sheer amount of them was staggering; as Joey had commented earlier, they looked just like Skye when transformed—except bigger, stouter and with a permanent snarl that marred their features. They came in all different sizes, different colours: grey, black, brown, white and russet. But in the twilight hours that had fallen upon the city, these great, bloodthirsty beasts were almost indistinguishable from one another. They had one aim: to kill, maim and destroy everyone and everything in their path. In her wolf form, Skye could sense their strong urge for destruction—a wild, carnal passion that marked the inexperience of these new Morphers. They, having only gained their ability that very night, had a poor sense of control over this new power. Their human mind was still yet to merge in temperance with their animal mind. The wolf was in control. The one that screamed murder, take none alive.

The overwhelming mass of raging, murderous intent that hit her senses with such powerful force secretly terrified her. But, standing by Raphael who yelled with thunderous vigour to fire arrows down, she showed no fear, her teeth bared, fangs glistening, calling upon her own animalistic urge to kill if they should break through.

It seemed like only seconds that they stood on the balcony, wolves dropping like flies beneath them. But in those few seconds, the inevitable happened. The wolves broke into the mansion; there was an ear-splitting sound of smashed glass as the first wolf threw itself through a downstairs window that led into the hallway.

And that was when Skye heard it—the scream.

Not just any scream. But the scream of someone she knew—someone she loved.

Someone who didn't escape as she was supposed to. Someone who had broken away from the evacuation party in order to find her daughter, no matter the cost.

Sick terror swooped through Skye's veins. She didn't even stop to acknowledge a swarm of General Jackson's soldiers that had fled to the scene of the smashed window, barricading it with all their might, slaying the wolves that viciously tried to jump through. Raphael's shouts and orders to his archers became deaf to her ears;

she fled on her heels and streaked from the balcony, snapping and snarling her way through the crowds, desperation tearing through her so she might reach her mother in time.

She found her in the hallway that led to the billiards room, taking no notice of the shouts, yells, howls and screams as wolves outside ripped into soldiers, as arrows continued firing down outside. Mrs. Archer stood in the dimly lit corridor alone, an expression of pure terror on her face, three enormous grey wolves surrounding her. She held a white vase in her trembling hands, swinging it in futile at the nearest wolf, which snapped at her heels.

Skye wasted no time. She lunged forwards, landing directly in front of her mother, the three wolves momentarily surprised by her appearance.

"SKYE!" her mother screamed.

The wolves, realizing she was not one of them, swiftly began snarling, edging towards her. Skye's back was arched, an expression of pure ferocity on her face.

Come and get me, she conveyed to them.

At the same time, Ricardo burst onto the scene.

"Mrs. Archer!" he bellowed, racing towards Skye's mother. "You must come with me—now!"

At the same time, the wolves dived at Skye. She was at the advantage in the fact that she had been morphing for many years now; her senses were sharper, her reflexes quicker, and her attack power stronger than this new vicious breed. She dodged here and there, snapping at the wolves, her teeth finding the neck of one of them; it howled as her fangs sank into it. The wolf, blood spurting from its jugular, collapsed to the floor, writhing uncontrollably. She was vaguely aware of her screaming mother being dragged away by Ricardo, the two disappearing down the hall.

You're dead, one of the wolves conveyed to her.

Maybe, she thought, *but if I'm going down, you're going down with me.*

The other two wolves leapt on her; one delivered a resounding blow with its teeth into her back; she howled, but quickly dismissed the pain, dodging a bite from the other wolf, which would have proven much more fatal. She could see, out of the corner of her eye, the General's soldiers desperately trying to close up the smashed window as more wolves tried entering the building. She knew there was only one way to get them as far away from her mother as possible and that was to lure them back outside.

With a wild snarl, she bounded over the wolf that had just tried plunging into her neck, dashing through the soldiers and out into the open. The wolves followed her. Outside, among the dimming twilight, she now found herself amidst clusters and clusters of the great canines. Her only chance of survival now was to mingle among them, to lose herself in their masses in the hope that she would not be recognized, and that she might scatter among them, chameleon-style, before succeeding in sneaking away and finding her way back inside the mansion.

The wolves were still on her tail; almost blindingly, she raced through the stampede of animals...right into the very area that Raphael's archers were firing a rainstorm of arrows down on their enemy.

With increasing helplessness, she watched as wolf after wolf was slain around her, their bodies piling in mounds. She had lost the two wolves that were determined to kill her; but now she faced a greater danger. To be pierced and struck dead by the man she loved.

She could think of no other way out.

RAPHAEL! She screamed in her mind.

And Raphael, at the top of the balcony, heard her cry.

"Skye?" he gasped.

He had not seen her leave; the past five minutes had been a desperate bid to defend the fortress, demanding all his attentions, all his strength. But he heard her in his head, as clearly as though she had been standing next to him, no different to when she had cried out to him as a prisoner in the cell.

And he knew in that one sickening instant that she was out there, among the wolves.

"STOP!" he bellowed. "STOP!"

But the archer unit continued firing arrows. Hundreds of them flew through the air. Fear gripped his entire being.

"STOP!" he bawled again. "DON'T SHOOT!"

But the arrows were relentless. The archers, desperate to stop the never-ending packs of wolves, fired arrow upon arrow, deaf to his orders, unable to hear him amidst the thunderous panic and howls beneath them.

He threw his armour from his body and transformed, roaring deafeningly.

The archers halted, their bows frozen in unison, arrows stationary between their fingers, all eyes swerving towards the enormous tiger that had suddenly materialized before them. Joey, who was standing at the back, rushed forwards.

"Raph!" he yelled, before turning to the archers.

"Hold your fire!" he shouted to them.

The tiger turned on his heel, his huge striped body bounding through the archers and down the stairs, desperate to reach his white wolf that was caught among the overwhelming might of the enemy.

Hurling himself down the staircase, he threw himself down three floors before landing on the bottom corridor. But his exit was blocked; ten wolves had succeeded in infiltrating the building, defying the soldiers' attempts at holding them back. He came to a halt, one tiger against the large pack of wolves, ready to fight to the death.

They lunged for him. Inexperienced as they were, he found it easy to fend off the first five that went straight for his neck, dodging and swerving, his own powerful feline teeth sinking into their throats, back and legs. But there were too many; two wolves jumped on his back, their fangs gripping his skin as he desperately tried shaking them off. One sprung towards him, its teeth finding his back leg; he roared, unwilling to give in or yield to the fact that this was a battle where loss seemed inevitable, where his own death seemed nearer than it had ever been...

Then there was another roar, but not from him. Out of the faintly lit corridor, another enormous, powerful creature came charging towards them.

Lord Renzo, in his purest tiger form, had come to the aid of his son. The magnificent beast threw himself at the remaining wolves that had pounced on Raphael, his fangs glistening. Four of them turned on the newcomer. A wild, ferocious fight between the two tigers and ten wolves ensued. Five to one, they battled as only powerful carnivores can. The wolves suddenly found themselves in dire straits, coming to the realization that two experienced tiger Morphers would be a lot more difficult to kill than originally expected. Teeth, claws and jaws flashed around the hallway; howls, snarls and roars blasted and echoed within the corridor; blood spattered the walls with ruthless fervour.

At last, defeated, seven wolves ran from the scene; three lay dead on the floor, deep claw wounds and tooth marks scattered across their lifeless bodies. At the same time, a platoon of soldiers burst into the hallway, several hurling daggers at the retreating wolves' backs. Raphael felt a surge of triumph as he watched the pack run howling from the mansion.

But the feeling was quickly stifled when he realized the three slain wolves were not the only bodies lying on the ground below him.

His heart stopped. A strange sensation bubbled inside him as time itself seemed to slow down, his sharp feline senses faltering and dissipating at an alarming rate. Lord Renzo, in his human form, lay beside one of the fallen wolves, sprawled on his front; he was nude, as a Morpher always is after making the transition from beast to man; a slow stream of blood trickled from beneath him, resulting in a small, sticky red pool that drenched his hands; he did not move; he was completely still, utterly silent.

Raphael swayed on the spot. He watched, in trance-like stupor, as several soldiers raced towards his father's unmoving body. A split-second later, he transformed.

"MOVE!" he roared, barging his way through the frantic soldiers.

"Dad!" He threw himself to the ground in the dim hallway,

kneeling by his father's side. One of the soldiers handed him a tunic and he snatched it with his shaking hand, wrapping it around his father, turning him on his back and staring into the old face; a red trickle oozed from Lord Renzo's lips. Raphael's blood ran cold as he saw numerous deep puncture wounds all over his body. He felt a heartbeat beneath his father's chest, a pulse in his veins.

Then, Lord Renzo's eyes fluttered open very faintly; when he spoke, his voice was weak and barely audible.

"Raphael…forgive me…"

"No—don't speak—you'll be fine—we'll get the doctor, don't worry—"

Raphael's trembling hands did their best to wrap the coat tighter around his father; the dark material absorbed the blood, red spillage oozing onto the floor.

"Forgive me…my son," murmured Lord Renzo; he could barely keep his eyes open as he found his son's distraught green ones. "The fault…is mine. I should…I should have…acted sooner…but I couldn't bear…the loss…of life…"

"Dad, don't talk. Please. Save your strength. WILL SOMEBODY GET A DOCTOR!" Raphael roared at the horror-stricken soldiers. Several immediately fled the room to find the physician, but Raphael would not allow himself to think that Doctor Jenson may not even still be with them, that he might be far from here by now, evacuating with the others…

"No…" Lord Renzo tried to lift his hand, but his weakened state would not allow it. Raphael grabbed it and clutched it tightly to his face. He gazed into his father's eyes, which still burned orange. Why did he look so pale? Where was that doctor? He had to hurry!

"It is too late…Raphael…"

"No!" said Raphael furiously. "No—the doctor's coming— you'll get better—"

"My son…listen to me. These wounds…they will not heal. Please…don't look that way. I go to a place…where there is no war…where your mother…and brother…wait for me…"

His fingertips gently brushed Raphael's bruised cheek, his eyes struggling to focus on his son's face. Raphael could not move; this couldn't be real…no…

"My dear son…you will be the man you were meant to be…Look after your brothers… Look after the people…"

"Dad…" Raphael's entire body was shaking; he was more afraid than he had ever been in his life and all he could do, as helpless tears formed in his eyes, was stare down at the face of the man who had raised him, cared for him, taught him, protected him, and now, sacrificed his life for him; all he could do was cower in fear, tremble at the might of the merciless power that continued to steal his father's life-force bit by bit, while he sat there, powerless to act. He, the fierce tiger, was reduced to a terrified cub; bewildered, petrified, unable to face the reality that presented itself; he could do nothing now, except beg; plead to his strong, powerful father not to leave, to be there always, just as he had been from the start…

"Dad, don't go," he whispered; the tears came slow and heavy, sliding onto his father's hand. "Please don't go. Don't leave me."

With one last great effort, the corners of Lord Renzo's mouth turned upwards in the smallest of smiles and he stared into Raphael's green, glittering eyes, his face full of a pride that needed no words.

"I will never leave you…my son…"

His hand became limp in Raphael's grasp; his eyes faded to their blue-green colour, like an old gentle ocean that had drawn its last wave; he gave a final shudder and then his chest lay still. Already, his skin felt cold as Raphael continued squeezing his hand, the tears coming swift and fast now as he stared into his father's motionless, expressionless face, realizing, even as his mind screamed at him that it couldn't be true, that Lord Renzo, his father, his leader, the man who made him what he was, was gone. He was gone. He was dead. He was not coming back.

Agony ripped through him; pain shot through his veins, slicing through him like daggers twisting ruthlessly into his skin; his chest burned as though alight with flames. The transformation from man to beast was inevitable as he shed his human skin for orange and black fur, fangs forming inside his mouth, claws protruding where fingernails should have been.

His roar shattered the earth beneath them; the soldiers almost fell to their knees, their hands flying to their ears; his grief spiralled in violent ripples throughout the mansion, felt by all, friend or foe. Death. It was irreversible. His mother…his brother…now his father…

Gone. Never to return.

General Jackson appeared, followed by a platoon of soldiers who stared in shock at the roaring tiger, a platoon that included Joey and Paddy.

"Lord Renzo, we must run, the mansion is lost—*Lord Renzo!*"

The General's red face paled at the sight of the lifeless body on the ground wrapped in the coat.

"No!" he gasped. "It can't be! My Lord!"

Joey had frozen; he stared at the motionless frame of his dead father, his turquoise eyes glittering strangely in the fluorescent hall.

"Dad...?" he whispered.

"It was the wolves!" choked the soldier who had given Raphael his tunic. "They—they killed him! There was nothing we could do!"

General Jackson's eyes flew towards Raphael whose roars continued to shatter through the building. He knew there was only seconds to act.

"Raphael!" he bellowed at him. "The Chinese forces have stormed the mansion, the wolves will be on us any moment now! We must evacuate—all of us!"

Joey continued staring blankly at his father's image; General Jackson, realizing the helplessness of the situation, took charge.

"You, you and you!" he barked at several soldiers who stood around, similarly at a loss. "Carry Lord Renzo! The rest of you— follow me!"

"Raphael!" yelled Paddy, approaching the tiger, but jerking backwards again when the huge feline turned on him, snarling wildly. "We have to go—please, we have to leave now!"

There was an almighty smashing sound mere metres away from them. Raphael in his tiger form could barely hear his friend screaming at him. He only knew one thing: the wolves had broken through. And he was going to kill them all.

He lunged forward among the mass of canines, deaf to the yells of Paddy and Joey behind him. His rage and grief combined gave him phenomenal strength, almost akin to the pill Doctor Jenson had provided him with earlier. In a flash, he killed five wolves as they rushed at him, biting and snarling.

"Raph!" Joey hollered. "We have to go—Raph, it's lost! We have to leave now!"

"We must move!" boomed General Jackson. "Everyone—run!"

There was a stampede of footsteps as the soldiers fled. Raphael barely noticed them go. He was going to kill the wolves, every one of them, and maybe he would die with them, but what did it matter? Death was no stranger; not now, not ever again.

"Raphael!" Joey bellowed again. "Let's *go!* We have to go—and find Skye!"

Something in his brain snapped.

Skye. She was still out there. She wasn't safe with the others.

"Skye needs you, Raph!" roared Paddy, shooting dead two wolves who threw themselves at him; they landed to the floor with a heavy thud "She still needs you!"

There was a deafening shout from outside as though someone was screaming into a megaphone.

"BACK TO STRATFORD, ALL OF YOU!" the voice thundered. "NOW! OR EVERY ONE OF YOU WILL BE KILLED!"

The wolves halted; four who had been trying to tear through Raphael's coat froze. They knew who had spoken. And they knew they had to obey.

There was a squealing sound outside; the wolves inside the mansion forgot the tiger and two men who were firing pistol shots at them; they fled. Raphael was quick on their heels, just as Joey and Paddy were quick on his.

They came to a sudden stop when they saw what was happening. Among the vast moonlight, hundreds of wolves were now retreating; those who attempted to break away from the withdrawing army were instantly killed by the Chinese forces, which now occupied much of the area. Arrows no longer fired down from the sky; the archers had disappeared along with General Jackson's army. The mansion was lost; the Pearsons were victorious.

Hidden among the shadows so as not to be spotted by the fleeing wolves, they saw him. Kai. He was the one yelling orders, the one ordering the instant elimination of any wolf who did not obey the command. They did not know why the wolves were being ordered to leave, not when the stronghold had fallen. But right then, Raphael didn't care. Murderous rage flooded him. The traitor. The bastard who was responsible for all of this. The one who had killed his brother. And his father.

His father was dead.

Dead. Gone.

He would tear Kai, limb from limb, rip his heart from his socket and eat it, and he would take the greatest pleasure doing so…

He snarled under his breath, crouching low, ready to spring into the open.

"Raphael, no!" hissed Paddy, laying a firm hand on the tiger's back. "If they see you, they'll kill you! Think of Skye! You have to stay alive for her! We'll get him—I swear. Just not now!"

It took every bit of control he had, every fibre of his being that loved her, for him to heed Paddy's words and recognize the truth in them. He could not think about his father right now…he had to concentrate on finding Skye, to think of a plan to get them away safely, to somehow salvage the devastating, catastrophic consequences that had occurred tonight.

Where was she? Was she still among the wolves? Was she even alive? Had she been slain by the enemy? By his own archers? His blood curdled. He couldn't think like that.

"That's her!" came Joey's frantic whisper. "I'm sure of it! Oh my God…they know…"

They all turned to stare at where Joey was pointing. Raphael's heart sank; it was definitely Skye. There were other white wolves in the vicinity, but Skye was the whitest of all and her almost-glowing coat was impossible to miss under the moonlight. Not only this, but she was being flanked by two grey wolves and four Chinese soldiers. They knew it was she—and that the enemy had captured her.

Immediately, both Paddy and Joey threw themselves in front of Raphael.

"If you go after her now, we're all dead!" hissed Joey to the tiger that was frothing at the mouth, his orange eyes blazing madly. "We have to wait, Raph!"

Wait? They were escorting her away, right before his eyes. Was his brother mad?

Violent tremors vibrated his entire body. Paddy bravely faced him, Raphael's fangs mere inches from his face.

"Joey's right!" he whispered frantically. "If we go to her now, we'll be killed! We were lucky enough to escape the mansion just now. They've captured her—there's a reason for that! If they wanted her dead they would have killed her!"

Then why hadn't they? What would they do to her? Torture her?

Make her suffer before they delivered the ultimate blow? The snarl emitted from his throat again; he watched, powerless, as she disappeared from sight among the sea of wolves that leaped and bounded away from the Renzo gardens, Kai and the Chinese forces mingled among them.

Raphael, restrained only by his brother's and friend's logic, felt his claws dig into the earth, his mind swirling with rampant ferocity and despair. In the space of a few hours, they had lost everything. The city...

The war...

His brother...

His father...

But by God...he would not lose her, too. Not even if he had to take the entire Pearson regime down with him and burn the City of London up in flames.

EPILOGUE

Fallen arrows and the slain bodies of dead wolves were all that remained outside the House of Renzo from the onslaught earlier. In the late hours of the night on the 27th September 2217, the war was over. A war that had lasted not even two days and resulted in a Pearson victory. It was a victory that expelled all hope and faith for the citizens within the city who swiftly came to the realization that the end was nigh. The Renzos had lost. Every innocent and civilian was rounded up and sent to East London to be used at the mercy of both Lord Pearson and the new order of the Chinese Empire. Thousands of wolves now patrolled the city, almost dancing in delight at the sudden turn of events that gave them the opportunity to sing victorious. The Renzo army had been vanquished, their leader destroyed. The city was theirs.

The House of Renzo lay deserted. Kai had laughed openly before his departure, mocking them. As he left, he shouted words that his nemesis, few as they were, could not fail to hear.

"Farewell, Lord Renzo! The island is mine!"

They were words that Raphael would never forget—that he swore he would avenge.

He stood now in his human form with Paddy and Joey, just outside Notting Hill Meadows, hidden amongst the shadows, the only protection they had against the force of the enemy. Skye had been taken, helpless in Pearson's clutches. Where she was now, he did not know. Only that she was with them—and he had to find her and bring her back.

His father was gone. No longer would Lord Renzo be there to guide him, to assist him. No longer would Trey speak in his calm, diplomatic way and reassure him when trouble found its way into their lives and hearts. He was alone. And he alone had to lead them…though broken as they were, there seemed little to lead.

"He's gone," Joey whispered, as though there was no one else around. "He's gone…"

The grief had to be quenched. To even have a shred of hope, there could be no grief. Not yet.

"We never stood a chance, you know," said Paddy, as the three lingered, silently, in the darkness of the early hours. "From the beginning, we'd lost. Kai had planned this all along—we'd lost before we'd even begun."

The gloom upon hearing these words was amplified and felt by the trio. They could only pray that the evacuees had made it out safely; that Ricardo had led them to a safe place outside the city, a place that Lord Renzo and his allies had previously arranged to be a haven in case things went drastically wrong. A place in the forests of the north of England. Joey had tried contacting his brother via tag device, but received no response. They could only pray the evacuation, at least, had been a success.

"How did you know?" Paddy asked, turning to Raphael, who

continued to stare silently into the dark streets that surrounded them.

"How did I know what?"

"That something was wrong. You received a second tag message earlier after the first one, telling us Kai's mission had been a success. You knew something wasn't right...how?"

Raphael cast his mind back. It seemed so meaningless and trivial to discuss it. But why not?

"I received a second message from Kai. It said, "We've got him. This is it. Have the wolves ready." I guess he sent it to the wrong person. That's when I knew, anyway..."

He swallowed, rage flooding through him once again before he continued.

"That's when I knew we'd been betrayed. That Trey was in danger."

Yes. His brother had been in danger.

And that danger had taken his life.

While he had been powerless to act.

There was a scuffling noise somewhere behind them.

"Watch it," said Joey warningly.

Out of the shadows of the street came a Renzo soldier; they did not know his name, but they recognized his face; they relaxed very slightly.

"Master Raphael," said the soldier, his voice trembling. "I have been searching for you. I have a message from General Jackson. It's—it's from Lord Renzo. In case things went... wrong."

He held his hand tentatively out to Raphael. There was an envelope in it.

Raphael took it wordlessly, opening it.

"What is it?" asked Paddy anxiously.

Raphael was silent for a long time after his eyes scanned the few words on the note inside the envelope.

"A message from my father," he said. "To travel north—to the Scottish borders. He arranged a resistance movement in the event of a successful invasion. The same place where the evacuees went."

There was a long pause, blinkered only by the sound of stray foxes scavenging amongst the bins. In the distance, jubilant, wild howls could be heard as many of the wolves celebrated their victory with euphoric mirth.

"What shall we do?" said Joey.

Raphael turned to them.

"Leave," he told them. "Go now. Find the resistance; help them. I'm staying here. I have to find Skye."

He turned away from them, determination eating away at his soul. He would find her, if it was the last thing he did.

A hand touched his shoulder.

"We're coming with you, Raph," said Paddy. "We're not leaving you."

He turned slowly. He looked at them. His brother and his friend. They stared back at him, their loyalty palpable, their fiercely resolved expressions burning into him.

"I want you to go—"

"No. We're with you. Till the end."

And, as one, they accepted their fate. Throughout the City of London, the sound of howling wolves echoed across the night sky.

ABOUT THE AUTHOR

Sarah Brownlee was born in London, England. She has been writing a wide variety of stories and literature from a young age, including penning letters to both President Clinton and the Duke of Northumberland when she was ten. Having failed miserably at her first attempt at college when she was seventeen, she fled to The Philippines for six months to pursue a life of adventure and excitement. She returned to England and, after failing a second attempt at college, she abandoned ship once more and immersed herself in a number of different jobs, ranging from working as a private investigator to performing as a sales executive for a trucking company; from being hired as a barmaid to being a World Cup Commentator. Her third attempt at college was met with success and she plunged into university where she trained to be a teacher. In typical fleeting fashion, however, she ultimately decided it was not for her and instead began her crusade as an author, her lifelong passion. She now spends her time writing, walking dogs and eating copious amounts of sashimi.

How the Tiger Faced His Challenge is the second novel in her Young Adult Dystopian series *How the Wolf Lost Her Heart.*

Find Sarah on Facebook here:

https://www.facebook.com/sarahbrownleeauthor